C.A. RUDOLPH

BOOK SIX OF THE WHAT'S LEFT OF MY WORLD SERIES

to: Superman
(Mr. Bill)

Cover Art by Deranged Doctor Design
Edited by Sabrina Jean
Blurb editing by Felicia Sullivan
Proofread by Pauline Nolet
Featured on the cover: Darja Filipovic of Deranged Doctor Design

ISBN: 9781086043259

For Stefanie, Delaney, Tristen, and Emma.

Though I've come to learn it was never in the stars, my intention has always been for this family to be closer than we've become. I realize much of the cause for division falls on me, and while no man is perfect, I've strived to make the best of things. Failures aside, nothing will ever change nor lessen the magnitude of my love for all of you.

Just as this series of books depicts in nearly every chapter, nothing is more uncertain than what our future holds for us. Still, I find myself having high hopes for it, and for us, all the same.

"A family doesn't need to be perfect; it just needs to be united."

ANONYMOUS

# PROLOGUE

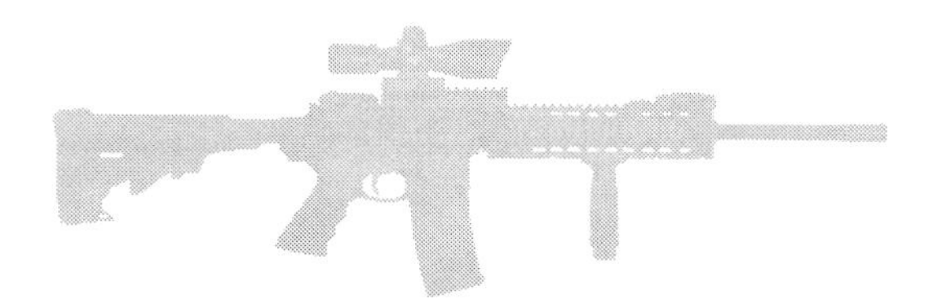

THE HILLY PATHWAY ON WHICH Butch had chosen to lead Alan and Jade was barely wide enough to travel. All told, it wasn't much of a path of any kind, but the terrain was proving no match for the massive Marauder armored APC. It hobbled about the snow-covered forest in stride, bouncing over everything it stumbled upon while paving its own path. It broke apart low-hanging tree limbs with ease, crushed full-grown fallen trees, and toppled live ones. It even fractured jutted-up portions of rocks it rumbled over. Its suspension system was doing a modest job of managing the ride, giving the impression it was built for this type of abuse, but the interior compartment wasn't exactly providing the most relaxing ride for its passengers.

Alan tightened his seatbelt and arranged himself in the passenger seat while holding tightly to the APC's 'oh-shit handle', a common nickname for the hand brace typically located inches above the side windows of most motor vehicles, to include exotic armored personnel carriers.

Jade's expression carried both looks of excitement and uncertainty. She was thrilled at the prospect of seeing Ken and Walter again after having presumed them dead. Evening had already begun to set in, and the pair had been on the 'road' for hours. Butch seemed to quite literally be leading them along the proverbial path to nowhere, and she was beginning to wonder if the choice to follow him and defer Alan's plan had been a mistake. It certainly hadn't been the best-laid plan in Alan's case, whom she looked upon with worry between bumps. "Hey, are you feeling okay? You're starting to look really pale."

Alan held his breath momentarily as his body tensed. "I don't know. For a minute there, I thought I had a…handle on it. Now I'm not so sure. We might have to stop, Jade."

"Motion sickness?"

"Yeah, I thi—"

Jade pushed hard on the accelerator, forcing the Marauder overtop a thick, petrified stump on her side, causing the enormous vehicle to pitch, then roll hard before leveling. "Uh…sorry about that," she said nervously. "I don't know where we are or how much farther we have to go to get to this White Rock place, but I wish it would hurry up and get here."

"From where I'm sitting, every rock I see looks white," Alan jested, doing what he could to will his stomach to settle. The ride itself was making him queasy, but Jade's nervy driving habits were exacerbating his ailment.

While she piloted the APC through the darkening, hilly forest under falling snow, with one hand on the wheel and barely half her attention, Jade fiddled with a unique digital touchscreen bounded by multicolored buttons. On each button was etched an indecipherable symbol, and the screen itself was mounted to a pivoting steel frame above a duo of ergonomic control levers near the center of the Marauder's dashboard.

Every so often, her eyes would jolt away from the screen, to the windshield, and back again, while Alan scrutinized her multitasking efforts, growing more unsettled as time passed. "Jade? I don't mean to… bug you or add another distraction, but what exactly are you doing?"

"Why? Isn't it obvious to you?"

"The only thing obvious is how it looks," Alan said, his stomach churning.

"And how *does* it look, Alan?"

"To me? It looks like you're struggling."

"Looks can sometimes be deceptive. And for the record, I'm not."

"I wasn't insinuating anything. But it might…benefit us both if you let me drive."

Jade sent along a snide glance. "Really? So soon? After what happened to Butch's *other* priceless indulgence?"

Alan leaned away, recalling the old vet's reaction to his accident scene. "Yeah, good point. Forget I said anything." He gestured to the device Jade was toying with. "What is that?"

"It's the UI for the Katlanit."

"The what?"

"The UI…the user interface for the remote weapon system mounted to this thing," she explained. "The one that runs the big machine gun."

"Oh."

"I'm trying to familiarize myself with the software and I'm not having any luck with it, which is frustrating. I've never seen anything like it before…the entire operating system is completely proprietary. I'm starting to think our new buddy is some kind of evil genius."

"You think he designed it himself?" Alan asked. "As in, Butch might also be a programmer?"

"Based upon what little we know about him and what he's divulged thus far? My money's on hacker."

Alan chuckled. "He *did* mention having more surprises. Maybe that's one of them."

Jade raised a brow. "Maybe. Anyway, since we're sashaying around in this monster, I reason it's best we know all there is to know about it."

"Yeah, *another* good point. You never know who or what we may encounter along the way. And a big machine gun could prove useful."

"Peace through superior firepower is always useful," Jade mused as they bounced hard over another obstacle. "Sorry."

Alan tensed again, reaching for his abdomen. "It's…okay."

"I'm seriously not trying to torture you," Jade said with kind eyes. "There's a first aid kit in that compartment above your knees. I probably should have told you about it earlier."

"Torture me some more, why don't you," jeered Alan, pointing ahead. "By compartment, I take it you mean this overengineered glove box?"

"That's the one. If you're lucky, you might find some Dramamine in there."

Alan opened the compartment door and extracted the first aid kit. As he did, a black nylon drawstring bag came along with it and tumbled to the floorboard under his feet. He retrieved it and gave the foreign manuscript printed on it a once-over.

"What's that?"

"It definitely isn't Dramamine."

Jade reached for it and Alan handed it over, resuming his search for antiemetics.

"What do you think it is?" he asked.

"Not sure." She jostled the bag's contents. "But the script looks like Hebrew."

"Hebrew? Like that thing you've been so distracted with? The catatonic?"

Jade smirked. "Katlanit."

Leaving the unmarked forest trail, Jade swerved right to follow Butch along a much wider, more exposed powerline right-of-way. She pondered for a second if it had been the identical one she and Alan had passed under along the Appalachian Trail the day before.

Both vehicles struggled to maintain traction along the snow-slickened uphill slope until the right-of-way intersected with another, this one appearing to be a snow-covered surface road. Taking another right, they travelled along the passage for a time until Butch signaled a left up ahead.

Alan pointed to a standard green sign with white lettering marking the turn. "Now, I'm no expert, but I'm going to assume this to be the final leg of our trip."

Jade squinted her eyes and the title 'White Rock Road' came into view. "Now *that's* marking your territory. Why not bother posting another one denoting 'Butch's fallback position'?"

"Probably overlooked it. He *is* a little…eccentric."

"Yeah. Just a little."

They followed Butch along the road, up a gradual incline and around a single mild switchback before coming to a stop at an in-ground reinforced barricade with diagonally painted white and black lines blocking the entrance. Butch hopped from his vehicle and entered the guard shack situated on the left-hand side, and a few seconds later, the barricade sank into the snow to become level with the pavement underneath.

Both vehicles pulled forward into a narrow parking lot. Butch hung his arm out and motioned for Jade to continue, so she pulled the Marauder forward to the reinforced entry door, which appeared to be held in place by the earth itself.

Jade shifted into park. "It isn't much to look at, is it?"

"Too soon to judge," Alan said. "Not enough daylight left for an accurate assessment."

"Maybe its beauty lies on the inside," Jade remarked. "Wonder how the other half of our team is getting along?"

A knock came before Alan could infer. He opened his door to find Butch standing below, his boots buried in snow.

"What do you all think?" Butch asked. "Home sweet home, for the time being, anyway. Jade, wait one or two while I motor open this herculean wretch of a door. You can pull the APC inside the bay; parking spots are a dime a dozen."

Once parked, Butch secured the door and led Alan and Jade through a spacious alcove with tall ceilings, mutedly illuminated by sporadically placed fluorescent lighting. Nearly every bulb in the ceiling flickered while ballasts within the fixtures retaining them buzzed a tune, either due to age, deterioration, or lack of suitable heat. Through a doorway, they followed him into a climate-controlled, carpeted hallway of furnished offices. Passing a kitchenette on one side and a lounge area on the other, they turned a corner into an office and found two familiar faces.

Ken and Walter were seated beside one another on a couch augmented with supplemental cushioning, mostly in the form of assorted pillows. A flat-screen television was mounted to the wall opposite them, and the pair were immersed in a two-player video game, each punching buttons on a joystick controller in their hands.

Butch, having entered first, presented them with an open hand. "Just like you ordered. Two marginally damaged, medium-rare roughnecks, right in time for Kwanzaa."

Jade beamed at them and darted into the room before either could make a move. "You two gave me a heart attack!" She dove between and embraced them, an arm encircling each man's neck.

"Hey there! Sorry 'bout that, fam," Walter said, patting Jade's back and struggling against her arm strength. "We surely di'n't mean nothin' by it. Not like we was tryin' ta git our butts burnt on purpose."

"Nice to see you, too. Both of you," Ken said, sending Alan a glance over Jade's shoulder. "But I don't get it…what are *you* doing here?"

Jade slid away, holding back tears as Alan moved in to shake hands.

Ken took Alan's hand first. "Seriously, what gives? I mean, I'm just surprised. What about the plan? Getting home and finding your family?"

"I made it home," Alan said flatly. "But everyone was long gone by the time we got there."

Walter reached for Alan's hand and shook it, a solemn expression befalling him. "What's that mean, bud? Somethin' happen to 'em? Think they might've vamoosed on their own?"

"Both," replied Alan. "Something did and they left a little over a year ago. My wife outlined it in a letter she left me. It filled in a lot of the blanks, even indicated where next to look for them."

"Welp, I'm sorry you didn't find 'em, bud. I truly am. But at least you picked y'self up some intel on where you'll be headin'." Walter winced in pain, attempting to sit up. "Point at issue is, why the heck did the y'all two come here 'stead of goin' there?"

Alan looked away to hunt for a convincing answer, only to have Jade provide it for him. "Because we wanted to. And the decision to do so was all Alan, so don't look at me. He didn't want to leave either of you behind."

"You don't say. Well, shit, Alan. I'm flattered," said Walter. "I truly am flattered to pieces. I mean, I knew you liked us a li'l, but I never woulda guessed me and ole Kenny here stacked so high up on yer list of priorities."

Ken reached for a beverage on the end table beside him and sipped from it. "I don't know, Walt. This might go somewhat *beyond* priorities. Maybe even deeper than, so to speak."

"Eh, how do you mean, deeper? And don't git gross, neither."

"It's not gross, Walt. Furthest thing from it, actually." A pause. "I think or, rather, I *feel*...that Alan's actions might be indicative of... love."

"*Love*?"

"Sure," said Ken. "Our man here could've very easily kept on going, but he didn't. Because he couldn't. He knew we were hurt and he felt for us, wanted to be with us. And then he came back for us. He couldn't let us go. It plays out like a love story. Alan loves us, even if only a little."

Butch let out an exhaustive sigh. "And this right here is where I smartly take my exit," he griped, disappearing through the doorway. "Off to bed I go. *Marines*...and their...*marineness*."

Jade giggled at the banter. "I never thought I'd confess this, but it's good to hear you two act like a couple of idiots again."

"What're you talkin' 'bout?" Walter unpaused the game. "Only idiot present in this here room is the likes of Kenny. Prolly somethin' we can all smoke the peace pipe 'bout...besides Kenny, of course. 'Cause he's an idiot."

"Shut up, Walt."

"You shut up."

Alan laughed. “All jokes aside, guys, one can’t help notice all the extra padding beneath you. What’s the extent of your injuries?”

“Extent of our injuries?” Ken mocked, pressing pause again. “All jokes aside there, high speed, but have you ever been shot in the ass?”

Alan shook his head. “Not…that I recall. But I believe I’ve taken some shrapnel in that vicinity before.”

“That’s right, but you were unconscious and couldn’t feel anything, so it doesn’t count.” Ken grinned. “When those tacticool Timmys blew Butch’s house all to hell, shards of burning plastic and liquified metal hit Walt and me directly in the goddamn buttocks, going Mach 1. Hurt worse than a steel-toed kick in the balls and burned hotter than the most offensive roasting yeast infection I ever caught. Then it festered too, like a—”

“Jesus, Ken, stop.” Jade covered her mouth. “You’re going to induce vomiting.”

Alan reached for his stomach, gauging the remnants of his bout with motion sickness.

“Fine. I’ll tone it down a little. But all that pain, burning, festering, scabbing, pus secretion and swelling aside, wasn’t shit compared to bending over and doing a facedown ass-up in front of someone like Butch while he played medic and extracted the shrapnel.” Ken leaned back and stared at the ceiling musingly. “A serviceman in combat can oftentimes see and experience horrifying things, events, and such. Some of these matters are so horrifying, they simply cannot be unseen. I know now the same holds true for that which he’s unable to see. Those matters can be haunting. And I have no doubt that mortal jolt of an ordeal will haunt me for the rest of my natural life.”

No one said anything for a long moment.

Walter finally peered over. “Kenny, that was crude as all get-out. An’ I reckon Alan had a reason for posin’ the question, and ’twernt to hear all that nonsense you jus’ retched. He’s askin’ ’cause he’d like to know when we can get back to followin’ his plan. Ain’t that right, Alan?”

Alan tucked his upper lip. “No, it’s not that. I mean, it is, but there’s no rush. And I certainly don’t expect either of you to go injured or unable.”

“Who said anything about unable?” Ken quipped. “We might be down, but we’re far from being out. Just let us know when you’re ready to get going and we’ll pack our shit and pop smoke.”

“That’s more like it. Tell ’im, Kenny,” Walter praised. “Cuts, scrapes, abrasions and gettin’ buttshot don’t change nuthin’. We’re with you, pard, or *will* be…soon as I can walk again and not before I git done whoopin' ole Kenny's ass in this here game."

"Walk again?" Alan parroted under his breath, sending Jade a curious glance.

"Wishful thinking, Walt," Ken said. "You'd better pack a lunch."

"Jokes on you, same as usual. I'm havin' you fer lunch."

"Okay, guys. We'll…leave you be a while so you can sort out… whatever this is." Jade smirked and reached for Alan's arm. "Come on, I'm dog-tired and I know you have to be."

Once in the hallway and out of range, Alan queried, "Did you catch what Walter said?"

Jade nodded while peeking into offices on either side of the hall.

"What did he mean by that?"

"I don't know for sure. They could be hurt worse than they're letting on. And if so, they'd never tell you to your face."

"Why wouldn't they?" Alan asked.

"Pride." Jade smiled gravely and tugged on his elbow. "Come on. I'll get the full story from Butch tomorrow. Let's find some suitable spots for some shut-eye."

# CHAPTER 1

**DHS Shenandoah Outpost**
**Woodstock, Virginia**
**Friday, December 31st**

DOUG BRONSON SLID TO THE bedside and placed a foot to the floor. He leaned forward and strained himself upright, feeling an immediate throbbing in his balding head. He groaned, reaching to a collection of pill bottles on his nightstand, and coughed through a dry mouth over a similarly parched, raspy throat.

Locating bottles of generic ibuprofen and acetaminophen, he tucked them under his right arm and went digging for more. Wheezing, he finally came across a bottle of aspirin, but he pushed it away upon sighting an orange-hued prescription bottle of oxycodone, bearing a name not his own on the faded label.

Bronson then staggered to his feet. Using his free hand for balance, he ambled to the bathroom, his vision becoming less blurry as the room got brighter, but the brightness of day caused his head to pound even more. Someone, very thoughtlessly, had left the blinds open the day previous to allow in the sun, for whatever reason. And now, to top it off, his bathrobe belt had come untied. *Great.* He was now exposing himself to the world in all his glory.

Cursing under his breath, Bronson stomped inside and dumped his armload of pill bottles into the sink. He then stretched for the window and adjusted the blinds, cancelling out the intruding, menacing daylight.

He regarded the door and considered giving it a kick to close it, but a second later, thought better of it. It was early, and all this morning-routine nonsense was taking far too much effort.

Bronson had felt this way about a thousand times before: unable to discern if he was more hungover than drunk, or more drunk than hungover. Either way, he went about closing the door in a gentle, less flamboyant fashion, one presenting a reduced chance of injuring himself.

His bathrobe still agape, Bronson waltzed to the commode and relieved himself in hands-free fashion with the seat down. Once finished, he adjusted his bathrobe and retied his belt, then turned to look himself over in the mirror. He scowled, gave himself the middle finger, and went about popping pill bottles open.

He twisted the faucet all the way to the blue and held his fingers under the stream to ascertain the temperature. He then made a bowl with his hands, filled them halfway, and splashed cool water on his face. Coughing and wheezing, he dried his face and hands with a towel, then arranged eight ibuprofen caplets on the counter. He added two tablets of naproxen sodium to the mix, then finalized the concoction with two white, circular Percocets. He filled a cloudy glass with water, scooped up the blend of pills, and dumped them on his tongue, forcing them down with multiple gulps and nearly spitting a few up in the process.

Bronson rubbed his eyes and took his leave of the bathroom, glass of water in hand. He forced his tongue between the dry skin of his inner mouth and gums, through the foul paste that had accumulated there while he slept. He poked at his teeth with his fingernails and rubbed his nose. Then his eyes fell onto a curvy, effeminate form beneath the silvery satin sheets covering his bed, and the bundle of tousled, flowing, golden hair on the pillow near the headboard.

Bronson was accustomed to entertaining companions of the female persuasion. Doing so was requisite for a man in his position, standard operating procedure for a person retaining his level of authority. Since the beginning of his post-collapse tenure as regional DHS commander, he'd taken pleasure in having his pick of the litter and had rarely spent a night alone. His initial options hadn't exactly been lowbrow, but had vastly improved as time passed, permitting him to give precedence to quality over quantity. Still, Bronson was no idiot. He knew both quality *and* quantity had their perks.

His most recent conquest was becoming his all-time favorite by a long shot. The woman was a ripe peach, a certified looker. She had a supple, curvaceous figure, ripened lips and a waist shaped like a dessert wine decanter. Her skin was unblemished and she had a full head of sunrise-gold hair, a rare, authentic blonde bombshell. And he couldn't remember ever having met someone so exquisite, calculating, and charming, who also happened to be an absolute firecracker in the sack.

The corners of Bronson's lips elevated into a sneer. He sniggered to himself and took a sip of water, swishing it through his teeth. The sculpted body beneath the covers made purring sounds like a newborn kitten. The woman rolled over onto her belly, and the sheets slid from her, exposing a portion of her lower body. Bronson didn't know when she'd wake up, but assumed she was dreaming, probably about their previous night together. As it had been one for the record books.

She had approached him in the weeks leading up to this to discuss topics on a strictly professional level. Bronson had thought her attractive since the moment he'd first perused her personnel file and noticed her head shot. She could've been a model, for all he'd known then. As it turned out, she was married, but he wasn't about to let that hinder their relationship as colleagues from taking the next fruitful step.

Bronson was in command. This was his world now and the Plantation was the apple of his eye. The region belonged to him, and what he said goes. But she'd worked her way in and he'd been powerless to stop her. The woman had a way about her unlike any other, and he could feel himself being pulled in for the kill. With simmering galaxy-blue eyes, glowing skin, a toned body and flawless breasts, Bronson had become obsessed with her in no time, and the rest was history. She had since become a frequent visitor to his home and a recurrent participant in his bed. He used to spend so much time in his office that sleeping there had become standard, but having her around made doing so impractical and foolhardy. Their interludes together had thus taken place in his home for privacy's sake.

Bronson watched her body stir again. She rolled to her side and slid the well-manicured fingers of her left hand onto her hip. Through moderately blurred vision, he noticed she'd left her wedding band on. Had the blasted thing been on her finger all night? The bitch. Alas, try as he might, he couldn't remember. The majority of the night had been a distortion in time, partially due to drunkenness, but mostly ecstasy. He inhaled, blowing a sigh of disgust from his nostrils, then left the bedroom and closed the door.

Bronson went to the kitchen and opened the freezer to remove a frost-covered glass bottle of Stolichnaya vodka. He dumped his glass of water in the sink and tossed a handful of ice cubes in it before filling it, capping the bottle and returning it to the freezer. He then opened the refrigerator to search for a suitable mixer while he yawned periodically and tried to remember what day it was.

After mixing himself a semi-decent Bloody Mary, sans the celery and garnishes that had become nearly impossible to find in this day and age, Bronson left the kitchen and sauntered into the living room, where he sat on a plush leather sofa, propping his feet on an ottoman. He reached for his laptop with his free hand, opened it and began perusing his office intranet, deciding to put off checking his messages after seeing the mail icon blinking in the taskbar with a two-digit number overtop.

Bronson took a drink, swishing the liquid around his mouth before downing it. He knew it wouldn't be long before he began feeling the effects of the narcotics in his system, especially after the addition of distilled liquor to the mix. But he knew even more how incapable he was of functioning at any capacity while hungover, and anything was better than feeling like this. Without being narcotized, drunk, or a combination of both, the stress of life in the post-apocalypse was oftentimes too much for him to bear.

Bronson took another drink before setting his glass down and fumbling for the television remote and clicking it on. A menu of windows soon appeared on the sixty-inch screen, and he navigated to one that presented a list of motion pictures available to watch. He then scrolled through the catalog of westerns.

Bronson had always been a fan of them. He enjoyed seeing the typical good guy versus bad guy plots that depicted the latter as being a rich, heartless, power-mad oil investor, railroad owner, or cattle baron who committed atrocities to assert and retain his power over a town. He did so with the help of a group of dingy, nefarious men who were anything from professional gunslingers to common criminals, all willing to kill with impunity at the drop of a hat. And the law didn't apply to them because their boss owned local law enforcement.

There always seemed to be a fair maiden or damsel in distress, who'd been victimized somehow, and then there was always a hero—a poor, lonely traveler who migrated from town to town, possibly a Civil War veteran or someone who'd had his family savagely murdered by Indians, or perhaps even by other power-mad ringleaders in other towns. The hero always kept to himself initially, with no intentions of getting involved in town business. He was oftentimes looking to start a new life, but always managed to find himself wrangled into the plot, most often due to his decision to play Dudley Do-Right and rescue the damsel.

In the past while watching westerns, Bronson had often compared himself to the hero in the plot. He was the one who'd been brought in to help people deal with circumstances and save them from bad things, because bad things happen to good people. Now he believed he was more like the oil investor or the railroad owner, or even the power-hungry cattle baron, because he'd come to the conclusion that no good people were left in the world. And no heroes were, either. There was only a job to do and a mess to clean up; a mission to accomplish and problems to hinder the process along the way.

The bedroom door swung open. Bronson turned right to see the woman who'd occupied his bed in one of his freshly pressed button-up shirts, and it appeared to be all she was wearing.

She yawned and tiptoed into the living room in her bare feet, combing through lengths of her hair with a brush. She smiled at him and squinted as she pranced over and took a seat cozily beside him.

The fragrant scent of light roses wafted past Bronson's nose. He recognized her perfume from the night before, although he had to admit, it wasn't nearly so pungent then. He assumed she'd either put on more this morning, or it'd been attenuated by perspiration from the night before.

"Do you mind?" Beatrice Carter asked, reaching for a two-tone box of Virginia Slims on the coffee table. "I presume this isn't a nonsmoking room…"

Bronson slurped his breakfast pick-me-up. "You presume correctly, as made evident last night, maybe even the night before, after all the fumes the two of us generated."

Beatrice sat back into the couch and lit up. "Hmm…you mean, from all the…friction? Would that be an accurate statement?"

Bronson slid his hips forward, reclining his body further. "Indeed." He gestured to the ceiling. "I'm surprised that scorching hot ass of yours didn't set off these smoke detectors."

"Ha! Now, that would've been a trifle embarrassing." Beatrice giggled, exhaling smoke from her nose and mouth. She placed her cigarette neatly on the edge of a glass ashtray. "You're a riot, Doug."

As the seconds slid by, Bronson's companion made slight efforts to glide her body closer to him. She was giving him plenty to look at, but the only thing with which he concerned himself was the wedding band on the hand she was now using to rub his inner thigh.

Bronson took another sip of his cocktail, then reached for Beatrice's hand, curling his fingers around hers. He then held it in the air. "Looks as though you might've forgotten to take something off before you came to bed."

Beatrice's first instinct was to recoil and defensively pull her hand away, but she refrained and relaxed. "Oh, hell. I do apologize for that. It must've slipped my mind in the…*heat* of the moment. Of course, I take it you *did* pick up on how I managed to take off most everything else."

Doug Bronson burped inadvertently after a valiant effort to hold it in. "Oh, I noticed all right," he said. "There's clothing and whatnot scattered all over the bedroom floor. Looks like two grown adults just walked in and exploded in there."

Beatrice slid her hand away from his, placing it beneath Bronson's bathrobe. "Well, that might be how it looks, but I know of only one of us who did any exploding in there." She squeezed his thigh, slid herself even closer and placed her lips inches from his neck. "And I relished every millisecond of it."

Bronson smirked and shook his head. This woman was undeniably good. His attraction to her had only begun to heighten, but he couldn't help that something still bothered him, even with the delicate touch of her hand perilously close to the point of no return. "I think the time has come for the two of us to discuss the ramifications of our affinity with one another."

Beatrice pulled her hand away in an instant. Reaching for her cigarette, she brought it to her lips and scuttled her butt away from him, taking a few puffs. "Well, since obviously you aren't in the mood for anything else, might as well get it over with, then," she quipped.

"Though, Lord knows, last thing I wanna do is spend all day long harping over it."

Bronson snorted and swallowed a wad of phlegm that had built up between his throat and lower sinuses. "Don't worry about that. This should be a brief chat. All I'm looking for from you is some reassurance."

"Pertaining to what?"

"Pertaining to your plans…for the unavoidable. The day your husband finds out about us."

Beatrice scoffed. "Really now, Doug. I don't see any point in discussing that."

"I beg to differ."

"Douglas, I'm here right now, with you, for a reason. I hold nothing against August. He's a good man, but he's not a great man. And the relationship you and I have is far too recondite. I assure you, he hasn't the aptitude to figure us out."

"Are you kidding me? Did I just hear you right?" Doug retorted. "Your husband was a DHS special investigator, Beatrice—a highly decorated one at that. He worked for Customs Enforcement and his career is replete with positions not handed off to just anyone. I'm sorry, but I respectfully dispute your competence appraisal of Special Agent August Carter, significant other, spouse or otherwise."

Beatrice slid her hindquarters to the other end of the couch, pulling her legs in close, covering herself with a pillow. "Doug, if you intend to speak to me in that manner, then I intend to bring this discussion to a close, toot sweet. You and I have started something here, and I find that I now care about you deeply. I do not want to allow this frivolous nonsense to come between us."

Bronson jerked his head in her direction. "Why? Why wouldn't you want anything to come between us? You're a married woman, Beatrice. You're still married to August and you even forget you're wearing his wedding band on the rare occasion you spend the night. And I'm sorry, but that bothers me."

"Well, it shouldn't."

"Why shouldn't it?"

Beatrice blew out a puff of smoke and produced an ivory-coated smile. "Because…you're the boss, Doug. You are the man with the plan, and everyone here, up to and including myself, must answer to you.

There's no one else. You run the whole kit and caboodle, and there isn't a reason why you should be intimidated by any man." She sucked out another drag through the filter. "Or woman."

Bronson knew full well what Beatrice was doing. She was catering to his ego, something a woman does when she wants her man to toe the line, follow her lead, or become docile, unassuming and submit. He was an alpha. Normally, he would take the standoffish approach to being treated this way. He'd assert his position, become verbally abusive, and things would escalate, eventually opening a doorway to physical harm and violence. The same, repetitive, abusive scenario that caused his wife of many years to finally pack her things and leave his ass.

But with this seductress of a woman, it was different. He felt differently. Bronson knew the tactics well and he knew what she was doing to him; he just didn't mind it. He had never met anyone like Beatrice before. She was the most dangerous drug and the sweetest candy in the universe—the one confection so pleasurable, yet so sinful, each serving carried with it a death sentence.

Bronson had elected this woman a man-eater from the moment he had set eyes on her, but he liked the way she was with him, loved the way she made him feel. She intrigued him and he desired her more than any woman he had ever met. "So what's your...*not so* better half been doing lately while you've been spending all your time elsewhere? I assume he's been asking questions."

"You assume incorrectly, Doug. He's been devoting much of his *time* elsewhere too. I've been keeping him rather busy."

"Busy doing what?"

"This and that. Errands, mostly. Assignments outside the fence. He's been on foot a lot."

"On foot?"

"Mm-hmm." Beatrice sat on her feet. "Not long after this *Solve for X* thingamajig brainchild of yours commenced, we put together a crew of men for him to lead, their first assignment being to fully investigate that crime scene in the forest and look for clues that might lead to the whereabouts of the remaining infiltrator. You know, the one who got away. The bodies of our fallen have all since been retrieved, including that of your ex-brother-in-law. I'm afraid they were far too decomposed and gnawed on by mongrels to fret with a proper burial, so I took the liberty of having them cremated. But we did bring them back home to HQ beforehand, however." Beatrice sighed contritely. "We didn't find any signs of those mangy dogs before the bad weather came, though. Shame."

Bronson lifted a brow, eyeballing her. "Let me get this straight. You've had him tasked with duties outside the wire all this time?"

"I most certainly have, ever since you first interviewed him," Beatrice said. "August is loyal to a fault. He doesn't ask questions, he just acquiesces. He's been leading those other men up and into the woods all over the place…following the plans you laid out pretty much to the letter. It's kept him out of the house overnight countless times now, which has afforded me some much-needed time…to myself." She puffed on her cigarette. "I can't have him hanging around here with nothing to do. Boredom is the devil's playground, Doug."

"Without a doubt."

"Well, hopefully, this'll put your mind at ease a bit. And we can get back to gossiping about the things that matter, like what the two of us are gonna do with our day." Beatrice scooted closer once more. "Doug, darlin', please don't worry yourself about anything. If it's anyone's problem, it's mine, and I will handle it my own way and on my own time." She ran her fingers through her hair and nestled it over an ear. "I used to go face-to-face with international terrorists, some of the most dodgy fellas ever captured alive. I've hunted down hajjis in their diminutive little caves and dragged them out kicking and screaming right beside the operator team tasked with acquiring them. I pledge to you, I am not the least bit petrified of August Carter. And Doug, you dear, should not be either."

Bronson relented, unwilling to carry on the argument. He smiled at her and rose, heading for the kitchen. He acquired a bottle of brandy and two snifters and held the bottle aloft. "Want to have a drink with me, gorgeous?"

Beatrice butted her cigarette out and stood, then pranced into the kitchen, modestly pulling on the ends of the shirt with her fingers. "I don't usually, but I don't suppose one little drink is going to affect my work too awful lot today. So why not?"

Bronson made their drinks and handed her one. The two tapped glasses and Beatrice took several small sips while Bronson pounded his like a shot. "Damn, that's good shit. I'm going to miss it when it's gone."

The half-nude blonde chuckled. "Well, maybe you'll start drinking bourbon instead, once that point is reached."

"What?"

Beatrice set her snifter on the counter, gesturing to the bottle of brandy. "You don't exactly drink it like you're *trying* to conserve it. You guzzle it—like a cancer patient swigging Oramorph with two days left to live, Doug. Not that there's anything wrong with it, I mean, we *are* living through a great tribulation. These are purportedly the last days." She winked at him and licked her lips as they parted. "We have to make the best of them while we still can."

Bronson chuckled, hesitated then chuckled again, deciding to pour himself another glass. "You know something, you're right. Fuck it. There's no sense in putting anything off or taking anything for granted. We found ourselves in a position of grand importance, Beatrice, not to mention one of extraordinarily good fortune. I mean, look around you. From where we're standing, it's almost like nothing life-threatening ever happened. While the incorrigibles, needy peasants and useless eaters outside the fence are scrounging for bugs and eating plants and toadstools, dying of dysentery and God knows whatever else, here we are, enjoying the finer things in life, getting everything we deserve. The lesser gives way to the greater; it's the way civilization has always been. The way it's going to stay."

"It will if *we* have anything to say about it." Beatrice giggled like a schoolgirl on nitrous. "Oh, Doug, you say the most outrageous things from time to time, and I gotta say, you are by far one of the most handsome men I have ever fallen for." She lifted her drink in a toasting gesture, her closed-mouth smile extending from ear to ear. "I see eye to eye with everything you said. Today, we run the region. Next week, the country, and who knows, maybe a year from now, the continent." She gulped down the remainder of her drink. "The sky is the limit."

# CHAPTER 2

THE EXPANSE SEEMED TO DIM and flicker like a lantern running treacherously low on fuel, becoming increasingly dark, impervious and unyielding. It was peaceful, though. Serene. Soundless, but alarmingly so.

By her best estimate, it was nighttime and she was outdoors. The sky overhead was black, virtually impersonating that which surrounded her on all sides. Nothing was discernible or detectable: no stars, no moon, no heavenly bodies, nothing serving to assist her course of travel. The blinds had been pulled in every conceivable bearing of the universe in which she was immersed. She might as well have been sightless.

After a time, the darkness began to mysteriously dissolve, leaving behind in its wake an ominous gray residue that draped lazily over the landscape. It felt warm and humid now, similarly to an evening in midsummer, but no insects were buzzing, no frogs were croaking, and no birds were chirping. She could barely feel the clammy air touch her face, even as she took her first step and then another, and pushed her way through the nothingness, advancing deeper and farther into the void.

The familiarity of an M4 carbine became perceptible before long, the texture of its knurled grip in her left hand and the slotted surface of the Pic rail foregrip in her right. She glanced down a moment to validate and caught a blurred, near indistinguishable snapshot of the weapon, enough to know it was there.

That datum in itself gave her pause, but she was dying to know where she was, where she was going, and why she was even here. All she could feel in the instant was a need to keep walking, to keep moving forward in the direction she had chosen. Or rather, the direction that had chosen her.

Lauren Russell couldn't see five feet in front of her, but the farther she went, the more the darkness continued to evaporate, in similar fashion whereby night covertly metamorphosed into day. Able to see more clearly now, she crested a hill of low-cut grass, and the ground beneath her converted into a paved road. A moment later, her house came into view. The one in which she and her family had lived before everything had gone so horribly wrong, before their move to the valley, prior to her father going absent without leave. Back before everything had collapsed, taking her world along with it.

The structure seemed to materialize from a vacuum as would an apparition, causing Lauren to halt her advance. She scrutinized the scene a moment while undergoing a temporary sensation of unsteadiness, as if wearing roller skates on uneven terrain, but the vertigo subsided quickly. She knew where she was now.

Lauren was home.

The sight of her old house and neighborhood was startling and practically inconceivable, compelling her not to rush and exercise caution before going any farther. She spent time taking in her surroundings. Everything in view other than her house appeared indistinct and blurry. Even her neighbors' homes didn't look exactly as she remembered them.

*Dammit.* Nothing she was feeling, seeing or was experiencing in that instant was tangible. Lauren was dreaming again. She knew that now, but still felt drawn to this place. Seeing her home appear so suddenly coerced her to explore it further and learn just how deep this rabbit hole would take her.

In no time, she was standing on her front porch. Lauren's hand slipped away from the rifle's foregrip and reached for the front door, finding it ajar. All the lights were on inside, from the bright LED daylight-imitating floods in the hall directly above, to those lining the staircase leading upstairs. She carefully trotted into the kitchen, finding nothing out of place upon entry. The room was laid out exactly as she remembered the last time she'd seen it, only it was empty now, devoid of life, familiar smells, smiles and colors, vibrant or otherwise.

Lauren spun and tried uttering a word, learning she wasn't able. She tried again without success, her intention being to call for her mother;

then she tried again for her sister, Grace. She even chanced a call for her dad, but she couldn't find any way to pry out the words. She tried forcing them into a scream and pushed with all her might to make a noise emit from her lungs. She even felt pressure build within her chest from the exertion, but every effort she put forth was fruitless.

*None of this is making any sense.*

Frustrated, Lauren departed the kitchen and traveled through the house in haste, going door-to-door in search of clues as her purpose for being here scrolled through her mind. Clothes were folded in piles, towels were dangling from racks, and every bed was made. Nothing was out of place, disturbed or in disarray; the opposite extreme of how they'd forsaken it. It was eerie and unsettling, like watching a slow-motion horror film move forward in first person.

Lauren's skin was starting to crawl and the hairs on the back of her neck stood at attention. An urge to leave thumped in her chest as would a heart palpitation. She dashed down the stairs, out the door and into the front yard, and there before her was a terrifying scene. It stretched across the street into neighboring yards as far as she could see and chilled her to the bone. Rows of bodies, practically hundreds of them, lay prone in every direction. All were bloodied, mutilated and unmoving. They were corpses.

Lauren gasped, her heart jumped, and her forward velocity divebombed to zero. She fell to her knees and her jaw went slack as she absorbed the gruesome scene in its entirety. How many were there? Who had done this? How had this happened? When?

Was anyone she knew among the dead?

Her rifle pulled close in the nature of being her only security blanket, Lauren gathered herself, rose and coursed her way through the drove of dead. It seemed to stretch for miles, but she didn't go far before coming upon a familiar face, one belonging to a newfound friend. He was a person of character, and though their amity carried with it a peculiar opposition imitating that of sibling rivalry, she trusted and believed in him. She had known him for only a few months, but in that time he had fought alongside her and managed to save her life and her sister's to boot.

Lauren fell to her knees again. "Oh, no. Not you, Christian…not you," she said in despair, now able to utter the words. "What happened to you?" She found his cheeks cold to the touch and gently lifted his eyelids, finding both pupils fixed and dilated. Entry wounds riddling his chest were all seeping thick crimson blood. He'd been shot to death, but by whom? Who had done this to him?

Lauren brought her rifle even closer, then rose and studied the scene again. There was nothing she could do for Christian, but seeing him like this frightened her to death of who might come next.

Minutes later, several yards and rows of bodies away, her eyes exploded into tears when she saw John's face. Convulsing, sobbing, she dove to him and, while doing so, noticed even more familiar faces: those belonging to his brother, Lee, and their father, Norman. Someone had murdered them all.

Lauren wept and sobbed uncontrollably, but her anger was building now, and it would soon be beyond her ability to control it. People she knew and loved were dead—but why?

She placed a trembling hand on John's head, finding him cold, frigid, devoid of life. The only person to whom she had ever given her heart had also been shot to death, much in the same manner Christian had. And now, he lay prone in the grass atop a pool of his own blood. Had he suffered? Had he fought for his last breaths? Had he called for her? Had his last thoughts been for her?

"Stop this," she told herself. "Stop this now, Lauren. This is just a dream, you know that. It's *only* a dream." But it didn't feel like one. Not this time.

Lauren rose and inhaled hard, exhaled even harder. She tried drying her tears, but they wouldn't go away. Trying to convince herself this wasn't real was becoming a moot point. John's lifeless body at her feet was as real as anything she'd ever beheld. Her breathing became rapid and shallow and her body tensed while she gripped her rifle with every ounce of strength she owned.

Dream or not, recess was over. "Whoever's responsible for this, I'm coming. Don't bother hiding. I won't stop until I find you. I'll pursue you into the depths of hell if I have to. And I swear, before God…I will *watch you burn*."

Lauren turned away from the fallen. She couldn't stand to look at them anymore. She took a step forward, then another, and stopped at the point of feeling something hard and unyielding touch the back of her head. It was strangely familiar to her…because it had happened to her before. It could only be one thing, the barrel of a gun. She knew what that felt like.

"Like what I've done with the place?" a voice from her six o'clock droned in a gruesome, undulating tenor. "Did some decorating since the last time you were here."

Lauren gritted her teeth. "You killed them all?"

"Yep," he replied, exhaling. "Did it just for you. Like a welcome-home gift. Impressed?"

She swallowed hard. "No."

"No?"

Lauren shook her head, feeling the pistol's muzzle drift through her hair.

"Oh well, gave it my best shot. Can't please everyone. But it makes a hell of a statement, doesn't it?"

"Who are you?" she asked, now feeling the being's slimy grip on her shoulder.

His fingers caressed her neck. "Who am I? Well, I'm your enemy, of course. I'm the one who…got away. You had your chance to stop me and put an end to all of this before it started, but you didn't." He chuckled. "Pretty dumb move on your part. You realize that now, don't you? And you had to know I'd eventually come for you. Didn't you?"

Lauren shuddered. "Yes."

"Life's all about lessons, little one. And this chance meeting of ours is no different. That's…why I'm here. To teach you."

Lauren nodded again, her fury well on display now.

"It's quite a shame, really. All these lives, including yours, could have been spared had everything gone another way." The man chuckled under his breath again. "Our decisions…and even our *indecisions*, do indeed have consequences."

Lauren felt his grip tighten. She could feel him putting pressure on the trigger. She closed her eyes and resigned herself to her fate, knowing only seconds remained before the firing pin impacted the primer of the chambered round.

A span of time passed, but the gun never went off. Then Lauren felt his hand suddenly pull away from her shoulder.

"L, move out of the way, sweetheart. I got him."

Her eyes went alight at the sound of one of the most familiar voices she'd ever known. Lauren dropped low, ducked and rotated, tried aligning her rifle on her foe, but what came into view instead nearly took her breath away.

With one hand holding her attacker at bay and the other pressing a Glock's muzzle to her would-be assailant's neck, Lauren's father had somehow appeared in the nick of time. He had saved her.

Lauren trembled. "Dad? Dad, is it really you?"

"Yeah, it's me, L. The one and only."

"This is crazy…I don't believe it." She shook her head in suspicion. "We all thought you were—"

"Dead? That's not at all surprising."

Lauren simpered. "You've been gone for so long."

"I know I have. And I'm sorry, L." He regarded her with loving eyes and smiled. "I know I've been gone. A lot of distance has been between us. But you should know…I've never left you." Then he squeezed the trigger.

*KAPOW!*

Lauren shot up from bed in a cold sweat, her bedsheets nearly awash in perspiration, twisted in knots around her tensing outline. Her heart was pounding with exertion and she felt her chest expand with each successive beat. She slid to the side of the bed, rapidly assessed her surroundings, and found that at first, she didn't recognize where she was. She took a moment to gather herself and examine the room in consort with its painted antique furniture and ornate decorations. She was in the guestroom provided to her for her stay in Bernie and Ruth's home on the farm.

*KAPOW!*

Another gunshot followed by a loud smack on the wood siding inches outside her window. Lauren's head snapped right where the panes were allowing early morning sunlight to bleed between the brown cotton drapes. That shot was genuine—it hadn't occurred partially in a dream, as had the one serving to rouse her.

Echoes of shouts and men calling out to each other outside penetrated the old walls as the home's interior came alive. Lauren detected people of all sizes stirring below, the audible creaking of hardwood on the lower levels of the colonial-era home. She dressed and arranged herself as fast as she could, donned her sidearm, spare magazines, and retrieved her Zastava AK-47, then sprinted from the room, the dampened tresses of her hair flinging from side to side behind her.

When Lauren reached the bottom of the staircase, she scoured the main level of the farmhouse, finding it was now vacant. All those heard scurrying around minutes before had seemingly made their exits. On her way into the kitchen, the door leading down into the cellar opened several inches, and she stopped before passing it by.

Ruth peeked through the cracked-open doorway, what color the elderly woman's face retained having dissolved. She breathed heavily, and strands of silver and white hair swayed over her eyes. "Heavens to Betsy, Lauren! You startled me," she said, putting a hand to her chest. "I didn't think anyone was up here." She looked Lauren over and ran her fingers through the teen's sweat-moistened bangs. "My, you're all whitish and sweaty, looks like you've seen a ghost."

Lauren jumped slightly at the sound of more gunshots rattling off outside. "I'm okay, Ruth, but what's going on? What's with all the shooting?"

Ruth looked away, urgency building on her face. "Another skirmish, I imagine."

"A skirmish?" Lauren moved past the woman, closer to the front door. "You're awfully passive about it." Approaching the window, she split the drapes apart to get a view of the driveway. "Does this happen often around here?"

Ruth tiptoed over and closed the gap between them. "Seldom. Most times it's the Sons just doing their thing…but the bullets are usually going in the other direction."

"Sons? Oh…the *Sons of the Second*, you mean. The militia."

"Mm-hmm," Ruth hummed. "We're blessed to have them boys around. We've had a good thing going with them for many a year. They protect the farm and keep us up to our ears in wild game; lots of elk in these hills. But all the good they afford doesn't come without a random measure of not so good."

Another flurry of gunshots went off, and areas of compacted snow erupted and spun into the air as errant bullets collided. "The shots are getting closer. What about the kids? They're sitting ducks out there."

Ruth patted Lauren's shoulder. "Easy, dear. Calm down. They're fine, all safe down in the cellar. We'd never let a thing happen to them, trust me. They mean the world to us, same as you."

Lauren exhaled a sigh of relief, but this skirmish thing was hitting a little too close to home. "Have you seen Dave this morning? Or any of his crew?"

Ruth chuckled slightly under her breath. "Afraid I haven't. He doesn't grace us with his presence unless there's a plate of food waiting for him on the table. Even then, there's no guarantee. I'd wager he's right smack-dab in the middle of all that back-and-forth. He's tried hard to help keep the peace whenever he comes around, but most of the boys from these parts are pretty darn hardheaded. If this old woman's intuition hasn't failed her yet, I'm starting to get the feeling his patience is waning."

"I didn't think Dave had *any* patience." Lauren snickered, spotting motion through the window. Bernie had exited the barn with an armload of freshly split firewood and looked oblivious to the danger surrounding him. "What does Bernie think he's doing?"

Ruth put her nose to the window. "Oh my stars, that man is forever losing his marbles." She wiped her hands on her apron and fiddled with her hair. "Don't worry with him, Lauren. I'll go fetch him."

"No, you won't," Lauren said, holding onto Ruth's arm. "I'll go. You stay here and watch the kids." Without another word, she exited and ran down the porch steps to the shoveled walkway, into the snowy yard. It had hardened somewhat since it had fallen, and a sheet of ice sheltered the top, making a chomping sound with each step.

Bernie smiled and crinkled his nose when he noticed her approach. "Young lady, what on earth are you doing? Coming out here like that with no jacket on? You're gonna catch a cold." He grunted under the wood's weight. "I don't know what's gotten into you young people these days."

Lauren turned slightly, ducking at another rattle of gunshots in the distance. "I'll be fine. I don't plan to be out here any longer than I have to." She slung the AK over her shoulder and offered to carry some of the wood. "I only came out to get you."

Bernie looked confused. "You did, did you? Somebody's got to get this firewood in the house, and I don't see no one else doing it. If that old house gets cold, it'll take forever and a day to warm her back up." Three impressively loud gunshots rang out, having zero effect on the old man. "But since you're out here, why don't you grab another armload from the barn and bring it inside for me? I'd be much obliged."

Lauren reached for his forearm, her resolve mounting. "I will—I'll do that. But you really need to head inside. I think Ruth needs you for something."

"Ruthie? She say what she wants this time?"

"She…didn't specify."

"I see—probably somethin' I forgot. My better half's honey-do list is about a hundred miles long—but don't tell her I said that. If she hears me complainin', she'll only add more to it." A toothy grin slid across Bernie's face and he gestured to the house. "Oh well, go on then. We'd better go see what she wants. Knowing her, it's probably important. Important to her, at any rate."

Lauren smiled at him, and the two walked side by side back to the porch. She escorted Bernie inside and handed him off to Ruth, then rotated and headed back.

"Lauren," Ruth rattled, "dear, where are you going?"

"To find Dave. And put an end to this."

Ruth instructed Bernie to stay put and gave chase. "Dear, listen to me, please…don't go back out there." She clung gently to Lauren's arm. "There are enough angry men, danger and guns outside already. You don't need to be getting yourself involved in that mess."

Lauren turned to face the old woman, her unfettered hair falling into elegant layers along and over her shoulder. "I'm already involved." She offered a firm, reassuring smile, a visible indication of the strength of character she'd attained in recent months.

For Lauren, being who she was now, it wasn't a conscious choice or a voluntary option; it had become a calling. "It's okay. Keep everyone inside, especially that mischievous husband of yours. I'll be back shortly. I promise."

# CHAPTER 3

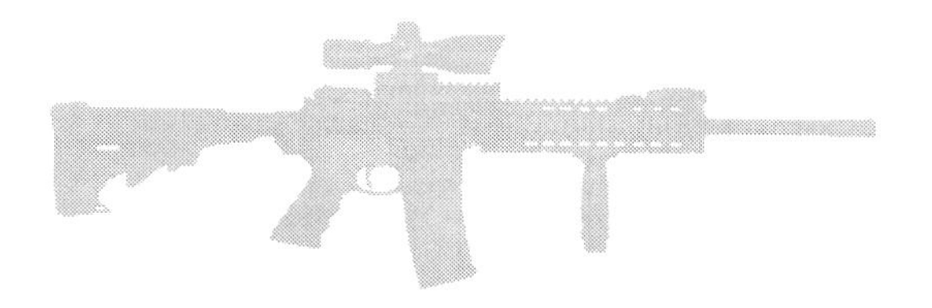

**The cabin**
**Trout Run Valley**
**Saturday, January 1st. Present day**

THE LOOK ON HIS FACE was smug, to say the least. There was simply no other way to describe it. Richie Rich, as he'd been baptized by those who'd known him the longest, was the walking, chattering epitome of sanctimonious. A whole melting pot of it, reaching the point of damn near boiling over and spilling whatever surplus he retained onto Grace's freshly mopped hardwood floors. One of his eyebrows was arched ever so slightly, and his lips were scarcely curled into a smirk, as if he were using only the absolute bare minimum effort to implement the gestures.

With her chin resting in her palms, her elbows on the table, and a scorching stare capable of setting anything remotely flammable in the room ablaze, Grace inspected the young man sitting across from her. The air of arrogance he gave off was causing her to develop nausea beyond any level experienced thus far in the final month of her first trimester. With every subsequent pompous word he uttered, every insensitive syllable that spewed from the orifice of lips, gums and teeth that fashioned his stupid mouth, Grace didn't just want to hurt him; she wanted to wound him, murder him, tear the skin from his face and chew on it like licorice, all the while clawing his goddamn eyes out.

The young soldier had impulsively joined Grace and Christian for breakfast this morning on a whim and without invitation, and was now helping himself to a serving of waffles that Grace had made specifically for herself, Christian, and the handful of others living in the cabin. And everyone who lived there, especially now that she was consuming sustenance for a sum of two, knew how much Grace relished her waffles.

As Richie tilted a glass of water to his lips, Grace reached forward, to his astonishment, and intercepted it. She relieved him of it following a trivial tugging match and placed it firmly onto the table. "Richie, stop a second. Wait. Refrain from taking another bite or sip and kindly reiterate what you just said...only, do so *sans* the attitude. And when I say 'sans the attitude,' I mean *without* it. You know, shorn of it. Completely deficient thereof—as in lacking said attitude entirely. As in leave it at the fucking doormat where you should've left those crusty boots when you barged into my home unannounced."

Richie's eyebrows shot up. "Um...o-kay."

Grace held up her index finger. "Halt. Don't speak. Not yet," she purred. "Cherry-pick the words you're about to use wisely—and I mean *very* wisely. Keep in mind the person about whom you're gushing off at the mouth just so happens to be my sister. And I *love* my sister."

"I know that," Richie replied. "And I always choose my words wisely. And what attitude, by the way? I don't think I hav—"

Grace snapped her fingers, her eyes slamming shut. "Yes, you do. You do, in fact, possess an attitude. A particularly shitty one. And if you keep brandishing it while speaking to me in this house, I swear before God the father himself, I will become aggressive, perhaps excessively so."

Richie sniggered and fell back into the chair. "Aggressive? Really?"

Grace elevated her brows. "Mm-hmm. I'm sure by now it's highly likely you've heard that I'm...with child. To be accurate, I'm nearing the final stages of my first trimester—my first one *ever*. I'm insanely hyperemotional, sick to my stomach every goddamn minute of every goddamn day, and for some unearthly reason, I retch every morsel of food I put down like some pitiful bulimic on an extended masochistic binge-purge cycle. Consequently, my tolerance level for bullshit has arrived at an all-time low, as in taking a head-first plummet into some foreign, unexplored gestationally fabricated abyss." Her glare went sour. "That all being said, I swear as sure as we're all sitting here, if you don't mislay that...childish arrogance of yours and address me with some...measure of courtesy, I will *cut* you."

Richie turned to Christian. "Um, dude? Is your girl for real?"

Christian glanced at his love, pursed his lips and sent a single nod. "Yeah, *dude*. I believe her to be just that." He watched Grace's hand disappear from the table and reappear with a Victorinox Swiss Army knife.

Grace overturned her hand, presented the knife for all to see, then brought it close to her chest and sent Christian a set of googly eyes. "Gosh, do you see why I love this man so? This knife was the first gift he ever gave me, I'm sorry…I mean, aside from his colossal, exquisite heart. He's such the loverboy, always doing the sweetest little things for me, always when I least expect it." Now on the verge of tears, Grace set the knife down and affixed her gaze to Richie again, chin landing in her palms. "Sorry—got caught up in the moment. Where were we? You were saying?"

Richie set down his fork and eyed Grace's knife. "Okay, okay. I can pretty much see where this is headed. The only reason I even chose to come here and say anything about this was because I assumed it would help us get to know each other a little better…maybe even ease the tension."

Christian folded his arms. "The only tension I'm aware of is the tension you created on the day we came here, and I'm over it. But since we're on the topic, let me hand you off a little advice. What you say is nowhere near as important as *how* you choose to say it. You strolled in here this morning, unannounced and uninvited, with an agenda of some kind knowing full well what, or more to the point, *who* you'd encounter. This is Lauren's house. Her family lives here."

"A lot of people live here, and not all of them are family," the young soldier said with a slight eye roll. "At least, from what I've…gathered."

"*Exsqueeze* me?" Grace barked.

Christian intervened with a hand. "Yes, that's correct. It's a full house. I live here now, and Norman and his sons are close family friends who've been living here since the beginning."

"Close family friends." Richie sniggered. "The blond guy…the one who doesn't talk a lot. That's Lauren's boyfriend, correct?"

Grace's nostrils flared.

Christian hesitated before responding, at a loss for where this was going. "Correct."

Richie jutted his chin out. "Yeah. I gathered that, too." A pause. "So, do they sleep in separate rooms?"

"I beg your pardon?" Grace asked, her eyes darkening.

"Sorry, I mean…well…what I'm asking is—"

Grace snapped her fingers again. "Don't, Richie. No. You stop right there. Don't you dare ask that."

"Huh? Why not? How do you know what I was planning to ask?"

"Because I'm telepathic, *stupid*," Grace fizzed. "The preliminary stages of motherhood have generously enriched all *six* of my senses. That's right, six. And you…you were about to touch on whether my sister and her man are…occupying the same bed—nightly. Right?"

Richie shrugged. "Well, yeah. I guess. But—"

"And the resolution to that…brazen, tremendously inconsiderate question would be none of your goddamn business. *I guess*," Grace said, mocking both his answer and tone. "Now, finalize your train of thought—for good, if you even have one, then kindly remove your ass from that chair *and* yourself from this house directly thereafter. We, meaning those living beneath this roof, have lots of…things to do today."

Richie sighed. He shook his head and rolled his eyes. "Fine. Whatever. I just don't understand…makes no sense to me why your sister's never mentioned *us* before—to anyone. It's confusing. That's all."

"That's all?" Grace queried. "Are you sure that's *all*, Richie?"

Richie shrugged again. "Yeah, I mean, I guess there's a little more to it than that. I mean…she *was* seriously head over heels infatuated with me."

Grace grabbed the Swiss Army knife and shot a glance to Christian. "That's it. I'm cutting him." She rose, knocking the chair away behind her.

Richie jumped from his seat and backed away, his right hand moving instinctively to his holstered sidearm.

Christian held Grace at bay by the arm and pointed at Richie. "Easy, bud. Hand away from the backstrap," he ordered, then looked to Grace. "And you…sit down and relax." A pause. "Please?"

"I'll back down when she does," Richie squawked. "Jesus…what the hell's her problem anyway?"

Grace's retort was instant. "My problem?" She chuckled maniacally. "*My problem?* Well, kind sir, my…*problem* happens to be you and your stupid…face and…words. Lauren has never been infatuated with anything or anyone, for that matter. Especially some self-important, urchin dickwad like *you*."

"Oh really?" Richie said. "Well, I beg to differ. You weren't there. Neither of you were. And your sister was downright crazy for me. We spent an incredible evening together, but in the end, I knew it wouldn't work out for us. We were way too…different. And I knew it was up to me to make the adult decision. I had to let her down easy."

"Asshole! Let go of me, Christian!" Grace yanked away, rounded the table and used its leverage to slingshot herself at Richie.

The young soldier dodged her advance with ease. He slid out of the danger zone and went on the defensive.

The situation looking to spiral beyond frenetic, Christian grabbed the table and slid it behind him, then jumped between the arrogant soldier and the highly agitated mother of his child. He stuck a hand in Richie's face while struggling with Grace, barely able to prevent her from gaining ground. "That's it, this is done! Through! Over! Richie, get out, now. While you still can."

Richie smirked. "Heh. No problem. I'll just be on my way," he said, and turned. "I guess sometimes the truth really does hurt, doesn't it?"

"You motherfucker!" Grace yelped. "I'll show you hurt! I'll show you oodles of fucking hurt, you spineless, hopeless, dickless, donkey-molesting shit feeder! I'm gonna—"

Stopping her mid-thought and mid-sentence, the front door suddenly flung open before Richie could reach for the handle. Junior Brady stepped inside accompanied by his brother Ricky, their boots caked with snow. Their eyes fell immediately upon Grace, who was in the process of opening several of the Swiss Army knife's accessories, including the knife blade, the saw and the fish scaler, while she battled Christian's grasp.

Junior Brady spoke first. "Might we be…interrupting somethin'?"

Christian forced a smile. "No, not at all. Just a little…family business. Got a hair out of hand, but everything's under control now."

"Yeah, looks like it," Junior said, wide-eyed and unconvinced.

"*Out of hand* hasn't quite arrived yet," Grace spat. She muscled open the scissors, bottle opener and Phillips screwdriver on the knife. "Oh, wait, there it is. There's *out of hand*, right on time. And now you're all about to witness something extraordinary. First-degree homicide, right before your very eyes."

Richie scoffed. "You're full of it. You couldn't kill a mosquito with that kid knife."

"Maybe not. But I could castrate one."

"Maybe…we should come back later," Junior said, his expression signaling nervousness. "When you actually *do* have things under control."

"Nonsense," said Christian. He passed cold stares and verbally admonished Richie and Grace under his breath while judging the newest arrivals' overall demeanor. As a rule, they were known for knocking and awaiting a response before making entry. Something was up. "What can we help you with?"

Ricky sent strange glances to all parties excluding his brother. "Is Michelle around?"

"Not at the moment."

"Where might she be, then? We're lookin' for her."

"It's difficult to know for sure," Christian said. "She keeps herself busy these days. Our…most recent unwanted guests left us a hell of a mess to clean up."

"Interesting way to put that," Junior said, holding his head solemnly. "We, uh, don't mean to come across as being pushy, but we really need to speak with her today. Any clue where we're likely to find her?"

Christian shrugged. "Across the road at the Masons' would be my first guess. Or next door at the Ackermann place where Dr. Vincent and his wife are staying."

"He means the provisional ob-gyn clinic," Grace hissed. "If you will."

"The what?" prompted Ricky.

"I suppose we'll head out and check both places, then," Junior said. "Thanks, and sorry to bother you."

"Junior, wait. What exactly is going on?" asked Christian. "I mean, what's this in reference to?"

The Brady brothers traded looks before Junior tendered a response. "Well, I suppose we could call it a matter of…family business."

"Family business?" Christian echoed, unable to discern if he was being mocked.

"It regards our deal," Ricky added.

Christian closed his eyes and sighed. He'd had a feeling this was coming. "What about it?"

Junior glanced at his brother once more. "No offense to you, Christian, but you haven't lived here as long as some of these other folks. And we prefer to discuss this with someone who has a little more…sway. Normally, our paw would be in the spot to handle this; then the right would fall to Bo. It…kind of goes without saying, in light of recent…events, our situation's changed."

Ricky's eyes darted into the hallway. "What about ole Norm? He around?"

Christian shook his head. "No, he's at the Masons'. Still tending to Lee."

"How's the boy doing, by the way?" Junior asked. "Figured he'd be back home by now."

"He's recovering well, but the docs want to keep him immobile a while longer," Christian said. "He and the others were lucky. Thanks for asking."

Ricky Brady huffed, sending Christian an insistent glare. "Well, ain't that swell. So nice to know how lucky they all were and how they're all gettin' better. Just so you know, not every injury is the healin' type."

"I realize that," Christian said.

"It's best you should," Ricky grumbled. "Don't ever be forgettin' it, neither."

Christian looked confused. "I won't, haven't, and wouldn't. And as I've said before, I'm very sorry for your loss."

Ricky sneered. "Mm-hmm."

"Excuse me," Grace cut in, "sorry to interrupt this squarejerk, but did either of you yokels come here intending to divulge anything of worth? Because if so, spit it the fuck out already and then let yourselves the hell out of my house." She pointed to the floor. "You two twats tracked friggin' mud and snow in all over the friggin' floor I only just finished friggin' mopping. And you both smell god-awful—like two men who've recently been intimate with livestock."

"Eh, sorry about that," Junior said, eyeing the floor and putting a nose to his underarm.

Grace fake smiled. "Oh, that's okay, really. I'm not really that mad about the floor. Just…peeved. And really nauseous. Everything makes me nauseous. And my poor stomach is once again on the verge of emptying itself of what little acid remains there…for the fifth damn time today."

Ricky stepped forward with the intent to offer a retort, but his brother halted him.

"Grace, we apologize, we do. For the intrusion and for the mess on your floor." Junior slid his hands into his pockets and turned away, headed for the door.

Ricky opened the door for him. After his brother slid past, he remained in the threshold. "In case y'all are wonderin', our deal is over. Ain't gonna be no more guardin' barricades or doin' patrols or makin' road trips. We're goin' back to keepin' to ourselves and takin' care of ourselves—like we shoulda done in the first place before we got tangled up with y'all."

Feeling more needed to be said, Junior rotated in the doorway. "Sorry we have to be this abrupt, but we can't stand to lose anyone else. We don't want any more blood. Probably should've never gotten involved in this little war in the first place, but that was our paw's doing." A pause. "He isn't around anymore to make family decisions, and Bo's not here either, so it all falls on me now. Puts me in charge of this family. And those of us left have to take care of ourselves the best way we know how. Good luck to all of you."

Grace snapped her fingers, nabbing both Christian's and Richie's combined attention as the door closed. "What the hell, you two? Are you just going to stand there?"

Richie looked dumbfounded. He said nothing while remaining transfixed on Grace's hand and the splayed-out tools of the Swiss Army knife.

"What?" asked Christian.

"What do you mean, *what*? This is sort of a big deal, Christian."

"I know that. In fact, I'm pretty sure it was me who told *you* that."

"Whatever. This isn't a pissing contest. If we lose our arrangement with the Bradys, we lose the help we've been getting at the barricades—not to mention the *major* help we stand to get with all that food they have access to at that place down the road. So, go. Now. Talk to them."

Richie sneered. "And let me guess. You want me to go with him, right?"

"Nope," Grace said, urging him along with a shooing gesture. "I don't want *you* to do anything other than leave. Oh, and never return."

Christian sighed. He went to the door, opened it and allowed Richie to stroll out. He walked to the edge of the porch and called out to the Brady brothers a moment after.

Ricky Brady waved Christian off with his back turned while slogging through the snow to his truck. His sons Tommy and Wayne were standing outside, appearing to have been waiting for him near the midway point of the Russells' driveway.

Christian continued to give chase, unaware if Ricky's boys had just arrived or if they'd accompanied their father here, but he took note that they were no longer manning their posts. And with Chad and Mark Mason having gone missing, it meant that no one was guarding the barricade at Wolf Gap.

One of Ricky's sons strolled directly to his father while the other followed a short way behind. "Paw, everything go all right?"

"Sure did. In fact, I'm real glad to see you both here. We were about ready to head up the hill and get you. We'll be takin' our leave of these folks and all their hitches and snags for good, beginnin' today."

Tommy Brady looked back at his brother. "Okay, I guess. But, Paw, there's somethin' else. Somethin' we know. A glitch we're facin'."

"You're telling me, boy," Ricky said. "We got lots of those, don't we…and one real big one. Well, don't you worry. We'll be fixing them all real shortly."

The two younger Bradys traded nervous looks.

Tommy began again. "Paw…listen to me, please. Me and Wayne wanted to tell you this weeks ago, but we didn't. With the family so tore up, we was afraid to. And now since we're partin' ways with everyone, like you said, we should probably say somethin' to them about it. You know, before."

Ricky looked upon his sons with a set of perplexed, bitter eyes, but offered nothing in response.

Christian homed in on the young man's words. "What is it you want to tell us, Tommy?"

Ricky pointed a stern finger at Christian. "Now you just hold on there. You don't get to talk to my boys. They're *my* sons. And that makes it *my* job."

"Fine." Christian relented.

"Well, go on then," Ricky urged them. "Say what you got to say so we can get a move on."

Tommy spoke hesitantly. "It's about the Mason brothers, Chad and Mark. Back before they went missin', they told us they were headin' to Virginia to do some huntin', said they'd be back in a day or so. Then they asked if we could keep it a secret about them leaving and cover for them. We thought it was strange they'd ask us to do that, but we said yes anyways."

"Secret? Damn right it's strange," Ricky scolded. "That shoulda smacked you in the noggin right there. What's the matter with you?"

Junior Brady intervened on the young man's behalf. "Easy, Rick. Let the boy speak."

Wayne finally moved forward to stand in solidarity with his brother. "I told him not to say anything. I didn't want anyone to get mad for what we did. It was my fault, Paw."

Ricky hung his head. "I taught you better than that, boy."

"I know, and I'm sorry." Wayne paused to gather his thoughts. "Anyway, Tommy and me, we got suspicious. So we snuck out of the hide and watched them right before they left. It probably wasn't right to do it, but we did." Another pause. "We saw three of them."

"Three?" Christian probed.

"That's right," Wayne timidly replied. "Chad, Mark, and another person. A woman. Each one had a motorbike…three of the ones we kept from that gang. We…didn't know who the woman was, at first. Thought it might've been one of y'all, until Tommy pointed out the color in her hair. Then we knew it had to be that biker woman."

"What biker woman?" Junior asked, his tone brasher than before.

"The one who showed up to the barricade the night before the attack to warn us," Tommy filled in. "The one who got shot."

Christian stepped closer into the fray with arms folded. "Wait a second, that woman died on the road that day. I thought we buried her in the mass grave with the rest of her posse."

"I reckon she must've risen from the dead," Wayne said. "'Cause it was her."

"Sounds like y'all have yourselves a mystery to solve," Junior said. "It's a shame those boys are missing; no doubt in my mind it's…difficult. But that doesn't really change much for us."

Christian nodded. "I know. And for what it's worth, I'm sorry for the way things have gone down. And I'm truly sorry about what happened to Bo. I honestly wish there was something I could've done. We were all in a really bad spot that day; any one of us could've been handed the same fate."

Junior elevated his gaze. "I get that. I personally don't blame you or anyone else for what happened. But we…just can't take any more chances."

"Mother of p-pearl on a p-pogo stick! It's frigid as fuck out here!" Grace shrieked, exiting the cabin, bundled in a winter jacket and a scarf securely wrapping her neck and face. "Perplexing…the polar air seems to have a thwarting effect on my nausea." She approached her onlookers. "Gentlemen, did we manage to work out our differences?"

Every man in present company took turns staring at one another and offering his version of a negative response.

"Well, great. That's great…freaking swell," Grace quipped through the woolen material concealing her mouth. "I love how everything is just falling to freaking pieces today." She angled her head backward and adjusted her scarf to expose her nose; then a curious look befell her.

"What is it?" Christian inquired. "That buzzing sound again?"

Grace shook her head, sniffing the air above. "No. No buzzing. It's just this…smell."

Christian pivoted. "I don't smell anything."

Richie edged forward after remaining mostly apart from the others. "What exactly do you smell? Something that doesn't belong?"

Grace pointed a finger at him. "Whoa, maintain your distance, GI joker. Remember, I don't like you. But since you asked, my answer would be not really, but maybe. It's like…men's cologne or something."

"I don't wear cologne," said Christian. "I don't think anyone in the valley does."

"Trust me, they don't," Grace spat. "That's a certainty."

"Are you sure it's not perfume?" Richie persisted.

"Yes, I'm sure. No way it's perfume; it's not fruity or flowery. It's more like…aftershave. Nothing girly about it at all."

"Grace," Christian began, now able to predict where Richie was going with this, "is it foreign to you? As in something you haven't smelled before around these parts?"

"Around these parts," Grace teased. "Listen to you, you're turning into a country boy. It's so cute."

"Grace…"

"Sorry." She thought a moment, then nodded. "Yes. Definitely. I have never smelled this smell before in my life…well, since living here, I mean."

Richie got a sudden serious look on his face, doing away with his characteristic superior one. He stuck his finger in his mouth and held it aloft to feel the direction in which the wind was gusting. "Okay, right now everybody needs to move. Get out of the open and find cover, now!"

Christian's look filled with urgency. "Do as he says!" With resolve, he scanned the trees and sprinted to Grace. "Come on. Get back in the cabin."

"What? The cabin? Why?" she asked, her hands aloft to her sides. "Why do I—"

A penetrating zip tore through the air, and a split second later, Ricky Brady grabbed his chest and collapsed to the ground, screaming and writhing in agony. Junior yelled for his brother and moved to render aid, only to make it several feet before he was taken down by a second shot.

Richie went into action. He pushed both Wayne and Tommy to the ground near their father's truck and hit the deck with his rifle pointed westward, then pulled a radio from a pouch on his plate carrier. "Break! Break! This is romeo-one-actual. Sniper in the woods! I say again, sniper in the woods! Danger imminent! I need all eyes open to the west!"

Christian latched onto Grace and hoisted her onto the porch, making quick work of escorting her safely indoors as several other barely audible shots whizzed by.

"My hero," she cooed, her hands gripping his shoulders. "You saved me again, my daring knight. And now I love you even more than I did a minute ago." She smiled, kissed him, and her expression contorted. "Did you hear what that douche bagel said to his radio? *Romeo*...like it was his name or something. Can you believe that shit? Romeo. As if."

"I heard him," Christian said, pulling away from her and sliding to the door to chance a look outside. "Junior's bleeding pretty bad from the shoulder. And Ricky doesn't look good. That shot hit him dead center...he isn't moving."

"Jeez, *more* hurt Bradys?" Grace mused. "We're running low on them for real now."

"Grace...Jesus."

"What? It's true. And you know as well as I do, it won't go over well. Who do you think is shooting at us?"

"By my best estimate? Undoubtedly one of your buddy's friends."

"My...buddy?"

Christian sighed. "Pornstache Max, whom you resolved to keep alive, for whatever reason."

Grace moved to her knees and crawled closer, halting upon receiving visual reprimand. "Oh, him. I thought I told you why I did that."

"And I thought I told you why you shouldn't have," Christian barked.

"Hmm. Christian, I'm sensing a certain off-color tone…I really don't wish to quarrel with you," Grace said, puckering her lips. "Not now. Not with people shooting at us."

"Nor I you." He took one last look outside, then secured the door and hurried down the hallway, hurdling Grace along the way. Christian reemerged a moment after with the Savage .300 Win Mag retrieved from the gun safe.

Grace sent him an odd look. "Is this the best time to go hunting?"

"Depends on the prey. I need something that can reach out and touch someone," he said, then knelt and placed a gentle kiss on Grace's waiting lips. "Stay here, please. And stay down. Protect yourself and that baby at all costs."

Grace brushed his cheek with her fingertips. "I will. No funny business on my part, I promise. Be careful, please. And don't get shot again."

"I'll try not to." Christian turned away and cracked open the door, and the added volume of sporadic gunfire became instantly noticeable.

"And by the way, it's *our* baby, never *that* baby," Grace exclaimed, watching helplessly as he took his leave, running daringly back into danger.

# CHAPTER 4

**Little Germany Farms**
**Riverton, West Virginia**
**Saturday, January 1st. Present day**

THROUGH VARYING DEPTHS OF DENSE snow, Lauren dashed away from the farmhouse in the direction of the shots. She ran low and lunged into snowdrifts to prevent being hit as bullets whizzed rebelliously overhead, most times with intent, a handful of times purely by accident.

During a brief intermission between reports, she began to hear rustling and panting from behind as two pairs of legs sifted through the tracks she'd made. Lauren had a feeling she wasn't alone anymore and saw a furry brown face upon whirling around to verify. "Dammit! Cyrus, no! Bad dog! Go back!"

She pled with him, but it wasn't any use. The young retriever was locked on now, as oblivious to the circumambient hazards as his owner. His snout lowered, Cyrus slowed his gallop and casually strolled to Lauren without a care in the world before pushing his cold, soggy nose into her face. He licked her and plopped down in the snow, offering his paw.

Lauren sighed, taking it with her free hand. She smiled at him, unable to help herself. "You're a lovely pup, Cyrus. No doubt about it. But you're also a big idiot," she said, petting him and rubbing his head and ears. "You know that, right?"

Soon, the erratic spurts of gunfire returned. The morning sky was bright and overcast, providing adequate light to move about, though

Lauren still couldn't see or discern from precisely where the shots were originating. She rubbed Cyrus's head. "I don't suppose I'm going to be able to talk you into staying put, am I?"

His tongue dangling and panting merrily, Cyrus merely cocked his head and pricked his ears.

"Yeah." Lauren sighed. "I didn't think so."

The muzzle of her AK-47 leading the way, Lauren darted ahead through the snowy orchard, mostly in a crawl. As expected, Cyrus edged closely behind, moving when she moved, stopping when she stopped, and before long the pair arrived at the driveway's intersection with the main road.

Lauren took cover behind one of the ancient oaks marking the gated entrance to the farm, and instructed her companion to lie down. The dog heeded her command this time, much to her surprise. She turned away from him and glanced right, then left. As unplowed and undisturbed as the driveway she'd paralleled to get here, US 33 was a washout. It appeared now only as an ample, meandering disruption between the trees in either direction, blanketed by drifts of frozen white powder.

Then a new problem became evident. Lauren could now hear gunshots both before and behind her. Some even seemed to originate from her flanks. She ducked lower, inched closer to the oak and plotted the scene, dismayed that she might've inadvertently positioned herself and Bernie's dog in a deadly crossfire. She spent a long moment contemplating which direction to go next and outlined what would serve as her safest path back to the house and away from danger.

But before Lauren could arrive at a conclusion, Cyrus alerted. His ears pricked; then he rose to his feet, barked and made the decision on her behalf. The young Lab jetted off along the orchard's tree line after something he had either seen, heard, or caught wind of.

Still utilizing the oak and surrounding snow for cover and concealment, Lauren rotated right and brought the AK to her cheek, glancing through the aperture of the magnified optic Santa had supplied to see where the pup was headed. A moment later, amidst a cloud of kicked-up snow, she saw what the fuss was about.

Huddled together approximately fifty yards distant, in what looked to be an arbitrarily hand-dug entrenchment in the snow, were Dave Graham, Santa, Woo Tang and Sanchez. And another man was sitting with them whom Lauren didn't recognize.

Amidst the ongoing sporadic gunfire, she studied their behavior, aided by her optic's magnification, and took notice of something uncharacteristic. Aside from the stranger, for whom Lauren had no comparative basis, the rest appeared wholly out of formation, perhaps even a hundred klicks slight of being so.

While Dave spoke with terribly tired eyes and loosely animated hands with the stranger, Sanchez and Santa were taking turns aimlessly firing their rifles over the snowbank cover on which they were sluggishly reclining. They were goofing off, smiling at each other and even laughing at times. Woo Tang's expression was indiscernible; he was either feeling out of sorts or dead to the world.

Lauren lowered her rifle, exhaling through her nostrils as her expression clouded with disdain. "I must have caught them at a bad time."

Shaking her head in disgust, she chanced another look through her optic, choosing this time to single out Dave Graham. He *was* the unit commander, after all. The pillar of the group, the one ultimately responsible. The upstanding gentleman, eternal defender of the defenseless. The former US Army first sergeant and company leader with the impeccable service record who never quite made it to officer, the whys and wherefores having never been disclosed. Mister Special Forces veteran, Point Blank Range instructor, protector and upholder of the Constitution of the former United States of America himself.

Today, that man looked downright knackered, a run-of-the-mill rendering of the Dave Graham Lauren knew. And the discussion he was entertaining with the stranger appeared to take precedence, for some inexplicable reason, over the ensuing gun battle, or whatever this was.

Insofar as Lauren was concerned, this was completely out of character for Dave and his men. She had never seen them this far gone before; it contradicted everything they stood for and believed in. Somewhere out there, a hostile force was shooting at them—sending lethal volleys of rounds toward a house occupied by defenseless friendlies. And Dave and his men were taking it in stride, doing next to nothing about it, barely batting an eyelid.

Lauren didn't know what was off beam with them or what was serving as a reason for nonaction, but felt determined to find out. She kept her profile as low as she could, broke cover, and crawled through the snowpack to the entrenchment. She made entry, pouncing on them abruptly as each man reeled back in surprise.

Sanchez was aghast and put a hand to his chest. "*Aye de mi!* Scared the shit out of me, *chica.*"

"Guess you're lucky I'm not the enemy, then." Lauren tugged the Marine's hand to where his rifle lay nearby. "Lose something?"

Sanchez palmed the M4's grip. "Hey, stop screwing around. What's your deal?"

"My *deal*?" Lauren studied the group. "Would any of you care to clue me in on what the hell is going on?"

Santa coughed and cleared his throat. "Sounds like a smidgen of a firefight to me." He nudged Woo Tang. "Wouldn't you agree, squiddy?"

Woo Tang shrugged. "I find I can offer no disagreement."

Lauren shook her head back and forth, her misperception mounting. "Well, do we know who's shooting at us?"

Dave Graham finally spoke, jutting his thumb over the snowbank. "Them."

"Brilliant. And who would *them* be?"

"Oh, well, *them* would be our mortal enemies," said the stranger seated beside Dave, with long, stringy, straight hair. "The Snyder clan, out of Harman. A hopeless bunch of usurpers, thieves, turncoats and jerks of the foulest degree."

Lauren squinted at the man.

"I sense some confusion there, so let me explain. It's a sordid relationship…kind of like a modern-day Hatfield-McCoy affair." He reached to pet Cyrus, but the dog scuttled away. "Guess he don't like how good I smell. Whatever. Anyway, this here's what happens when two sets of folks come to blows over…well, I suppose we'll call it irreconcilable differences. Them boys drew a line in the sand with us about a century and a half ago, and not a whole lot's changed since then."

An errant bullet smacked the snow near the trench's edge, showering the group in a fine coating of powder.

Lauren ducked instinctively and brushed the snow from her face. "Right. And is that some up-country way of saying that what's happening now is because of some…long-standing feud?"

"Yepper," the long-haired stranger said colloquially, accompanied by an equally colloquial nod. "That's what I'm telling you." He turned to Dave, nudging him with his elbow. "She's a smart one, ain't she?"

Dave nodded indifferently. "That she is."

"Mighty cute too," added the stranger.

Dave scooted closer to Lauren, holding out a rather shaky introductory hand. "Janey, meet Lazarus. He's the…reigning high priestess of the Sons of the Second, the militia I told you about that protects these parts."

"And that's 'cause it's the *only* militia anywhere around these parts," the newly introduced added. "And *high priestess*? Really, Graham? That's charming."

"Your name's Lazarus?" asked Lauren.

"Yepper. That it is. Pleasure to meet you."

"And that's your *real* name?"

"Absolutely, why? Is Janey yours?"

Lauren huffed and turned her attention away, gesturing to the ongoing sporadic pops of gunfire. "Dave, this is insane. We have to do something about this…there are bullets flying all over the place back there. This isn't any way to live."

Before Dave could respond, Lazarus chimed in, "Hang on a second…hop down off that high horse of yours, city girl. There's no need in making a fuss out of it. Out here in the country, this type of thing just sort of happens every so often. Stay a while, you'll get used to it."

"And how…*every so often* does this…*type of thing just sort of happen*?" Lauren challenged, mocking his diction.

"Eh…come to think of it, it's been a while since we've exchanged niceties," replied Lazarus, rubbing his chin. "This one popped off over a little argument. Before that, we'd been enjoyin' a long-lasting ceasefire. But the boys were up kind of late last night, and things got a little riled up, and insults started getting tossed back and forth. Next thing you know, one of 'em pulled a gun and shot another. And usually, when one gun goes off, another goes off not long after. Kind of like the circle of life and such."

"Right." Lauren monitored the man's shifty eyes closely. Her negative opinion of him in mid-development, she turned away and sent her concern back to the others. "Why do you guys look like you collectively crawled out from under a random rock this morning?"

No one spoke for a moment as the shots continued to ring out overhead.

"It's called fatigue, Janey," Dave moaned. "It's an occupational hazard for all-nighters, and just plain staying up too damn late."

"What were you guys doing besides sleeping? If it's okay for me to ask."

Dave shrugged. “Enjoying a measure of highly craved R and R. And being…festive.”

“Festive?” Lauren darted her eyes around. “Are you guys drunk?”

The men all shared a barrage of uncommon looks.

Woo Tang sighed, rubbing the bridge of his nose. “I think what you are witnessing in this moment are the unpleasant aftereffects of drunk.”

Lauren’s mouth fell open. She cut her eyes at him. “Jae!”

He shrugged. “Lauren Russell, though I do, in fact, feel horrible, both internally and externally, I can offer no apology for the damage imposed. We are all grown men and warriors alike, and all men and warriors the same necessitate leisure time. It sponsors morale.” From there, he coughed himself into a gagging fit.

Lauren rolled her eyes and ran her fingers through her hair. “Unbelievable. You guys are *un*believable.”

“Come on now, what did you expect?” Sanchez queried. “*Era La Nochevieja, chica.*”

“What?”

“New Year’s,” Santa filled in curtly, his eyes half-shut. “Or New Year’s Eve, rather.”

“Fuckin’ A,” Sanchez said. “Haven’t you ever burned the midnight oil and grooved all night long before a new year rolls in?”

“No.” Lauren snapped her fingers, beckoning Cyrus. “I haven’t.”

“Really? It’s a blast. Lots of drinking, dancing…Hawaiian shirts, pigs roasting…”

“And Spam,” Santa inserted.

“Shit yeah,” Sanchez hooted. “I fuckin’ love Spam.” He wearily considered Lauren with his handsome eyes. “So why haven’t you?”

“Um, probably because I’m *only* eighteen, Sanchez.”

The Marine snickered. “Well, you’ve missed out, then.”

“Yeah, I can see that. So far, I’m real impressed.” She glowered all through an elongated pause. “And I suppose *this* would be our New Year’s resolution…giggling and acting stupid, taking potshots at the jerks shooting at us along with random catnaps to nurse our headaches. A real innovative, asinine strategy for the unit. Well done, Dave. I’m hereby rendered speechless.”

Dave peered over at her from the corner of a bloodshot eye. “Just what exactly do you fancy we do about it, Janey? Hop on the radio and call in an airstrike?”

The others chuckled while Lauren only bristled. "Don't be ridiculous. What I *fancy*…is for all of you to somehow resurrect yourselves and find some way to put a stop to it. Expeditiously, if it isn't asking too much." She pointed down the driveway in the direction of the house, her eyes alight. "There are over seventy kids back there, all huddled in a basement, too scared to come out."

"I'm aware of that—and that's good," Dave said. "The cellar's the safest place for them for the time being until whatever this is dies down."

Lauren scowled. "Dave, stray bullets are hitting the house. One even smacked the siding next to my bedroom window. Woke me up out of a dead sleep."

Dave raised a shrewd brow. "And conversely, I was *not* aware of that," he said, changing his tune. He regarded their long-haired companion. "What the actual fuck, Lazarus? This dispute of yours doesn't involve those folks. Why are those shitwits shelling the house?"

"I don't know. They shouldn't be," Lazarus said. "I mean…they've never done anything like that before. They must really be ticked off this time."

"Ticked off, livid, or blood boiling, that's no cause to send fire toward civilians," remarked Santa with a pointed finger. "Especially them kids back there."

"I realize that and I agree with you fully," the long-haired militiaman said. "But they could also be doing so because of the presence of y'all's army-variety trucks parked in the driveway. Could've easily given them the wrong idea…probably think we've hired ourselves some mercenaries, a private army or something. Won't know for sure until I talk to them."

"*Talk* to them?" Lauren snapped.

Lazarus shrugged. "Yepper. You see, the leaders have these roundtables every few months or so. Helps scale back hostilities and keep the peace."

She pointed over the snowbank. "Want to give it a try now?"

He ducked suddenly when a shot smacked the snow inches above his head. "Nah. I'm thinking it might be better to wait."

Lauren sighed and cradled her AK, staring coldly at Dave and the others.

After a time, Dave stirred and inhaled a deep breath. "All right, boys, front and center. Janey's not happy with us, and for good reason. Let's get a move on." He slapped Santa on the shoulder, sent a fist into

Sanchez's arm, and tapped Woo Tang with his finger. "Let's shut this shit down before somebody gets hurt."

With a puzzled look, Lazarus reached for Dave's arm. "Whoa, wait a second there, Graham. Exactly what are you planning to do? You can't just go out there and get in the middle; it's not your place."

"It *wasn't* our place until they selected those kind folks back there as targets," Dave barked. "That's unwarranted collateral damage, Lazarus." He moved to his knees, adjusted his gear and reached for his rifle. "Santa, I take it you saw to bringing along some heavier-than-routine ordnance?"

Lazarus's eyes grew wide. "Heavier-than-routine ordnance? Graham, wait."

Santa rubbed his eyes. "Damn skippy," he said, yawning. "There's some under-barrel forty mike-mikes and one heavy-as-the-dickens mark nineteen sitting in one of them five-tons. And there should be a Gustaf bazooka buried in there somewhere, too. I think."

Lauren's eyes broadened and glistened.

"I got the light fifty tucked behind the seat of the transport I rode in," Sanchez added. "I'll drag it out if someone finds me some vitamin I and something to stuff in my ears."

"Use your socks, taco. Weapons check in five." Dave rotated to Lauren. "Janey, I need you to amscray. Take the mutt with you; ready the household for something a touch more overstated."

"Overstated?" she repeated timidly.

"That's a roger."

Lauren nodded hesitantly, deducing the connotation. "Okay, and thank you. I'm sorry you guys don't feel well."

"Your empathy is both acknowledged and appreciated," muttered the typically infallible Woo Tang. "But we earned it."

Lazarus slid into the middle, doing his best to make his presence clear. "Don't ignore me, Graham. I need to know exactly what you're planning to do here. Mutually assured destruction has kept us from all-out war for decades. Using artillery on them is only going to escalate this, and believe you me, they'll find a way to retaliate. I swear to you, there's going to be backlash for this."

"Have ye no fear, Lazarus," Dave said satirically. "For verily I say unto you, I have called upon my faithful disciples to go forth and deliver a sufficient response unto our aggressors."

The militia leader looked at Dave sideways.

"Secure your concern," Dave said. "We're not going to hurt anyone—deliberately, anyway. We're just going to put the fear of God into them."

"The *fear of God*?" Lazarus responded. "What does that mean?"

Dave's tone turned gruff. "It means we're going to engage in some posturing…a tactically induced cease-fire using bigger, louder, meaner guns. If we send just enough boom in their general direction, I hypothesize they'll err on the side of prudence and de-escalate this nonsense. In other words, if we posture hard enough, they'll roll over and submit like good little dogs."

Lazarus didn't seem convinced. "Fine. If you say so. Just…don't let it get out of hand. Please."

Santa chuckled. "Listen to him. You do realize who you're schmoozing with, right? That there is former US Army top kick David R. Graham, getting-out-of-hand's patron saint."

# CHAPTER 5

LAUREN HOISTED LILY, THE YOUNG girl she'd rescued during the Christmas Eve assault, into her arms and ascended the cellar stairs on the heels of Bernie, Ruth and a panting, tail-wagging Cyrus. Her brother, Daniel, followed, trailed by several parallel rows of wide-eyed, yawning young persons, all of whom had been hunkered belowground for safety.

Lauren glided into the living room, spun Lily around a few times, then sat down on the couch, arranging the cackling girl on her lap.

Daniel took a seat beside them. Peering around the room, he waved at familiar faces as they filed past the entrance. "Do you think it's over?" he pondered as the front door was heard creaking open. "Is it safe to go back to our rooms?"

"It's over," Lauren said.

Her arms not quite long enough to enfold her, Lily latched onto Lauren and nuzzled her head under Lauren's chin amidst near-silent whispers.

"Sorry, honey. I couldn't hear you. What was that?"

The youngster repeated herself in a matching whisper.

"She says those noises scared her," her brother filled in. "Lily never liked loud noises. But they never bothered me. When Mommy and Daddy took us to see fireworks on the Fourth of July, I liked it, but Lily didn't. The noises made her cry a lot."

"That's understandable. Not everyone is a fan of abrupt sounds," Lauren said. "I was the same way when I was a kid, Lily. But you want to know what used to scare me to death?"

The child gestured her interest.

"Thunderstorms. They used to scare me more than anything. My dad told me to try learning about them, so I did. Now I find them comforting, even sleep through them."

Daniel peered over. "You were afraid of thunder? What about lightning? It's way more dangerous."

"That's a good point. I wasn't allowed outside during storms for that reason, and thunder can't exist without lightning. So, I suppose in a way, I was scared of both."

The little boy studied her. "I didn't think you were afraid of anything."

Lauren beamed at him. "I don't believe it's possible to be fearless, Daniel. And if I gave you that impression, I probably did so by accident."

Lily pulled away and turned to her brother, poking him on the shoulder.

Daniel sighed and leaned in so she could whisper into his ear, pulling away a few seconds later. "Lily says superheroes aren't afraid of anything, and maybe you just need more time."

Lauren smirked. "Maybe she's right. We'll wait and see what happens, Lily. But I think your expectations of me might be set a little too high."

The young girl's brows drew together in curious fashion.

"Never mind," Lauren said. "I'll work on it."

Lily smiled and rested her head against Lauren's chest.

"Daniel, how long has your sister been like this?" Lauren asked, combing the bangs from her eyes.

"Like what?"

"Withdrawn."

"I don't know what that means," said Daniel, shaking his head.

"She's incredibly quiet. And when she *does* speak, it's in whispers, and the only person with whom she directly communicates is you," Lauren explained. "It's not a bad thing, so don't take it that way, that's not why I'm asking. We all do things to make ourselves feel comfortable for reasons only we know. I was just curious…and a little concerned is all."

Daniel shrugged. He looked down to his shoes, realizing one of them had become untied, then leaned over to address it. "I don't know. My sister's always been quiet. I think she used all her voice when they took us."

"*Used* all her voice?" Lauren queried.

Daniel nodded, pulling tight the final knot in his laces. "Yeah. She yelled and cried and screamed a lot then. And I think maybe her voice ran out. I haven't heard her talk regular ever since that day."

Lauren drew her lips in a tight line. She rubbed Lily's back and gently combed Lily's hair with the tips of her fingers. "I'm sorry I brought it up…and even more sorry the two of you had to go through that."

Daniel shrugged again. "It's okay, you weren't there and you didn't know. Nobody knows. Nobody here knows anything about us." He went silent as his attention followed Ruth's voice. She could be heard rummaging about in the kitchen with several others, assigning duties for breakfast. "Lauren? Do you think…we'll ever see them again?"

"Your parents?"

Daniel nodded.

Lauren sighed and reached for him. "I wish I knew the answer to that. I wish I knew the answer to a lot of difficult questions, but I don't. Knowing the future isn't one of the superpowers I was born with. But if I did know, I would tell you."

"That's okay," said Daniel. "I…see them in my dreams sometimes, so I think maybe they're still out there looking for us. I just hope they find us."

Lauren patted Daniel's shoulder, smiled grimly and squeezed his neck. She knew precisely how he felt. "I'm not a parent, but I know for a fact that a parent's number one job is looking after their children. If you and Lily were my kids and I lost you guys, nothing would stop me from getting you back. I'm sure your parents are doing just that…and if you can see them in your dreams, they can probably see you in theirs."

"You think so?"

Lauren nodded. "I do."

A dishtowel in her hands, Ruth then slid into the room, making her presence known with a grand smile. "Daniel? Lily? Would the two of you like to join us in the kitchen? I need some help with the gravy, and I know how much that pretty young lady there likes to churn fresh butter."

Daniel nodded and rose, both eager to assist and switch topics. "Yes, ma'am." He turned to his sister. "Come on, Lily. Let's go help."

Lily turned away from Daniel's outstretched hand, clamping on to Lauren like a vice.

Daniel scowled at her. "Really? Come on, don't act like that. Mrs. Ruth needs help in the kitchen."

Lily only snubbed him.

"Daniel, it's okay. I got her," Lauren said. "She might need a little more coaxing this morning."

Ruth smiled and reached for Daniel's hand, but before she could haul him away, Lily summoned him.

"What is it this time?" He slid back to his sister, and she put her mouth to his ear once more. "You really need to say these things yourself, Lily."

Lauren looked to Daniel expectantly.

"My sister says you make her feel safe."

Bernie reemerged after disappearing to the home's upper level for reasons unknown. "Good gracious. I'm starving to death," he said, passing by the living room in a rush and sticking his nose into the kitchen. "I smell food, but I don't detect anything cooking, Ruthie. By my estimation, that'd make you a smidgeon behind on your chores for the day."

Ruth angled her head at him. "Look who's talking. It's rather difficult getting anything done around here from all the way down in the basement. I would've thought to come up a while ago, but I was more concerned with trying *not* to meet my maker. I figure I'm more use to you alive and kicking than the other way around."

Bernie chuckled. "Well, if I don't get some vittles in me before long, alive and kicking might be out of the question. What do you think about them apples?"

"If you're that famished, I reckon you'd better get your stubborn backside in here and lend assistance. I can only work miracles as fast as these two rickety old hands move, you lowly geezer."

"Eh, I reckon I'm not *that* afflicted. Never have been keen on the idea of slogging what little time I have left away in the galley."

"Then kindly put some space between your detestable self and my *galley* before I make use of those butcher knives you were kind enough to sharpen for me."

Bernie shook his head and took a few steps into the living room, sending Lily a kind wave. "I'm sorry you had to witness that, girls. But do you see what I gotta put up with? Makes no sense why a wife would speak to her husband in such ways. What do you think?"

Lauren shrugged. "I think the two of you are cute, meant for each other, and it's really none of my business."

Bernie huffed. "I see. Takin' her side, then. Figures."

"No…I…"

Bernie let out a cackle and headed towards the front door. "It's all right. I'm used to it." He raised his voice for all to hear. "If anyone needs me, I'll be out in the barn…getting us some fresh milk to go along with breakfast!" He then angled his head towards the kitchen on his way out. "Assuming we get any today."

Once breakfast was made and served, the children were called inside in groups. It was a standing rule in Bernie and Ruth's home that the younger generations receive their meals first and foremost, and no adult be allowed to partake until they were through.

About an hour after they'd finished and scattered back to their chores and daily routines, Lauren took a seat at the dining room table with a plate of fresh scrambled eggs, two strips of uncured bacon, and a generous portion of biscuits and gravy—a rather uncommon meal for the times until arriving here.

A stainless-steel percolator in hand, Ruth took a seat across from her, setting a plate of food down on a handwoven placemat. She situated the percolator on a ceramic pad near the center of the table. "Lauren, care for a cup of coffee?"

Lauren shook her head slightly, stuffing a slice of bacon in her mouth and savoring the briny flavor. "No, thank you."

"You sure? It's the good stuff—whole bean dark roast. Bernard and me never could stomach instant."

Lauren nodded. "I'm sure. Truth is, I've never been much of a coffee drinker. Now, my sister, on the other hand, she could probably live on the stuff."

"Your sister and I share something in common," Ruth said, grinning. "Just like a million other folks, I expect. Perhaps one day you'll come to your senses."

"Perhaps."

"Coffee was one of the items the old fart and I decided to invest in when we started planning for the long term. As much of it as we drank before the fall, I'm certain without it the two of us would've given up the ghost a long time ago. It sure keeps these old bones and joints moving. I suspect it might have a related effect on young ones." Ruth filled her mug. "Lauren, I do want to thank you…for your help in the kitchen this morning and all the other times you've chipped in. Putting together meals for all these kids can be awfully trying some days. These hands of mine don't seem to want to move like they used to."

"It's the least I can do," Lauren said graciously, "in return for room and board."

Ruth grinned and took a sip from her mug. "That's sweet of you. Just know that we don't expect it. We'd never ask you for anything we wouldn't ask of anyone else. After all, you're a guest here." She paused. "I know you're far away from home and family. The old fart more or less alluded to me a little of what you two spoke about the other night. I hope you don't mind."

"No, I don't mind," Lauren said, though not fully certain. "He did kind of catch me in a…weak moment."

"That's how he described it." Ruth hesitated, regarding her younger counterpart a moment. "Lauren, dear, are you doing all right?"

"I think so," Lauren said, a slight, awkward chuckle accompanying her words. "I mean, considering the circumstances."

Ruth's grin was cloaked in a similar unease. "Indeed. In-deed. I understand your pining for home. Any idea how long you plan to stay? I'm not asking because we're thinking of kicking you out or anything, so don't get the wrong idea. You're welcome here as long as you like, just like the old fart's probably told you. You can consider this house your home. And I do mean that."

Lauren swallowed a mouthful of eggs and washed them down with a gulp of water. "I appreciate that, Ruth. I do. And everything else you've done and said. And thank you. But to answer your question…I haven't really given much thought to it." She glanced out the window to the endless knolls and drifts of snow bleaching the landscape.

"Mm-hmm," Ruth rattled. "Well, it's no rush. It's not like you could just run along down that road right about now with all that chilly white crud out there." She paused, sending a glance to the ticking grandfather clock in the corner. "I wonder when David and the boys plan on joining us and helping themselves to some of this grub. If they don't get in here soon, it'll all get cold, and that dang microwave of ours stopped working a while back…for some reason."

Lauren snickered. "I'm sure they'll be dragging their feet in before long."

"How's that?"

"I...don't think they're feeling too hot," Lauren said, leering. "They definitely didn't look it when I ran into them earlier."

Ruth looked inquisitive. "You think they're catchin' some sorta bug?"

Lauren's expression turned hangdog. "No, it's more like the *bug* caught them."

"Oh. Okay, then."

The pair went silent a moment. When the woman across from her wasn't looking, Lauren stealthily slipped a slice of bacon under the table to where Cyrus had been waiting patiently, his snout nestled between her knees. "Ruth, Dave acquainted me with someone this morning...he was with them when I found them out near the highway."

Ruth rolled her lips between her teeth and nodded. "Probably Lazarus, wasn't it?"

"You know him?"

"Very well, I'm afraid. Knew his daddy, too. His daddy was a good man, passed away a few years back from cancer." Ruth sipped her coffee. "Lazarus has himself quite the unusual personality, if you catch my meaning. He's a good person though, from what I've seen of him. A little rough around the edges, but I reckon he means well. What did you think of him?"

Lauren considered the question. "He's...peculiar. And bothersome."

Ruth chuckled. "He was probably just testing you, dear. His family founded the Sons in the late nineteenth century and's been leading them ever since, kind of in the vein of a monarchy. Those men follow his orders now, same as they did when his daddy was alive. And that makes him an ally."

Lauren nodded. "He said something I found a little hard to believe, something about a feud between his group and another. He said this morning's skirmish was between the Sons and their...mortal enemies."

Ruth used a free hand to rub the soreness in her knuckles. "Yes, ma'am, the Snyders. Those two troupes have been at each other's throats for going on several generations now."

"I wasn't aware feuds even existed in today's world," Lauren said, "or in yesterday's world, for that matter."

"There's a lot that goes on in the hills and valleys of Appalachia that isn't talked about anywheres else," Ruth said. "Lots of secrets and skeletons in the cupboard…many of them even I don't know much about. And I was born and raised here."

Lauren leaned forward curiously. "Any idea what the feud is about? Or how it started?"

Ruth sipped her coffee. "From what I recall, it all started over a girl."

"A girl?"

"Mm-hmm, a beautiful girl," Ruth purred. "Gorgeous girl. Native American…Saponi, from what I recall. Curvy hips, silky black hair all the way down to the backs of her knees. If memory serves, it was Lazarus's great-grandfather and one of the Snyder elders. They got in a spat over who was going to marry her—and she was far from the… polyamorous nature. But she *was* a floozy, strung both men along for months until they fell head over heels for her, then told them both she wasn't going to choose between them. Said they had to decide.

"She played them both like fiddles, and it didn't take too long before things got ugly." Ruth hesitated, looking awkwardly towards the kitchen. "Lauren, honey, I hate to break up a good chat, but I had better take a plate out to the old fart while the food's still relatively warm. He's too darn stubborn to come in and get it himself, and if he eats it cold, he'll never let me hear the end of it."

Lauren smiled at her. "No, go ahead. It's no problem. I look forward to hearing the rest. It was just getting good."

"I'll save the best for last," the old woman said, and rose. "Listen, you make sure to help yourself to more before Dave's soldier boys come in here and wipe it all out. You hear?"

Several minutes following Ruth's departure, the front door opened, and Lauren could hear Dave Graham's commanding voice intermixed with several others. He passed by the dining room, making a beeline for the kitchen, with Woo Tang, Santa, and Sanchez marching in sequence behind him.

A few seconds later, Lazarus passed by in the process of shedding his jacket. He wavered before strolling into the kitchen and held a hand out, twiddling his fingers in Lauren's direction. Then, after passing, he angled his body backward, leaned his head into the entryway and winked at her.

Lauren scowled and shooed him away. "Breakfast is on the stove. Help yourself. It *might* still be warm."

Lazarus joined the others while mouthing something Lauren couldn't make out, and several minutes after, all five men merged in the dining room, each with a brimming plate of food and a beverage glass in hand.

Dave scanned the room as he took his seat and his eyes soon perked up. "I must be delirious. My partially obstructed snot box is detecting a familiar yet tantalizing bouquet. Rather difficult to validate, but it reeks an awful lot like Colombian rocket fuel."

"Why Colombian?" Sanchez rubbed his eyes and pointed to the percolator. "*Mis ojos* can't focus on nearby objects for shit, but that shiny contraption looks like a pot of November Juliet to me, LT."

Dave and Sanchez both went for the coffeepot at the exact moment, but the sniper's hand sequestered the handle, leaving Dave's calloused palm to settle for a lid landing.

"Fine reflexes, *jarine*," Dave grunted, sending along a tarnished look. "Care to fall back?"

Sanchez grinned coyly and shook his head. "Jarines never fall back."

"I suppose they don't." Dave relinquished his hand with fierce hesitancy. "Go on then, warfighter. Get your subpar IQ recon on."

"Oorah." Sanchez pulled the pot close and put his nose to it. "Damn. It's heaven in there. Presence of November Juliet confirmed."

"Well, wonders never cease, do they?" Dave said. "The missus went and whipped up a whole batch of wine flu therapy."

"Permission to decant?" Sanchez queried.

"Granted. But no gorging," replied Dave. "Be charitable and leave a goblet or two for each of your fellow disadvantaged brethren."

"No worries, LT, I got this." Sanchez filled his mug, ribbons of steam wafting into the air, then brought it to his lips. "Target acquired, standing by to ingest."

"Um, what's...November Juliet?" Lauren pondered, a delicate pattern of caution marking her tone.

Sanchez set down his mug, leaned casually over, and whispered into her ear to provide enlightenment.

"Really?" She rebounded, grimacing. "Jesus, Sanchez. That's horrible."

"Not to mention racist as hell," Sanchez said, offering no disagreement. "Sorry for the coarse language, chica. But you should be used to it by now with me. And you *did* ask."

"And now I'm wishing I hadn't."

Santa rubbed the bridge of his nose, closing his eyes amidst a yawn. "You all go right ahead with that diluted swill," he said. "Unless it's denser than sludge or has a pH low enough to trigger contact burns on human tissue, it ain't gonna touch what's ailing me." His hand disappeared under the table and reemerged with a two-milligram single-use morphine syringe. "This little jewel right here is what I had in mind. I must've got into a bad batch last night or something. Everything hurts…even the hair on my chinny-chin-chin."

Lazarus stepped into the dining room and plopped down on a chair at the opposite end of the table from where the others were sitting. With his plate hovering over his lap, he casually tossed his feet on another chair nearby and began eating with his hands.

Lauren's brows drew together as she scrutinized him. "Make yourself at home."

Lazarus stuffed two strips of bacon in his mouth, licked his fingertips and started to chew. "Isn't that what I just did?"

She shook her head at him distastefully and looked away. "You are a piece of work."

"Look who's talking," he said, his eyebrows dancing, chewing his food with his mouth agape. He motioned to Dave. "She gets cuter every time she says something."

Dave took possession of the percolator. "You should see her operate a battle rifle. It might have an abating effect on your impression."

"On the contrary," replied Lazarus. "Being witness to that could result in something more along the lines of…arousal."

Lauren dropped her fork to the table. "Are you done?"

Lazarus slowly shook his head with a tantalizing grin. "Nope. I'm just getting started."

The group ate together mostly in silence from that point forward, while only sharing the occasional anecdote. While some enjoyed second helpings, Lauren and Woo Tang cleared off portions of the table, washed and rinsed some of Ruth's dishes, and returned to their seats amidst a discussion in progress.

"Oh, shit. I almost forgot again, Graham. Something I've been meaning to tell you." Lazarus pulled a tattered sheet of lined paper from an interior pocket of his field jacket and glided it across the table in

Dave's direction. "We got a message from your guy the other day…I meant to give it to you yesterday, but it slipped my mind."

"The other day?" Dave griped.

"Yepper," Lazarus said. "Picked him up on the AmRRON frequency on forty meters, which surprised the hell out of me, as bad as the bands have been. Damn solar minimum has been murdering them. His signal was weak, but I heard him call out foxtrot-alpha-nineteen plain as day."

Lauren's eyes widened. "Isn't that Neo's call sign?"

"It's one of them," Dave said, unfolding the message while refraining from reading it. "Did the sender authenticate?"

Lazarus nodded nonchalantly and snorted. "Really, Graham? What is this? Amateur hour?"

Dave sighed. "Lazarus, kindly provide a response to my question before I eternally misplace what little tolerance for you I have left," he thundered. "You have already riled me once today to the crux of utilizing artillery in spite of what could verifiably be the worst hangover I've had in decades. And now you're handing me off a radiogram purportedly received more than twenty-four hours ago from my numero uno RTO."

"Okay, Graham, back off. Don't start with me," Lazarus stated, his finger pointed. "Seems to me after the use of that artillery this morning, despite my objections, that we both have some beef with each other."

"Shut your yap," Dave commanded, uprighting in his seat. "I won't repeat myself, so pin your ears back and listen." He held the message aloft tightly between his fingers. "If the info contained within turns out to be in any way time sensitive, whatever beef there is between us will cease to be. For I will arrange to have your beloved sweetbreads whittled off, steamed to edibility and served on Mrs. Ruth's finest china right here on this table, deficient of garnish."

Santa chortled. "Yummy."

"Sweetbreads?" Lazarus posed. "Just what are you talking about?"

"*Huevos*." Sanchez chuckled. "*Por supuesto*."

Lazarus still looked muddled.

"He means balls," Santa filled in casually, his fork held up, mouth half-full of eggs. "*Your* balls specifically. Testicles. Gonads. Kangaroo apples. Crotch nugs. Jizz berries. The two amigos—"

"Santa," Woo Tang cut in, a finger to his temple.

The bearded one gulped down his food. "Go for Santa."

"Cease and desist."

Santa awkwardly regarded his company. "Oh…yeah. Roger that, forgot where I was. Sorry…"

Lauren put a hand to her mouth and sent a stare to the table, half-amused, half-disgusted, endeavoring to recuse herself.

Sending Dave a set of jumbled eyes, Lazarus said, "You can't be serious."

Woo Tang motioned to Lauren. "You might aspire to cover your ears a moment." He then regarded Lazarus. "The removal of appendages is a form of intertribal warfare that has been in practice for a millennia. LT has contributed to this custom for most of his career and already possesses a grandiose collection of enemy scrotums. He preserves them and suspends them as accolades, much in the same manner as Pawnee and Sioux warriors…after taking scalps."

Lauren's face contorted. "Gross."

"Okay, look. I'm sorry," Lazarus said, swallowing hard. "My apologies, okay? I was just…messing around. I didn't mean to take so long to get you the message. And the authentication was legit."

Dave cut his eyes at him, awaiting validation deficient of ambiguities.

"Using the methods previously agreed upon," Lazarus continued, holding two fingers in the air. "Swear on my pop's grave." He paused. "Just, eh, back to my point…don't forget…using your damn artillery despite my warnings is going to cause problems. The Snyders will retaliate, mark my words. So I'm pretty riled about everything right there along with you."

Dave rolled his eyes. "We'll deal with it." He then spent the next few minutes reading through the message.

Lauren leaned forward, anticipation getting the best of her. "Well? What does it say? Is everything okay at home?"

Dave slid his free hand over and gestured for her to relax.

"Don't do that, Dave," Lauren snapped. "Don't placate me. I haven't been home in a month, and that's the first message we've gotten from them." She tried to snatch the letter, but the Green Beret's reflexes won the match.

"Janey, stow it. Take it easy." Dave slid his chair back to gain some distance while reaching for the percolator for a refill. "Allow me a few more precious sips of this fine emulsion and I'll divulge everything within."

Lauren huffed angrily and enfolded her arms. "Fine."

Dave raised his mug and drank from it. "Oh man. That is some damn fine mud," he said. "Looks as though everybody's good and settled in, but they had a little hiccup upon arrival…some sort of invasion."

Lauren furrowed her brow. She stood, a look of intense worry washing over her. "An invasion? By who? What happened? Is anyone hurt?"

Dave held up a hand. "Two. Both since deceased. An elderly couple—husband and wife," Dave said, glancing up at her. "George and Elizabeth Brady. I assume you knew them?"

Lauren sighed, hanging her head. "Yeah, I knew them. They were Austin's grandparents. They lived in the valley a long time, long before any of us." She hesitated a lengthy moment. "What happened to them?"

"Neo didn't include specifics. I'm sorry, Janey."

"I am sorry, too," Woo Tang echoed.

The others sent along condolences in chorus.

"It's okay, I barely knew them," said Lauren. "The whole family kept to themselves, but we had an alliance with them. After what happened to Bo and Austin and now this, I doubt that'll be the case anymore. Did he mention anything else? Or if anyone else was hurt?"

"Neo would've advised," Dave replied. "Evidently, the invaders were put down not long *before* the convoy arrived." He took another sip of his coffee, then continued. "He says the doctors are settled in, staying at a farm adjacent to your family's place. Food and supplies have been evenly distributed. Also says here that those previously stricken with illness are now symptomless."

The sadness that had amassed on Lauren's countenance dissipated. "You're kidding. All of them? They're all better?"

Dave nodded again. "It appears that way. Looks like they got there just in time to help. This is good news, Janey, all the way around."

"It's fantastic news." Lauren let out a long breath of relief. Her deepest inner anxieties began to dispel. The plan to leave the valley in search of food and medical assistance had ultimately been a success, despite encountering a handful of dire setbacks. "Thank God."

"That's not a bad idea, bearing in mind He probably had a hand in it," Dave remarked. He sipped his coffee again as his brows knitted. "Janey, there's a postscript here. Neo's requested to go direct with you."

Lauren looked at him sideways. “Meaning what?”

Lazarus spoke with another mouthful of food. “Oh, that means he wants to tell you something himself—directly. Like with your pretty face in front of the radio and your dainty hand holding the mic.” He held up a hand and squeezed his thumb between his fingers, as if holding an imaginary radio microphone.

Lauren looked to him briefly, her curiosity gaining ground.

Dave set the letter down. “Is your comms setup close by, Lazarus?”

Lazarus shrugged indifferently. “Now, just hold on there. What leads you to believe my equipment is available for public use?”

Dave halted before sipping his coffee and set his mug down. After a moment’s hesitation, he stood, made his way over to his long-haired acquaintance and yanked the chair away he’d been using as a footstool. “Don’t make me ask you again.”

Lazarus recoiled, his eyes wide. “Hey, I was just joking with you. Relax. There’s no need for any of that.”

“On the contrary,” Woo Tang began, his fractious stare finding the man with longer-than-usual hair, “from what I recollect, Ruth is not fond of her furniture being misused. Nor is she fond of the use of profanity in her home. I recommend you show some respect and watch your language.”

Lazarus took a quick scan of the room, seeing now that all eyes staring at him had joined forces, and with that, he’d become the minority. “Hey, look. It’s no problem. If you want to use the radios, you’re welcome to them. And the shack’s not far away. I’ll take you there…we can even go right now if you want.”

Dave leaned in. “I want.”

# CHAPTER 6

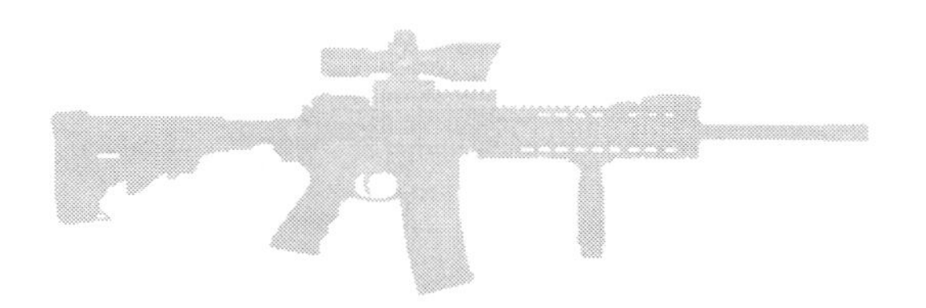

**Mason residence**
**Trout Run Valley**
**Saturday, January 1st. Present day**

MICHELLE RUSSELL ASCENDED THE STAIRCASE, entered the hall, and found her way to the formal dining room, where Kim Mason was folding and arranging a load of laundry. Kim glanced up and smiled upon noticing Michelle's entry, but her concentration remained adhered to the meticulousness of her efforts.

Michelle, who had entered empty-handed, made her approach and gestured to the table halfway covered in folded garments and bath towels. "I'd offer my help, but my folding skills are considerably lacking compared to yours. I've done laundry most of my life, and I don't think I'll ever be able to fold clothes anywhere as well as you can."

Kim absorbed the praise and proffered thanks with her body language. "It's nothing special, really."

"Maybe not from your perspective, but it sure is to mine," Michelle said, smiling.

"Well, if you think this is something special, you should see my husband's rendition. His folds and stacks are plumb, level, and square… darn near close to being engineered. It is a sight to see, let me tell you."

Michelle nodded. "Did he acquire those skills in the Army?"

Kim emitted a barely audible snicker. "Hardly. BCT, AIT and Ranger indoctrination notwithstanding, the only thing the Army taught Fred to arrange or stack was bodies." She set a perfectly aligned crease in a bath towel and placed it neatly onto a pile of others. "How long have you been here?"

"Not long," Michelle began. "I was over at the Vincents', chatting with the good doctor and his wife about their…wishes, up until all hell broke loose. We sheltered in place for a good while, not knowing what was happening, until one of those tan trucks pulled up with two soldiers inside. They came to the door in a hurry, talking about casualties and needing his assistance. He left with them, and I walked over here to nose around in your basement after hearing on the radio it was safe to go back outside."

"Any word on them?"

"The Bradys?" Michelle prompted, glowering. "It isn't good, but it wasn't good to begin with. Ricky…passed away on the scene, right in my front yard, in front of his sons. Junior lost a lot of blood but will most likely pull through. But that family is seriously reeling after this."

"They were reeling before it," Kim said. "But a lot of others are, too. I'd offer to help them if they weren't so damn proud." She paused. "What about *our* remaining patients? I assume you're informed after nosing around in my basement…"

Michelle exhaled. "Clean bills of health. Peter and Liam are preparing to leave, pending arrival of their armed chariot. Amy is downstairs with Jake right this moment, packing their things. Everyone else is out of the woods, it would seem."

"That's good. I'm glad they're all better now. It's been a long road for them."

"It's been a long road for all of us, especially them. It'll be nice to get everyone back home where they belong…and I'm sure you'll appreciate having the house back to yourself," Michelle said, stumbling over her words. "Shit. I'm sorry, Kim. I misspoke. I didn't realize what I was saying."

Kim leaned over on the table and hung her head. "It's all right, Michelle. Sometimes it all doesn't seem real to me either. Having folks coming in and out of here like they have these past few weeks has been one of the few things keeping my mind off my boys." Kim sniffled. "Ever since Fred found out they were missing, nothing I've been able to say or do has served to keep him home. He hasn't even given a damn about his own recovery, just been out there every day looking for them.

And now he's got Megan involved. Once everyone goes back home and we stop emulating Grand Central Station, it'll just be me here in this big old house by myself with my thoughts."

"The Schmidts will still be around, won't they?"

Kim sent a narrowed glance. "I get the feeling they don't much want to be anymore. Once Scott started coming around, Whitney's been scouring the valley for options, though she hasn't exactly been forthright about it. Can't blame them, really. It's not easy sharing space like we have."

"I didn't know that," Michelle said. "Strange of her not to say anything to you or discuss her plans."

"It's her prerogative. This arrangement wasn't ever meant to be permanent."

Michelle nodded. "I suppose. So you really will be alone. How long do Fred and Megan stay gone during the day?"

"Better part of it, most times. And ever since the shooter threat began, they've been leaving before sunup and barely getting home until after twilight. Fred says it's safer that way. I don't even know where they go anymore; he won't discuss it. He just packs his things, kisses me on the cheek, utters a few words to Megan, and they leave. That's become our routine."

"How long do you expect that'll go on?"

"How long do I expect *what* to go on?" Kim snapped. "How long would you look for Lauren if *she* were missing, Michelle? Do you not recall a few months back when she didn't come home for a couple of nights? Do you not recall your worry? Your demeanor? The vicious looks you were handing everyone? Because I do. She was gone for just a few days and you were ready to tear the world apart to find her. My boys have been gone for a month. No signs of them anywhere, and other than what them two Brady boys have told us, which borders on ludicrous, nobody knows nothing. And my family has been torn apart over it. My husband came home a broken man after that road trip, limping and beaten to bits by some psycho killer son of a bitch…" Kim drifted off and started to cry. Her hand moved to her nose and she wiped her tears. "I'm sorry, Michelle. I'm sorry, for heaven's sake, I don't mean to be crude."

"It's okay. I probably deserve that after what I said," Michelle said. "For what it's worth, Lauren's doing it to me again. She hasn't been home in a month and I have no idea how she's doing, what her plans are, or if she even wants to come home. My family isn't exactly in one piece right now either."

"I suppose we can find some peculiar way of empathizing with one another over our predicaments," Kim said with a despairing sigh. "You know what my biggest fear is? That Mark and Chad have gotten themselves captured…and both my boys are now confined in that godforsaken FEMA camp. I tried talking to Fred about it, but he won't hear of it. Keeps telling me I don't know what I'm talking about—that something else must've happened to them, that there's some other explanation. He thinks they're out there helping somebody and got in over their heads. And I think he's delusional.

"I think he's looking for a happy ending where none exists. In fact, I'm about ready to take those pain meds he's been choking down and flush them…if I knew of a working toilet." Kim paused. "I know he's only taking them because he needs them, though. And my husband's no addict. This strength he's exuding…it's counterfeited and seems to be having an encouraging effect on Megan, and in some weird way, it's doing the same for me. I don't know, I just don't know anymore. I'm growing exhausted of playing the tough mom…being the leader…running this family. And I'd like to see something good happen for a change."

Michelle only nodded. She couldn't agree more with her friend. She just didn't know what advice she could offer that would provide benefit. Kim had never made a conscious choice to lean on anyone before. It had always been the other way around. She'd remained steadfast during tough times, offering herself to others in need. Now she was the one in need, like so many others.

"I don't like being like this, Michelle," Kim said. "I'm not comfortable being a worrywart or a wet blanket. I wasn't raised that way. I was raised to be headstrong, independent, and self-sufficient." She locked eyes with her friend. "I know we've yet to chat much about it, but my brother and I were raised in the same manner by the same woman. You might find some consolation in knowing that. From what we've gathered, your Lauren is with David. Fred and Christian have confirmed that, though no one's really alluded as to why, but I'm sure there's a reason. If she sticks by him, she'll be fine. He'll protect her like his own, rest assured, and see to it she gets home safe."

Michelle's expression fell flat. "If she wants to come home."

"Stop that. Everybody wants to come home, Michelle, even Lauren. She's a tough kid who's had to endure a lot, but she's no different. Right now, I imagine she's just following a path of her choosing or perhaps one that's calling out to her. A lot of things have happened to her since this all started, and I expect the loss of her father hasn't helped much."

Michelle bit her lower lip. *Disappearance, you mean.* "No. I suppose it hasn't."

Kim looked up at her, returning to her toil with a pile of unfolded clothes. "It *has* been over a year."

Michelle squinted. "I'm aware of that," she said. "I've counted the days."

Her friend sent Michelle a brief look of uncertainty.

"Four hundred sixty-three. Not counting today."

Kim's eyes grew wide at Michelle rattling off the figure as if it were her social security number. "Has it really been that many?"

Michelle didn't answer.

"Sorry, that was more of a reaction than a question, anyway," Kim said. "Have you ever given any thought to…moving on, someday?"

Michelle's eyes narrowed even further. "Moving on?"

Kim nodded. "Yes. As in finding another and opening your heart to him, and of course, allowing that person, whoever it may be, to open theirs in return."

Michelle backed away from the table and folded her arms. "I don't think I like where this conversation is going."

"It's not a comfortable topic to discuss, so that's not surprising. But it *is* a valid question…between friends."

Michelle gritted her teeth slightly. "No. The answer is no, Kim. I haven't."

"Okay, that's fine," Kim said. "I suppose it's possible I might've gotten the wrong idea, then."

"About what?"

Kim leaned onto the table again. "Look, I realize this is far from being any of my business, and I'm sorry if saying this bothers or offends you, but I could've sworn there for a little while that you and Norman were getting kind of…chummy."

Michelle's arms fell to her sides. "Chummy?"

"Mm-hmm."

"Kim, Norman and I have always been *chummy*. But it has never once gone any further than that. He's one of Alan's closest friends—and it's been that way for the better part of two decades. Both his sons have grown up around Lauren and Grace. We know each other like family. For the love of God, Alan made arrangements with them to unite with us on the off chance he wouldn't be around if the world decided to turn to shit…and we all know how that turned out." Michelle took a long pause. "Norman…is a decent man, dependable to a fault. He's protective and I do, in fact, love him…platonically. But I am still very much a married woman. I'm married to my husband."

"Like I said, I misinterpreted," said Kim. "I got the wrong idea, and I'm sorry. I probably shouldn't've said anything, I just don't like seeing you alone. I don't like seeing anyone alone. Companionship is hard to come by, especially these days. And it's awfully hard to replace."

"My relationship with Alan could never be replaced," Michelle said coldly. "Yes, he never came home to us. He's missing and sometimes I do think the worst. But it doesn't matter because I just can't give up on him. If by some miracle he's still alive, he's still out there, I pray to God he hasn't given up on me." A pause. "I can't give up on him—I've tried…and I just can't do it. I'm still married to the man. Even if he were dead, I wouldn't dare desecrate our marriage, and that makes moving on impossible for me. I don't think I'm built that way."

Kim smiled grimly. "That's good to know. You're an upright woman, Michelle. I think I like you even more now."

"Besides, I'm pretty sure Norman has other plans in mind. I think he's developed a bit of a liking for Kristen."

Kim let go of the shirt she was tending to. "Pardon? Did I hear you right?"

Michelle nodded. "I probably shouldn't say anything. I've never been one to gossip about other people's business or spread rumors, but we're friends and I haven't endured any decent girl-talk in weeks, so why the hell not? Grace and I used to engage in it daily; it was one of our morning rituals. But lately she's been otherwise engaged."

"What? Grace got engaged? Christian popped the question?"

Michelle jerked her head back and forth. "No, that's not what I said. They're not engaged, I mean, not that I know of, anyway." She laughed. "Bad choice of words."

"That, or my ears need cleaning," Kim said, laughing along with her. "Girl-talk can sometimes be inappropriate, but I'd wager it's good for you. Look at us now, both laughing through life's difficulties. It's already helping us relieve some stress." She switched to a whisper. "Now, fill me in on the Norman-Kristen affair."

Michelle closed the distance between them. "He hasn't been around the house as much as he used to be, and I know that's attributed to the temporary infirmary we erected in your basement. Like clockwork, Norman's been here to look in on Lee every day since he's been back, but he's also been spending a lot of his time elsewhere."

"And how do you know that?"

"I just know."

"You've been spying on him? Michelle…"

Michelle looked embarrassed. "Not spying per se. I was worried about him. He wasn't himself after he got back, didn't talk much to me or anyone, and that isn't like him. Grasping the extent of Fred's injuries, I considered the possibility of post-traumatic stress or depression of some kind. Christian told me not to bother with him, that he was fine, but his behavior was so erratic. It was like he was purposefully hiding something from me."

"And that's when your investigative instincts shifted into high gear." Kim looked at her coyly. "He's been over to Kristen's place, hasn't he?"

Michelle nodded. "Norman's been single for a really long time, and he's always seemed contented to be. I never bothered asking him why—never pondered about his romantic interests or if he even had any. He just always seemed fine with being alone."

Kim nodded acknowledgment. "Well, I hope it doesn't sound like I'm repeating myself, but I don't believe anyone is ever fully *fine* with being alone."

Michelle smiled at her. "I wouldn't disagree," she said. "You know, Kim, after your basement tenants take their leave, I think we should do something about that. As in get together periodically, maybe even a few times daily. For some…girl-talk."

Kim smiled genuinely. "I believe I'd like that. There's far too much negative nonsense in the valley. Some gossip should spice things right up…and maybe help take my mind off things."

# CHAPTER 7

**Riverton, West Virginia**
**Saturday, January 1st. Present day**

THE COMMS SHACK EMPLOYED BY Lazarus and his militia was a ten-minute walk outside the farm to a nearby residence, making it just over a half-hour's trudge in the snow. The shack itself was indeed little more than a shed once used for housing gardening and farming equipment, some of which remained today. It was powered by an array of mismatched solar panels mounted to the tin roof on both of its eastward- and westward-facing slopes.

Upon arrival, Lazarus reached for a shop broom leaning near the doorway. PVC tubing had been attached to it with a variety of zip ties and duct tape, effectively extending the handle and lengthening its reach. He hoisted it over the shack and gruffly mumbled while sweeping a dusting of snow off the panels.

Inside, the militia leader took his seat first and gestured for Dave, Woo Tang, and Lauren to pull up a stool from a stack of dust-covered ones in the corner. Then from a table of haphazardly scattered, mostly antique, glowing radios, Lazarus took hold of a microphone and made a call. "Foxtrot-alpha-nineteen, foxtrot-alpha-nineteen, this is five-lima-echo calling. I repeat, five-lima-echo calling from maidenhead grid foxtrot-mike-zero-eight, hotel sierra. We are live from Riverton, West Virginia. That's Germany Valley, Pendleton County. Over." He repeated the call in similar fashion and unkeyed, allowing static to fill the speaker.

“So much for COMSEC,” Dave griped.

Lazarus rotated. “What’s that?”

“Communications security, numbnuts. Either you don’t know or don’t give a shit about it. Why not just announce our exact position down to easting and northing to anyone paying attention?”

“Should I?”

Dave cut his eyes at the militiaman. “You already did.”

Lauren ignored their banter, finding herself transfixed on the assortment of transceivers and their chattering speakers. She recollected hearing similar sounds from radios in her father’s office in times past. Scanning the room, she found a framed, well-faded amateur radio license mounted to the wall. “You’re a ham radio operator?”

Lazarus nodded while toying with some knobs. “No, not me. My pop was, though. He taught me a lot, and I know my fair share about it, but I never took the test.” He paused. “Not like it matters anymore; everybody’s a pirate operator these days.” He turned to her and posed, with the top of the mic near his lips. “Works for me, right? I know, I just have that *look*. Like one of those badass lead singers in a heavy metal band.”

“You look more like the bass player type to me,” Lauren mocked him. “And I’m betting your luck with women reflects it.”

“You’d be surprised,” countered Lazarus. “Most ladyfolk who encounter me find me irresistible.”

“Not this one.”

“So abrasive,” Lazarus quipped. “Damn, I swear. Every time you say something witty like that, it puts butterflies in my stomach.”

Lauren rolled her eyes. “Stifle it and call Neo again, or I’ll release those butterflies.”

“Your wish is my command.” Lazarus made the call and, after several minutes of waiting with no reply, did so again.

After an unnerving moment of silence, a weak signal carrying a distorted version of a familiar voice broke through the layers of static. *“Five-lima-echo, this is foxtrot-alpha-nineteen returning. How do you receive this station? Over.”*

Lazarus keyed the mic. “Foxtrot-alpha-nineteen, this is five-lima-echo. Rough copy, over. I repeat, rough copy. Your signal is weak and fading, but you are readable. Over.”

*"Roger. Your signal is both strong and readable. Go with authentication. Sum method, please. Positions romeo, golf, and november. Over."*

"Romeo, golf, and november. Roger." Lazarus's attention fell upon a notebook nearby with notes scribbled in pencil on the cover. "Sum method," he griped. "Of course."

Lauren leaned in so she could observe the radio operator's index finger as it traced the word *Armageddon* written in capital letters, each having a corresponding number beneath from one to ten.

Lazarus began counting with his fingers. "Seventeen?" He turned to the men behind him. "Seventeen, right?"

Dave and Woo Tang both nodded.

"Thought so," Lazarus said, seemingly proud of himself, and keyed the mic. "I authenticate seventeen. I repeat, seventeen, over."

A burst of static, then, *"Confirmed. Hello again, Leper. Proceed with your traffic. Over."*

"Leper?" Lauren asked, sending a glance to a shrugging, highly apathetic Dave Graham.

Lazarus keyed the mic again. "Good morning back at you. I have two of your fellow…brethren here with me along with…" He trailed off, turning to Lauren. "Wait one." He lowered the mic. "What's your handle?"

Lauren tilted her head. "My handle?"

"Can't be using your *real* name over the air, shnookums. Never know who's listening."

"I don't have a handle."

"Well, think one up, quick-like."

Lauren looked to the others, uncertain.

Woo Tang looked sheepish, appearing to roll his eyes. "Orchid."

Lauren smiled at him. "Right. Use that one."

"What, Orchid?" Lazarus looked at her sideways. "What kind of handle is that?"

"All the same, what kind of handle is Leper?" Lauren shot back.

"A cool one. Started out as a nickname my friends gave me back in college," Lazarus explained.

"*You* went to college?"

"Yepper. Got a degree in veterinary medicine from WVU, believe it or not," Lazarus replied proudly. "Impressed?"

Lauren shook her head. "Not really. And I think your friends might've gotten their biblical characters mixed up."

"What do you mean by that?" Lazarus candidly asked, though Lauren failed to tender a reply. He keyed the microphone again. "Neo, I have…Orchid here with me."

Neo's voice came back immediately, requesting to have Lauren speak directly to him.

Lazarus handed her the mic, and she keyed up without delay. "Neo? Hi, it's me. It's good to hear you…we got your message. What's going on? Is everything okay? What did you need to tell me?"

*"Affirmative, all is well here. First things first, I need to know if you're sitting down or standing up. Over."*

"Why would he need to know that?" Lauren asked herself, her eyes darting around. "I don't know why you're asking, or why it even matters…but for the record, I'm sitting down. Over."

*"Good. That's good. Because it does matter."* The static crashes and fading in and out became more persistent. *"Next question is, are you alone? The topic is somewhat personal. Over."*

"Personal?" Lauren pondered what it could be. "How personal, Neo? I don't understand. Over."

A few seconds passed before reply. *"I don't know how to answer that."*

Lauren ruminated a moment. Neo's methods of rationalizing were unlike most people she knew, and for him, took on a whole new meaning. He identified with radios, logic and numbers—maybe that was it. "Neo, try this for me. Assign how personal you consider it to be to a number, on a linear scale from one to ten. Over."

Neo returned almost instantly with, *"Roger that. The number is eight. Over."*

Eight out of ten. Lauren hadn't any clue what it could be, and couldn't fathom any reason to request Dave and Woo Tang provide her with privacy. She didn't particularly care for her newest acquaintance, but he didn't know her and didn't know the least bit about her family, and this was his shed and his radios.

She was far too anxious now to think it through any further. She gave Neo the go-ahead.

*"Okay, so, here goes. I was told to divulge this because you needed to know."* Static crashed through the speaker. *"Grace learned a few*

*weeks back that..."* Then the signal faded and Neo's voice fell below the noise floor.

Lauren looked frantic. "Wait...what did he say?" She keyed the mic. "Neo? Neo, come back. I didn't copy all of that." She unkeyed, but nothing save squelch noise exited the radio's speaker. "He said something about Grace. Did any of you catch that?"

Lazarus began fumbling with some knobs. "It's these damn band conditions," he said. "They've been awfully funky lately. Just tell him to repeat his last, and if you still can't copy him, tell him again. He's a radio operator, he'll know what to do."

Lauren sighed loudly and keyed the mic again. "Neo, this is Orchid. Repeat your last. I say again, repeat your last. I didn't hear you. Over."

A couple of seconds later with a much weaker signal, Neo came back to her. *"Roger. I say again, your sister is..."* The signal then faded once more.

"This is bullshit!" Lauren went to toss the microphone, but Lazarus intercepted. "Get him back!"

"Hey! Be careful! We can't just drive down to the nearest Radio Shack and get another one of these." Lazarus twisted a few more knobs, then reached for an antenna selector switch. "We can try the full-wave loop. It's not resonant on this band, but it's a hell of a lot quieter, and who knows, maybe it'll do us some justice today." He keyed the mic. "Foxtrot-alpha-nineteen, this is five-lima-echo. Do you copy? How copy now? Over."

Neo came back almost immediately. *"Five-lima-echo, foxtrot-alpha-nineteen. Full copy, five over nine. Lima charlie. Strong signal. Over."*

Lazarus turned his head and made eye contact with Lauren before keying up again. "Very well. Now would you please, for the love of God, repeat your last."

*"Roger that. Orchid, are you still direct with me? Over."*

Lauren seized the mic from Lazarus. "Yes—I mean, affirmative. I copy you direct, Neo. Go...with your traffic."

*"Very well."* A pause. *"Your sister, Grace, says hello and she misses you. And...she wanted me to inform you that she's...with child. I say again, Grace is going to have a baby..."*

Lauren set the mic down gently. She placed a hand to her chest and her posture slumped. "A baby," she mumbled, exhaling slowly. "Oh my God...Grace is pregnant..."

Dave folded his arms over his chest and lowered his head, an eccentric scowl creeping across his face.

Lauren's expression gradually filled with joy and her cheeks flushed with color. "I don't believe this," she cooed. "Grace is a mom…I'm going to be an aunt."

"Congratulations," Woo Tang said, doing what he could to share her excitement.

"Yeah, congrats," Lazarus chimed in. "That's some amazing news. I think I got some cigars around here somewhere. We should smoke them."

Lauren eagerly keyed the mic. "Neo, this is all wonderful news. I can't tell you how good it is to hear and know that everyone's doing okay. If you could, please, tell everyone…I miss them. And tell Grace I'm super happy for her…I love her and I'll be home as soon as I can. Over."

The speaker expelled several bursts of static. *"Actually, you can tell her yourself. She's here now, sitting beside me."*

Even through the static, fading and distortion, the sound of her sister's voice made Lauren's heart flutter. *"Hey you! Happy New Year. Just where the hell have you been? You were supposed to be home a month ago. Oh, never mind...you don't have to answer that. Christian told me what happened. Talk about scary. I'm really, really glad you're both okay."* A pause. *"Excuse me, I was just informed that I didn't say 'over'. As if radio decorum was ever my thing. So, over."*

Lauren went to key up again, noticing now that her hand was shaking. She steadied it with her other hand and brought the mic close. "Hey yourself. It's good to hear your voice…even a warped version of it. Congratulations, by the way. God…I'm *so* proud of you. I guess everything you told me about—well, I won't go into detail. Too many extraneous listeners. Either way, I guess it's confirmed. Over."

*"Oh, yeah. It's most definitely confirmed. At present I have a humanoid parasite sprouting inside me, soaking up every extra nutrient and every last modicum of energy I can spare, as if I had any of either to begin with. Life is uproarious, no? I don't know what God decided to allow this to happen or even thought it would be a good idea. Guess I should be thankful...I can't exactly take it back, now, can I? Over."*

Lauren squeezed the microphone and spoke with heavy eyelids and an even heavier heart. "Kind of fortuitous how Dr. Vincent's wife turned out to be an obstetrician." She hesitated. "You probably won't agree with me, but I know you'll be a great mom. You'll own it like you own everything else. And despite his…abnormalities, I think Christian will prove to be a wonderful father; *and* a respectable boyfriend, significant other, or whatever, if the two of you can keep from murdering each other. Listen, there's so much I want to say to you and talk about, but it's not easy right now where I'm sitting. So I'm going to save it for when I come home, okay? Over."

A long moment went by before Grace replied, *"Okay, whatever. That's fine. I didn't want to sit in this frigid shed any longer than I had to, anyway. And when do you expect your extended sabbatical from home to conclude? I know you miss us. We all miss you too. Over."*

"I don't know right now, I…don't have much control over the timing. But I promise as soon as I'm able to, I'll be there."

*"Okay, love. I'll hold you to that. Stay safe."*

The sisters then said their goodbyes and ended the call.

Lauren spent a few moments pushing her tears away, then rotated in her seat, casting a stare to the only man in the room yet to say anything or offer the slightest reaction. "Dave? Is something wrong? Your reserve is deafening…not to mention, killing the mood."

Dave exhaled through his nostrils. "That's certainly not my intention. I can take my leave if it suits you."

"No, that would *not* suit me." Lauren rose. "I don't get it…you look…I don't know, like you're peeved with me or something."

He pressed his lips together. "I'm not peeved with you, Janey. Far from it."

"And even so, not the least bit happy either," Lauren said, her excitement over the news heard losing ground by the second. "If you're not peeved with me and not happy, what are you, then?"

Dave deferred his reply. "Apprehensive."

"Apprehensive. About…"

"About what I know is destined to come to pass after this…update," he grumbled.

"And that is?"

"An insistent yet semi-dutiful request to return home, I imagine."

Lauren stepped closer to him, nodding acknowledgment with an uncomfortable smile. "So you're a mind reader now. Can you blame me? After what I just heard?"

"No, I surely cannot."

"Then what's the problem? Do you think it's unreasonable for me to want to go home?"

The venerable Green Beret hesitated a long moment. "Feeling that way or any other way you want to feel isn't unreasonable, Janey…to yourself or anyone else. And neither is feeling strongly compelled to act on those feelings. But taking action that is genuinely, consciously acting on those feelings when we are fully engaged in the predicament at hand would most certainly be unreasonable, no doubt about it. Let alone vastly imprudent."

"Imprudent," Lauren repeated flatly.

"That's affirmative." Dave gestured to the snow clinging to his trousers and boot laces. "Look what we had to plow through just to get here through the fields. You think road conditions in surrounding West by God are any different? Think they're better? Or worse? The white stuff was falling at a blizzard's pace for no less than two consecutive days by my count, and I can offer assurance the department of transportation isn't maintaining them. I theorize almost every road between here and wherever meets with the very definition of impassable. We passed by and maneuvered around countless stalled-out vehicles on our way here prior to the storm. There could be countless trees and defunct power poles down, and Lord knows what else blocking our path. If I did not categorically believe this to be the case without reservation, we would've departed for Rocket Center days ago."

Lauren looked away. "Okay, I get all that, I do. But I don't get why you've given up looking for options."

"Careful there," Dave muttered. "You know me better than that. I possess a finely tuned opportunity-detecting radar under my hood. And if there was a viable, expedient alternative for us, it would've been on the table. As of this moment, I've yet to see any."

"Impossible is a lie," Lauren began, "told by those eager to control us. It's only purpose, to make us weak and subservient. It's a programmed method of thinking we must learn to rise above."

"Come again?"

"Elevate your frame of mind. Know your enemy, know and take responsibility for yourself and assume control, and you'll find *impossible* to be nothing more than a figment of your imagination." Lauren grinned, her unease on display. "You don't remember? Those are *your* words. You used to drill them into me whenever I said something was too hard."

"While I do appreciate the rehashing of times past, there's more to it than that, Janey," Dave said. "Our original plans involved coming here to deliver a package. Getting stuck here and dividing the unit up all over God's green earth was never our intention, but Mother Nature had other plans in mind for us...and as it stands, we can't do much about that. Getting word from Neo is advantageous, it alleviates a few tidbits of butt pucker, but we've yet to hear anything out of Tim and the boys since we left, and I have no idea how they've been getting along with Major Pain and his miscreants in our absence.

"There's no way of knowing what else the weather has in store for us, and winter hasn't even started yet. Staying warm, preventing frostbite, and cuddling up with our loved ones is important, and I'm not discounting it, but maintaining an adequate level of security within our AO is a primary concern. With the unit split up like it is, it fucks us...I mean, really screws the pooch. And I can't consent to any more fragments."

Lazarus tapped his fingers on the radio bench. "This is just the beginning of January. Even the valleys around here are highlands and sit up high, like around fifteen hundred feet or thereabouts. By my best guess, we have a couple more months before seeing any snowmelt, if any."

"Thanks," Lauren slurred.

"Don't mention it," said Lazarus, not sensing the sarcasm in her tone.

Lauren rolled her eyes. "I get that we're divided, Dave. And I can see it's weighing on you. It would weigh on me too if I were in your shoes. But I'm *not* in your shoes. I live in mine. And mine want to go home, and I'm not sorry for that."

"I know, young lady," Dave said. "And I get it, I do. And I know you're anxious, and I know it sucks, but the only choice we have, at least for now, is to hope and pray for some good weather and conditions to improve. Yes, we're divvied up far beyond my liking. And we're teeter-tottering on the brink of far too many goddamn allowable risks. Taking you home would necessitate personnel, transportation, supplies, and weaponry. We'd be staring down another split and a lot more risks. And doing that would—"

"Defy prudence," Lauren broke in.

Dave squinted. "It would defy logic."

Lauren felt ready to draw out the argument, but opted against. She turned her head away, folding her arms. "I see. And I guess I understand."

"I'm sorry, Janey. I really am, but this simply cannot happen right now."

Dave went on and on, but Lauren only ignored him. Soon, she put her jacket on, zipped it up and exited the comm shack without another word said.

# CHAPTER 8

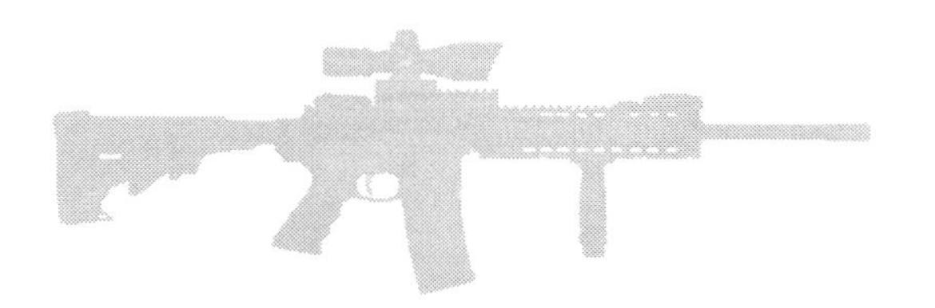

IN A PASSION-FUELED STUPOR, LAUREN STORMED out of Lazarus's radio shack. She hustled through the snow, finding that Cyrus had been waiting for her not far away. The dog ran to her with enthusiasm, ready to play, but Lauren paid him little mind. She passed by without so much as petting him, and dejected, he plopped down in the snow, pricking his ears. Then, after a moment, he followed in her footsteps all the way back to the farmhouse, making sure to maintain his distance.

Lauren stomped up the porch stairs to the front door, kicked the caked-on snow from her boots, and went inside, holding the storm door open long enough for Cyrus to slide in. She untied her boots and kicked them off one by one near the door, then ran upstairs to her room.

As she went to seal herself alone inside, she hesitated, noticing that Cyrus seemed intent on accompanying her. "You're not going to let me be, are you?"

Cyrus sat on his haunches and tilted his head to the side.

"I like you, but this really isn't the best time. My mood has gone to shit today. You should probably go find your master."

Cyrus only panted and whined a little bit.

Lauren rolled her eyes and sighed. "Fine. You can come in, but I don't know how much company I'm going to be." She then bade him enter and closed the door behind him.

She strolled to the other side of the room, past an assortment of clothing, gear and a few weapons, some of which had arrived with her, others she'd recently acquired from stacks of tubs and bins her father had stored in the barn, having delivered it himself years before. Cyrus took a seat nearby and put his nose to the floor, sniffing at some of the items. His paws slid forward and he rested his head on them, exhaling a breath from his nostrils that sounded more like a sigh.

"I can relate," Lauren said, looking upon him.

If there was one thing Lauren could not tolerate, it was being told she couldn't do something. Not necessarily being told no or that she wasn't able to, but being informed that she wasn't allowed, as if some invisible force existed serving only to prevent her from following her will. And Lauren's will wasn't just stubborn, it was on the periphery of being superhuman.

But she knew Dave Graham and how accommodating he could be, or downright inflexible he could be when it suited him. He was just as obstinate as she was, and his resolve was unparalleled. After this latest face-off, Lauren wondered how long it would be before she woke to find armed guards stationed at her bedroom door.

"Guess there's no point in waiting to find out," Lauren muttered. "You always put so much emphasis on the import of perseverance. Permit me to show *you* some." She then rotated to regard her nightstand, where she'd placed a stack of topographical maps printed on waterproof paper. Each map contained a USGS grid of the areas surrounding Bernie and Ruth's farm and beyond. She'd found them amongst a stack of other paper items in the gun safe her father had also evidently transported here with Norman's assistance, per Bernie's account.

Lauren began arranging the grids on the floor, sliding and aligning them together like puzzle pieces, stopping after she had created a path between her current location and home. Cyrus watched her intently with his head between his paws, blowing the occasional exhale through his nose.

Lauren studied the maps, running her fingernail over them in a straight line from point A to point B. She reached beside her into the pile of gear for a hank of 550 paracord, unrolled a few feet then cut off several inches using the folding Kershaw Induction knife she had clipped to her pocket. She sliced through the outer sheathing, separated it from the core, and extricated one of the interwoven strands.

When she flicked the unused remnants to the floor, Cyrus raised and tilted his head.

"Oh, sorry." She scooted the strings to him, and he began merrily toying with them, employing both paws. "Is this your way of telling me that cats aren't the *only* pets who fancy strings?"

Lauren tied a knot in one end of her strand and placed the knot on her current location on the map, then stretched it taut and tied another knot where the strand met with Trout Run Valley. She then compared the length between the knots to the map scale and approximated the line-of-sight distance to home.

"The shortest distance between two points is a straight line, right?" Lauren prompted the dog, causing him to alert. "You don't have to answer, it was rhetorical." She sighed. "Just over forty miles, sixty not omitting elevation changes. And no direct path or trail to get there. Just a shitload of ups and downs—steep ones, in very unfamiliar territory." She studied the map closely while Cyrus monitored her every movement and murmur. "From the looks of it, the straight-line approach won't be an option on foot; it goes against the grain the entire way. The Alleghenies run southwest to northeast, they're rugged and most of their ridges are sheer, especially this far west. I count at least five major river crossings to contend with, and it goes without saying that roads are off-limits. So that sixty miles just became eighty or more. Still better than a hundred on the road, I suppose."

Lauren leaned back on her hands and exhaled. "Five to six days tops in satisfactory conditions, but we don't have those, do we?" She paused. "There's at least a foot to eighteen inches of snow on the ground, and there's no telling how deep it'll be at the higher elevations. Might need to locate or put together a pair of snowshoes…but either way, those six days could very easily become a week and a half. Water wouldn't be an issue, but food procurement could be. Can't forage, hunting and fishing would be time consuming, and trapping isn't viable when you're on the move… and I'm definitely no Daniel Boone. I'd have to carry everything. And a week's worth of food is a lot of weight to shoulder, especially since this would become the longest trip I've ever done on foot."

Lauren's eyes met with the dog's, who lazily stared up at her from the floor. "It's doable, though—" she chuckled to herself "—for a crazy person, anyway. Seriously, I must be losing my mind. I have to be nuts to even consider this." She exhaled. "I should probably complete a gear assessment before conjuring any more dumb ideas. Let's see what Dad left us."

Lauren's inventory of prized backpacking and hiking equipment had been left behind in the mountains of Hampshire County on the day she and Austin Brady had been captured. Subsequently, she'd only managed to acquire replacements for her forsaken firearms and tattered clothing.

Among the particulars previously delivered and stored in the barn, Alan Russell had left a sealed bin of gear explicitly for her, that, failing some aesthetic, functional and a few itemization differences, closely resembled her former loadout.

Lauren's previous catalog of gear had been perfectly suitable for backpacking. But the items in this collection looked more robust and heavy duty, appropriate for mountaineering and bushcraft, or rather wilderness survival and subsistence, thriving for extended periods in natural environments.

While the backpacker carries in all items needed for the trip and packs out everything that cannot be burned or decomposed, the bushcrafter only carries in those items that cannot be feasibly constructed or recreated by nature. Backpackers bring along only what's needed for the trip, and plan their inventory specifically for it in advance, along with some extra padding in case of emergency. But their preference is to keep their loadout as light as possible, and for good reason. Backpackers are usually on the move and tend to hike for long distances on hilly, adverse terrain, and extra weight takes a righteous toll on the body.

The bushcrafter has no specific itinerary and brings along only the basics, but those basic items serve multiple purposes and have various uses, including the construction of other items. For these reasons, these basic items should therefore by all means be capable of withstanding a lifetime of abuse, making weight requirements of little to no consequence. The bushcrafter focuses instead on knowledge and skills—the ability to make or build whatever is needed. And neither knowledge nor skills afforded superfluous weight.

While having fallen somewhere between the average backpacker and the run-of-the-mill bushcrafter on the outdoorsman spectrum, Lauren's father had always prioritized functionality, while remaining a stickler for keeping things light. She recalled him testing outdoor gear purchases on numerous occasions either at home or on the trail. Items that passed his tests remained in his inventory and, as well, in his good graces. Others that didn't were either sold for pennies on the dollar or given away, discarded, or even reduced to ashes in ritualistic fashion.

As she visually inspected the items strewn about in no particular order, Lauren was reminded of 'the five Cs of survivability', as deliberated by author Dave Canterbury in his *Bushcraft* book series. Those being cutting tools, combustion, cover, containers and, finally, cordage.

To her right, Lauren palmed the first of the five, a stout survival knife, its full-tang blade safely shrouded in a black MOLLE sheath. She carefully slid it out to examine it, noting both the breadth and sharpness of its coated blade, along with the letters spelling out the word ROWEN etched near the hilt. She flipped the knife over, finding a company logo for Randall's Adventure Training and Equipment Group and ESEE, seeing now that the knife model was an ESEE-5.

Lauren admired the knife. She'd never seen or held anything quite like it before. It was of similar length and slightly heavier than the KA-BAR with which Woo Tang had entrusted her in prior weeks. It was stoutly built and she imagined its usages were virtually limitless. "I think we stand to become good friends," she said, sheathing the knife and setting it aside.

The second 'C' of the five was combustion, or fire-making gear. Lauren was already highly proficient at multiple fire-starting methods, and though it remained possible to use items found in nature to do so, it wasn't always practical. Bearing this in mind, her father had left her a kit consisting of a six-inch ferrocerium rod and a ceramic striker, a credit-card-sized plastic Fresnel lens, and two mini Bic lighters. A tinder kit comprised of petroleum-jelly-dipped cotton balls, waxed wood, fatwood sticks and shavings, waxed and unwaxed jute twine, and a tea candle accompanied it. By using these items and building upon them with other fuels obtained in the field, a fire could be had just about anywhere and in any environment.

In terms of cover, a woodland camouflage Gore-Tex bivy lay nearby, rolled tightly in a cylinder, bound by a hook and loop strap. Cover, or shelter, can be re-created in nature. But doing so requires both time and effort, and in any survival situation, time is of the essence. As such, any outdoorsperson of merit knows well the import of toting shelter provisions. They can be used conditionally until a more permanent means is constructed from natural materials, or in conjunction with them.

Lauren ran her fingers along the material, recognizing it as a standard-issue bivy cover, a component of the MSS, the military's modular sleep system. Her dad had purchased a number of them both online and in surplus stores, most of which had been previously issued. They were sturdy and both wind and waterproof. An inflatable sleeping pad lie beside it, rolled into a matching cylinder right next to a brand-spanking-new winter-weight down sleeping bag.

Lauren ogled the bag, on the verge of unpacking it, fluffing it up and sliding herself inside. At long last, she'd found a surrogate to her highly cherished Marmot Ion down sleeping bag after having been forced to leave it behind.

Alan, as it turned out, hadn't skimped on the fourth or fifth 'Cs' either, but that didn't exactly knock Lauren for six. She inferred that for obvious reasons, he'd chosen to omit the standard cookstove and iso-butane fuel cannisters. Gas was a consumable and therefore finite, making it impractical to carry in ample supply or rely on beyond the short term. Nature made available both the positions on which to cook food and bring water to a boil and the fuel necessary to make it happen.

Cooking pots and the like simply cannot be recreated using natural materials. Instead of standard single-purpose containers like the polyethylene water bottles he typically carried on backpacking trips, Alan had substituted stainless-steel single-wall Klean Kanteens. They were multipurpose by construction and could be used for drinking or carrying water, boiling it, or even as a cooking vessel.

Lauren counted at least ten randomly branded hanks of paracord amongst the gear pile to round out the list, but there were also bails of jute and hemp twine, and tarred, braided nylon bank line intermixed within. Cordage was something else that could be re-created in nature, but since its uses were practically limitless, it never hurt to pack plenty of your own.

Setting all other items aside, Lauren pulled closer a uniquely designed ripstop nylon backpack that still had the retail tags dangling from it. It was an uncommon, checkerboard-patterned blend of black and gray, and the embroidered threading near the bottom bore the model Ohm 2.0 by ULA. It was an ultralight, no-frills, minimalist backpack, one that was rugged and built to last.

Lauren looked it over while removing the tags and recalling ULA stood for Ultralight Adventure Equipment, a company based in Utah that her dad had mentioned before. He'd referred to it and a host of others as 'cottage industry', as they were located domestically and manufactured their products in-house, mostly by hand.

Then she recalled the ULA pack he'd purchased and had taken along on their last backpacking trip together, one that had quickly become his favorite. It was slightly larger than this one, but the overall design looked remarkably similar. Lauren remembered how skeptical he'd been. It was unlike any pack of big-name manufacturers he'd ever owned, but after loading it up and putting it to the test, the pack had made him a believer. Empty, it weighed virtually nothing; full of gear, it was bulky while remaining incredibly easy to carry and gentle on the shoulders, lower back, and hips. And, much to his amazement, it was remarkably quiet, no squeaking or hissing like most all of his other backpacks.

Lauren guessed he had purchased this one for her and had brought it here for her use not long after. "You've done it again, haven't you?" she asked aloud. "My dad, the master planner. I just wish you would've done a better job planning to get home." She exhaled and reclined onto the floor, stretching her arms above her head. "And I wish you were here now. You're probably the only person in the world who could talk me out of this."

An unexpected knock on the door spawned a raucous bark from Cyrus. He ran to it with his tail wagging and scratched at it, acting as if he knew who was on the other side.

"It must be a friendly," Lauren said quietly, then sat up. "Come in."

The handle twisted and Bernie opened the door, slipping his head through the crack. "Excuse me, Lauren." He smiled at her, then at Cyrus, whose tail wagged furiously at the sight of his owner. "Hey, pooch. I was wondering where you got off to. Usually, he's running around the house terrorizing everyone. He isn't pestering you, is he?"

Lauren shook her head. "No, not at all. He's just keeping me company."

Bernie took a step inside as Cyrus ran to him. "He's gotten awful close to you, hasn't he?" He took the dog's paw and glared. "Traitor. Can't say as I blame him, dogs know character, and you've got yourself a good one going for you. But they're also empathic and have a special way of knowing when someone they're fond of is feeling blue. You… doing all right?"

Lauren chuckled. "Yeah, I'm fine. Maybe a little more homesick than usual."

"I imagine that's to be expected. I'll try not to take offense." He gestured with his head to the mess on the floor. "Did you dig all that stuff up from the barn?"

Lauren nodded. "Most of it."

"Looks like a good assortment of loot. Your old man leave you anything decent?"

"No complaints thus far." She reached for a three-ring binder. "Dad had a notebook similar to this one in his gun safe at home. We got it out a few days after the blackout." Lauren opened it and flipped through the first few laminated pages. "But this one, near as I can tell, is unique. It has a section that wasn't in the one we had."

"That so?" Bernie prompted. "What about?"

"There's maps, itineraries, lists of names and addresses, even a page of coordinates entitled 'Resupply'. Probably his plans for getting back home, a copy of them, anyway." Lauren folded the notebook closed. "I've been reluctant to delve into it."

Bernie moved in closer, his curiosity on display. "Think you might find something in there you won't like?"

She didn't answer him.

"Lauren, not everything always works out the way we plan or want it to," Bernie said. "That's a fact of life, dear. And that isn't going to change in your lifetime, I can pretty much guarantee. By my best guesstimate, your dad left that there notebook here so someone else out there would know what he was up to."

"I get that," Lauren said. "And it makes sense, but why *here* and not for us? Mom, Grace, and I never knew anything, almost as if that portion of his plan was omitted by design."

"Eh…I'm thinking there might be a plainer explanation."

"Such as?"

Bernie tilted his head. "Such as he might've just plum ran out of time, sweetheart. It's easy knowing the right things to do and the right times to do them after the fact. That's the science of hindsight. Your dad's a smart fella, but no one besides the big man upstairs can predict what's going to come to pass. Guys like your dad are always planning things out. Maybe he intended to do more and just never had the chance.

"Look, I don't want to bug you anymore about it unless you want me to. If so, great. Gather up what you got there and bring it downstairs, and we'll go over it together. I'll try to recall the things he told me, and maybe we'll make some sense out of it." He chuckled. "No guarantees, mind you…not with this old-timer's of mine. But the better half's sweet tea tends to get my noggin moving. I might even steal you a glass to season the pot."

Lauren sighed and took a softer line. "I think I'd like that. But I'm feeling a little burned out today. Would tomorrow morning work for you?"

"Certainly," said Bernie. "Bright and early suit you?"

Lauren nodded.

"Okeydokey. I'll leave you to it, then…but, how about a glass of tea directly, at any rate?"

"Tea sounds delightful."

"Coming right up," Bernie said. "Be back in a minute. Come on, Cyrus. Let's leave the young lady to herself."

# CHAPTER 9

AFTER HAVING TAKEN THEIR LEAVE of Lazarus and his comm shack, Dave and Woo Tang encountered Sanchez and Santa near a saggy, corroded barbed-wire fence marking the property line on their return trip to the farm.

After hurdling the fence and kicking the snow about, Dave rubbed his hands to warm them. "What brings you ladies out this far?"

"Felt like going for a walk," replied Sanchez. "I've been slacking on the cardio something fierce lately."

"Exercise does a body good, even second-rate ones," Santa added. "Also, we wanted to get a better picture of the AO as it stands. The surveillance posts are in place…fire watchers are designated, and rotating patrols have been arranged for the duration of our stay, per your instructions, LT. NVDs are charged, operational and distributed, and we're doing fairly well on ammo. We got enough eyes to see what's coming and enough firepower to put it down for good if it does."

Sanchez nodded agreeance. "Everybody is asses and elbows, the way you like it."

"I'm captivated," Dave said, his chest expanding. "Guesstimated perimeter defense strength?"

Santa shrugged slightly. "It's a big damn perimeter. And the hills around these parts are as sheer as the ones we saw near Tora Bora. We got a few of the Sons working with us, though. And that's good 'cause we don't have shit for personnel. Still, I'd rate our defenses somewhere between Ferrigno and that *mountain* fella, though Riki-tik Martin here might regale us with his assessments."

"Riki-tik Martin? Really?" Sanchez discreetly gestured to some nearby mountaintops. "My guys are hoofing it to some dicey spots in those hills as we speak. Places I would choose myself to take potshots at some unsuspecting tangos. So far, negative contacts and zero evidence of hostile activity. Coast is clear to this point, LT."

Dave sent a look of approval. "Outstanding."

"Anything else of note to report?" Woo Tang asked.

Both men seemed hesitant, neither tendering a reply.

"Fine business," muttered Dave. "Carry on, then."

Dave went to move past, but Sanchez slid over to obstruct him. "LT, it's a little off-topic, but we do have something to report."

"Oh?"

"Yeah. So…Santa and I had a brief Orchid sighting a few mikes back. I think she was on her way to the farm…the old man's brown dog was shadowing her…and she looked awfully pissed."

"Mm-hmm. If she looked that way, then I suspect she most likely is."

Sanchez hesitated and shared a look with Santa. "You have any notion as to why?"

Dave pushed out a breath. "I might."

"Feel like divulging it? So we can all be on the same page?" Santa asked. "She blew by us in quite a hissy. Looked to me like a storm was brewing, like one of them bad ones with golf-ball-sized hail, lots of lightning and shit. The kind that'll put a hurtin' to your house if you don't batten down the hatches."

Dave folded his arms and sulked, opting to take his time to respond. "She got off the horn with Neo a little while ago. He passed along to her some particularly personal intel regarding a family member, whom she was then able to speak with directly. Shortly thereafter, our young miss Janey made it clear that she aspires for nothing more than to galivant home on the double. And I subsequently informed her that doing so was out of the question."

One of Santa's brows lifted. "You did what?"

"I told her no. As in one big, corpulent negative."

"Why?" Santa probed.

"What do you mean, *why*?" Dave yapped. "You already know why, or *should*, at the very least. There are about a hundred levelheaded reasons why a trip like that makes zero sense and would be borderline foolhardy at this juncture."

Sanchez cocked his head. "And I'm betting not any one of those reasons matter to her."

"It doesn't matter what matters to her," Dave said. "My reasoning is sound. And the last time I checked, she wasn't the one in command."

"LT, no one is challenging that," Sanchez said. "But how did she react to hearing what you said?"

"She was…" Dave trailed off, sighing. "Disappointed."

Santa sniggered. "Yeah, she looked it."

"Well, I am very sorry to hear that. I truly am. Now, if there's nothing else, I'll be on my way."

"LT, wait. Another question," Sanchez said. "Other than stewing in disappointment, what do you think is going on in her mind right now? I mean…what do you think she's doing presently in response to what you said to her?"

"Sanchez, I don't know," Dave growled. "I mean, I really don't have the faintest clue. Why?"

"LT, come on, man, think it through. She isn't one of us. I mean, she is, but at the same time, she isn't. She fits in here and meshes with us because of our history and because we all love her." Sanchez paused to gather his thoughts. "But she's far from being a Marine. She's not a soldier or an operator. She doesn't know a CO and she doesn't comprehend the chain of command. She was never trained to obey orders without question. She—"

"Okay, stop. Halt chatter." Dave held up a hand. "Check your fire, taco…are you high? Did your cock holster resign from audible range? You are by and far the most insubordinate of any subordinate I have ever had under my charge. Your own comprehension of the chain of command is nigh on equivalent to *my* understanding of the latest pre-collapse federal tax code. Exactly what point are you endeavoring to get across to me?"

Sanchez rubbed his chin. "Eh, maybe I'm using bad examples."

"Nah, I think the examples are on point," jeered Santa. "It's the delivery that's lacking, or maybe the deliveryman."

"*Chinga tu madre*, Santa."

"Only if it's *your* madre," Santa countered with a grin. "Love me some Latina girls."

"*Mi mamá está muerta*. She's dead, *cabrón*."

"So's mine. What makes you special?"

Sanchez humbly tilted his head. "Shit, I never knew that. Knee-jerk reactions, you know? I'm sorry, man."

"Me too, brother."

The two men fist-bumped and shared a moment.

Dave scoffed at them both. "Oh, that's real darlin'. Do you two sissies intend to finish this inconsequential circle jerk sometime *before* the second coming? I'd really like to get on with my day."

Santa offered his apologies while thumbing his beard.

"Sorry, LT," Sanchez said. "Look, I'm trying hard to say something, and I guess I haven't had time to think it through. The original idea or plan was for us to teach her things…but I feel like somehow we've all learned things from her at the same time. She's helped us see from a young person's perspective, only she's not just a typical young person. She's built differently. The girl never gives up, LT. What kind of teenager does what she does and keeps the kind of company she keeps?"

"The kid's lost a lot, Dave," Santa added. "But she takes a beating and keeps coming back for more. Now, far be it from me to tell you how to run your unit, but if Miss Jane is looking for a way of getting home with something substantial weighing on her heart, I suggest we find a way to accommodate her. 'Cause getting in her way is only going to make her do something you don't want her to."

"And that's something none of us want to see," Sanchez appended.

"You two think she's going to head off on her own? On foot? Through *those* hills in the snow for a hundred miles with a pack strapped to her back?" Dave harrumphed. "No way. She's deliberate, no doubt. And maybe somewhat irrational. But not nearly enough to do something like that."

"Yeah, that's what I used to think about her too," said Sanchez. "Until I saw her run down a mountain in the middle of a firefight to save two kids from getting killed in spite of herself."

"And let's not forget the home-run swing she put on that dude in New Creek," added Santa. "If it weren't for that, we might be talking to a *soft* taco right about now."

Sanchez elbowed the bearded one. "That's fucked up, Santa."

Santa patted his shoulder. "Quit. You know I didn't mean nothing by it."

"Whatever, *pinche*."

Woo Tang spoke up, interrupting their banter. "I was present to observe her willfully confront a menacing enemy. She did so despite my warnings, conscious that her life and the lives of others hung in the balance. After my men were killed in action, she persisted still, seemingly detached from fear."

Sanchez beheld his shorter cohort, then his leader. "Exactly. Either she was born with it or she developed it somehow because of us and what we taught her, but that girl has the heart of a lion. Right now she fears nothing, and a total absence of fear like that can be a slow route to greatness or a quick one to a grave. You can't just tell her no, she can't go home. Not after what she's been through. Not after almost becoming hell's next victim. Don't forget where we found her."

"Damn it all," Dave expelled. "Catch fucking twenty-two, same as always. You're telling me it's not okay to tell her no, but it isn't exactly okay to allow her to pack her shit and leave either, Sanchez."

"Okay, what then? Want to post sentries at her bedroom door?" Sanchez asked. "Treat her like a prisoner? Give the order."

Dave bit his lip. "No. I can't do that, either. And I wouldn't do that to her. But I can't just allow her to march home on her own along the trail of frozen tears. Too many unknowns that could get her killed—if the weather doesn't do her in first."

"Maybe you should go talk to her, bud," Santa said.

"Yeah, sit down with her and explain it like her father would," Sanchez agreed. "I know that sounds strange as hell; it feels strange to say it. But in his absence, who does she look up to more than you? I don't want to see her get hurt, LT. I'd sooner carry her home piggyback before I would let that happen."

"I find I am in agreement," Woo Tang said. "It would serve her best interests and that of our own if we intervened."

"Right," Dave said, nodding. "Message received, gents. I do very much appreciate the conflab. I'll do some thinking on this and we'll go over our overall lack of options tomorrow morning at the breakfast table. Carry on."

Lazarus stood discreetly yards away from Dave Graham and his men. He'd listened in on their conversation and had heard every word spoken between them while refraining to make known his presence, an auspiciously placed ancient oak having afforded him concealment. As the four men went their separate ways, he jerked himself behind the tree a little further to remain hidden.

Once certain they had all moved far enough away, Lazarus stepped out in to the open. He sucked on his teeth, turned and started back to the comms shack, a contemplative look befalling him. He crossed his arms, sent a hand to his chin, and assumed a thinker's pose just as two of his men strode to him, interrupting his train of thought.

Lazarus dropped his arms to his sides and studied them. "Well? Are the two of you just going to stand there? Speak."

The one on the left wearing a wool cap with earflaps was the first to open his mouth, doing so with trepidation in his voice. "It's…well, worse than we thought."

"Worse?" probed Lazarus. "How worse?"

"Shit's gone to hell in a handbasket, sir."

"It's bad. Real bad," the other man said, wiping his nose. "Much more bad than what we thought it would be."

"Much more bad, huh?" parroted Lazarus. "Exactly how *much more bad* are we talking? Give me details. I want to know what was said, since I couldn't be there to hear it myself."

"I dare say it was the most heated meeting I've ever seen," wool cap said. "Everyone was arguing, and I mean everyone. A couple of fights even broke out…it's like the entire group's done gone and fell into a civil war over all this."

"A civil war?" Lazarus tilted his head. "You're exaggerating."

"No, I'm not. Sorry to say."

Lazarus began to pace. "What about Claudio? Was he there?"

"Oh yeah," the man on the right said. "He was there."

"And…did he say anything?"

"Oh, yeah. He said lots of things. Had lots to say, like usual. But mostly, he was just tryin' to calm folks down and keep order."

"Did he say anything about me?" Lazarus asked.

"Well, yeah," wool cap replied. "He said what you did was unwarranted and unprovoked, and a whole bunch of other words I forget. He said he never started nothing and all that coup talk was just rumors. He's always been fine with being the Sons' number two in command and never wanted more than that. But he also said after what happened…after what you did, everything's going to change. Then he started a show-of-hands voting thing…to see who was going to side with who, you or him. Some stayed with you, said they wouldn't betray your family name. But a bunch of guys went to his side of the room; then even more followed. After that, lots of fellas were saying what you did was inexcusable. And you needed to pay for it."

Lazarus's eyes got wide. "What? *Me* pay for it? Pay for what? I don't have to pay for anything! I'm the motherfreaking commander-in-chief of the whole damn chapter!"

"Not no more," the other man said. "Claudio said he's assumed command, and no one challenged it. He said you're guilty of a crime… an offense against a brother. And you know what that means."

Lazarus threw his hands in the air. "Great. That's just great! Talk about the fuckup of all fuckups. I should've just done it myself."

"Sir? I'm sorry all this has happened, I really am," wool cap began, taking a good look around. "But this ain't going to die down anytime soon. And until it does, it's not going to be safe for you around here."

"Around here?" Lazarus barked, his eyes alight. "And by 'around here' you mean the whole damn state, right? Yeah, trust me…I'm aware." He let out a long, undulating sigh and paused a moment. "By the looks of things, how many of us would you estimate remain loyal to my family?"

The two men shared a blank stare.

"Maybe about…I don't know…less than half," the man on the right said.

"Less than half," Lazarus uttered in a chuckle.

"To be fair, sir," wool cap began, "there were quite a few undecideds as well. I don't think Claudio has much more siding with him than you have siding with you."

"Great," Lazarus said, putting his forehead to the tree. He began recalling the discussion he'd only minutes ago overheard between Dave Graham and his men. "I'm working on something…I might be leaving for a while, taking an extended sabbatical. I'll fill you both in once I've finalized my plans." He turned to face them, choosing to stuff his hair into his hat. "In the meantime, I'm going to be relying on you both to sift through this for me. Find out who's still loyal and make a list. Then make a list of undecideds and find out their grievances. I want as many men as we can get. Offer them whatever they want, I don't care what it is. I'll find a way of getting it to them. I need them to pick our side. If Claudio wants a war, we'll give him one."

Wool cap looked concerned. "Sir? Are you sure that's a good idea?"

Lazarus laughed. "No! No, I don't. I think it's a horrible idea. But, like it or not, this isn't going to go away on its own. Now, we got to finish it."

# CHAPTER 10

**Loudoun County, Virginia**
**Sunday, January 2nd. Present day**

WHEN ALAN AWOKE, HE YAWNED deeply, rolled onto his back and stretched, and tried willing open his eyes. The room was mostly dark, and only a minute amount of light was peeking through the cracks in the doorway. He hadn't any idea what time it was, when he'd fallen asleep, or how long he'd been sleeping, but he felt well rested.

A week had elapsed since arriving at Butch's underground fallback position. Though their original itinerary had involved an earlier departure, circumstances beyond his control had made doing so difficult for him. Alan desired nothing more now than to track down and reconnect with his family. Nothing ranked higher on his list of concerns. But he couldn't do it alone, that much was obvious. And though the choice was his own, he simply couldn't bring himself to leave without those who'd made getting this far possible for him. At odds with himself, he wrestled with the conundrum he'd created, to his wit's end.

Alan felt rejuvenated for the first time in a long while. In only a day's time of being here, he'd grasped the need to engage in activity. He had to locate ways of killing time before time found a way of doing him in. When he was idle, errant thoughts of his family's welfare and whereabouts ate away at him in conjunction with the soreness in his middle-aged muscles. He began a stretching regimen, and those stretches, a day later, turned into calisthenics. He started running, very slowly at first, mostly in vacant, low-lit corridors in the facility's lower levels, careful that no one was watching him. And he began reading whatever books he could find strewn about the facility.

Nearly all remnants of joint pain and muscle soreness from his on-foot adventure had all but evaporated. Physically, Alan felt like a man again, but his conditioning did nothing for his aching soul.

Today's schedule, as far as he knew, remained up in the air, and not seeing any point in rising just yet, he decided to snooze a little while longer. A side sleeper, Alan's ideal resting position was on his left with his arm supporting his head beneath his pillow. He closed his eyes, rolled over and yawned again.

The bed wobbled a bit. Then Alan felt an unusually familiar, sultry warmth brush past his face. His eyes reopened and he learned that he wasn't alone where he slumbered. An attractive female face, half burrowed in a pillow, was mere inches away from his own.

For reasons unknown to him, Jade was now sound asleep in the same bed, emanating soft purring sounds with each breath. And though Alan knew her, trusted her and cared deeply for her, a feeling of distinct unease began to consume him. He was a married man. He had a wife and a family with whom he was desperately trying to reconnect, and no man should ever be caught dead lying with *any* woman not his wife, no matter the circumstance. And here he was.

Alarmed and mortified, Alan scooted away and sat up, the suddenness of his movements serving to rouse Jade. She rubbed her eyes, then opened them wide and sent a stare directly into his.

They froze at first sight of one another. Neither said anything at first, not a word.

Alan began feeling around for the bed's edge, attempting to flee, escape, or dodge whatever the hell was happening, had happened, or whatever he held destined to happen.

Jade came to life and reached for him. "Alan, wait. It's okay, let me explain."

"No, I don't think so. This is far from being okay." His legs now draped over the edge, Alan sent his focus to the floor below the sleeper sofa that he and Jade had discovered days ago in one of the larger offices within the White Rock facility.

Jade sat up and flipped on a light fixture mounted to the wall. "I know this looks…horrible. But it isn't. I mean, it's not as bad as it looks.

You didn't do anything wrong...neither did I, technically. You don't have to feel bad about this."

Alan rose to his feet and took several steps from the bed without responding.

"Where are you going?"

"Nowhere. I just...need to add some distance. That's all." Alan rubbed the matter from his eyes. "I remember falling asleep, but what I don't remember is how the two of us ended up in this fold-out bed together. This...isn't right."

Jade nodded. "I realize that, and I'm sorry. Just please...let me explain."

"Fine. Explain, then."

"This is awkward for me to admit, so bear with me," she began, sighing. "I...watched you fall asleep last night. I've been doing it every night since we got here. I stand in the hall just outside the doorway when you go to bed and I watch you. Call me a stalker or a creeper if you like, but I can't help it. I took care of you for months when you were comatose and used to worry myself to fucking death not knowing if you were going to stop breathing or...die on me. So, consequently, watching you sleep and listening to you breathe became a habit. It's just something I do. And I know it sounds strange."

Jade ran her fingers through her hair. "I've been running on adrenaline for weeks. I crashed hard yesterday. And there's nowhere to sack out in this place other than a floor covered in festering rat shit. Ken and Walter need the couches they claimed, and there's zero appeal in the thought of closing my eyes anywhere in Butch's vicinity. So I've been sleeping in the APC all week, and now my back and neck are absolutely killing me. I...just wanted to feel the comfort of a real bed, or something close to one for a change. I knew there was room in here, and you...are without a doubt, a safe bet. And I trust you. I'm sorry, I didn't think things all the way through. I promise it'll never happen again."

Alan glanced over at her with his head low, realizing now that Jade was fully clothed. She hadn't even bothered to remove her boots. And he was still wearing nearly every article of clothing he'd had on the previous day. "Thank you for telling me that. It makes this little...ordeal seem permissible, in a way." A pause. "Why haven't you said anything about your sleeping arrangements...or the lack thereof?"

"I didn't want to bother you with it," Jade said. "It's stupid to complain about, and you have enough on your mind as it is."

"Well, that may be true, mostly, but tonight we're finding you a bed to sleep in," Alan said. "Only, alone and *not* with me…in this one. I'll dig around and find something for you."

"You don't have to do that."

"You're right, I don't. But I want to, so let me."

Jade smiled. "Okay, just this once, then. But don't fuss over me. I'm a big girl."

Alan sent a nod along.

"Thank you, by the way. For hearing me out." Jade threw what remained of the covers off and rose, then pranced to the door. "Back to the Marauder for me."

"Jade."

"Yeah?"

"I'm…sorry."

She rested her head against the doorjamb. "For?"

"For…getting the wrong idea," Alan said. "And I don't want you to feel uncomfortable now around me…because of this."

Tiredness evident in her eyes, Jade smiled at him. "You're a good man, Alan Russell. Far too good for someone like me. And don't worry about me, worry about you. Get some more rest if you can. I'll see you in a little while for coffee, assuming Butch has more stored somewhere in this dump."

Weary of beating each other at video games and bored to death with almost everything else, hellhounds Ken and Walter were in urgent need of entertainment. Not long after taking their first sips of Butch's acrid-as-hell instant coffee and griping about the taste, the pair had gone on a grand tour of the complex and wound up finding more than they'd bargained for.

Customarily under stringent lock and key, the former troposcatter relay site turned datacenter turned federal continuity-of-operations facility's armory was jam-packed with NATO small arms. A variety of automatic rifles and carbines, pistols, shotguns and machine guns, all pristine, were neatly organized within. Uncertain if they were dreaming or dead, they took turns pinching each other for validation, then acted out like two kids in a candy store with a blank check.

What little self-control they held cast aside, Ken and Walter helped themselves to a grandiose share of the arsenal, ogling each weapon with a peculiar bloodlust branded only to them.

And much to Butch's chagrin, after having amassed them, they'd relocated their spoils to the main bay for inspection, proper cleaning and care, and to render affection.

"Hey, ground pounder," Walter called to Butch. "I hate bein' one of 'em folks, err, rather, *guests* I s'pose I should say, who's forever askin' fer stuff." He held aloft a midnight black Heckler and Koch M27 IAR, or infantry automatic rifle. "But would you mind terribly if I borrowed one of these? It's been an *año* or two since I held one of 'em, and by golly, I missed it."

A perturbed Butch shook his head without bothering to look up. "Depends. How long do you plan to hold on to it?"

"What's that?"

"You said *borrow*," grumbled Butch. "The term implies intent to return the merchandise."

Walter turned to face Ken. "Why does he always feel the need to git so dang technical?"

"It *is* his house, Walt," Ken said, shrugging, "and it's his stuff, kind of. I think that might give him the right."

"I claimed it. And that makes *it* and everything within *mine*, no *kind ofs* about it," Butch retorted.

Ken grinned. "See?"

"And while we're on the subject of that which is mine, I don't recall either of you soliciting permission to pull a whole hog Grenada on my armory, never mind lug all that usurped hardware up here."

"Anythin's better than leavin' 'em neglected," Walter spat.

"Come again?"

"I said there ain't no sense in leavin' all this here exquisite standard-issue hardware in the nasty cold an' pitch dark by its lonesome," Walter quipped. "It's reckless endangerment and it makes me sick. Weapons like these ones deserve better, you gotta keep 'em warm, clean and happy...let 'em know they're loved." He presented the M27 once more. "Look here, Butch. Take a gander at this rifle."

The man in camo didn't move a muscle.

"Butch! You fuckin' lanky tenderfoot! Don't you ignore me! I said lookit this here rifle!"

"Keep that shit up, gyrene, and your tender ass will rendezvous with my size eleven not-so-tender foot." Butch sent the rifle in question a reluctant stare and sighed. "What about it?"

"I'll tell you what about it—it's smilin' now, but 'twernt before. 'Cause e'rbody done forgot about it," Walter began. "This here rifle is mint, ain't once been fed or shot, same as most of these other ones. And that is one supreme abomination in demand of a generous unfuckin' on the double, compadre."

"You don't say."

"I do say. Ain't none of 'em ever had no good ole-fashioned cleanin' neither, not until me and Kenny brought 'em into our fold. Now, all of 'em are cozy and content, and up here with folks who care about 'em; and they even reek like TUF-Glide. Warms my heart." Walter sighed and took a few breaths.

Butch smirked and shook his head apathetically. "Not like you're leaving anytime soon, but if it generates an upsurge in your shrinking serotonin levels, borrow it for as long as you like, jarnuts. Just...spare me another one of those...whatever the fuck that was."

Alan emerged from the hall, and the sight of the pile of guns caught his interest. He wandered over to study the assortment and bid his friends a good morning.

"We already know what you're going to ask," Ken said, "and the answer is, we're both feeling fine. Same as we were yesterday and the day before, and the day before that. Both our asses are still leaking a foul-smelling blood and pus combo and still hurt like hell, just like yesterday and the day previous. And yes, I'm still ready to go. In fact, I've been cleared. Got my clean bill of health. So I'm not the one holding you up anymore."

Alan was stunned. "Ken...have I been repeating myself? Or asking the same questions every day?"

"You have, only it's been somewhere around five to ten *times* a day." Ken set down the rifle he was cleaning. "Look, man, I get it. We all get it. You're stir-crazy. Hell, we're all stir-crazy. Do you think any of us likes being stuck in this pit? My skin has lost every bit of tan I worked so hard to get at Camp Hill. It's like I'm back in the cavern, stuck in another underground hellhole all over again."

"Easy," Butch moaned from his spot at the bench.

"Sorry, Butch. I was going for emphasis, not description."

"As far as holdin' you up is concerned," Walter began, "'fraid there ain't much I can do 'bout it." He tapped on the frame of the wheelchair in which he was seated. "For the foreseeable future, I've switched my stems up for wheels. Sorry, pard. When y'all leave, I don't expect I'll be goin' with."

"You have nothing to be sorry about, Walter," said Alan. "There's a chance moving about could paralyze you, and we can't risk it. I don't need that weighing on my conscience any more than you."

"Hey," Butch's voice bellowed.

Alan didn't hear his name, so he dismissed it. Then, a moment after, Butch repeated himself.

"I think you're being summoned," said Ken, a brow raised.

"Careful," Walter said. "Ole boy's in one of 'em moods today."

Ken arched a brow. "Only because *you* set him off."

"Shut yer face, Kenny."

Alan could see the man in camo eyeballing him. Brows raised, he pointed at himself inquiringly.

"Yeah, you. Who'd you think I was talking to? Get over here. I got a bone to pick with you."

Alan strolled to where Butch was sitting on a stool behind a workbench, where before him lay Alan's pack and emptied out contents. "That's my backpack."

"Very astute."

"Why do you have it? And why is everything dumped out of it?"

"Can it. You're in my house. And my questions come first." Butch held aloft a walkie-talkie in each hand. "Now, where exactly did you acquire these?"

Alan looked strangely at him. "They were in the armored truck."

"What armored truck?"

"Yours. The one I took down the mountain," Alan said.

"Took?"

"Well, borrowed."

"*Borrowed*?"

"Butch, are you going to repeat every word I say back to me?"

"I'm asking the questions," Butch griped. "You stole them, didn't you?"

"The radios? No, I didn't steal them. I removed them from the truck after I...wrecked it."

Butch pursed his chapped lips. “The APC, you mean.”

“Right.”

“*My* APC.”

Alan nodded once. “That’s the one.”

“The one you managed to somehow miraculously overturn.”

“Yes.”

Butch set both radios down. “What were you going to do with them?”

Alan’s face contorted. “Um, use them, I guess?”

“For *what*?”

“Communication,” Alan stated, now himself sounding perturbed. “Since that’s what radios do.”

“Communication with *who*?”

Alan sent his arms outward at his sides. “I don’t know, Butch. With people. Maybe Jade or Walter or Ken. Or you or someone else. They were there, so I took them. I thought they might prove useful to us.”

“Have you used them yet?”

“No…”

“That’s what you get for thinking,” Butch grunted. “Do you even know *how* to use them?”

Alan sighed. “No, but I haven’t had time to play with them or learn what makes them tick. I just assumed I would. I was an amateur radio operator in my previous life, so I—”

“In your previous life?” Butch butted in. “Exactly how many lives have you had?”

“There’s a lot you don’t know about me, Butch.”

The warhorse smirked. “Likewise, I’m sure. You can…stand at ease, there. I’m not really that miffed. It’s just that when I decide to go through your provisions, like a friend would, to see what could be done to supplement them, I wind up coming across some items that don’t quite belong. Raises a few question marks.” Butch pointed to one of the handhelds. “They aren’t the best rigs in the world, but they’re weatherproof and use regular batteries, something I have quite a stockpile of. That’s why I keep them around. They’re also something I like to call ‘frequency agile’.

“They receive *and* transmit on multiple bands, but as far as range goes, they’re not exactly the best performers, especially with these goofy rubber duck antennas. You’re welcome to hang on to them if you like, but before you leave, I'll be installing a mobile transceiver in the Marauder Jade's keeping warm over there. Something with a little more oomph coupled with a decent antenna. It'll have preset memories in it, and we'll decide which ones to use ahead of your departure, so we can communicate if the need arises."

Alan folded his arms and sent along a gracious expression. "I appreciate that. I guess this means you won't be going with us."

Butch narrowed his eyes and sighed. "As much as I would love to join your crusade, I can't. Too many loose ends around here in which to tie granny knots and scorch the ends, and one ho bitch in dire need of a final snuffing out. But at some point down the road, I'll be looking you up to retrieve all which I have so cordially imparted unto you."

"Butch," Jade called from the Marauder's driver's seat, "stop bullying Alan before you get hurt. I need you front and center. I have some questions for you."

"Must be *your* turn now; imagine that. What sort of questions?"

"The kind only a gentleman of class like yourself, bearing your considerable knowledge, can answer."

Butch directed a suspicious look Alan's way. "Is she trying to butter me up? Because it's working."

Alan shrugged. "You heard the lady."

"'Deed I did." Butch rose and led the way over the bay's unadorned concrete floor with Alan following in tow.

Jade leaned out from her driver's side perch as they approached, gesturing to the Katlanit's interface and fire control. "What precisely is *death blossom*?"

Butch ascended the ladder and observed the screen with a cautious eye, dubiously noting how deep she'd been able to delve into the system on her own. "Now, I put a considerable amount of effort into making that software the absolute inverse of intuitive, as in beyond the deciphering capacity of most random persons."

"I'm not most random persons, Butch," Jade said.

"So I'm gathering. How did you manage to gain access to the admin menu? Hack the passphrase? Locate a backdoor? Create your own?"

"Hardly."

"Okay. How, then?"

Jade went expressionless. "Persistence."

Butch smirked at her. "Persistence? Really. Well, aren't you something else? You can't fool me, megababe. I know weapons-grade aptitude when I see it. Exactly what was your MOS? Crypto? Electronic warfare? Psyops?"

Jade responded shyly, "I never had an MOS."

"You never had one? Well, well, no shit." Butch backed away and stood at attention. "Should I be tendering a salute to you, ma'am?"

"Butch, quit," Jade said. "And read me in on death blossom before I knock you off that ladder."

"My apologies, ma'am." The veteran tilted his head to the side. "I take it you've never seen *The Last Starfighter*?"

"What?"

"The flick about that boy who got sucked into an arcade game and ends up a couple of hundred years in the future. They hustle him into fighting a bunch of nasty alien types in a badass spaceship."

"What year did it release?"

"Uh…nineteen eighty-four or thereabouts, if I recall."

Jade snorted. "Yeah," she said, drawing out the word. "Butch, I just turned thirty-five."

"Right. Of course, you did. Sure they didn't come out with some new-age, millennial-ized, CGI'd-to-death remake of it?"

Jade smirked and shook her head slowly in the negative.

Butch sighed. "Astonishing. They sure did with everything else." He then went into a synoptically formatted explanation of the movie from memory.

Jade listened intently, somewhat enthralled with hearing the movie's similarities with the remote weapon system's capabilities.

"In the sandbox," he continued, "we used to call hajjis firing weapons in the air at random with little hope and zero aim a death blossom. Mine is a highly improved rendering. It acquires hostile targets in any environment, day or night, and downright terminates the ever-loving shit out of them, with hate and purpose. Perfect if you're up shit creek with no paddle or pinned down in some unwinnable SNAFU."

Jade presented the nylon bag that Alan had discovered in the Marauder's glove box. Butch took the bag and removed some small colorful round discs with holes in the centers.

"What are they?" Jade asked.

"Lifesavers."

Jade squinted at him, chuckling. "Right. Because of their likeness to the candy?"

"No," Butch corrected. "Because, used appropriately, they'll save your goddamned life."

"Oh."

"Don't let those cute, girly, Skittles colors fool you. Each of these bad boys is an encrypted transponder. If the Mini Samson picks up the signal, the software classifies a one-meter bubble around the bearer a nontarget. If you're a hapless friendly downrange while DB is running, one of these in your hand, pocket, stomach, rectum, or any other orifice will safeguard you from a really shitty death."

Jade sent a thin smile. "Got it. Good to know."

"And all the same, very good *not* to forget," Butch said. "So don't. Keep one in your pocket, give Alan one, and coax your hellpooch into gulping one down with his next crayon meal." A pause. "Similarly, it's good not to overlook the system's limitations. I'm sure you're already privy to the M2's particulars, so I won't windbag you with them. The ammo box is oversized and holds two full links, both standard combat mixes of AP incendiaries and tracers, one hundred five rounds each. DB will blow through every damn one of them without stopping, but after, the barrel is wasted. Anything else leaving the muzzle will spray all over the place with zero accuracy, like the flight path of a bumblebee. The Ma Deuce is cooked."

# CHAPTER 11

**Little Germany Farms**
**Riverton, West Virginia**
**Sunday, January 2nd. Present day**

HAVING GONE TO BED EARLY the evening previous, Lauren rose long before sunup and met with the home's other infamous early riser. Bernie led her into the living room, a freshly poured cup of coffee in one hand and a Rand McNally street atlas in the other. He made his way around the coffee table and took a seat on the sofa.

Lauren chose a seat in the chair to Bernie's left and scooted it closer to the table, watching Bernie unfold the atlas.

"Now, this old thing is about as decrepit as the fella holding it, but it's all we got, so don't poke fun at it," Bernie joked, mashing the crease with his palm.

Lauren leaned in closer. "I'd recognize that inverted-pentagram street layout anywhere. That's Washington, DC."

"Indeed it is," Bernie said, tracing his finger along the downtown area while squinting behind his bifocals. "Okay, let's see here. Here's the Capitol, the Washington Monument, the mall, and there's where the White House is, or was, anyway. So about one or two blocks north of there…" He trailed off, tapping his finger on the map. "That's where your dad was, or where he said he was going to be."

Lauren slipped to the chair's edge to get a better look. "Right there?" Her index finger joined the old man's. "That's where my dad was working?"

Bernie nodded. He took a sip of his coffee and leaned away. "Yes, ma'am, if memory serves. I've been there hundreds of times, though I don't recall what the building looks like, or looked like."

Lauren snickered. "And I guess Google Street View is out of the question."

"I reckon so."

"You said it was a federal building?"

"State Department, I believe," replied Bernie. "What did your dad do for a living?"

"He wrote code, mostly," Lauren said. "He was a logic programmer for a building management company, but I think there was a lot more to it than that. He used to say he wore lots of hats. He worked so much overtime, picked it up whenever he could. He never wanted to work only to pay bills, he wanted us to have more than what we needed."

Bernie sipped his coffee again. "Well, don't forget. A lot of that time away and money spent was for your future."

Lauren smiled. "How could I? Especially now." She rearranged the items she'd brought with her on the table, placing some photocopied maps alongside the atlas.

"I see what you're doing," Bernie chided. "You're tryin' to replace my old map."

Lauren shook her head, grinning. "Quit. These maps show several views of routes out of the city. They're copies and printed in grayscale, but if you look closer, each one has a route highlighted. Could be his exit strategy. Maybe even a plan A and B."

"Exit strategy," Bernie repeated with a nod. "I see. I do remember him talking about his plan a little. He mentioned something about staying off the highways and main roads, not leaving any tracks behind. Oh hell, he might've been talking about railroad tracks, for all I know."

Lauren looked up at him while she concentrated on the topic. "Funny to hear you say that. One route looks like it follows the W&OD trail from Alexandria all the way to Purcellville. It used to be a railroad a long time ago and was paved over when it became a national park. Knowing him, this was probably plan B."

Bernie looked at Lauren, intrigued. "What makes you say that?"

"Because my dad could smell danger a mile away," Lauren remarked. "He hated being around crowds, even before the shit hit the fan. He used to preach about how dangerous populated areas were." She placed her finger on the map and traced the W&OD from its eastern terminus to the edge of the page. "The trail takes you westward to rural areas but travels straight through Northern Virginia…some of the most populated areas in the country, at one time. This was an option for him, but only a slightly better one than hiking home as a pedestrian on the interstate."

Bernie placed his coffee mug between his hands and leaned forward, rubbing the lip of the mug on his chin. "That sounds about right. Your dad did have quite the knack for this type of thing—predicting human behavior, that is. Especially in bad situations."

Lauren nodded slightly, flipping several pages of Bernie's atlas to match her maps. "Which leads us to his preferred option." She pointed to the Georgetown area of western DC at the eastern terminus of the C&O Canal.

Bernie raised an eyebrow. "Now you're cooking with oil. Folks used to call that monstrosity the *Grand Old Ditch*, especially all through construction, for obvious reasons. I used to lead a scout troop back in the day, and we took a bike trip along the towpath every year."

"So you're familiar."

"Indeed I am. Done the whole thing on a bicycle. For the most part, she's nice and flat. Goes through a lot of farming areas, too. Runs alongside the Potomac River for the duration." Bernie paused. "You think your old man might've gone that way?"

The two began perusing the assortment of maps, aiming to make some sense of it all. Lauren had known her father to be a problem solver and, as well, a complex individual. When he'd encounter a problem or a topic of interest, he'd dissect it, divide it into subtasks, and attack each one individually until a solution was found, instead of working the entire problem as a whole. Following this method was his nature and one of the features that intrigued her about him the most.

Looking away from the table a moment, Lauren sent a glance to the mantel on the opposite wall. She studied the mass of photo frames, soon finding a faded color likeness of a much younger Bernie and Ruth flanking a teenage girl with long dark brown hair. "Bernie, sorry to interrupt, but I have to ask. Is that your daughter?" She pointed to the frame.

Bernie's gaze followed her finger. "Yes, indeed," he said, nodding. "That's her. That's my Sasha."

"She's pretty."

A strange smile crept across Bernie's face. "Oh, she's magnificent. One of those pure, rare, cornfed country girls. The kind you just can't find growing native anymore."

"I've been here for days and it's the first time I've noticed her picture. I guess it never dawned on me until now who she was." Lauren pressed her lips together. "Sorry, I know it's a tough subject."

Bernie interlaced his fingers. "Sometimes, it still is. And for a while there, especially right after we lost her, it felt like the end of the world for Ruthie and me." He paused. "She used to love being outside, love to play in the woods and climb trees. If she wasn't picking apples and grapes, Sasha was off riding horses or cliff jumping off that riverbank behind the barn. I don't recall her ever being afraid of anything, and I mean *anything*. If Ruthie and her were out in the garden planting seeds and a black racer slithered up, Ruthie would scream and run like the dickens. But not Sasha.

"She'd grab a-holt of it by the tail and fling it, without even thinking. She used to clear the house of wolf spiders for us, them nasty brown, biting buggers. She'd grab them by their legs and stare in their beady little eyes right before tossing them outside. Yep, that girl was fearless. But pleasing, though. Never had any intention of doing wrong or getting in trouble, and when she did and knew a spanking was coming, she'd always sit with us and promise she'd never do wrong again, even though she would eventually. But she sure did mean well." Bernie took a pause to wipe away the errant tears brought about by recollections of the past. "We sure do miss her and love her. And we always will."

Lauren smiled at him. "You'll see her again someday."

Bernie nodded and cracked a smile. "Young lady, you are right about that. As much as I love living, that is one thought that brings me joy. Knowing the day will soon come when I permanently depart the earth. Because that'll be the day I can see my Sasha again." He paused and looked to her sternly. "But in the meantime, I do value my life and the lives of those around me. And if anyone, I don't care who it is, ever tries to harm somebody I care about, well, they'll feel my wrath."

Lauren beamed. "I believe you. And I'll lend some of my own."

"You would, would you?"

She nodded.

"Young lady, you sure do have a fire burning inside you. I hope you're able to control it when the day comes."

"When what day comes?"

Bernie's smile went flat. "The day you're put to the test."

The morning routine was adhered to by all the farm's residents. Chores were tended to and breakfast was put together courtesy of Ruth and a small army of young people who had all graciously volunteered to chip in. Every one of Ruth and Bernie's 'refugees', as they were sometimes dotingly termed, finished their meals and handwashed their dishes, then returned to their routines, which consisted of daily chores, farm tasks, reading, education, and a strict regimen of playtime.

They were children, after all, the majority of them, at any rate. And above all, the most important thing for them, in both Bernie's and Ruth's opinions, was the enjoyment of their childhood or, at least, what had become of it.

The pursuit of happiness within the boundaries of Little Germany Farms was a premise of particular import. The couple saw no point in applying time to anything lacking the promise of contentment on the other side. Bernie sometimes referred to it as 'a second horizon'. For most, if not all of these children, their lives had been turned upside down, and the days of old, those belonging to their lives prior on this earth, had concluded. Therefore, a new horizon had been established for them, the dawning of a new day, one they could each use to start over and afresh. The couple believed that leading lost souls along this path of theirs had become their calling now. That they had been placed here exclusively to watch over others less fortunate, despite that it had taken them until their sunset years to learn of it. Some learn their true purpose in life later in life versus sooner.

The crowds of young people vacated the farmhouse after having finished breakfast, and not long after, Lauren and Bernie relocated into the dining room.

Ruth's smiling face entered as well and brought them each a plate, then set one for herself along with a full carafe of black, steaming coffee. "That should be all it takes to get their attention, I expect," she droned. "The smell of coffee is like ringing a dinner bell whenever Dave and his boys are around."

Bernie gnawed on a slightly overcooked slice of bacon, then held it aloft with a frown. "What the dickens happened here, Ruthie? You havin' problems with the stove temperature again?"

"It was an accident, you old coot. And don't you start with me or you'll be the one slaving over your own stove from here on out."

Bernie stuffed the remainder of the slice in his mouth and crunched down on it. "See that, Lauren? See that right there? See how quickly old women resort to threats? Ain't no sense in it."

Lauren giggled. "Actually, for the record, it was me who ruined the bacon. I'm still learning how to cook with cast iron and a wood-fired stove."

"Oh. Why didn't you say so?" said Bernie. "All's forgiven, then."

Ruth poured her mug full from the carafe. "Forget him pointing out my behavior…take a look at how *he* acts, Lauren. See how he resorts to name-callin' and curries favor? One of these days, I just know it, he's gonna find himself a younger woman and leave me for her."

Lauren didn't respond, only watched as the couple sent each other scowls. Though it didn't take long for them to convert to smiles.

Sanchez, Santa, and Woo Tang entered the home several minutes after. They waved and sent smiles when they passed by the dining room and returned moments after, each with a heaping plate of food. They took their seats, placed their hands together for a short, silent, somewhat irreverent prayer, then attacked their meals.

Bernie studied them in silence for a minute before asking, "Morning, gentlemen. You fellas…missing somebody?"

Sanchez pointed his fork in the direction of the front door. "LT's still playing footsies with Lazarus."

"Playing footsies?" Bernie prompted.

"*Claro*. They've been together all morning, discussing something no one knows jack shi—sorry, not a darn thing about. A half hour before chow time we tried to pull him away, but he shot us the bird. Obviously, we thought what he did was disrespectful and went our separate ways."

"Good move, young man," Ruth said. "I'm proud of you."

"*Gracias*, Miss Ruth. Anyway, last time we saw them, they were headed back to that commo shack to make a call."

"Commo shack?" Bernie responded.

"Sorry…communications facility," Sanchez revised, drawing out the words.

"You mean that little shanty down the road with all the wires clinging to it? Looking like some gigantic spiderweb?"

"That's the one," Santa said, nodding.

"Heh. Thought so. That Godforsaken eyesore has been disgracing the landscape for decades. Can't believe it's still standing, much less in operation."

"Were they planning to join us for breakfast? Should we wait on them?" Ruth asked.

"Uncertain at this time, ma'am," Sanchez responded, his tone as respectful as anyone had ever witnessed. "But it would not surprise me either way."

"Well, suppose we'll keep some food out for them, then."

While the remaining men stayed at the table to eat and polish off what was left of Ruth's coffee, Lauren helped Ruth gather up dirty dishes. It wasn't long after when the front door opened again and Dave Graham entered with Lazarus following. Both men moved hastily into the dining room.

"Good morning," Ruth greeted them from the kitchen. "Glad you could join us. We saved some vittles for you."

"That's very much appreciated, ma'am. But I won't be partaking this morning." Dave pointed to the carafe of coffee on the dining room table. "I need all the brainpower I can muster, so I'll be fasting and adhering to a liquid diet today, assuming there's any left." A set of brownish eyes unwilling to look at him provided an answer.

"Don't worry, I'll put on another pot," said Ruth. "My coffee has been known to cause spells of overconsumption."

Santa poked Sanchez's arm. "Ain't that the truth."

"That's okay, ma'am. Don't put yourself out on account of me," Dave grunted. "I can do without."

"Don't be ridiculous, David Graham…it won't take but a minute."

"Very well." Dave then rounded the table and took a seat beside Woo Tang.

Lazarus, as usual, found his place at the foot of the table, opposite Bernie, choosing this time to forgo misusing the family furniture.

Dave was barely able to pour enough coffee to coat his mug's bottom. He turned to verify Ruth had moved out of earshot. "You know, this here cock bag fuckery should be dealt with severely, as in nothing short of a treasonous act," he ranted, his eyes locked on Sanchez. "Pardon my French, sir. But impetuosity gets the better of me when there's too much plasma extant in my caffeine system."

Bernie only sniggered. "No apologies necessary. Happens to the best of us. Though, not so sure my better half feels the same."

Dave put the mug to his lips and downed the speck of coffee like a shot of tequila. "Gentlemen, and…you too, Sanchez, one of our many prayers have been answered. I just got off the horn with Tim. He advises everything at Rocket Center has been going smoothly, if you can believe it. There hasn't been one single, solitary issue. Major Pain and his yokels have been cooperative, receptive, and willing to work with us." He chuckled. "Talk about a bolt from the blue."

Santa thumbed his whiskers. "Well, that should certainly serve to take a load off your mind."

"That it does," Dave said, then sent a glance over the table to Lazarus. "Additionally, there stands to be some…augmentations to our plans in the days coming. I figured it best to present them here and now for examination and endorsement. It's no secret the weather has put a damper on things for us. I'm proud to announce though, after some comprehensive discussions with our rather unconventional ally, who's so courteously graced us with his presence, there now exists some new options on the table."

"What brand of options, LT?" Santa posed.

"The transportation brand," Dave grumbled. "The brand fluent in relocation, to grid coordinates of a particular necessity. And these options appear viable. We can implement them now and move forward, or sit here with our thumbs up our butts until spring arrives. I'm partial to the former of those choices."

Lazarus scooted closer to the table just as Lauren reentered the room. "I know road conditions have been a major concern for you. Well, those days are over," he began. "This mountain weather might be a hindrance to y'all, but it isn't to us. We just get up and deal with it. We have four-wheel-drive, custom-lifted diesels that can drive over it, and equipment to push it out of the way so we can get on with life. Winter never shuts us down around here, and I'm willing to make available what I have to you, out of the kindness of my heart."

Lauren slipped gracefully into her seat and eyeballed Lazarus conspiratorially. No one else said anything for a time.

Dave Graham held his tongue as Ruth entered to offer him fresh coffee. "Thank you much," he said, chancing a sip. "Well, don't everyone speak up at once. Doesn't matter anyway. The decision's been made. In lieu of this unexpected stroke of…charity, the offer has been accepted."

"So you're leaving?" Lauren studied Dave's expression with sharp eyes. "I don't understand."

"What's not to understand?" Lazarus queried. "I'm making it all happen. I'm going to get everyone where they need to be, young lady."

"Are you?"

"Yepper. I get it, trust me. Progress has reached a standstill because of the weather and a certain lack of means. And while I can't do much about the weather, I do know ways to affect those means." Lazarus sat up in his seat. "Folks in the mountains don't hibernate like the bears when the weather gets crappy. We just shovel it, go over it, or push our way through it, and keep on working. Now, after talking with Dave, I'm figuring on four trucks total with a snowplow on each one, two of them being V-plows, the kind that don't quit. Two of them will pave the way for the convoy back to y'all's HQ, and the other two will do the same for the secondary destination."

"What secondary destination?" Lauren asked, her tone becoming agitated.

Dave took a slow sip of coffee. "*Your* destination, Janey. Home."

"Home," she echoed.

"That's right. In addendum to helping us reassemble the unit, Lazarus and the Sons have courteously extended an…ancillary offer. One that involves hauling you back to your family."

Ruth frowned. "What? Wait, you're going home, Lauren? So soon? W-why haven't you said anything?"

"Ruthie…" Bernie hushed her. "She didn't know till now. Simmer down."

Lauren sent Dave a jumbled look, then stared Lazarus down. "Why?"

The long-haired militiaman shrugged dispassionately. "Kinda felt obligated, like I had to. After that heartfelt convo on my radio yesterday and your emotional outburst that followed, I…just couldn't help myself."

"I didn't have an emotional outburst."

"Okay, I know what I saw. Call it what you want, but it looked pretty clear to me how bad you were yearning for home." He sneered. "I'm doing this as a favor to you. You really should thank me."

Lauren delayed, seeming dead set against. "Thank you."

"You're welcome—oh, crap, I forgot," Lazarus said. "Your thanks might've been a tad premature. I…haven't had a chance to inform you about what's set to happen once we get there."

"Perhaps you should, then," Lauren hissed.

"Darlin', we're goin' to the chapel, that's you and me. We're fixin' to have ourselves an arranged marriage."

Lauren rose and thumped the table with her palms. "There isn't a chance in hell!"

"Easy there, don't be a spoilsport, it's unbecoming," Lazarus teased. "Besides, I was only joking with you."

Lauren tensed up, glowered and leaned in further, her left hand shifting precariously close to her holstered Glock, a weapon that, from the point she'd taken possession of it, had literally never left her side. "I am *not* amused."

Ruth gasped and turned away, shielding her eyes. Bernie seemed unsurprised, as if knowing all along that the teenager's dormant wrath would eventually surface in his home. Sanchez and Santa looked giddy and expectant, their expressions like those of children waiting to open birthday gifts. Woo Tang wasn't fazed in the least, and Lazarus sat frozen in place, conveying the impression of a person who'd wet himself.

"Janey." Dave snapped his fingers, lassoing her attention. "It would gratify me greatly if you would kindly unruffle those feathers." He eyeballed Lazarus intensely for several seconds, then locked eyes with her. "Apart from this mistimed, particularly tactless spell of clowning around, this offer is a particularly generous one. The Sons are under no compulsion whatsoever to make this available to any of us. Consequently, we might want to consider refraining from looking this particular gift horse in the mouth, if you catch my drift."

Lauren backed away and hovered elegantly into her seat. As would a lady, she wiped the corners of her mouth with a cloth napkin, folded it and returned it to the table. She spoke delicately, giving the impression that her mood had gone full circle. "Dave, may I have a word with you, please? Alone?" She excused herself, stood and pointed a rigid finger toward the living room.

Dave sighed raucously while uprighting himself. He tracked her and the two squared off with one another, neither speaking until out of earshot and certain a conversation had resumed in the dining room.

"All right, state your business," Dave muttered.

Lauren's hands went in motion. "Forgive me, I'm lost here. Exactly what reaction were you looking to get from me in there just now?"

Dave put his shoulder against the wall. "I don't know, gratitude, possibly? Maybe a smile, a thank-you…maybe an 'I can't believe this is happening, Dave' or something along those lines? I wasn't trying to put you on the spot, but there's an offer on the table now to get you where you want to be. I could've sworn that's what you wanted."

"Of course it's what I want. You know that," Lauren said. "But you could've told me about it devoid of the…mixed company."

"You're probably right about that. Might've gotten ahead of myself. Guess I'm anxious to get this show on the road."

"So am I, more than you know. But, Dave…I don't feel comfortable with this."

"*This*? Meaning what?"

Lauren hesitated, then whispered, "Lazarus."

Dave nodded his head slightly. "Okay, I get that. He's not everyone's cup of tea."

"Forget tea," Lauren stated. "He's shady and I don't trust him. And I don't find any comfort whatsoever in the thought of him or any of his underlings taking me home. I'd just as soon go by myself."

"Received, but as sure as I'm standing here, going by yourself is not and unequivocally *will not* be an option," Dave grumbled. "I recognize he isn't your favorite person, but he's given us no reason not to trust him and neither have the Sons. These folks have confidence in them and have worked alongside them for years without quandary. For those reasons, I deem this offer and the altruism behind it legit. You say you don't trust him, and I'm sure you possess a valid reason for that, and I supposed there's no point harping on you for feeling that way."

Lauren folded her arms and rolled her eyes. "Thanks for the validation."

Dave expelled a sigh. "Look, Janey. I'll level with you. I've been dreading the point of going our separate ways since we stumbled upon you caged up in that shithole. These eyes never want to witness anything resembling that again. In view of that, ever since, your protection and welfare have fallen under my already overextended list of duties. And since I aspire to see you get what you've been longing for in the most carefree manner conceivable, I'm going to work with you."

"Work with me?" Lauren's features softened. "Dave, I—"

"Let me finish," he said, holding a hand up. "Since I haven't discovered any viable way of accompanying you home myself, some other arrangements have been put in place."

Lauren looked confused.

"I was approached last evening by a certain someone." Dave gestured with his head into the dining room. "We chitchatted a good while about this. He's since requested a new detail....and a transfer."

Lauren adjusted to see diagonally through the hall into the dining room. Woo Tang was the only person in the room staring back at her, as if knowing she'd be looking for him.

"Tang volunteered," Dave said. "His feelings for you and his position on the matters at hand are on par with my own. He wasn't wild about finding you in that cage."

Lauren smiled grimly. "I wasn't wild about *being* in that cage."

"Even those born into slavery comprehend deprivation of freedom," Dave said, "and, young lady, you are the furthest thing from being a slave." A pause. "Listen, I get it, dealing with Lazarus can be trying. The man's got a slimy personality and he could definitely use a haircut. But this offer of his is your ticket home. So do yourself a favor and go there. Talk to your mother, hug your sister, spend some time with your family. Put your mind at ease and your heart at peace. My men are there watching the place already, and Tang won't let anything come near you. He'll be under strict orders not to. Where you go, he goes, and with him around, you'll have nothing to worry about. And neither will I."

"I don't know what to say," Lauren said, a smile emerging. She reached for him, and Dave pulled her into an embrace. "Thank you. And I guess I should apologize for getting so angry. And for my...emotional outburst."

"No need." Dave held her like the daughter he never had. "I comprehend things a lot better than what I let on. After we part ways, we'll keep the communication and supply lines open, and I'll be looking in on you before long. I need to check in on Fred at some point and verify Richie isn't being too much of a cosmic prick. And that means personal visits, so this won't exactly be goodbye."

Lauren could feel her excitement building. "When are we leaving?"

"We still have some kinks to work out. I'm not a hundred percent keen on how long it'll take for Lazarus and crew to saddle up and organize. I'm supposing another day, maybe two, but as you are already well aware, that's subject to change."

# CHAPTER 12

**Trout Run Valley**
**Sunday, January 2nd. Present day**

CHRISTIAN KISSED A SNOOZING GRACE on her forehead and left her to sleep in. He ascended the stairs quietly so as not to wake her, then entered the kitchen and gathered some pine kindling for the stove. He set it alight and prepared the family's coffeepot, recalling how doing so had once been a part of Grace's morning routine. Now the only duties with which she concerned herself were the vital ones: getting in as much sleep as time allowed, and ingestion of calories.

The sun had begun to overtake Great North Mountain's horizon, filling the cabin's rearward-facing windows with amber-hued daylight. Satisfied the fire wouldn't wither out, Christian left the percolator to do its thing. He put on his boots, took hold of Grace's AR-15, and stepped out onto the porch, surprised to find John in his usual spot.

The two men, who seldom interacted, greeted one another, then sent cautious gazes into the snow-covered, forested landscape beyond.

"It was quiet last night," said Christian. "No shots since late yesterday afternoon. Might be a good sign."

John chuckled. "I wouldn't know. Nobody tells me anything." He spit on the ground. "After what happened, I honestly don't know what to think or expect anymore. The same things keep happening around here. We work our way out of one bad situation only to find our way into another one, and now we have to worry about people hiding in the hills on either side of the valley taking shots at us. I've been thinking about it all night while sitting here, waiting for someone to take a shot at me… wondering why they haven't."

Christian regarded him but said nothing, perceiving he was set to expound even more than he had already, which was uncommon for him.

"What's stopping them right now? From shooting either one of us right this second? Their aim? Timing? Are they sleeping? How many of them are there? I've been doing this watch thing since we moved in here to keep us safe. I've done it because…what else is there? And now I'm almost scared to." He sent a solemn look Christian's way. "That's it, man. That's my life. Just sitting here on the porch waiting to die. A man died yesterday right in our driveway, and his brother almost died right after he did. Today it could be me or my brother or my dad…or you. It's no way to live. This world is just…shit."

Christian nodded, leaning his weight onto one of the porch columns. "You'll forgive me if I fail to respond to that, John. I don't exactly know how to. I'm about to become a father and raise a child one way or another in this shit world."

John expelled a sigh. "I know, and I don't condemn you for it. I'm just spent. After watching what Lee went through, dealing with those taker assholes, then hearing Dad's story and worrying myself to death about Lauren every minute of every day, and now this…I don't know how much more I can take."

Christian nodded. "I feel your pain," he said, endeavoring to empathize.

"No, I don't think you do," John said. "Ever since we got here, my place has been protecting us, protecting what we have…whatever it is. But I'm beginning to fail to see what the use of it is. If all the effort we put into living can be taken by a sniper's bullet, by some fugitive hiding in the woods with a rifle…then what the hell is the point to all this?"

Christian slung the AR over his shoulder and inched closer to John. "Bud, you think entirely too much."

"Tell me about it."

"Sitting out here by yourself alone all night long is getting to you. Maybe you should take a break from it. There're about twenty military-trained men parading around the valley now with selective fire weapons and armored vehicles. With them around, security is tighter than it's ever been."

"Yeah. All thanks to Lauren, right? We should thank her for everything she's done for us," John huffed, then looked to the sky and exclaimed, "Thank you Lauren, wherever you are! We all thank you! Very fucking much!"

Christian shifted his weight to a heel. "I know you're mad at her. I was pretty pissed when she told me she wasn't coming home…really threw me for a loop. But in the end, she *did* come through. People we know and love are still alive because of her, including your brother *and* your dad, and me, uniquely enough."

"I know that," John groaned, "and I'm grateful, believe me. But her being gone is killing me a slow death. And I can't overlook this whole… Richie thing."

Christian's eyes narrowed. Had John overheard Richie's assertions? "So you know about—"

"Speak of the goddamn devil," John snarled, pointing, as a desert tan JLTV turned the corner into the driveway. "Christian, if you'll excuse me, I'm going to bed. If I see that guy right now, I'm likely to kill him."

Christian watched John trudge inside. The JLTV slid to a stop and the driver's door flung open. Richie shut the engine off, but remained inside.

"Sorry to disappoint you, but breakfast isn't ready yet," jeered Christian. "And you're too soon for coffee. I think that makes you shit out of luck."

Richie only smirked at him. "I didn't come by for breakfast or coffee. I need to have a discussion with you and Grace, though. If you have a minute."

"Grace is sleeping, so you'll have to settle for me." Christian gestured to him. "I'd invite you inside, but I think you wore out your welcome yesterday."

"That's okay, I prefer the armored can I'm sitting in. I don't have to worry about snipers picking me off or getting stabbed by your crazy girlfriend."

"Don't be so sure."

Richie rolled his eyes. "Look, man. That prisoner we have, Max… he's made a request. The request is reasonable and I think we should honor it. He's asking to talk to Grace."

"What? No. No way."

"The people sniping us from the mountains are his men, Christian."

Christian chuckled. "No shit."

"And if we don't do something soon to stop them, they're going to keep coming at us and eventually pick us off one by one. My men and I are doing what we can, but it isn't enough. I don't have the personnel to cover all those acres, and normal life can't continue around here with everyone staying inside all the time because they're afraid of getting shot."

"They *should* be afraid. Getting shot isn't fun," Christian mused. "It's cold as hell up there during the day and even colder at night. Temps are already dropping below freezing and winter hasn't started yet. No rifle-toting human can handle that kind of cold for days on end. Give it a few more days for exposure to set in…and we might win by attrition."

"Come on, man…work with me, please?" Richie pled. "He just wants to have a few words with her. And if we can find a way to settle this, wouldn't that be worth it? We'll keep it civil, I swear."

Christian deliberated. "What if the tone were to dip below civil?"

"Then we would intervene."

"On a physical level?"

"As required," the soldier said.

"Harshly?"

Richie sneered. "We don't sanction the use of torture on detainees, Christian."

"Who said anything about torture?" Christian went to the door. "I'm still leaning against it, but I'll run it by Grace and see what she thinks."

With Richie leading the way and Christian acting as chaperone, Grace strolled inside the room being used to retain the first prisoner ever to be taken in the valley. Richie went to him and removed the gag covering his mouth, then adjusted the window blind to brighten the room.

Christian remained at the doorway and reluctantly allowed Grace to continue in without him. She stepped hesitantly ahead, keeping her distance, while the man seated on the floor stared hard at her.

She had originally bound him with remnants of rope, but his wrists and ankles were now in shackles. She looked him up and down and smirked. "I like the new jewelry. I never took you for a bracelet and anklet man, Max. It suits you."

Max cast a sardonic look. "That's funny. You're hilarious. I see you haven't lost your sass." He peered around her at Christian, then sent a glance to the young soldier feet away. "And you've brought friends along. That's nice. That's real, real nice. My request was for the two of us to speak. I didn't intend for our conversation to extend to every Tom, Dick and Harry extant in your fleapit."

"Sorry to disappoint you. But we don't always get what we want, do we? You of all people should recognize that. Anyway, since we're all here now, allow me to introduce you." Grace gestured to Christian—"I'd like you to meet Tom"—then to Richie—"and that's Dick."

Richie slumped and frowned at her.

Max pressed his lips together. "Well, it's a pleasure to meet you both. Such a shame that Harry couldn't make it. Now, would the two of you kindly vacate the space and allow Grace and I to be alone for this chat?"

"No fucking way," Christian muttered from behind.

"Really? It's a simple request, Tom. Fully innocent. Look at me. I'm no threat to Grace. She knows that. She knows I wouldn't be a threat to her even if I weren't bound by chains to the floor. I would never hurt a hair on her pretty little head."

"Doesn't matter what you say or what she knows," Christian said. "It's not going to happen. So whatever it is you wanted to say to her, spit it out. We don't have all day."

Max smiled. "Oh, but I do." He paused extensively. "I seem to have plenty of time. Well, I suppose the added audience won't be too much of a bother, other than a mild disenchantment. I was just hoping it could be you and me, Grace. Like old times."

Grace scratched her head. "Old times? Forgive me, but we only knew each other for a couple of days, so I'm a little misplaced here."

"You'll have to forgive *me*, Grace," said Max. "You see, *I* was under the impression that you and I had developed a rapport during those *couple of days*. And that's why it only makes sense for you and me to speak and discuss our current circumstances."

Grace giggled. "You and I have a rapport? Max, you're being silly. I cooked all of your men dinner and fed them poisoned food. They're all dead because of me. Do you not recall that? Your invasion failed, your laughable plan failed, so whatever rapport we had or didn't have should be null and void."

Max's smile evaporated. "Yes, I recall. How could I forget something so…catastrophic. But I seem to also recall that for some inexplicable reason, I am still here. You spared me, Grace."

Christian let out an expansive sigh, coupled with an eye roll.

Max continued. "I see something in you, something principled. I saw it when you showed me where my late young niece was interred. There's honor in you. You keep it hidden well behind that unremitting sass of yours, but that honor is the prime reason I wanted you here."

Grace covered her mouth and yawned. "Sorry, just feeling a little tired. I'm always tired these days. It's not you boring me."

"Yes. I suppose you would be, wouldn't you? How is the pregnancy going, by the way? Have you properly geared up to raise a child by your lonesome?"

"Nope. I won't have to," Grace quipped. "Alas, my baby daddy, the knight in shining armor that he is, has returned to spare me the agony." She gestured to Christian again.

"That so? Well, good. Congratulations, Tom. I'm sure the two of you will make fine parents. How divine for there to be one fewer amongst the world's list of bastards." Max paused. "Now that we've gotten those trifles out of the way, allow me to get down to business. I want you to tell these people to cut me loose. I want out of here. And I want out of here today."

Grace laughed uproariously. "You'd like that, wouldn't you? Well, I want stuff too, Max. Like a new car with four doors and an infant car seat…and a sunroof, and some new furniture for the baby's room…oh, and a stomach that keeps food down."

"I'm not joking with you," said Max, his tone deepening. "Those gunshots I'm hearing, I know it's not target practice, Grace. I know what it is; more to the point, I know who's doing it. It's my people, the ones who remained behind. They're coming for me, to retrieve me. Precisely as planned."

Grace looked around the room, then motioned to Max's restraints. "They're not doing a very good job of it."

"Allow me to be blunt. Until I am released, my people will not stop. They will keep shooting into this valley until every one of you is dead. And then, we will resume the acquisition we started, with nothing in our way to stop us. Now, if you let me go, I promise to let bygones be bygones. We can draw up a treaty of sorts and share everything. Work everything out between our communities by other means. It's on the table. And that means it's all up to you, Grace."

Grace stepped closer and knelt. "Allow me to be blunt*er*," she cooed. "I. Don't. Care. We're keeping you here until hell freezes over, and I'm not implying Hell, Michigan, either. I mean the hell Satan calls home, the one with the lake of fire and all the screaming sinners drowning in it."

Max pursed his lips. "Are you certain that's how you want to play this?"

Grace pointed at Richie. "See Dick? See Dick's camo Army getup? See Dick's guns? Since taking you down, we've added a few fortifications—lots of other guys and guns just like Dick and his. So you don't scare me. And your people don't worry me. Because with Dick and all Dick's friends around, eventually your people won't be."

"You can talk tough all you want," said Max. "And you might not care now, but you will. You'll care when one of my shooters picks you off or picks off Tom or someone else you love. It would be wise of you to take me seriously. Don't underestimate me."

Grace rose and went to Christian, sulking. "You were sooo right about him."

"I was?"

"Yup." She pointed to the handgun on Christian's belt. "Give me that."

"What? You want to shoot him? Here? Right now?"

"Damn right I'm going to shoot him, right here, right now!" she snapped.

Max expanded and shouted indecencies at everyone in the room. Richie stuffed his gag back in place, stifling him shortly thereafter.

Christian halted Grace's advance with his hand over his weapon. "No, wait. Not like this."

"Okay, how then? You mean take him outside first? So we don't have to clean his stupid blood and brains off the floor? Good thinking, man of mine."

Christian shook his head. "No...something else entirely. Mr. Pornstache might still have some value to us alive. I have a better idea."

# CHAPTER 13

**Riverton, West Virginia**
**Monday, January 3rd. Present day**

BERNIE AND RUTH REMAINED INDOORS after saying their goodbyes to keep Cyrus from scratching his way through the door after Lauren. That, and it'd already been an emotionally trying morning, and seeing her leave would've decidedly been too much for them. Instead, they passed the remaining time in the living room, surrounded by a handful of youthful spirits offering their support.

The driveway had been cleared, and every vehicle in the convoy was now facing away from the house with their engines idling. An oversized diesel truck—its knobby tires wrapped in chains, sporting a massive yellow snowplow—was parked in the lead, and another, practically indistinguishable from the lead truck, was positioned in the middle. Still two more, equally large and similarly outfitted, sat idling in the rear.

After conveying undying thanks to Dave Graham and hugging Sanchez and Santa goodbye, Lauren descended the porch stairs and strode to the pair of diesels closest to her, marveling over their size. There had been no exaggeration on the part of Lazarus, who'd spewed claims about them in abundance, devoid of any lucidity. Seeing them now left little doubt that they were fully capable of fulfilling his assertions, and with that, transporting her over miles of mountainous, snow-covered terrain, and eventually home.

From the corner of her eye, Lauren could see three figures on approach. Lazarus and a male and female couple, both wearing near-matching insulated flannel shirts and leather gloves.

He strolled directly to her, his lengthy hair as staticky as ever, and introduced them. "This is my cousin Francis and his wife, Jean. They were kind enough to offer a few of these trucks on loan, so they'll be going with us to make sure we don't insult 'em too much."

The couple were simple and fresh-faced in appearance. They sent along friendly nods and benevolent looks Lauren's way.

Lazarus pointed. "Guys, this is Janey."

"Lauren," she revised.

Jean slipped off her glove and offered a calloused hand. "Hi, Lauren. Good to meet you. Lookin' forward to your trip?"

"Very much so." Lauren shook Jean's hand, followed by her husband's.

"Don't pay no attention to anything Lazarus says," Francis alleged in a joking manner. "We're happy to help out."

The couple then moved off to load their gear.

"You and your bodyguard can put your stuff in this one," Lazarus said, pointing to the far rear truck, then to the couple. "They'll be riding in the other one with me, and y'all will follow us. It's got a big ole V-plow on it, just like the one leading Graham's parade in the front. So it just makes sense."

His portrayal in mind, Lauren inspected the differences between each snowplow.

"Anyway, won't be long before we head out. I hope you're packed and ready. It'll be a longer than usual trip, but don't you worry. I've added a few shortcuts."

"Marvelous," she said, and hoisted her pack into the truck bed along with a duffel of random contents.

Her long-haired acquaintance having moved off and away, Lauren opened the passenger-side door to examine the cab. She stowed her AK-47 and a sling pack of magazines on the floorboard, both of which were covered in layers of dirt, gravel and chunks of soiled snow. The heater was on and pumping mellow warmth through the vents. A glance at the gas gauge evidenced a full tank. Upon spotting a switch denoting a second, Lauren flipped it and the truck's secondary tank, similarly topped off, took over.

A steel spare diesel tank was permanently mounted to the bed of each truck, along with a toolbox filled with hand tools, shovels, axes, saws and chainsaws, with fuel and maintenance items for those as well.

Everything, as far as she could tell, appeared legitimate, but it wasn't enough to settle Lauren's apprehensions for the trip, nor quell her trust issues with the trip's organizer.

"Lauren?" a child's voice called from behind.

Lauren found Daniel and his sister, Lily, running through the snow to her. They'd been absent earlier during the send-off ceremony, and she'd wondered where they'd run off to. "Hey, you two." She knelt and welcomed them with open arms and they barreled into her embrace. "I missed you this morning. Where were you? And why are neither of you wearing jackets?"

"Lily didn't want to come," Daniel admitted. "She said it would make her sad to see you. We don't want you to go, Lauren. We want you to stay longer. Please stay."

Lauren squeezed her eyes shut. Her lower lip trembled. "Honey, I wish I could stay, but I can't. I have a family…I have to go home to them."

"Then take us with you. Can't we just go with you? It's a big truck; there has to be room for us."

"I'm sure there is. But getting there could be dangerous. It's a long trip and the roads are horrible. Something could happen to you, and I can't let that happen."

"Then why are you going? Something could happen to you too."

"Bad things can happen to anyone," Lauren said. "And in your cases, they're avoidable. You both need to stay here with Bernie and Ruth and the other kids. It's safe here."

"We don't want to," Daniel whined.

"God…Daniel." Lauren's eyes welled up. "Leaving here…leaving all of you, isn't easy for me, okay? Don't make this harder on me. Please?"

"We don't mean to make you sad. We're just really going to miss you. Will you even come back?"

Lauren smiled and squeezed them. "Of course I will. Once everything is settled and the weather gets better, I'll visit you guys, and you can visit me if you want. I promise." She pulled away from them and held aloft her finger. "I'll even pinky swear to it."

The boy smiled broadly and hooked his finger around Lauren's. A moment after, Lily did so as well.

"Now get back to whatever you were doing. It's cold out here, and don't ever come outside again without a jacket on."

The pair started off and Lauren turned back to the truck, but before she could get away, Lily broke free from her brother and ran to her, shouting her name in a petite tenor. "Lauren! Lauren, wait! I have to tell you something!"

Stupefied at hearing her, Lauren got down on a knee and took Lily by the hand. "Listen to that voice! Lily, I could listen to you talk all day."

Lily sniffled and rubbed her nose. She spoke with hesitation. "I… just wanted to say…thank you. For…helping us."

Lauren went limp. "You're welcome. But it isn't necessary to thank me. I'd do it all over again if I had to." She kissed Lily's forehead. "Now go. So I can." She urged the little girl along, doing her best to keep it together.

Watching the interaction ensue between Lauren and the pair of youngsters from his perch atop the farmhouse porch, Dave Graham waited semi-patiently for Woo Tang to join him. When the former SEAL reached the porch stoop, Dave began descending each stair, one at a time. "All packed and ready to skedaddle?"

Woo Tang nodded. "I believe most if not all of the proverbial bases are covered."

"Fine business. I expected nothing short of it," Dave said, regarding the line of running vehicles, their exhaust fumes noticeable in the parched, wintry air.

"Any final orders before the official parting of ways?"

Dave squinted an eye. "One. Don't let anything happen to her, Tang."

Woo Tang's eyes narrowed. "I will see to it that she is delivered home safely."

"I realize it's near goddamn axiomatic at this point, but I'm saying it anyway. That young lady is priceless cargo. No harm is to befall her." Dave paused, his hands falling to his hips. "And it's my intention it remain that way, that no harm or ill will ever befall her again, and I mean zero fucking harm. I don't care what it is, not an itsy-bitsy spider bite, not even an indirect one, nothing within a minefield's distance of her. I don't want anyone to even dare send a cross look her way. You get her home, and after, you watch her like a hawk. You've been promoted to guardian angel until further notice."

Woo Tang tilted his head and leered. "I am genuinely honored. You do realize, of course, that I have never before been granted a field promotion."

"That I do. And I suppose, in light of that, congratulations are in order. So, congratulations. Wish we had the time stretch to throw a full-on celebration for you, but we're burning diesel."

"And daylight," said Woo Tang. He regarded Lauren over his shoulder, who stared wryly at them.

Dave conveyed a wave and received one from her in reply, then held out his hand. "It's been a pleasure, Tang. Until we meet again."

"In this world or the next," Woo Tang said with a fleeting grin. "Good luck." Turning on his heel, made simpler by the slick coating of wintry mix beneath, he marched Lauren's way.

"What was that about?" She studied Dave as he withdrew back into command mode, converging on his men.

Woo Tang casually disregarded her query as he loaded a heavy nylon rucksack swollen with contents into the truck bed.

Lauren gestured to the jingum, his Korean combat sword of choice, melded to the MOLLE. "Couldn't help yourself, could you? You just *had* to bring it."

"I never leave home without it," he said colloquially. "Any questions for me before we...sally forth?"

"Sally forth?" Lauren pulled her beanie snugly below her ears. "Yeah, one." She smiled. "Who's driving?"

Woo Tang peered into the truck cab. "Hmm. I was of the impression a chauffeur, of sorts, was to be provided."

"Yeah, I thought so too," Lauren said. "Lazarus came by a few minutes ago and introduced me to the couple who own the trucks, or some of them, anyway. Evidently, they're coming with us, but riding with him. Guess it's just you and me again, pal."

Woo Tang nodded acceptance. "I am not displeased at hearing this, as I have never been one who enjoys extensive outings in confined spaces accompanied by persons unfamiliar. At any rate, unless you object, I will take the wheel and you can act as copilot. Advise at any point if you wish those roles to reverse."

"Sounds fair to me. I don't like driving in snow, anyway. Then again"—she pointed to the truck—"I've never guided one of these."

"Ditto."

The pair broke off and entered the cab on either side, then went about finding comfortable spots in their seats.

Lauren fidgeted with the heating vent. “What about you? Any questions for me?”

Woo Tang shrugged his shoulders to some extent. “Only one. Are you suitably packed?”

“I think so.”

“You think so or you kn—”

“I *know* so,” Lauren blurted. “Sorry, I should’ve seen that coming.”

Woo Tang grinned. “Plenty of food and snacks? Potable water and filtering mechanisms?”

“I thought you only had *one* question…”

“Clothing appropriate for the environment for which we are headed? Gear to provide adequate shelter and protection from the elements?” A pause. “Copious quantities of feminine hygiene products?”

Lauren’s face knotted up. “Excuse me?”

“I am only asking in jest.”

“Yeah, I get that, now. But I’m not used to this side of you; feed me a little warning next time.”

“Enhancing levity of dialogue was never my forte,” Woo Tang said, then asked, “Weapons and kit?”

“More questions. We’re headed into potentially hostile territory, so I overpacked.” She gestured to the holster on her hip, then pointed to her ankle. “Omnipresent G19 and a Beretta PX4 strapped to my good ankle. I relieved it from the gun safe my dad left here. I like how it feels in my hand. Only one extra mag for the PX4, but plenty for the Glock.” She jostled the Zastava M70 to her left, its muzzle supported by the floorboard. “Santa would tase me in my sleep if I left his precious Dragana behind. And I brought a duffel of mags, ammo and Lord knows what else.” Lauren pulled her knees to her chest. “Now that we’re past that, think you can answer my question?”

“What question was that?”

“The one I asked earlier, pertaining to the exchange between you and…you-know-who.”

“Exchange? That was nothing.”

“Nothing?” Lauren reacted. “By the look on his face, I couldn’t tell if he was going to hug you or pull a knife on you.”

“It would appear neither option was chosen. Though, in place of them, a tertiary was selected. It seems I have found my way into a promotion.”

Lauren looked surprised. "Really? To what? Master chief? Or something like that?"

"It was not one of rank, but rather, of supplementary duty. One of which I am certain you will develop an understanding in due course."

Lauren didn't say anything for a moment, but the words he spoke, much in the same manner most things Woo Tang conveyed, carried a notable hint of momentousness. "Well, I'm sure whatever Dave ordered or promoted you to or whatever…he knows you're capable. You'll do fine."

"Thank you, Lauren Russell. I can only hope you are right. You know Dave as I do. He has inordinately high expectations, which I can only strive to achieve."

Lauren nodded. "Don't I know it. It's one of the first things I learned about him. I think Dad noticed it, too. People like Dave have a way of bettering other people. He doesn't give you any other option. He was the first person to ever look me in the eyes and tell me I couldn't fail because he wouldn't allow me to."

As the convoy began to move up the driveway, Woo Tang pressed the accelerator and the diesel engine came to life. "Never once has he said or implied the same to me. His encouragement has always come by way of an order. And, Lauren Russell, it is imperative that all orders be followed." He regarded her from the corner of his eye. "Do you…understand?"

Lauren took notice of the graveness in her companion's voice. For some reason, he'd stepped it up again. "I do." She looked through her window as they pulled onto the highway, effectively departing Little Germany Farms. "Thank you for doing this, Jae. For coming along."

Woo Tang smiled grimly. "You are welcome. And, you should know, I would have accompanied you regardless. Even if LT had ordered me not to."

"But you just said all orders must be followed."

"As with most things in life, sometimes, though it is rare, there can be exceptions."

# CHAPTER 14

**Pendleton County, West Virginia**
**Monday, January 3rd. Present day**

LAZARUS LED THE WAY ALONG US Route 33 in the lead custom diesel, its immense V-shaped snowplow carving a path for itself and the truck tailing vehicle lengths behind. Both vehicles upheld a less-than-meager pace, slowing even more so at particularly large snowdrifts and upon obstacles met in the roadway.

They crossed over a bridge spanning the Potomac and wandered through the low-lying ranges of Judy Gap just before the highway began the greater than three-thousand-foot ascent over North Fork Mountain. Road conditions there were nothing short of atrocious, but the oversized diesels took no issue overcoming them. The heavy-duty chains encircling the trucks' all-terrain tires seemed to more than make up for the lack of traction. It wasn't long, though, before a daunting obstruction presented itself.

Seeing the lead truck's brake lights redden, Lauren sat up in the seat. "Whoa. Now *that* is one big tree."

Woo Tang pulled their diesel to a stop behind the lead truck. He and Lauren got out and went to meet with Lazarus, Francis, and Jean, who were already in the process of examining the inconvenient natural roadblock.

Lauren scanned the woods with her AK at the ready, then took note of the fallen tree's unique, furrowed bark. "Guess it's safe to say this old guy came down naturally. It probably would've taken forever to cut it down."

"You got that right. Forever and about ten brand-spanking-new saw chains," Francis said. "That's a black locust, about two centuries old by the looks of it, and these mountains are almost all sandstone. Means there's sand in the dirt. Trees soak it into their roots all the way to the inner grain. Makes sawing a real pain in the butt. You wouldn't get six inches before wasting a perfectly good blade."

"And that means there's no point in us bothering with it," Lazarus said. "We'd kill every saw and extra chain we got if we tried."

"What's the plan, then?" Francis asked.

"We only got one other choice," replied Lazarus. "Head back and go the other direction." He went to his truck and returned with a rolled-up map of the surrounding areas, then unrolled it atop the warmth of the hood. "Already got that trip figured out too. And the good news is, we can still make good time going this way. It'll be faster driving through places we already plowed, and after we pass the starting point, we'll be on the path the other trucks made ahead of Graham's convoy."

Lauren inspected the alternate route. "Let's not overlook the bad news. This adds at least fifty miles to the trip."

"How do you know that, honey?" Jean asked.

"The southern route is the longer of the two, omitting the detours added to the northern one. We only went this way to give those two unsecured areas neighboring the northern route a wide berth." Lauren indicated the zones with her index finger. "Dave said, and I quote, 'No one goes any-fucking-where near there.'"

Lazarus grinned deviously. "Look, I got his message loud and clear, and I'm telling you, I got it covered. We won't go anywhere near those places, promise. Last thing any of us needs is getting in over our heads with a bunch of raving lunatics." He grabbed the map and started off. "Come on, let's giddyup. We'll just need a minute to get turned around."

Lauren rolled her eyes and twirled her index finger defiantly. "*Come on, let's giddyup*," she said, mocking Lazarus such that only Woo Tang could perceive.

After some maneuvering, the pair of vehicles and their passengers pulled away in the reverse direction whence they'd come, passing by Bernie and Ruth's farm on the right-hand side not long after. They made good use of the pre-plowed roads, both their own and those previously cut by the plows leading Dave's convoy. As such, their pace was amplified, thereby making up for lost time after setting a new course.

Several miles after the new route began, Woo Tang glanced over at his young companion. “Lauren Russell, forgive me for putting an end to the silence, but something has been vexing me. I would like to air my concerns with you, though I am reluctant.”

Lauren looked expectantly at him. “Why? How bad can it be?”

Woo Tang spoke solemnly. “Depends on your reaction. I observed a discussion prior to our exodus, during which several theories concerning your recent behavior were presented, and as well your potential reaction to a certain…ultimatum. One of those theories portrayed you consciously selecting to gather your belongings and take your leave of us on foot without a trace, deprived of farewell.”

“And…you only *observed* this…discussion?”

“Admittedly, I was an…unenthusiastic collaborator.”

“Mm-hmm. Right.” Lauren clenched her jaw.

Woo Tang glanced at her, but remained silent, allowing her time to respond, if she chose.

After a time, she said, “I won’t lie to you, I considered it. I had everything I needed, almost. And I knew I could do it. But that didn’t stop me from trying to talk myself out of it.” She paused. “If you were to ask me if I’d have actually gone through with it, the answer is, I don’t know, Jae. Maybe.”

Woo Tang nodded recognition. “Understood. And thank you for answering openly. Allow me to convey how thankful I am that you chose smartly.”

Lauren glimmered.

“Because had you not,” he continued, “there is little doubt I would have been tasked to pursue and retrieve you. And I am far too out of shape for such a fatiguing chore.”

“Nice one,” Lauren said, pursing her lips. “You failed to warn me, again.”

“I am working on it.” Woo Tang took an extended pause. “I do wish to ask…do you justly believe in your ability to endure such a trip on your own?”

Lauren chuckled slightly. She wiped clean a portion of frozen condensation on her window using a finger. “Of course I do. I was born hardheaded. The gene was directly inherited from my father.”

“A notably motivated individual,” said Woo Tang. “Determined, though not nearly so hardheaded as you believe yourself to be.”

Lauren nodded. "He and Dave are a lot alike. In the same way Dave held failure untenable, Dad never allowed me to quit. He hated excuses—*hated* them. He always told me never to give up, no matter what, and that no matter what I believed, there was always a solution to every problem. But that was him, the ever-enduring problem-solver. He used to obsess over them to the point of unapproachability. If he was in the middle of one, it was impossible to break his concentration, let alone talk to him."

"Even for you? His own descendant?"

"Even for me," Lauren said. "And he didn't prioritize much over his family. I guess I'm a little like him when it comes to obsessing over solutions." She rotated in her seat. "Jae, you should know, if I hadn't felt an immediate need to go home, I swear I wouldn't have acted out. I wouldn't have pushed so hard, and I never would have been so disrespectful to Dave. I just know I need to be home. Something…some feeling or force is pulling me there."

Woo Tang peered over. "This feeling or force, is it equivalent to the one that compelled you to remain with the unit when you could have and most likely should have gone home?"

Lauren thought a moment. "It's…similar."

"Then I understand. And even though he is one of the best at concealing his inward state of mind, I believe LT understands as well."

"Yeah, maybe."

"Dave Graham is a complicated man. He, akin to your father, is also a solver of problems. And there exists an abundance of nuisances he is desperately attempting to resolve, all of which seem very much unsolvable in our current predicament. As such, he concentrates on that which he fears stands to trigger the worst headache. Though, it is my belief, his doing so has created a migraine for him in and of itself."

Lauren rolled her lips. "And I'm not trying to add to that, but I suppose I have, involuntarily." She paused contemplatively. "What do you think is destined to happen…in the future?"

"I remain highly uncertain. But, in the end, it does not matter what I think."

"It matters to me."

Woo Tang regarded his young friend with unstiffened eyes. "Lauren Russell, you know as I do how inexact the future is. What I think or believe could happen is irrelevant. What I want for it…or rather, what I wish for it, is that it someday achieves equilibrium."

"Equilibrium?"

"Yes." Woo Tang nodded. "It is my belief that this will come to pass eventually, one way or another. Nature is an omnipotent force vastly proficient at self-renewal. It consistently regains ground despite humankind's efforts to thwart it. It is also my belief that one day peace will come, as well. But there is only one way to achieve peace, and that is through the perfection, that is, the comprehensive understanding of war and of evils extant in our world.

"Your generation will someday pick up where mine leaves off, and I pray that by then, we will have at least reached a rebuilding stage and there is little fighting left. That is another mystery LT contends with daily. Zero Dark Armageddon was set to commence by this time. And it looks as though we will never see that commencement. For much of the country, a collapse has begun. It is currently in full swing, possibly even on a downslope. And it must reach a terminus before reestablishment of government in any form is considered."

Lauren measured Woo Tang's introspective remarks for several miles, until the point Lazarus made an unexpected right-hand turn.

She pointed ahead. "What is he doing? That's not right, he's deviating from the planned route."

"You are certain?" asked Woo Tang, turning right to follow.

"Positive. We weren't supposed to make any turns until after Hopeville."

A concerned look etching his face, Woo Tang reached for the microphone attached to a citizens band radio mounted under the dash. "Do we know if Lazarus is monitoring this channel?"

Lauren looked uncertain. "I don't know. He never mentioned anything to me about it."

"Nor me." Woo Tang pressed the PTT. "Leper, do you copy? This is Barracuda. Over."

Lauren's brow shot up. "Barracuda?"

"It is my handle. What do you think of it?"

"I'm more partial to it than *Leper*."

The radio came to life, breaking squelch. *"Yeah, go for Leper, whoever you are."*

"We have reached the conclusion that you have chosen to deviate from the planned route. Is this accurate? Over."

*"Yepper. That is accurate,"* Lazarus came back. *"Is that a problem?"*

Woo Tang sneered. "Whether or not a problem exists or manifests remains to be seen. That said, the occupants in the vehicle trailing you would welcome an explanation."

Laughter emanated from the speaker. *"Oh, they would, would they? Okay, here's your explanation—I set this rodeo up and I'm in command. I made the decision to go this way and we're going this way. Leper out."*

Woo Tang slowly set the mic down. "And there you have it."

"Asshole," Lauren hissed.

Both trucks continued along the incredibly narrow, steep mountain pathway through multiple sets of tight switchbacks and eventually over a steep pass before descending sharply on the other side. It took about an hour for the trip's deviation to pass from start to finish, where the unmarked road ended, intersecting with another.

The trucks veered left, pushing the snow forward and away to either side. The CB came to life as Lazarus's voice poured from the speaker. *"This is the one and only Leper in the lead. That little unplanned deviation back there you two got so riled up about shaved around twenty minutes off our total trip time. And to top it off, lo and behold, we made it out of there alive. Like magic...all in one piece. Leper out."*

Lauren scoffed, casting a cruel stare to the inanimate radio. "Seriously? How many more rounds of 'Lazarus knows best' are we to endure?"

She received her answer not even a half-hour following. Once again, the lead truck made another right-hand turn onto another road not matching the planned route. Woo Tang whipped the wheel to follow, but this time both he and Lauren decided to refrain from protest.

Twenty minutes in, after two sets of incredibly narrow, steep hairpins, the road leveled out and began a gradual ascent to the ridgeline. As they got closer, both trucks were forced to stop at the point of encountering a hefty rotten oak that had split near its base and fallen over the road under the snow's weight.

Lazarus, Francis, and his wife exited and trudged over to investigate. They returned not long after, donned gloves and gathered tools and began priming chainsaws.

Francis checked the gas level in his saw. "Looks like we got our work cut out for us today."

"Quite frankly, I'm surprised there hasn't been more of them," Jean added.

Woo Tang rolled down his window and called out, "Need any assistance?"

"No, we got this," Lazarus dismissed. "You two stay in there and keep warm. It might be a while."

Lauren took turns watching the trio process the tree while sending cautious gazes into the forest. "Are you thinking what I'm thinking?"

Woo Tang nodded. "Since the moment I shifted into park. The tree looks to have fallen naturally. Still, it would behoove us to secure our location. We should set a perimeter while our friends play lumberjack."

Lauren nodded avowal. She slid her AK close, snapped the safety down and slid back the bolt a tinge to verify the chambered round.

Woo Tang shut off the engine, exited and circled to the front, where Lauren joined him. He scanned the scene, then pointed due south, indicating a snow-covered outcropping. "There. It towers over most everything. I will cover your advance. Send a signal once you are in place."

Lauren nodded her understanding and pranced away, hurdling the wall of snow formed by the plows. Reaching the rock's base, she brushed off layers of frozen snow until finding traction then pulled herself onto it. Struggling against its slick surface, she scaled it with all four limbs until she could hoist herself onto the peak.

Once she was in position, Woo Tang scampered up the opposite embankment to a spot of his choosing. The duo shared a nod, then with rifles ready, stood on alert for whatever might come, even if nothing.

Once the tree was fully processed and all remnants were removed or otherwise relocated, Lauren and Woo Tang relinquished their chosen posts and rejoined the others.

While handing his saw off to Francis, Lazarus said, "What the hell were you two doing? I told you both to stay in the truck. We're in the middle of nowhere, for God's sake. There's nothing out here. You both could've been all warm and cozy the whole time. But nooo, no sir. Don't take my advice."

"There is no harm in maintaining vigilance," Woo Tang said. "And, Lazarus, not all advice is sound advice."

"Well, maybe it ain't," Lazarus shot back. "But in my experience, the best advice comes from the ones who know best."

Woo Tang's voice went coarse. "And in my own experience...the worst typically happens to those who believe...that it simply cannot."

Lazarus shook his head. "Whatever." He extended himself to get a look at the freshly stacked woodpile beside the road, his feet supported by the truck's rear tire. "Frank, make a note of this one. That's some damn good firewood there. Hot-burning chestnut oak. After all that work, I hate to just leave it here. Damn shame we can't take it all with us."

"I don't know why you're so bothered by it," Jean hissed. "It's not like were staying wherever we're going, right? We got two trucks now, and we'll still have them when we leave. Why can't we just pick it up on our way back?"

Lazarus and Francis shared an unusual look, both making certain Jean couldn't see.

Lauren caught on instantly, but suppressed any reaction.

Francis shrugged after a moment. "She's got a good point, Laz."

"Yes she does," Lazarus said. "Goood point, Jean. We'll worry on this later. It'll be dark before long. Let's giddyup on down this mountain and find a spot to camp. I need to get some food in me. I'm as hungry as a bear."

"Food sounds good," Francis said. "And after all that work, a nap sounds mighty good, too."

# CHAPTER 15

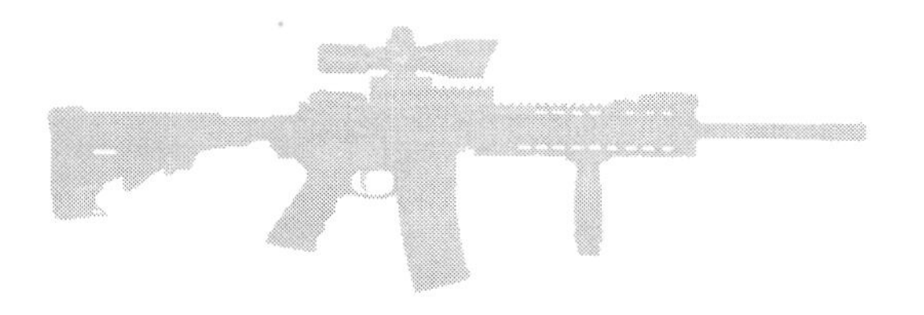

**The cabin**
**Trout Run Valley**
**Monday, January 3rd. Present day**

WITH THE THREAT OF SHARPSHOOTERS still active and weighing on her mind, Grace remained indoors to await Christian's arrival. He was set to be here any minute to take her to see Dr. Pamela Vincent for her prenatal care appointment, in what he'd referred to as a 'very safe' method of transport. She hadn't a clue what that meant, but whatever he was doing seemed to be taking an excessive amount of time to get done.

Grace folded her arms and tapped her foot on the floor as she grew more impatient, then went to search for signs of him through the windows. The last window she checked, the one closest to the front door, provided a view that made her gulp and almost swallow her tongue. "Oh…snap."

Incredulous and wide-eyed after a double take, Grace shuffled backward, her fingers touching parted lips. She stood there in shock and waited for Christian to come inside and retrieve her. No way she was about to walk out to him after what she'd just witnessed.

The approaching truck's rumbling engine and chugging exhaust grew louder and soon vanished. A metal door squeaked shut, and the cabin's front door opened a minute after.

Seeing Grace, Christian's face lit up. "Hey. All ready to go?" He reached for her, but she backed away. "Uh-oh, what's wrong now? I know I'm late, but don't be mad, okay? That project took a lot lon—"

"Stop." Grace halted him, then slowly extended a finger. "Don't say another word. Just…tell me what the hell I just saw."

Christian looked all around the room. "I'm…not sure. I just got here. I wasn't here before that, so how am I supposed to know?"

"Okay, fine, play games. Be a…bonerhead, then. See if I care."

"Grace, I'm lost."

"You are? Really? Do you wish for a guide, Christian? You want to know what I saw? Here, I'll show you. I'll show you what I…*saw*." Grace marched to the front door, opened it and pointed to the two-tone 1975 Ford F-150 parked outside. "*That's* what I saw. That right there." A hand fell to her hip. "What the hell is that, Christian?"

He peered out the door. "Um, that would be Peter's truck. I'm pretty sure you've seen it before…"

"Yes, I have. I have seen the truck before, many times," Grace said. "But what I haven't seen before, *ever* before…is Peter's truck with *that*—that newly installed…hood…ornament." She pointed again with her finger twitching, her eyes half open.

"Oh, that." Christian sniggered. "That's what you meant. Sorry, I'm an idiot."

Grace exhaled deeply, back of her hand to her forehead. "Christian, honey, I realize that you are indeed a troubled soul. It's one of the reasons I fell for you so quickly. But could you please explain this to me in the best way you know how? I mean, babe, for the love of the blessed Virgin Mary—what is that?"

Christian's brow furrowed. "Grace, you know what *that* is, or rather *who* that is. That would be Max, the guy you didn't want to kill, until a couple of days ago, anyway."

"Yes." Grace bobbed her head. "I realize that, I know who it is. But…why is he…there? Why is he now lashed to the hood of Peter's truck? And are those cargo straps?"

"And a few ropes." Christian said, sounding pleased with himself. "I said I had other plans for him, remember? I've been mulling over the best way to…use him to our advantage. On my way to borrow Peter's truck for your appointment this morning, it just hit me."

"This. *This* hit you?" Grace badgered. "Strapping him to Peter's truck hit you? How is doing this using Max to our advantage? I-I'm literally punch-drunk. Discombobulated…and, a little disturbed, being honest. This is crazy. What were you thinking?"

"It's not crazy, Grace. It's genius. Think it through," Christian said casually. "See the way he's splayed out? With him strapped there like he is, we can drive around without worrying about his so-called people taking shots at us."

Grace rubbed her temples. "No, no, no…this is a stupid idea. It's so stupid, I can't even bring myself to add all the stupid up within. This isn't how you're supposed to treat people. You don't use them as targets."

"Targets? Come on, give me some credit. I would never do that. This is deploying him as a human shield, and that's a totally different thing."

Grace forced her eyes shut. "I believe…I mean, I know you're only trying to help. But this idea…it's sooo wrong. It looks wrong. It feels sooo wrong."

"But everything about it is right. Give it a chance and me a chance. I know what I'm doing," Christian began, pushing the door near-closed. "Those are his men in the hills who're shooting at us. Now, I doubt they're highly skilled marksman, probably just a couple of guys with scoped deer rifles, but even trained sharpshooters don't particularly care to fire on moving targets. The truck is a moving target when it's in motion. And with Max strapped to the hood while it's in motion, it's unlikely his people will fire on us and take the chance of hitting him. It's a pretty safe bet, in my opinion."

"A pretty safe bet, huh?" Grace asked.

"I think so. You're carrying our child, Grace. Your safety is vital to me."

"And you love me enough to strap a guy to a truck for me?" Grace blushed. "That's adorable." She looked ready to endorse the idea, but went skeptical again as her beau guided her arms into her coat. "Christian?"

"Yeah?"

"How does he pee?"

Christian sent Grace an odd look, then cracked the door open and peered outside. He shrugged. "I don't know. I guess…if he has to go, he pisses himself."

"Oh, that's lovely. A grown man peeing himself while spread out and strapped to the hood of an antique pickup. That's real dignified." She paused. "And what about the other…thing."

"The other *thing*?"

"You know what I mean, the other…product, consisting of…waste. Christ, I can't even bring myself to articulate the word without upchucking."

Christian surveyed Max and rubbed his chin. "Admittedly, I haven't given any thought to that."

"Well, you might want to. Before nature calls and effects permanent stains on a vehicle that doesn't belong to us."

"I can't argue with that," Christian said, then snapped his fingers. "You know, when we moved the docs in at the Ackermann place, I'm pretty sure I remember seeing a few boxes of adult diapers. Maybe that's the ticket."

"Eww, enough." Grace shuddered. "No more talking about this. Let's just go already. I've been a nervous wreck all morning—I hate doctor visits…absolutely detest them. And now, I have to endure them for the foreseeable future, and that prospect brings me no joy." She reached for him. "I crave validation and affection—and pickles, all of a sudden. Find pickles for me."

"I'll do what I can," Christian said, holding her just as Michelle made an entrance.

She closed the door and pointed astern with bulging eyes. "Okay, you two. Under most circumstances, I'm capable of handling just about anything. But who's responsible for that…act of barbarism I just witnessed in our driveway?"

Grace pulled away from Christian. "Take a wild guess."

# CHAPTER 16

**Hardy County, West Virginia**
**Tuesday, January 4th. Present day**

AT THE BREAK OF DAWN, LAZARUS led the truck duo out of mountainous terrain and into a spacious valley. They forded a shallow portion of Mill Creek and climbed onto a snowy thoroughfare flanked by corroded steel fencing and wooden poles bearing a triad of forlorn power lines. Plowing their path through wafting snowdrifts, they moved north at a paltry stride, and before long, a familiar sign came into view.

Lauren took notice of it, even under a veil of frozen precipitation obscuring most of its purview. They were now traveling north on US Highway 220. "Wonderful," she quipped.

Woo Tang peered over. "What is?"

"Nothing…in particular. It's this road, again."

"Care to illustrate?"

"Not every encounter I've had with it has been pleasant," Lauren began. "My first memory of *that* sign"—she pointed ahead—"was when Dad took me for an extended drive to have one of his father-daughter talks with me. And tour some prisons."

Woo Tang peered curiously over, but said nothing.

"We didn't tour them from the inside or anything. Just parked across the road for a little while and took in the view, which was unnerving. Before that, I never paid much attention to highway signs, or anything else, really. I think I was living life with blinders on in those days."

Woo Tang deliberated a moment. "And penitentiaries, or rather, the mere prospect of them, had been selected to bring you about. Very innovative."

"Dad never did anything the conventional way," Lauren replied, her head beside the window. "He laid emphasis on the importance of freedom that day and went on to explain how freedom as we knew it then really wasn't." She paused. "And *that* was a pleasant encounter. The last time I saw one of those signs was right before the ambush at the overpass…barely a day before Austin and I were captured. Ironic."

As the lead truck made a sudden right ahead, Woo Tang said, "It would appear Lazarus endeavors to relieve your reservations."

Lauren sighed. "With another shortcut, no less. What would we do without him?"

Woo Tang moved their truck in to follow, and the pair wandered along another narrow, thickly forested path as it rounded hairpins and snaked up and over a ridgeline by way of a variety of zigzags on either side.

After a time, the path leveled off and they exited the forest into a field, only to enter another densely wooded area where the road became notably treacherous. It dipped into a gulley and wound through patches of evergreens and laurel, and as it began a gentle climb, ridges rose on either side, nestling the backwoods pathway in a trench.

Lazarus slowed to a crawl to compete with the terrain, and Woo Tang matched his pace. A number of minutes in, steam suddenly began erupting from the lead truck's radiator, creating a dense cloud that melded with the frigid ambient air, degrading visibility to almost zero.

Lauren shuddered when shards of rubber pelted the windshield. "What was that?"

Brake lights went luminous as the lead truck swerved and skidded erratically, forcing Woo Tang to take evasive maneuvers to prevent a collision. With well-timed hard cuts on the wheel and diligent use of the brake, he brought the diesel to a stop, lodging the plow and rear bumper into walls of snow on either side.

With seemingly no traction, the oversized truck carrying Lazarus, Francis, and Jean skated forward and collided with the road's edge, crushing the snowplow and scattering tree debris atop both vehicles.

Lauren unsnapped her seatbelt and looked herself over, then froze when something rigid smacked the windshield, fracturing it into a spiderweb.

Woo Tang took action, directing her to duck low into the footwell. "Stay down." He shut off the ignition, and with the rattling of diesel engines no longer invading the ambience, several more rifle shots could be heard impacting the chassis.

Lauren shrieked, "Who the hell is shooting at us in the middle of nowhere?"

"Irrelevant. But we *must* exit the kill box. An intermission approaches; be ready for it. We will break during the lull and reposition behind cover." Woo Tang's eyes narrowed. "Then...we will sort this out."

"Okay."

"On my signal, open your door and go to ground. Utilize the truck for cover and stay low. I will follow after."

A long moment passed by. Then, as he'd predicted, the rate of fire declined and finally subsided.

Woo Tang tapped her shoulder. "Go."

Lauren pulled the lever and pushed open the door with her foot. She shoved her AK and sling pack of spare mags into the snow and crept out after them.

Woo Tang then slinked his way out like a serpent. "Origin of fire is due east...we must retreat west. Standard protocol, Lauren Russell, center peel. I will move first. You suppress them until I set a base of fire, then you retreat under my cover. Do you understand?"

"I know the drill, Jae," she said, and moved her weapon into position.

His head low, Woo Tang rose to a knee and waited.

Lauren snapped off the safety and fired once—"Go!"—then sent a volley of rounds downrange.

"Moving!" The SEAL scaled the embankment, then hotfooted backward through the varying snow with his M4 pulled to his shoulder to thicker forest. He found cover behind a fallen petrified tree, crouched and aligned himself for Lauren's retreat. "Set!" he shouted, and commenced fire.

But Lauren didn't move. She remained in position, watching, listening, gauging from where the shots were originating.

"Orchid! Peel! Break contact!"

Lauren didn't respond. She crawled underneath the truck and repositioned between the grille and the crooked snowplow, a location appearing to offer adequate ballistic protection. Then, under muted daylight, made so by a canopy of ancient conifers, she waited for the first sign of a muzzle blast.

A moment passed by in silence, and Lauren thought she'd overheard chattering at one point. Then her eyes tracked left, spotting a flash the instant a rifle's report cracked off. She squinted through her optic, made a slight adjustment, and brought a middle-aged man's scruffy beard, half-hidden behind a tree, into focus. A magazine-fed rifle of some variety rested in his hands and, though it wasn't aimed directly at her, was pointed in her vicinity.

The shooter was preparing another shot, but Lauren already had him dead to rights. She aligned the optic's red dot on the bridge of his nose and squeezed the trigger. The M70 burped, and the slug struck the man with force enough to knock him from his perch as his weapon fell and tumbled into the snowy road.

Right after Lauren dropped him, a surplus of panicked shouts was heard.

"Woody! Woody! Oh shit!"

"What is it? What happened?"

"Woody's hit! Oh, man…he's hit bad! He's…oh no, man, no! He's not moving! I think they killed him!"

The men's chattering did nothing to help their cause, only gave their positions away to the tenacious young woman huddled below them in her improvised sniper's roost.

Lauren waited tolerantly, and when one of them broke cover to check on Woody the corpse, she fired twice at center mass, sending him to meet his maker. "And that leaves one of you."

"Zero," a voice beside her whispered.

Startled, Lauren whipped around to see Woo Tang had rejoined her. His rifle was secured to his shoulder, and its suppressed muzzle was braced on the diesel's hood. The final shot from his weapon seconds after sealed the deal, putting an end to the skirmish.

Lauren brushed the caked snow from her pants and slowly stood while remaining in place to watch for additional threats. When she chanced a stare at her companion, she found a vacant, humorless one being sent her way; and for the moment, she felt like Daniel LaRusso being visually scolded by Mr. Miyagi himself.

She awaited an earful over this, but Woo Tang merely strolled off to inspect the damage inflicted. He wasn't content with her performance, but something or perhaps *someone* else was displeasing him even more.

Lauren drew her attention to the lead vehicle's empty cab, and reality collided with her. "Where did *they* go?"

"Did you not see them withdraw?"

"I haven't seen much of anything since that shot hit the windshield." She expected to see the trio shot dead, having been pinned down inside the cab at the onset, but there were no signs of them inside or out. Foot tracks were nearly impossible to make out, and there were no indications of blood trails. Lauren edged closer and shot a look into the bed, finding all their tools, equipment, gear and personal items still in place. "Wherever they went, they left all their stuff here."

Woo Tang nodded slightly. "Curious."

Concern mounting for her own personal effects, Lauren went to verify them. She jumped into the bed, and several minutes in, she heard chattering again. She turned to track it and found Lazarus and Francis standing behind the tree where the first man had gone down after she'd put a bullet in his face.

Francis was holding a rifle, which he hadn't been in possession of prior to the surprise attack. Though they spoke softly, their conversation looked heated, like the two men had fallen into conflict over something, and they were pointing at the fallen man and using animated gestures to convey their opinions.

Lauren then detected Jean pulling herself from under the front axle, where a cavern of snow had been formed when the truck had run aground. She sped over to help the woman to her feet.

"Thank you, sweetie," Jean said. "Sorry I couldn't do much to help. Did we get them all?"

"I think so." Lauren motioned to Lazarus and Jean's husband. "How did you end up here and not with them?"

Jean brushed snow and gravel from her jacket and pants. "I don't know, it all happened so fast. I was sitting in the middle, so I was the last one to get out. They ran off and I would've ran with them, but all I could think about was not dying. So I found a hiding spot."

Her look displayed a certain genuineness. Lauren believed what Jean was saying, but the combined behaviors of the other two coupled with Lazarus's unruly conduct from the get-go was raising red flags.

Lazarus jerked his head awkwardly and waved to Woo Tang upon seeing him approach from below. "Oh hey, bud. Sorry…we'll be done in a second."

Woo Tang's expression went colder and darker than Lauren had ever seen it. His voice seared as he spoke. "Lazarus, admittedly,

I am exasperated at the moment. This route should never have been considered, as it is one of distinct disadvantage."

Lazarus stared strangely at him. "Do what?"

"Look around you. Study the landscape. The environment in which we are situated is textbook for ambush. You took it upon yourself to lead four individuals into a three-dimensional target area. Up until now, your use of ad hoc, circuitous routes has been benign, but this one could have very easily killed every one of us."

"Okay, I get that. But it didn't, right? So take it easy. I understand your being upset, but—"

"There will be *no* more of this," Woo Tang roared, cutting him off. Then he stomped away to cool off.

Lazarus shrugged and resumed a disposition of complete indifference and went back to whispering with Francis. The men slowly made their way back to the scene only to have Lauren approach them.

Lazarus rolled his eyes. "Here we go. I guess now it's *your* turn to yell at me, right?"

Lauren ogled him. "Where were you?"

"What? What do you mean? You saw us. We were right up there."

"And *why* were you up there?" Lauren sent impugning looks at both men. "And you left Jean behind…you both dumped her in the middle of a firefight. Why?"

Francis looked away, guilty as charged. He sidestepped away and went to join his wife, now visibly troubled.

"You know…I'm getting really tired of this shit from you," Lazarus began. "You're always badgering me. You've been doing it since before the trip started, and you really need to stop it. Just…get off my ass already. This is close to being harassment."

Lauren didn't waver. "Did you know those men?"

"Who?"

"The ones *we just killed*."

"What? Hell no! I've never seen them before in my life," he pled, failing to look her in the eyes.

Lauren watched him fidget anxiously. "Every indicator you're sending tells me you're full of shit."

"Oh, come on. What are you? A cop?" Lazarus reacted. "I'm not lying, give me a lie detector test if you want. Truth is, I don't give a shit what you think. I'm telling you, I don't know those guys. They sneaked up on us in the middle of nowhere, probably because they wanted the trucks, our gear, guns or something. That's it. It's a simple explanation. And now they're dead. It's over. And we can giddyup."

But it wasn't as simple as he was making it out to be, Lauren was certain of it. She vacated his presence and went back to arranging her gear, knowing now that the remainder of the trip home was destined to occur on foot.

Both vehicles rendered undrivable, the group soon converged on them amidst the cavernous tracks spawned by the subsequent mishap.

Lazarus looked the most hopeless of the bunch. "Well, dare I say this creates a slight disadvantage for us."

"Slight?" added Jean.

"Not a whole heck of a lot we can do about them," Francis said. "The radiator's busted on ours, and both front tires are shredded. It ain't going nowhere." He pointed to the other truck. "That one looks drivable, but it's wedged in pretty good. The plow is wasted, though. So even if we somehow got it out, we wouldn't get far with it."

"So what are we going to do, then?" Jean asked, looking around at the trees.

Francis regarded his cousin. "Whereabouts are we, Laz?"

Lazarus shrugged. "Somewhere between Brake and Bass, west of Elkhorn Mountain. Near the falls, I expect."

Lauren folded a map she'd been perusing and slid it into her pack, then jumped down from the truck bed and pointed up the path. "It stands to reason had we *not* been ambushed, our journey would've continued on this route. The only difference is we're on foot now."

"On foot?" Jean retorted.

"How far are we talking?" Francis asked.

Lauren deliberated. "Twenty miles or so, maybe a few more. We're not far from Lost River State Park. We can hike into it and follow trails from there."

Francis ridiculed, "We're all gonna get frostbite on our toes. We might want to try hunting down whatever them fellas drove in."

Jean scowled. "And how long would doing that take?"

"Too long," Lazarus said. "On foot's the only way we're getting out of here, there's no ifs, ands, or buts about it. Let's go see what gear we have to take with us."

When the group reconvened, Lazarus was lugging an ancient external-frame backpack nearly as tall as he was, and Francis had a small day pack hanging from a shoulder, leaving Jean with little to nothing.

Lauren analyzed Lazarus's choice of gear. "Nice pack."

"Thanks. I think so too. You like it?"

Lauren slowly shook her head. "No."

"No?"

"Uh-uh."

"Why not? 'Cause it ain't camo? It's still a heck of a pack. Better than most of them newfangled things they used to sell in outdoor stores."

"More like residue from the nineteen-eighties Boy Scout era. In what thrift store did you find that thing?"

"It belonged to my pop," Lazarus said. "He was a scoutmaster back in the eighties, so you know."

Lauren grinned snarkily. "And I take it you were his proud little Eagle Scout?"

Lazarus smirked. "Actually, I was."

Jean sulked, gathering up what little she'd brought with her. "I didn't bring a damn thing for this, not no winter walk in the mountains. I don't even have a knife."

"You can use mine," Lauren called. "We can share what I have."

"I appreciate that," Jean said. "It's very generous, though it would've been nice to hear the same from my husband."

Francis stuttered. "Honey, you can use anything I got, you know that. I just figured I didn't have to say it for you to know it."

"No, that's okay. Seeing as how Lauren was kind enough to volunteer hers already, I won't be needing yours."

Lauren smiled at her. "For starters, we need to get you dressed for the occasion," she began, dipping into her pack for a fleece beanie and matching fleece neck gaiter. "We lose a ton of body heat from our heads, and the gaiter will keep your neck warm. It's long enough to cover your face, too. And keep you from getting wind burn."

As the two women went through gear options for Jean for the trip, the whispering between Lazarus and Francis began again and before long escalated into bickering.

"Any idea what that's about?" Lauren asked.

"I don't have the foggiest clue what it could be," Jean said.

"What it *could* be," Woo Tang said, reappearing seemingly at the last minute before departure, "is that our trip has distorted into a shitshow."

Lauren giggled and pulled her beanie over her head and ears. "Truer words were never spoken, my friend."

Lauren and Jean took the lead with Lazarus and Francis hiking alongside one another behind them, where they continued their strife. Woo Tang took up the rear, eyeballing both of them as their quarrel went on nonstop and intensified.

"Have they ever argued like this before, Jean?" Lauren asked, turning to check on them periodically.

Jean shook her head. "No, never. If they weren't cousins, you'd think they were best friends. They've known each other forever, and this is the first time I've ever seen them at each other's throats like that."

Lauren didn't say anything and kept her eyes on the prize, pushing forward through the mountain pass. Another mile underfoot, then another, and before long, the argument reached a fever pitch. Lazarus and Francis began pushing each other and a scuffle ensued. Both men wrapped each other up and fell into the snow, rolling over one another, throwing wild punches at each other's faces amidst curses and blasphemes.

Woo Tang went into action and tried separating them on his own, but the men were skinny and strong, entangled like steel cable. No sooner did he gain control of them did he misplace it.

Jean made her way over and moved in behind Francis. She pled with both of them, did what she could to help, and even tried stopping Lazarus's punches from striking her husband's face.

Growing frustrated with her interference, Lazarus took a break from his assault on Francis and switched targets. He drew back and belted Jean in her cheekbone with a right, sending her reeling backward into the snow.

Seeing this, Lauren lost every bit of her restraint. "No fucking way!" She dropped her rifle and pack and hurried into the fray, tackling Lazarus head-on to the frosty terrain.

The two men separated now, Woo Tang pulled Francis from the fight and held onto him, motioning for Jean to accompany him.

Lauren grabbed Lazarus by his jacket collar and rose, pulling him upright along with her. Still entranced by rage, Lazarus pushed her off him and swung on her wildly.

Lauren blocked the punch and the man's arm caved onto hers. She secured it, pulled hard and twisted it, then used its leverage to adroitly throw his body headlong over her shoulder, doing so as if he were weightless.

Lazarus landed fiercely with a loud grunt and lay flat on his back in a daze.

Lauren stood over him, awaiting a counteroffensive, but Lazarus only lay there like a slug, his chest pounding, whimpering and defeated.

She panted and pointed a finger in his face. "I don't care who you are, if you ever raise your hand to a woman again, I'll kill you. And that includes me."

Francis went to consoling his wife, and Woo Tang stood silent and alone for a moment, surveying the abomination his new mission had become.

After Lazarus gathered himself, he surveyed his options and came to the realization he was slowly but surely running out of supporters. He noticed that Woo Tang was by himself now, and cautiously slithered in beside him. "Hey, thanks for your help breaking that up. I know, I probably screwed up back there. I've been meaning to tell you thanks for coming along and I appreciate everything you've done so far. You're, uh…pretty impressive." He paused dramatically, motioning to Lauren. "Not sure about that one, though. Wish I knew what her deal was. You… got any idea?"

Woo Tang squared off with him but said nothing.

"It's just that…you seem to know her. Is she…bipolar? Have a rough childhood or something? Seems a might off-kilter to me."

The SEAL sent a searing glare to the long-haired man. His face went rigid as iron, and the scar on his face stiffened, giving the impression of a lightning bolt, jagged, encrusted with grime, ire, and brutal murder. "Lazarus…at present, you are standing in my personal space."

Lazarus stammered. His eyes went wide and his jaw dropped open; then he promptly measured the distance separating him and the shorter, much broader, now highly agitated man. Deciding it best not to push his luck, he backed away, palms held out in subtle surrender. "I'm…sorry to bother you."

# CHAPTER 17

**The cabin**
**Trout Run Valley**
**Tuesday, January 4th. Present day**

YOU WANT SOME HELP WITH that?" Grace called, rounding the rear corner of the cabin.

Michelle was using a scoop shovel to clear a path between the driveway, the cabin, and the shed. At present, she was working on the wooden bridge that stretched over Trout Run, and the soreness in her lower back was menacing. She'd taken breaks often, but there seemed little she could do to alleviate the pain.

Michelle dumped a shovelful of wet snow over the bridge's edge, sending clumps splashing into the icy water below. "I'll manage, Grace, thank you. I'm fairly certain it isn't advisable for pregnant women to engage in manual labor. Hope that doesn't sound too judgy."

"Oh, no," Grace responded clumsily. "I wasn't offering *my* help. No…I was going to have Christian put *his* back into it."

Michelle chuckled. "It's very kind of you to offer his assistance. I guess I should've known…considering your slight aversion to working with your hands."

"Slight?" Grace pulled the collar of her jacket tightly around her neck and observed the scene. "You've got a lot done. You've been out here all morning with that thing." She pointed at the shovel. "I bet you have blisters all over your hands."

"Actually, I do. And my blisters have given birth to more blisters."

"Baby blisters," Grace remarked. "Cute analogy. Why aren't you wearing gloves?"

"I can't find them, for some reason," Michelle said. "Looked over the house forever…I don't know what I did with them. Then again, knowing me, I probably moved them and set them somewhere they shouldn't be, making these blisters some form of penance."

Grace nodded and shivered. "Serves you right. Well, if you don't want any help, I'm going back inside where it's warm. Dr. Doolittle has me reading that *What to Expect…*pregnancy book."

"I didn't even know we had that one."

"We didn't. Kim had the paperback in her library, conveniently enough."

"I read it a long time ago." Michelle tilted her head. "What do you think of it?"

"What do *I* think of it?" Grace quipped. "I think it's bizarre. But then again, finding out I was with child was a pretty damn bizarre occurrence too." She rolled her eyes crazily. "Oh well, call me if you need me. You know where I'll be." She then turned and scuttled along the path Michelle had made back to the cabin.

Michelle smiled, watching her prance away. "If you only knew the half of it."

She resumed her work and finished clearing the bridge. A few minutes after, she heard an engine on the approach. As she turned toward the gate, a multicolored snowmobile with a driver and passenger came into view. It stopped at the gate and the rider hopped off and sent a wave to the driver while fumbling with the gate. The snowmobile made an incredibly tight U-turn and sped away in the opposite direction.

Michelle squinted over the snow's brightness as the figure moving toward her slipped off a protective ski mask, exposing the face of a friend.

Norman waved to her while making his way over. "Looks like you've been doing some trailblazing," he said, studying the path.

"Look who's talking. I didn't know anyone in the valley owned a snowmobile."

"Yeah, me neither. Kristen dragged it out a week or so ago," Norman said. "Evidently, Michael bought it a couple of years back with some of his 'mad money'. He has quite a collection of recreational goodies collecting dust in that metal shed behind their old place. Kristen's been reluctant to go in there since he passed…but she's coming around, slowly." He inched closer. "That's a lot of slogging there, Michelle. You didn't do all that by yourself, did you?"

Michelle pushed the shovel into the snow and leaned on it with both hands. "No, it's been all me. The holidays are over now. And we might as well get the routine going again…or some semblance of it, anyway."

Norman nodded. "Not a bad idea at all." Then he went silent for a time and stared at the ground.

"Norm? Did you come here to talk? Lend a hand? Or gawk at my boots?"

"Actually, I came by to ask you something."

"Then ask me."

"Sorry, just that I'm trying to find the right words," Norman said. "It's more of a favor I need to ask of you. Seeing as how I no longer have a vehicle of my own and we kind of lost both trailers a few weeks back, I was wondering if I could borrow the Suburban for a couple of days."

Michelle's posture stiffened and her brows drew in. "I…don't have a problem with that. What do you need it for? Actually, never mind that—why are you even asking? You're approaching me as if we don't know each other, and we do."

Norman hesitated a long moment. "Yeah, I know. And I'm sorry, it just feels funny asking to borrow it, that's all."

"Well, it shouldn't." Michelle looked away and lowered the shovel's handle for another scoop. "You know where the keys are."

Norman nodded. "I appreciate that. Thank you." He paused. "Michelle, I think it's only fair to tell you what the plan is. In the coming days, I'll be moving some things."

"Moving some things where? Such as?"

"Well, it's probably more accurate to say that I'll be moving everything."

Michelle stopped working and set the shovel aside. She began rubbing her hands. "I don't understand. You never hinted to this…or mentioned anything about doing this before."

"I know I haven't, though I probably should have a while back," Norman replied, digging his boot into the snow.

Michelle sent a gracious smile. "Is it Kristen?"

Norman hung his head, opting not to answer.

"Norm, it's okay—it's seriously okay. I'm not the only one who's taken notice, and it's nothing to be ashamed about. I think it's good that the two of you found each other. I certainly never expected you to hang around here and be alone the rest of your life. That wouldn't be fair."

Norman's head bobbed. "I appreciate you saying so. I don't want there to be any hard feelings, Michelle. And yes, a lot of this does have to do with Kristen. There's something there, though neither of us has been able to put our fingers on what exactly *it* is. But it's making us happy and we want to pursue it, and it'd be awkward doing so with me living here. Looking back, I probably should've said or done something about this…living arrangement sooner. I think it would've prevented some folks from getting…I don't know—"

"The wrong idea?"

"Yeah, that."

"It's ironic. I was just talking to Kim about that very thing the other day," Michelle explained. "Our…relationship hasn't been easy for those watching from the sidelines to comprehend. I blame Alan for that…I blame him for a lot of things. But what he asked you to do, he knew he couldn't ask of anyone else. Of all his friends, he trusted you more than any of them. And you know what? He was right about you. You dropped everything and helped us; you got us here and helped get us started. If you feel you need to leave, then please don't let us stand in your way. And don't feel like you owe us an explanation. We all love you. But you have a life to live and two sons to look after, and you almost lost one of them. If you feel this is for the best, then go. Do it. Live your life. And the Suburban is at your disposal."

Norman locked eyes with her. "Thank you, Michelle. That means a lot. I'll keep the truck in one piece, though it probably won't do me much good until we finish this little portage you started."

"Until *we* finish?"

Norman gestured for Michelle to hand the shovel over. "Give me that. You go inside and warm up. Put some comfy clothes on, prop your feet up, and slather some lotion on those hardworking hands. I'll take it from here."

# CHAPTER 18

**Hardy County, West Virginia**
**Wednesday, January 5th. Present day**

JEAN'S TERRIFIED ECHOES AWAKENED LAUREN from a short-lived slumber. She and the others had slept in shifts overnight to keep watch over the camp, and the latest one was presumed covered by the likes of Lazarus and Francis, allowing her, Jean and Woo Tang some time to rest.

When she pried her eyes open, she could see Jean scurrying about the camp, going through her husband's things as well as those belonging to the militia leader. Woo Tang had risen and was on his way to join her so he could ascertain just what in the hell was going on this time around.

"I don't know where my husband is," Jean snapped. "He and Lazarus got up to pee over an hour ago, and they haven't come back yet."

Lauren unzipped her bivy and pulled herself from her sleeping bag then went to stuffing overnight items into her backpack.

"In what direction?" asked Woo Tang.

Jean put the back of her hand to her forehead worriedly. "I don't rightly remember. I want to say they went down yonder, but I don't know. I was half asleep when Francis told me."

Jean indicated the deep gully below them. The camp had been selected on high ground so anything or anyone coming their way could be spotted long before becoming a threat.

Woo Tang walked to the embankment's edge. "The snow reveals two sets of overlapping tracks that persist beyond my line of sight."

He looked to Lauren. "Remain with Jean. I will look to this." He then gathered his weapon and rucksack and started off.

"What do you think he's going to do?" Jean asked.

Lauren put a hand on her shoulder. "Whatever he can. I'm going to make us some hot tea. Want some?"

She nodded, looking frazzled. "That sounds nice."

Woo Tang returned an hour later with a vinegary look on his face. "The tracks lead to an area of levelling terrain and converge with another set of tracks one half klick from here."

"What does that mean? Were they taken?" Jean asked.

"That is unclear. The tracks file into a portage that leads to a dilapidated wooden structure approximately one hundred meters south, possibly a dwelling. Wood smoke is rising from the chimney. I presume Lazarus and Francis to be held inside."

"Any idea who with?" Lauren asked.

"That is also unclear, as were signs of struggle," Woo Tang said. "The whole scenario has me puzzled, Lauren Russell. It is not adding up."

Jean's worry started to overtake her. "Well, puzzled or not, we're not just going to leave them there, are we? Can't we do something?"

Woo Tang didn't answer her, only stared malcontentedly into the forest.

Lauren squeezed Jean's shoulder, then pulled her friend aside.

"I know what you wish to ask," Woo Tang said. "And you should know my feelings on this matter are very much in conflict."

She frowned. "Jae, that's not like you."

"I do not believe either of us has been ourselves as of late."

"I can't argue with that."

Woo Tang's brows knitted. "I understand this may come across as sounding insensitive, but I do not desire to involve myself in these matters. That is not why I am here—this is not why *either* of us are here."

"And you think I do?" Lauren queried. "I never expected this trip to be easy, but the plan was cut and dry. I was going home, and for some reason, this whole thing has turned to shit since we left. Regardless, I can't in good conscience just stand here and do nothing about this. Lazarus is one thing, but I can't leave Jean's husband down there to die. Inaction has consequences too. And that means I have to go. And *that* means you have to go with me. Otherwise, you'll be disobeying orders."

Woo Tang squinted one eye. "Remind me not to be so forthcoming with you in the future," he said. "Point taken, Lauren Russell. However, hearken this: we have no support element of which to speak. It is only you and me. There is no way to estimate the size of the opposing force or their objectives. The environment in which we are located is both unfamiliar and unforgiving. Forget rules of engagement, as those rarely coincide with acting on sentiment, what we feel to be proper and just."

"It's not like we haven't done anything like this before," Lauren said somberly, recalling the time she and Woo Tang had gone together into coarse territory to take on Sir William.

"The situation to which you refer bore some similarities, though not many," said Woo Tang. "In retrospect, it was foolish to act as we did, without the advantage of support. Choosing to act on this situation now is one and the same, divergent of judiciousness."

"I know that," Lauren said. "And I know the risks. Going after baldy wasn't smart, but he's dead, we made it out of there alive, and I'm thankful." A pause. "I'm not Lazarus's biggest fan; the man repulses me. And I don't know the details about the arrangement the Sons have with Bernie and Ruth. If their leader gets hurt or killed or never makes it back, what happens to the protection they provide? If that goes away, what would happen to those kids? Where do they go without Bernie and Ruth and without that farm?"

Woo Tang exhaled and turned his head away. "You need not convince me further." He started off, gathered his things, and performed a weapons check.

"Hey, just wait, you two," Jean said. "Are you really going down there?"

"There is no other option," Woo Tang responded.

"Oh my," Jean reacted. "Listen, I don't want y'all to think I'm a coward. I love my husband, but I don't have a clue what to do here."

Woo Tang looked her over. "Are you capable of shooting and hitting targets from a distance?"

"I'm not a bad shot, but I'm not the best neither."

He gestured to a 1960s Springfield M14 they'd brought along, sequestered from one of the men who'd ambushed them the day previous. "That rifle is deadly accurate at long distances in the right hands. If you feel you are able to employ it properly, then remain here as overwatch. If that suits you."

Jean thought a moment. “Yeah, that suits me, I suppose. But what are y’all going to do?”

“Send hate downrange,” Lauren said. “A lot of it.”

“And effect the recovery of those taken from us.” Woo Tang sent his young counterpart a quick glance. “I take it you know where I want you?”

Lauren nodded. “Right behind you.”

When they arrived at the area surrounding the shack, Woo Tang and Lauren switched to nonverbal communication consisting of hand signals and sign language. The more experienced of the pair taking the lead, they moved from one position of concealment to the next and drew nearer for the purpose of gathering as much intel as possible without being discovered.

From behind a thick patch of mature laurel sheltered in iced-up snow, Lauren brought her rifle up and used the magnified optic to search for clues through the cloudy glass window. Several figures were seen standing, pacing and moving about while another, appearing to be Lazarus, was seated, conceivably in a chair. And from this angle, Francis was nowhere to be seen.

One hand glued to her weapon, she signed her findings to Woo Tang. He nodded and sent a hand signal to move out, and the pair continued in haste to another potential hiding spot, but only made it halfway before someone opened the door.

“What the hell?” A man raised his pistol and fired wildly at them.

Caught in the open, mere yards from cover, Woo Tang shoved Lauren forward into the snow and unleashed a flurry of rounds from his M4, slicing the shooter through his abdomen. The man folded and toppled, his eyes rolling into his forehead, just as a second man exited and hurdled him.

Woo Tang expended another burst of shots, catching the second man center mass. He spun and landed on his side in the opposite direction, his body twitching and his weapon landing safely several feet away. The former SEAL then went on the move, grabbing Lauren by her jacket collar and dragging her through the snow with him.

Flailing and attempting to set her feet, she sent Woo Tang a searing look. “What are you doing?”

“Following orders.”

"You're being ridiculous! Let go of me, Jae."

Woo Tang refused, his eyes locked on to the open doorway. "Not until we are behind cover."

The duo soon took position behind a stack of seasoned hardwood partially covered by a tarpaulin.

"Y'all know what you're doing?" a voice yelled. "This really ain't none of your concern."

Lauren peeked over the woodpile. Woo Tang remained in place with a finger over his lips.

"If you think we're coming out, you're crazy. And if you think we're letting you in, you're insane," the voice said. "This here is private business! And the only thing that needs to happen right now is for y'all to git!"

Lauren took a breath and rubbed her eyes. The men being held hostage were no one to her. She despised Lazarus and didn't know Francis from Adam. If it weren't for what Bernie and Ruth stood to lose, she wouldn't even be here. And neither would Woo Tang, who'd gone simply because she'd persuaded him.

Her recollections glided back to when she'd first encountered Brandon and Lily. She recalled their faces, how pained their expressions had been, how sad, dejected and lost they'd been. The farm had changed nearly all of that for them. In today's world, it was doubtful their parents would ever be found. Those types of happy endings were a rarity.

Christian had told her once about a place somewhere in the western portion of the country known as 'the redoubt' or 'the promised land', touted as a location of solitude, peace and order, where normal life had yet to be interrupted. She didn't know if such a place truly existed, but Little Germany Farms was real. And that was why she knew something needed to be done about this.

Woo Tang gestured for her to come close. "There exist two options. Wait them out, or breach." He slid off his rucksack, dug in and pulled out a single XM84 stun grenade. "In the essence of time, option two is applicable."

Lauren's eyes boggled. "There isn't a lot of room inside, Jae."

"I am mindful. I plan to move alone while you stand fast. The flashbang will incapacitate them, and you can cover the extraction. Do you understand?"

"Yeah, I underst—" Lauren heard a scream, a woman's scream, and her eyes darted into the trees to the incline whence she and Woo Tang had come. Sounds of a struggle switched to a woman yelping from the pain of being beaten cut through Lauren like a knife blade. Jean was being assaulted, and she looked to Woo Tang for what to do next.

He looked conflicted still. And he was fuming over this whole mess of a situation. He could hear Jean's cries for help as well as Lauren could, but he did not want to separate from her. Dave Graham had made it clear that no harm was to befall her, and Woo Tang couldn't protect Lauren if he couldn't see her. But he also couldn't see any other way out of this.

"You must help Jean," he said, sending a disputed gaze.

Lauren acknowledged him and readied herself.

Woo Tang trained his weapon on the building. "Break on my signal."

She broke cover as soon as Woo Tang's first shot was heard, and ran as hard as she could up the incline to the point of nearing exhaustion. When she crested the hill, she found Jean on the ground wrestling with a man in a camouflage hunting jacket.

Lauren raised her rifle in his direction, and the man jumped at the sight of her.

Panicked, he jerked Jean's body up with him, then twisted her into a fierce choke hold. "Watch it there…watch it! Don't come any closer! Do anythin' stupid and I'll break her neck!"

Lauren didn't bother slowing her pace. Her sights aligned on his shoulder, she snapped the trigger, sending a round tearing into him. He yelped and went limp, falling backward away from Jean, screeching and writhing from the pain.

Jean ran to her, but Lauren drove her away with her free hand, pressing on to the wounded man with purpose.

"Hey, stop! Stop, please!" he begged. "What is this? You already shot me once! What do you want?" He tried getting away, but only tripped over his own feet. When he finally got upright, Lauren throttled him in the solar plexus with a violent front kick, knocking the wind from his lungs and putting him down for the count.

"Stay down and don't move! That's what I want!" Lauren slowly backed away to verify Jean's welfare while keeping her gun trained on the bleeding man. "Are you all right?"

Jean spit blood on the ground. "He got me good a couple of times, but I'm all right now. Thank you."

"Do you know him?"

"No, I sure don't," she said, her voice hoarse. "But he seems to know us."

Lauren checked her expression. This attack wasn't staged, and Jean had no reason to lie. She was starting to put all this together now. Lazarus had been hiding a big secret. Francis seemed to know something about it and wasn't entirely in agreement. Jean seemed clueless, and the closer they got to their destination, the more the situation worsened. Members of their group had been shot at, abducted and now physically assaulted, yet not a hair had been harmed on a certain someone's head.

Lauren was going to get to the bottom of this, or leave every one of these people, save Woo Tang, behind in the forest.

When Woo Tang reentered the scene along with a salvaged Lazarus and Francis, husband and wife ran to one another and embraced, while the militia leader and the bleeding man shared a bitter glare that Lauren picked up on in seconds.

"Status?" Lauren asked her friend.

"Negative contacts," Woo Tang said, giving her and the scene a once-over. "Are you squared away?"

Lauren nodded affirmation.

"Then I suggest we carry on, unless there is other business or threats to cancel."

Still under her watchful eye, the man Lauren had shot worked to tie a bandana over his wound. "Threats? You *people* are the threats. All we was doin' was our jobs."

"There's an epiphany. And what jobs were those?" Lauren interrogated.

The man looked her way but didn't respond. "What's become of the boys down in the valley?"

"Deceased," Woo Tang replied, glaring.

"All of 'em?"

"Of course *all* of them." Lazarus sauntered over to his pack. "Damn, my ears are ringin'. Can't barely see shit, neither. Next time somebody tosses one of them flare bombs near me, send a warning. Copy?" He shouldered his pack and started off. "Now, with *that* junk out of the way, we can all giddyup and get the hell out of here. I'm freezing."

"Y'all ain't leavin' me here alone, are you?" the wounded man piped up.

"What else should we do? Make friends and take you with us?" Lazarus replied, his back to everyone. "After what you did?"

The man chortled. "You…you son of a bitch…"

Lazarus recoiled. "What was that?"

"You heard me. You son of a *bitch*!"

His dingy teeth showing, Lazarus twisted and bolted for the man in a frenzy.

But Woo Tang blocked his path in an instant. "Enough! What is this nonsense? This man is injured."

"I can see that! But he wouldn't be"—Lazarus pointed at Lauren—"if she would've killed him!"

Lauren set her jaw. "Do you two know each other?"

Lazarus pretended not to hear her and treaded away.

The bleeding man seethed. "What's the matter, Laz? Aren't you gonna answer her?"

No one said anything for a moment.

"That's all right, I'll answer for you. Yeah, we do. We know each other. We all go way back," the man said. "He knows why we're here, too. Go ahead, Laz. Tell 'em. Tell 'em why we're here."

"Somebody shut him up!" Lazarus hollered.

"Tell 'em what you did that got this whole mess started. Go on, tell 'em! You fuckin' traitor!"

"What is he talking about?" Lauren prodded.

Lazarus shrugged, his hands aloft to his sides. "I have no idea. He's in shock; he's talking out of his ass."

Lauren folded her arms. The truth was set to expose itself. "The man speaks from his ass, yet he knows your name."

"I know a lot more than that," the man said. "I know everythin'. I know you, your family, and I know its legacy too. And I know how you soiled it. They reigned over the militia for generations, but they were fair. All that changed the day your daddy died and you got the hot seat. And the second you thought your precious command was in jeopardy, you just had to do somethin' about it."

"Shut up!" Lazarus barked.

"Instead of handlin' things the right way and talkin' things out amongst brothers, you gave an order and sent two men to do your biddin'. You sent 'em to murder another brother. And now Claudio wants you dead for tryin' to have 'im killed."

"Claudio?" Jean pondered, casting a stare to a shrugging Francis.

Lauren sent Lazarus a fiery glare. "Is this true?"

"I only did what was needed to keep my family's legacy intact," Lazarus said. "It was within my power to do so."

"Power? Claudio never wanted no power and no nothin' from you," the bleeding man said. "You got jealous 'cause the boys respect him better than you. He's a combat vet. He knows how to fight and how to train men and you don't. People follow him and they like him, and they only do that to you because of your family name."

Woo Tang repositioned himself and stared at both men. "And now an internal power struggle exists?"

The other man nodded. "You could say that. There's been a lot of infightin', too."

"And how does this struggle impinge on the chain of command?"

Both Lazarus and the man tending his wound looked puzzled.

"I will rephrase," said Woo Tang, a finger pointed to Lazarus. "Who assumes command during this dispute over who reigns supreme?"

"Belay that," Lauren broke in. "What about Bernie and Ruth and their farm? And those children? And the protection your militia provides? What happens to them in the wake of this?"

Lazarus hesitated, shrugging his shoulders. "The answer's pretty simple. It goes away."

"What did you say?"

"I said it *goes away*, as in disappears," Lazarus said. "The protection was based on a mutual understanding, a handshake, between two men, both dead and buried. Nothing was ever in writing. There's no contract. And with me out of the loop, they're on their own now. Same as I am, same as all of us." He gazed around at his increasingly critical onlookers and sulked. "Whatever, y'all might as well know everything. I'm dead anyway, dead to everyone, so what difference does it make? It doesn't matter where I go, it's over for me. My life is shit."

Lauren shook her head in disgust. "So Lazarus isn't the philanthropist he pretends to be."

"What? I ain't no philanderer."

"All of this has been a charade—it's been bullshit from the word go, hasn't it?" Lauren demanded. "This wasn't about getting me home; it never was. And it wasn't about helping Dave either. It was about you—*saving* you. Protecting your ass. Keeping this Claudio from finding you and killing you over what *you* did. You set this whole thing up."

"That ain't the half of it," the bleeding man said. "Claudio is a decent man with morals. He's forthright and he don't have a reason to lie or hurt nobody. But Laz tried havin' 'im offed and failed. And when he found out Claudio wanted 'im dead, he got scared and ran off far away, hopin' to escape his fate. Even had us stage out here along his escape route…to clean his mess up for 'im."

As Lazarus turned his back to everyone, Lauren sent an inquisitive stare to his whistle-blower. "What mess?"

The man looked to Lazarus as if bidding the militia leader to respond, though nothing came of it.

Lauren repeated herself, stomping the ground. "*What* mess?"

"Witnesses." Francis spoke up and every eye fell on him. "Accomplices. Anyone with the slightest inkling about where he was headed." A pause. "Y'all…weren't supposed to make it out of the mountains."

Jean backed away from her husband. "Francis! Sweet Jesus, that's outrageous! How long have you known about this?"

"I didn't know anything till after we left," he admitted. "I swear it, Jean. And after he told me, I couldn't believe it. I didn't want to believe it, until we started gettin' shot at. After the first few went off, it was clear sailin' for us. Lazarus didn't even seem the least bit worried about it. Afterwards, it didn't take a fool to notice all the shots taken at us were just at the truck. All of theirs were aimed right where they were sittin'."

"Was this why you two were tusslin'?" Jean asked.

Francis nodded, then hung his head. "For what it's worth, Lauren and Mr. Woo Tang, sir, I deeply apologize and I'd like to ask your forgiveness. I didn't plan this, but I realize knowing about it makes me complicit. I'll accept whatever punishment you think is suitable."

Lauren rolled her eyes and stared at the sky, then ogled Woo Tang. "Do you believe this shit?"

"To a certain degree. Though, it does run alongside theatrics."

Jean looked lost. "What are we all to do now? Go our separate ways?"

Sporting a casual smirk, Lauren gracefully strolled to Lazarus. She reached forward and, with a finger, touched his cheek, causing him to flinch at the point of contact.

"What?" he asked, angling away. "What now?"

"None of this is acceptable," she hissed. "You grasp that, right? Good people put their trust in you, they relied on you, and you fucked them. And you don't even care."

"Oh, please! That's life, sweetheart! Do yourself a favor, judge someone else," Lazarus barked. "I've had my fill of you, young lady. I should've never offered to help someone so ungrateful."

Lauren didn't say anything. His actions were appalling, and the manner in which he verbally conveyed everything uttered in her presence exceeded deplorability by her standards. Her inner fury surged as would a volatile chemical reaction, as her smirk transmuted into a scheming smile.

Lauren drew back and throttled Lazarus with a bareknuckle jab, crushing his nose, then spun her hips and caught his lower jaw with a blinding left cross, lifting him off his feet. He fell rearward, landing flat and inert in a drift of powdery snow.

She was tuned-in now and wanted nothing more than to beat the man to within an inch of his life. His foolhardiness, selfishness, and reckless abandon had ostensibly placed hundreds of lives in unnecessary danger, including that of her own, and there was simply no justification for it.

Lauren stood there, ready to reach for him, drag him up by the collar and punch him again and again with everything she had, then watch his eyes sway into his head as crimson blood cascaded in rivulets from his shattered nose.

But instead, she found her restraint. She took a few deep breaths, exhaled slowly, and with her forearms tensing and hands still balled into tight fists, she backstepped away.

Woo Tang, who had decided not to intervene, strode to her and rested his strong, reassuring hand on her shoulder. "That was a pragmatic decision on your part. He is not worth chancing injury to yourself."

Lauren gritted her teeth and flexed her fingers. "He isn't worth anything."

Woo Tang nodded accord, then sent a gaze to the recently anesthetized. "What shall we do with him?"

"I don't care anymore, Jae. I just want to go home."

"I understand." Woo Tang broke away at the point Lazarus started to come around. He moved in quickly, and when the long-haired man reached for a hand, Woo Tang offered his and yanked him abruptly to his feet.

Lazarus wiped his nose and staggered, trying to find his balance. "What happened? I can barely see…feels like my nose is broken."

"You're lucky I didn't break your jaw." Lauren knelt and hoisted her pack.

Lazarus stared hard at her, then pointed. "Hey! Why'd you hit me?" He directed a related query to Woo Tang. "Why'd you *let* her hit me? This is great…this is just fucking great. I come clean and tell the truth and try to get us all on an even keel so we can work all this out, and what do I get for my efforts? Attacked! Assaulted! Punched in the face by some…violent, feral, half-breed bitch." He pointed at Lauren again, his finger shaking. "You…you're lucky your bodyguard is here to protect you, because if not, I would kick your scrawny ass up and down this mountain."

Lauren finished adjusting her pack straps, then prompted Woo Tang for input.

The frogman held up both hands. "I will stand aside."

"There you go. Opportunity knocks. My bodyguard is off duty, and you're fresh out of excuses." Lauren's tone went bitter. She stood solid and ready, legs shoulder-width apart with a menacing glower. "I'm waiting."

Lazarus sniffled and snorted and continued to manipulate his shattered nose. He looked to Woo Tang, then back to Lauren. She was standing her ground and hadn't so much as moved an inch. He wanted to call her bluff, but couldn't tell if she was bluffing, and he wasn't about to chance it.

A corner of Lauren's lips curled upward. "Hats off to you, Laz… you've proven yourself to be a coward *and* a fraud." She then turned her back and started off, never to look upon him again. "Good riddance."

Lazarus went to respond, but Woo Tang quickly squared off with him. "From this point forward," he began, sending Lazarus the iciest of stares, "we go our separate ways. You are hereby advised *not* to follow us. Doing so would be unwise on your part."

"W-what about them?" he inquired, a rigid finger pointed at the couple huddled together.

Woo Tang regarded them. "Francis? Jean? You are welcome to join us." He fell in to Lauren's boot tracks, tossing a small medical kit at the bleeding man's feet as he made his exit.

A moment later, under Lazarus's hateful gaze, Francis and Jean gave chase, abandoning him and his injured counterpart in the remote, unforgiving forest somewhere in the vicinity of Lost City, West Virginia.

Lauren had already gone a good length up the trail, but stopped to wait for Woo Tang to catch up. Once reconnected, and noticing that Jean and Francis were with him, she smiled and thanked him.

"Thank me for what?"

"For...backing me up. And doing what I would've done." She gestured to the couple.

"Lazarus is not an honorable man. Whatever negative outcome that is set to befall him is warranted, for he has brought it upon himself."

"We agree on that," Lauren said, now sounding anxious. "As soon as we get back, we have to find some way to warn Bernie and Ruth about this. They lost their safety net. And Dave needs to know too."

Woo Tang nodded his head with a detached gaze. "There is time. Neo will know how best to go about it, and LT can handle himself. I do not expect our friend to make it far from where he is now. There are many searching for him. I estimate fate will befall him long before he learns of a new way to postpone it."

"I guess."

"Guessing is immaterial," Woo Tang said. "For men such as Lazarus, there is no sanctuary, on this earth or beyond it."

# CHAPTER 19

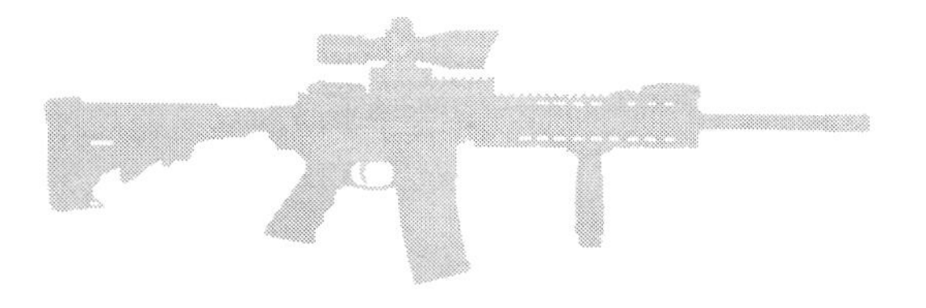

**Loudoun County, Virginia**
**Wednesday, January 5th. Present day**

ALAN'S EXCITEMENT HAD REACHED AN all-time high, for the day had finally arrived to depart White Rock and restart the search for home once again. He packed and repacked his gear, checked his weapons, twice, and loaded everything he owned into the Marauder APC's rear compartment, discovering that Butch had stashed some goodie bags in there as well. Alan hadn't felt the need to ask what was in them. Butch, despite his indelicate disposition, was shaping up to be quite the altruist, and he'd supplemented their inventory for good reason.

Butch had installed a mobile dual-band amateur radio in the APC and had pulled Alan aside and gone over the unit's controls with him. The rig had been preprogrammed with a specific list of memories, each frequency serving a particular purpose and bearing with it a set of limitations.

The embittered vet had gone on to explain the use of the 3-3-3 Radio Plan, as employed by preppers, survivalists, and SHTF emergency communications groups, where operators powered down most of the time or maintained radio silence to save power. Calling for stations or listening for calls occurred every three hours beginning at twelve o'clock until three minutes after the hour on channel three, whether citizens band, maritime or marine band, Family (FRS), General Mobile (GMRS), Multi-use Radio Service (MURS), or amateur radio simplex channels.

The plan's purpose was creating a communications rally point of sorts, where operators could meet if standard means of comms was interrupted or became obsolete. It was based on the Survival Rule of Threes, and therefore easily recalled by those savvy: theoretically, human beings can survive three weeks without food, three days without water, three hours without shelter, and three minutes without oxygen.

Butch had wittily added to this that *Homo sapiens* can also survive for three decades deprived of speaking directly to another, three years if doing so by radio, thereby bringing his opinion on the necessity of human interaction to the table.

After he and Alan had finished going over the encyclopedia of radio etiquette and protocol as scripted by Butch, the group gathered in the main bay to finish loading up and to sort out any last remaining details before departure.

With her gear dragging behind, Jade strode Alan's way, noticing he was in the process of rereading his wife's letter. She didn't say anything, not wanting to interrupt him.

Alan noticed her approaching him and glanced over. Soon after, he folded the letter and slid it into his shirt pocket. "Did I ever mention anything to you about writing a book?"

Jade pushed out her lower lip. "You mean, as in you think I should write one? I don't know, I don't think I have the patience for that."

Alan chuckled. "No. What I meant was, did I ever mention anything about *me* writing a book. As in being an author."

"Oh." Jade blushed. "No, not that I recall. Why? Are you?"

"It would appear. Michelle mentioned something about it in her letter and I've been trying to wrap my mind around it. She said my oldest, Grace, was with them on the day and had originally wanted to leave, but her car wasn't working. I take that to mean she lived elsewhere. At first, she was planning to walk home, but Lauren had her read this book I evidently wrote, and she changed her mind, for some reason."

"Well, that's a good thing, isn't it?"

"No doubt. But it begs the question, if I did in fact write a book… what could it've possibly been about?"

Jade dropped her things and took a seat next to him, folding her legs. "I can think of a few things."

"Care to share them? I'm drawing a blank."

"That Alan…such a smart guy, yet he knows nothing about nothing sometimes," Jade mused. "Maybe you could benefit from a little woman's intuition."

"Meaning…"

"Meaning, knowing you and who you were *then*, it was likely about something you obsessed over the most. Like guns, prepping, or the end of the world as we know it."

Alan's brows drew in.

"You said it yourself just now," Jade said. "Whatever your eldest read kept her from walking home. Something got her attention, or maybe even scared the daylights out of her. I'm going with the latter, knowing who her father is."

"Comforting."

"As far as subject matter is concerned, there are tons of possibilities. Maybe you wrote a doomsday blueprint or an outline to follow like Johnny Jacks did with *Absolute Anarchy*. Or a fictional story about something you believed destined to happen, to the tune of Orwell or Pat Frank, or maybe Motes, Steven Bird, or Horton."

"Okay, but I don't know who any of those people are, Jade."

"Authors—" she chuckled "—of apocalyptic fiction. One of my colleagues in the cavern was obsessed with the genre. She always had a pile of books on her desk, by those authors and a slew of others."

Alan sent a stare to the distance. "Me. A fiction author…"

"Why not? We could try Googling your name if one of Butch's computers could access the web, if it even still exists."

"It doesn't," Butch said, emerging from behind them. "Unless you're adept at packet switching and archaic ARPANET jive that predates the World Wide Web." He rapped his knuckles on the table while continuing past. "Minor change of plans, turtledoves. When the courting ritual's through with, kindly approach the bench."

Alan's face twisted. "Courting ritual?"

"Turtledoves?"

Alan and Jade stood and followed Butch to his workbench, where Ken was perched beside Walter in his wheelchair. At Butch's feet were two Pelican-style armored cases.

"Now that we're all here, there are a few things we need to gab about, so listen up," Butch began. "First topic is operational and personal security, subjects to which I doubt any one of you subscribes with any level of sobriety. It's fortuitous, in that regard, that you've become acquainted with yours truly." He lifted one of the cases onto his bench and opened it.

Ken was the first to chance a peek. "NVDs?"

"These are generation three, ultralight, unfilmed image intensifier binoculars with P45 white phosphor screens."

Ken shrugged. "Isn't that what I said?"

"This plan you've all been devising has you leaving and undergoing most of your…mission throughout the bright of day," Butch said. "Well, I'm squashing that right here, and I'll be the first to say that doing so is just fucking stupid. I won't allow it, no siree, no way in hell, not when my hardware's on the line. And me putting my fat foot down leaves you with one option—a nighttime departure and nighttime-only operations. As a caveat, the headlamps on that South African APC are underpowered as all get out and have the candlepower equivalent to a Mini Maglite."

Alan nodded his understanding, recalling his trip down the tunnel in the other Marauder, the one he'd subsequently overturned.

"In recourse, you'll be running lights out at all times and using these. Harris F5032s are perfect for rapid movement in not-so-ideal light conditions. They can be mounted anywhere, to a helmet or a skull crusher, break them apart and mount them to a weapon, whatever suits you. They use AA rechargeables that last around five to six hours and recharge with USB. And you'll find plenty of places to charge them in the APC. Run out or lose them, regular batteries work just as well, but don't last as long. Any questions?"

Ken lifted one of the devices from the case. "Do they come in green? I prefer the lighter shades."

Butch puckered his lips. "Any *other* questions?"

"What about thermal?" Jade spoke up.

Butch's lips transmuted from a pucker into a smile. "Damn, a lady who knows what she wants. I bet when a man takes you out for a steak dinner, you don't bother ordering ice water, do you, Jade?"

Jade slowly shook her head. "It's bourbon or bust for me."

Butch gritted his teeth. "Je-sus Christ. I am seriously starting to believe I'm might miss you a little bit after you're gone." He knelt and opened the other case. "Behold, ask and ye shall receive. There's only two of them, but they're FLIR, and at one time, they were the best multipurpose thermal scopes money could buy. However, same as all my other prized possessions, I want them back, so please try to take care of them."

"So we're not leaving until tonight now?" Alan pondered.

Butch sighed. "The sun ebbs at quarter till five today. It's only a couple more hours of waiting, Alan, Jesus…"

Alan nodded, his letdown on display, then pointed at the NVDs. "And we can drive with these on?"

"Field of view and depth perception is limited," said Jade, "so it's not easy for the untrained eye, or eyes, but it's doable. And a lot safer than parading around in a black monster truck with a big machine gun on top."

Ken nodded agreement, turning to the Marauder. "That thing does stick out like a sore thumb."

"More like a turd in a punch bowl," added Walter.

"Only now," Butch said, "sore thumb or…turd, as it were, it'll be sponsored by the cover of night."

The next few hours dragged on for Alan and felt more like several days had been added to further postpone departure. Ken had accused him earlier of being stir-crazy, but now, Alan felt ready to come out of his skin. The anticipation of leaving was like murder, having long ago bypassed disappointment. He paced a while, but that didn't occupy him long. Jade had brought him a plate of food, but Alan had turned it down, too excited to muster an appetite. He'd grown increasingly irritable, so much so that Butch had even kept his distance.

And then, a few minutes after sundown, the time came. Butch rolled in a half-dozen steel cans of diesel fuel on a cart and went to topping off the Marauder's tank after locking down others in mounts on the exterior chassis.

Alan was chomping at the bit to leave at this point and already had his door propped open awaiting his entry.

Ken and Jade hung out by Walter's side and waited for Butch to finish. All three had their arms folded and eyes locked on Alan's fidgeting form.

"What?" he asked, noticing their stares.

The trio deadpanned and impassively pursed their lips in chorus.

"Just a couple more things before you go," Butch growled, marching up to them, hearing another one of Alan's sighs. "Come on, reel that shit in. I promise it'll only take a minute."

"Sorry," Alan muttered.

"That's better. This regards the transceiver I installed in the dash, so you might care to listen in. If you find yourselves in trouble or you need assistance, hop on and make a call," Butch went on. "All you gotta do is push the button and talk. That's it. It's all set up and dummy proof. We'll be monitoring here, and with Walter on extended stay, he'll be listening for you if I'm not around. Stick to the comm plan we spoke about. You should hear us come back to you if you're within range. Just remember, most of the area you're headed into is valley, as in surrounded by mountains, and that means your signal might not get out.

"The channels I programmed into your rig are all VHF. RF waves in that range travel line of sight, so elevation is your friend. They do tend to bend around environmental obstacles somewhat, but not much. Occasionally, you'll get some magic, but keep your expectations low. And if you're parked in a metal or concrete building for whatever reason, all bets are off, so try to stay out of them. The GPS transponder remains operational, so wherever you go, I'll be looking you up, eventually."

"That's reassuring," Jade quipped.

"I'm sensing the sarcasm. Anyway, I realize time's a-wastin', so, Alan, good luck to you. If you make it home, fantastic. Give the wife and kids a kiss for me. But if you don't, mosey your butts back here and we'll figure something else out." Butch finished with a tone more candid than his usual. He sent waves to Ken and tipped his hat to Jade, then strode to his bench, where he went to occupying himself with a soldering iron.

Walter and Ken shook hands and gave each other a one-arm hug.

"Watch yer ass, Kenny," Walter said.

"Got to. You won't be there to watch it for me."

"Y'all realize I'm still 'bout half the notion to hook a tow strap to this wheelie chair and let y'all drag me 'round. Shame they don't make skis for these contraptions."

"Walt, this place is built into a mountain," said Jade. "The hills on either side are like double black diamonds, so forget it. We don't need you going kamikaze on us."

"Come on. You act like you know me or somethin'." Walter embraced her. "Jade, girl, I'd tell *you* to watch yer ass too. But that'd be silly. So instead, I'm jus' gonna say watch Kenny's for 'im. Since he sucks at it."

"That's a tall order, Walt," Jade said. "And not high on my list."

"Are you saying my bum isn't nice to look at?" Ken asked.

Jade smirked. "I wouldn't know firsthand. Shall I query Butch for his account?"

Ken sent her a middle finger and turned away.

"Eew, got me a visual on that." Walter laughed.

Alan moved in to take Walter's hand. "Take it easy, Marine. And I mean that. Get healed. You're no good to me like this."

"Roger that. You jus' go an' finish what you started, you hear? When the fiesta begins, don't forget my invite."

And with that, Alan, Jade, and Ken boarded the Marauder while Butch worked to open White Rock's two-ton entry door. Jade slipped on her skull-crusher head harness, then unstowed the night-vision binoculars and adjusted each diopter.

Ken spent a moment playing musical chairs in the APC's rear compartment, trying to decide which seat offered the most comfort. "All right, let's do this," he said, rubbing his hands together. "We're off, once again, to find Alan a home. Or have him committed to one."

Jade backed the APC out of the bay and began her turnabout. Once far enough from all sources of artificial light, she unstowed her goggles again, tossed her hair and rotated sideways. "How do I look, fellas?"

"Like a sight for sore eyes," Ken said.

"Better question is, how do *we* look?" Alan asked. "How well can you see?"

Jade killed the Marauder's headlamps and dimmed the dashboard backlighting. "I can see…everything. Trust me, you'll want to try this."

"Meaning you plan to let me drive eventually?"

"Meaning…maybe." She sniggered. "It takes time to get to get accustomed to these, so grab a set." Jade pressed the accelerator and sent the Marauder toward the main gate as the steel barricade sank into the pavement below. "What's our destination?"

"Woodstock," Alan replied, as if on the tip of his tongue.

"Woodstock it is," Jade said. "Of course, same as before, I don't know which way to go. So point me in the right direction, if you would."

"My navigational skills are at your disposal."

# CHAPTER 20

**George Washington National Forest**
**Hardy County, West Virginia**
**Wednesday, January 5th. Present day**

AFTER TRAVERSING LOST RIVER STATE Park using a system of slick, overgrown hiking trails, Lauren led the group along an unblemished rustic roadway for a mile before veering into an open, unfenced field. From there, they entered a thickly wooded trough and hiked in parallel to the icy cascades of Lower Cove Run, where they took a break, hydrated, and replenished their dwindling supplies of fresh water.

Lauren was back in familiar territory, encircled now by nothing but steep, rolling woodlands, timeworn cattle farms, and National Forest as far as the eye could see. The stream would lead them through and intersect with Judge Rye Road, which ascended and crested the three-thousand-foot elevation mark onto Devil's Hole Mountain.

As they moved through the arctic landscape of the higher elevations, limbs of trees, shrub and laurel, and individual needles on evergreens revealed a thin coating of ice. The frozen sheen refracted the sun's rays as it closed on the western horizon, superimposing a dazzling, tawny hue over the immediate panorama, in similar fashion to how a watercolorist might capture early twilight on canvas, as perceived amidst a miniature ice age.

Woo Tang went on alert when the group rounded a corner and came upon an overturned truck. As he passed by with caution, he studied it with a keen eye, chancing a look inside to find three corpses entangled with one another, all vastly decomposed. The windshield was cracked from one end to the other, replete with starbursts denoting where each bullet had struck and breached it. The driver and passengers appeared to have been killed in the cab, likely while the truck had been in motion.

A quarter mile later, the group stumbled upon another curious scene. Another truck, completely scorched, appearing either to have caught fire or exploded, was situated awkwardly in a drainage ditch halfway glazed with snow.

The former SEAL examined what remained of its tires with a raised brow, each one now a jumble of molten rubber and steel belts.

"Good gracious, what a mess," Jean remarked. "What on earth do y'all think could've happened here?"

"One could only speculate," Woo Tang said.

Lauren grinned uncomfortably. "No speculation necessary. I know what happened."

Woo Tang and the others regarded her with scrutiny.

"Me," Lauren said in monotone. "*I* happened here."

Jean grimaced. "I'm sorry, honey, but did you say *you* happened here?"

Lauren nodded and her expression congealed.

"What does she mean by that?" Francis asked his wife.

She swatted him. "Don't push her…if she wants to tell us, she'll tell us."

Lauren inhaled a deep breath. "It happened a few months ago. My friend Megan and I were riding together in her UTV. We'd been cleared to act as road patrol with her father's permission, but not up here though. We weren't supposed to leave the valley. She…had other plans in mind. She was determined to recon some areas below just north of here where she believed *the takers*—the faction that'd been attacking us—were camped out. We were on our way back and a truck came up behind us and started shooting. One of the shots hit Megan's mirror…it was inches from hitting her. They were gaining on us, and I knew I had to stop them before they killed us." Lauren locked eyes with Woo Tang. "So I did."

He looked upon her with sincerity, indicating at that point, he was all ears.

"After that, we thought we were good, like we'd gotten away." Lauren pointed to the charred pickup. "But *that* truck pulled out of the woods right in front of us and cut us off. Megan whipped the wheel; we skidded and overturned. I'd taken my seatbelt off to shoot at the truck behind us and hadn't put it back on, and was thrown into the bushes. I lost my rifle, my pack, everything but my sidearm. The Polaris was on its side and we used it for cover. The men who'd ambushed us...taunted us and said terrible things. If we hadn't fought them off, I don't think words could've described what they would've done to us."

"Oh, honey," Jean said, her expression allaying. "What an awful thing to go through."

"They were awful people, but every one of them died that day," Lauren said, "because they deserved to." She took a few steps away and stared hard at the truck. "I'd shot men before, but it was different that day. I knew it was all on me; no one was there to save me. I couldn't lean on my dad or call 911. The police couldn't help me; there weren't any rangers nearby, no security guard, no older brother, no bodyguard. Help was miles away, and a friend was with me who stood to suffer the same fate as me had I not refused to become a victim." She paused. "I chose to fight. And I elected to win that fight. It's been that way for me ever since."

Lauren turned away and started off again while the others stood in place, absorbing every moving word she'd said, attempting to imagine the day she'd described to them.

Woo Tang remained reticent and shot occasional glances Lauren's way. In witnessing her recent behavior and now, this latest exposé on a portion of her life for which he hadn't been present, he spent a moment mulling it over and outlining her backstory in his mind.

Lauren's predispositions aside, Woo Tang knew that he, Dave Graham, and the unit had enabled her in such ways and were therefore culpable to some degree. They'd all had a part in making her the person she had become, even in such a short amount of time. They'd provided the foundation, but she had built upon it, having gone far beyond what he had conceived possible. On her own and directly affected by the world's atrocities, by some exceptional means, the Lauren Russell he'd watched develop into a young warrior had become a revolutionary.

Before departing the road and reentering the woods along the wagon trail that would lead them two miles into the valley below, and Lauren home, she turned to observe the scene a final time. She stared hard at the destruction she'd elicited, calling into memory the life-altering crack of every shot.

Woo Tang affably bumped her shoulder with his. “Lauren Russell, I deem that we are merely a hop, skip, and a jump from our destination. Shall we break here or continue?”

She shuddered. “Sorry…just taking a few to reflect over this. It’s all somewhat difficult to believe, sometimes.”

“What is? That you are capable of such things? Surely the realization of that was broached long ago.”

“You’re right, it was. But it still surprises me.” Lauren looked to her feet. “Have I ever told you about how I wanted to be a veterinarian when I was younger?”

“Not that I recall.”

“It’s been on my mind ever since Lazarus bragged about his degree the other day,” she began. “Every semester in fifth grade, we had these ‘career days’. People would come in during class and discuss their careers with us, and by day’s end, we had to choose which one we wanted for ourselves. There was this woman in her twenties who came dressed in scrubs. She was happy and vibrant, always smiling; I could tell she was doing something she loved. She told us she was a veterinarian and that working with animals wasn’t always easy, but the good experiences by far outweighed the bad. She said her job, on the fundamental level, was simple.

“She used her strength to nurture the weak. She protected the vulnerable and fostered the helpless. She took away hurt and pain and saved lives, and doing those things gave her purpose. After her presentation, I wanted to be everything she was. I wanted to help animals like she did and look and feel happy like her. I told my parents about it, and for the longest time, I was convinced becoming a veterinarian was the only thing I ever wanted to do. I felt like I was born to do it. Then I got older and learned how wrong I was. And now, in retrospect, I don’t think I was ever born to do anything…apart from this.”

Woo Tang hesitated before responding. “An enchanting story. I wonder though, would it be untimely to offer another perspective?”

“No. Of course not.”

Woo Tang regarded her with kind eyes. “First and foremost, I disagree with your assertion, as I believe you were born for not one, but many reasons, all of which are distinctive, many of which have yet to be unearthed. My viewpoint is of a single element within a unit, the one who facilitated bringing your inherent gifts to the surface where they could be used. It brings me satisfaction knowing your capabilities have served to extend your lifespan and will likely continue to do so.

"You have proven yourself a capable fighter, proficient at self-preservation, and because of this, I believe you are naturally suited for the premise of combat. But being a natural at something is in no way uniform with being born for something." Woo Tang stepped closer. "I have never once alleged you as having a sole purpose on this earth. You are not a seed or a blade of grass; you are a human and therefore a keeper of many. But of them, it is my belief you and many others were born into this world for a highly celebrated purpose in particular; one that is far too often disregarded."

Lauren's eyes had begun to well up. "What, Jae? What purpose?"

He spoke firmly. "To live."

Nearing the wagon trail's midway point between Devil's Hole and the valley, Lauren slowed her pace upon smelling wood smoke. She rotated and, in the waning light, saw the flaming shimmer of what could only be a small fire burning in the forest.

Woo Tang took two steps to stand beside her. He'd noticed it as well and sent a questioning look her way, as if to ask if she knew anything about it.

Lauren shrugged her shoulders and pulled her rifle close. She motioned to Jean and Francis. "Wait here."

About twenty yards in, they came upon a small campsite with trash strewn about, intermixed with portions of muddied snow and slush. Two men—both with shaggy beards, long hair, and raggedy clothes—were sleeping soundly, bundled underneath wool blankets, their backs to each other, leaning against a tree. A scoped bolt-action rifle lay on the ground beside each of them.

"You've got to be kidding me," Lauren said under her breath.

Woo Tang scrutinized the scene and moved in closer with Lauren falling in behind him. Sliding their rifles away, he handed them off one by one. Lauren unloaded them and placed the live shells in a pocket, then slung both over a shoulder, snug to her pack.

The two men remained asleep, clueless that visitors had joined them. Their snoring disguised nearly every neighboring noise in the forest, effectively acting as would a lullaby.

Woo Tang felt around their blankets for the presence of other weapons and, upon finding none, rose and backed away. He unshouldered his rucksack and extracted two sets of restraints.

Lauren grinned satirically. She moved to within inches of the men, went to a knee and slapped her palms together with enough force to echo the sound into the hills.

Both men nearly flew out of their blankets.

"Hey, guys. What's shakin'?" Lauren probed. "Doing a little hunting?"

The men yawned and studied their predicament, then began whispering to each other.

"We have a right to be here," one said. "This land is ours too, you know."

Lauren rose. "I never said anything about whose land it was."

Woo Tang tossed each man a set of zip cuffs. "Put these on, gentlemen. The two of you will be joining us."

"Joinin' you? Where're we going?"

"Some of us are going home," Lauren said. "You boys are going to visit the constable."

"Constable?"

She nodded, still sending her grin along.

"And what if we don't wanna see no constable?"

Lauren backed away and leveled the AK at them. "Then we shoot you. And you both die right here."

The men deliberated with one another, soon deciding that compliance was their best option, but not before starting a round of multiple consecutive questions.

Removing a hank of paracord from his rucksack, Woo Tang unwound it and tied a knot in the end. "We will make a leash and tow them in while keeping our distance." He secured their bonds while they complained and voiced grievances with intermixed profanity while Woo Tang did his best to ignore them, though they were trying his patience. "Lauren Russell, would you happen to have any duct tape in your pack?"

About an hour later, the group made their official entrance into the valley at the point where the wagon trail came to a terminus at Trout Run Road.

"Is this home?" Francis pondered aloud. "Looks deserted."

Jean looked around. "I tend to agree…where's all the houses?"

"Down there, mostly," Lauren said, pointing north. "My house is just around the corner on the right."

The group trudged over crunchy layers of compacted, iced-over snow in the direction Lauren indicated. The road, appearing to have been plowed by some means, meandered through the woods exactly as she remembered, though coated now in a wafting blanket of whiteness, which served to reflect a set of approaching headlights.

"This trip's been rough. I hope that's somebody one of y'all know," Francis said.

The vehicle was soon identified as one of the larger dual-axle M1083 FMTVs belonging to Dave's unit. "It is," Woo Tang said, then neared it as it slowed.

The driver, a young soldier sporting a freshly shaven face and a broad smile, rolled down his window. "Well, look who it is. Evening, Chief"—he tipped his hat—"ma'am. When did you get into town?"

"We deplaned only moments ago."

"You did, did you? We weren't expecting a visit, but it's good to see you. Bring some friends along?"

Woo Tang gestured to the pair not in restraints. "This is Francis and Jean; they are friends. The other two were discovered on the way, armed with scoped rifles. They have since been disarmed. We brought them along for posterity."

The driver conversed with the other soldier in the passenger seat. "I wonder if those two are the shooters."

"What shooters?" Lauren pondered.

The soldier explained the issue that had been plaguing the valley over a span of days. "What caliber rifles did they have? Something with reach?"

Francis slid the men's guns from his shoulder and presented them.

The driver shook his head. "From the looks of it, these might be our culprits. Richie's liable to be happy as hell knowing they're in custody. Funny how you just stumbled on them. Were they sleeping?"

Lauren grinned. "Actually, they were."

"Better lucky than good, I guess. We got a good place to put them. Chief, you want to hitch a ride with us to the FOL and get checked in?"

Woo Tang nodded. "That is acceptable. We will also need to find accommodations for Francis and Jean. They were not expecting to stay long; however, it appears they will be."

“Roger that,” said the driver. “Well, hop in the back and we’ll get going on it.”

Woo Tang turned away and squared off with Lauren. “Lauren Russell, this is where I leave you. That is, unless you object.”

Lauren shook her head. “No, I don’t object. I couldn’t’ve asked for a nobler bodyguard.” She hugged him and gave him a peck on the cheek. “I’m going straight home, so you’re officially off duty. Look me up tomorrow if you want.”

“Very well. Oh, and by the way…”

“Yeah?”

He grinned sheepishly. “I have heard said before, though I fail to recall the source, that…there is no place like home.”

Lauren sniggered. “Funny. Real funny.”

Jean and Francis stopped on their way to the truck to bid their thanks. “Lauren, just so you know, Francis and I…we know Claudio,” Jean said. “There’s a slight chance we might be able to fix this mess. No promises, but we can sure give it a try.”

Lauren smiled grimly. “That would be great, thank you, Jean. Whatever you can do.”

The trio boarded the transport, and the truck made a turnabout and headed north, soon disappearing into the darkness; and Lauren trudged the remaining distance between herself and home.

# CHAPTER 21

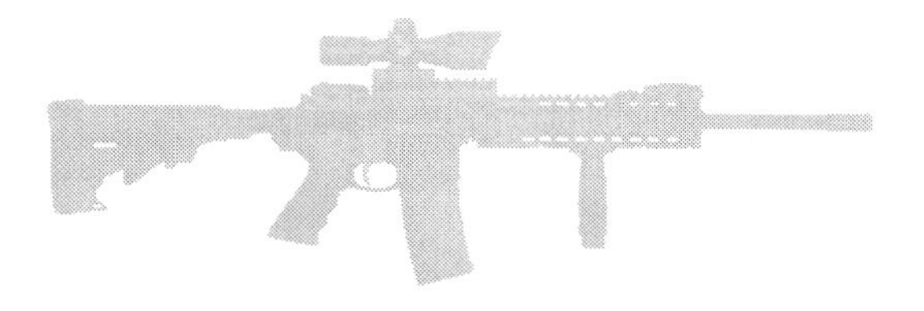

**Shenandoah Valley, Virginia**
**Wednesday, January 5th. Present day**

JADE LURCHED THE APC TO a stop at the bottom of White Rock Road, then looked either way along the snowy break denoting the thoroughfare beneath. "Which path shall we take, boys?" She pointed ahead to a pair of parallel, concave grooves in the snow. "Alan, we *could* follow those back to Butch's barely beaten woodland corridor if you want."

"I'll pass," Alan said, fiddling with a set of night-vision goggles. "I don't think my stomach could survive another jaunt like that one. Unless either of you oppose, I vote we stick to the roads."

Jade shrugged and took a left-hand turn. "We're running NVDs at night in a blacked-out, armored tin can now. So it's all the same to me. Ken?"

"All the same, sure. Bearing in mind the limitations of said NVDs," Ken remarked.

"So far, I haven't found any," Alan mused. "These things are incredible. I can see stars and planets in the sky I never knew were there."

Jade leered. "After you finish stargazing, unpack the FLIR thermals and acquaint yourself with one. They focus on infrared light and make heat signatures visible. What night vision can't distinguish, thermals can, and effectively, vice versa. Night vision can't see through smoke or fog, but thermals can. Using both, we should see anything coming our way."

"Anything coming our way not capable of defeating either technology," Ken added.

Alan grinned and shook his head. "There he goes again. I knew it wouldn't be long before Mr. Winter's pessimism made an appearance."

"Realism," Ken corrected, taking possession of the last remaining NVD from the case. "And asymmetric tactics are very real thing, Mr. Russell, sir."

"Asymmetric tactics?" Alan prompted.

"Would that be your way of expressing interest?"

"It's my way of expressing that I don't know what the term means, Ken."

"I assumed as much. You might want to write this down," Ken said. "It means fighting smarter as opposed to harder, especially when confronted by a larger, more technologically advanced aggressor, by pitting his strengths against him. If your enemy relies on his tanks, make him fight you in mountainous terrain where that shit is impractical. If he has air superiority, make him look for you under a thick canopy, in deep gullies or in caves, where he can't see dick and it's dangerous to fly, land and refuel.

"If his troops are wearing body armor or heavy loadouts, make them pursue you uphill so the extra weight tires them out. And if he's got the best surveillance tech, make use of countermeasures; provide false positives out the ass and make him doubt his own alert systems. If he's heavily reliant on tech, find a way to make it useless to him. Intelligence and skill always prevail over million-dollar toys. They only offer an advantage, they're not foolproof."

Alan looked to Jade for clarification and received a nod. He shrugged. "Maybe I *should've* written that down."

"I doubt I'll ever repeat it, so you missed your chance. Tangos in the sandbox used to light fires and burn random shit where they were moving about, and wore emergency mylar blankets between clothing layers to lessen and obscure their heat signatures. It wasn't perfect, but it did a damn good job of making their bipod frames look more like blobs through a thermal scope. Glass windows, depending on their age and makeup, are opaque to thermal. Vehicles are a lot harder to hide from a thermograph, but if there's a will, there's a way." Ken paused. "And high-intensity strobes, pyrotechnics and even this torch on my belt can overwhelm NVDs and shut them down."

"Temporarily," said Jade. "These aren't the gen-two hand-me-downs the Corps issued you."

"Excuse me, I was First Platoon, Lima Company, Third Battalion of the Second. We had the good stuff, thank you," Ken rebuked. "And temporarily is plenty of time to get a shot off." He propped his feet on the side row of seats and leaned back, intertwining his fingers. "So, how far away is this 'Woodstock'? That's a town, I take it?"

"Just over sixty miles or so," replied Alan.

"And that's where you think the fam is now?"

"I don't know for certain," Alan began. "But my wife mentioned they were headed to my parents' place in her letter. I don't have anything in my plans that correlates, but I did find a spot indicated on one of the topo maps between the Shenandoah River and the town limits. There's also a deed in the folder for a twenty-five-acre parcel and a five-bedroom cabin near a town called Perry in West Virginia."

"And *that* would be the family's top-secret, off-grid, bug-out estate," Ken proposed.

"It's conceivable. By road, it's about fifteen miles away from my parents' place. Three names are on the deed: mine, and a Samuel and Faith Gallo. Ownership is a dead-even three-way split."

"Gallo?" Jade queried and glanced over.

Alan nodded.

"So you were adopted, big deal," Ken jeered. "It's okay, man, happens to a lot of tykes. Nothing to be ashamed about."

"Or it *could* mean his mother is remarried, Kenneth," Jade advised.

Ken thought a moment. "Yeah, there is that."

"The property is paid for, and I was entrusted to hold the deed, for some reason. We must've had a joint venture at some point, like a real estate investment of some kind. Michelle said they went to their house first. So I reason we should too. If we find them there, great. If not, we'll rule it out and head west."

The Marauder's tires whirred over US Route 11's undermaintained asphalt roads just south of the nearly abandoned town of Strasburg, Virginia. The APC's width exceeded that of a single lane, and depending on the obstacles encountered, detours had been taken. Some were short and sweet, utilizing the median on either side, while others were something of the opposite and required a reroute along a paved or gravel road for several miles before returning to the original course.

Alan had requested to drive the remaining length of the trip to his parents' home, hoping that doing so would serve to jar his memory in some manner, though it hadn't, yet. Most of his concentration had been utilized to pilot the oversized APC around numerous obstructions.

While Ken offered sporadic wisecracks and occasional advice from the rear deck, Jade sat inaudibly in the passenger seat, scanning the environment surrounding them, switching between her NVDs and a thermal monocular. "Guys, I don't mean to put a damper on what's become a rather mundane drive for us, but I'm getting this…eerie feeling."

"You're late to the game." Alan glanced over. "Mine started twenty miles ago."

Ken stuck his head between the driver and passenger seats. "Did you spot something?"

"No…"

"Okay, spell it out, then. Or would you rather us draw conclusions based on your tone?" Ken quipped.

Jade exhaled. "Sorry. It's just that, after coming this far…it feels like we've set down in some strange universe, like in a world that's become one big ghost town. This whole way it's been nothing but miles of unused roads with tall grass growing between the cracks, sporadic abandoned cars and tree branches in the way. I haven't seen a single light on anywhere, not even a candle. Suffering an overall lack of maintenance is one thing, but no signs of life anywhere? That's another. It's as if life itself is just…gone."

Alan turned the wheel hard to negotiate around an abandoned tractor-trailer blocking half the road. "It's a worthy assessment. All things being equal though, we *have* been driving through a directly affected disaster zone a year and several months subsequent to an apocalyptic-magnitude event."

Ken chortled. "*Apocalyptic magnitude*…listen to the professor. Hang on, let me get comfortable for your incoming dissertation."

"Not a dissertation per se, Ken, but how else should we describe it?" Alan said. "I mean, it petrifies the hell out of me to even think about it, much less pontificate over it, knowing my family was around to see and experience what happened. Most people then were fully dependent on technology and lived lives that couldn't exist without it. Electricity made it all possible, and I'm betting next to no one gave any thought to what it might be like if a day came when electricity just…ceased to be."

Jade peered right as they passed an old farmhouse with its front door missing, its wooden siding shredded, and every window shattered. "I think we, meaning Walter and the three of us, missed the worst of it. We were riding out a tidal wave of initial reactions underground in the cavern. Millions of people everywhere else were trying to make sense of everything, then had to fight their way through it, and many of them learned they weren't able to.

"When I was a kid, I remember how much fun it was when thunderstorms knocked out the power for a couple of hours. We'd light candles and pretend we lived in the Old West. Sometimes snowstorms would move in, and the power would be off for days. It was always so cool and fun at first, but after a day or two, it got scary. And all we wanted was the lights to come back on so we could watch TV and cartoons again…and see in the dark. Anything to break the monotony and cancel our fears." Jade paused. "Did either of you ever watch *Little House on the Prairie*?"

"Nope," Ken said.

Alan shrugged. "I'd answer honestly if I could remember."

"It was about a family living on a small farm near Walnut Grove, Minnesota, in the late nineteen century," Jade went on. "It was based on a true story. I watched it all the time when I was little. I couldn't get over how simple life was then and how hard work provided so much satisfaction for them, even though most families struggled for everything then, even money. Electricity was in its infancy, and they didn't have anything to use for light other than oil lanterns and candles, and those things ran on a finite fuel source.

"Lamp oil had to be bought, and candles had to be made, and both had to be conserved; you couldn't burn them forever. Eventually, it just got dark and they dealt with it. Being afraid wasn't an option. If something went bump in the night, their alternatives for lighting up the fields outside were vastly limited. I imagine that was pretty damn scary for them. But I'm betting it had to've been far worse for the people living in these areas a day or so after the EMP struck. Apocalyptic-magnitude event, no doubt."

"While my memory remains of no help," Alan began, "for reasons I feel pointless to rehash or disclose to present company, my imagination remains operational. I have no doubt that the days and weeks directly following this event had to have been something of an atrocious nightmare for most. I've, very reluctantly, given a lot of thought to it. Every day waiting in Butch's hideaway provided me too much time to consider it." He sighed despondently. "There's no way of knowing for sure, but after what we've seen since leaving the bunker, it looks like this little section of the country was left decimated."

Jade reached for Alan's hand where it rested on the shifter. "Hey, chin up…they're okay. You did nothing short of a stellar job preparing your family for this."

Alan nodded a tinge. "Thank you. I pray that's the case."

"Guys? Not that this isn't enthralling, but can we change the subject?" Ken asked. "It's really bringing me down. I've been trying to concentrate on better places and better things, but now all I can think about is this hell on earth the two of you are portraying. It's depressing. And my hunger is making it worse. Did anyone pack any finger foods in this brute?"

Jade grinned. "Should be a whole duffel of snacks back there, Ken."

"Holding out on me as usual, I see." Ken acquired the bag and explored its contents. "Oh my. Oh my, my, my. I was expecting to see the same old crapola—SOS, Mainstay rations, maybe a package of stale M&Ms. But this thing's full of potato chips, pretzels, crackers, and cookies."

"Cookies?" Alan asked.

"Goddamn right, cookies."

"Any Oreos? I'm dying for an Oreo," said Alan.

Jade put a palm to her belly. "Mmm…Double Stuf. Seventy calories of blissful oral indulgence. If you find any, you'd better pass them forward."

"There might be," replied Ken. "But both of you can wait your turn."

At the point of reaching what was believed to be his parents' house, Alan applied the brake and slowed the Marauder to a stop. Even through the hue of night vision, it was apparent the property had become nothing short of unlivable. Doors were missing, windows and their frames were smashed to pieces, and portions of the home had collapsed, perhaps having done so long ago. There were faded orange notices affixed to the foundation and peculiar markings spray-painted on the brick exterior.

"Whoa. This can't be your parents' place," said Ken, biting into a pretzel. "I was expecting something a little more...I don't know, uptown. With some fancy raised gardens, hibiscus bushes and flower beds, maybe a birdbath or two, something. But definitely not this."

Alan reached for his map. "There's no other homes nearby, so this has to be the place." He sighed. "My family can't be in there, can they? It looks condemned...like the place caught fire."

"Or got struck by lightning," Ken commented.

"There's no way to be certain unless we go in." Jade gestured for Ken to pass her kit forward. "Nothing showing on thermal. I'll run this one solo. Ken, stay with Alan, but if you hear shots—"

"I'll be there faster than a speeding ticket."

"Back in a few."

"Be careful," Alan said.

Jade smirked at him then descended the ladder and made her entry into the asunder residence. After several minutes inside, she made her exit, and the look on her face was all that was needed to surmise what she'd found, or hadn't.

"There's nothing in there," she said, stowing her NVDs. "The whole place is ransacked, it looks like a bomb went off inside."

Alan rolled his lips together. "No signs of my family, then."

"No, nothing. It's a real mess. What walls remain have holes in them the size of someone's boot. There's trash everywhere, and paper notices all over the floor...martial law declarations and several tattered no-knock warrants. I would've brought one back, but like everything else, they're covered in black mold and rodent shit." Jade took a breath. "It all looks official too. Typed on Homeland Security letterhead or stock that bears the logo. Everything Valerie said about what we might find here looks to be accurate. We might've driven ourselves smack-dab into occupied territory."

Alan slumped and his expression filled with burden. "Jesus...if they were taken by the feds, what the hell do we do? How would I ever know for sure? How would we get them out?"

"Don't jump to conclusions," Jade said. "We don't know they were taken. And we still have one more place to check before we run out of places. Hang in there."

Alan nodded, but looked as though his nerves were about to get the best of him.

"Do you want me to drive?"

Feeling overcome by their most recent discovery, Alan graciously accepted her offer and traded seats, then worked to resume his role as navigator.

Jade drove on for several miles until returning once again to US Route 11. They continued southbound, passing through another quaint, seemingly uninhabited town before long. A burned-down convenience store came into view on the right, followed not long after by a car dealership on the left, situated amidst a lot of late-model vehicles, all inoperative and motionless. Then, a mile or so after, she tensed and unexpectedly pushed on the brakes. "Alan, trade places with Ken."

"What?"

"Do it," Jade urged. "Ken, I need you up here…get on the thermal."

Ken inserted himself between the seats. "What did you see? A glint?"

"It was only there for a split second. But it hit us."

"IR?" Ken set his bag of chips down and slid past Alan into the passenger seat. "It's too cold for lightning bugs. Think someone painted us?"

"Possibly."

Alan righted himself in the rear compartment. "Painted?"

"With a laser designator," Ken said. "Used to indicate targets for bombs, rockets, missiles, practically anything guided by laser." He brought the FLIR to his eye. "Most times though, it's simpler, like a rifle-mounted IR targeting module or a keychain gadget."

"And no one uses infrared unless they're able to see it," Jade said. "Anything?"

Ken provided a negative reply at first. "Fuck, scratch that. I have multiple inbound heat sigs, all white-hot."

"Engines?"

"And exhaust fumes. They're running as we are—all dark. Three contacts, my count. Parallel course, heading…damn near zero."

"Time to intercept?"

"Two minutes, tops. Turn this bitch around and haul ass, Jade."

"No time." Jade shifted into reverse and forced the accelerator to the floor, backing the Marauder off-road through scrub and a handful of trees. She veered into a gulley that led to a drainage ditch, parked and shut off the engine.

Several edgy minutes passed by in total silence while the trio waited with sweaty palms and pounding hearts. Their disquiet reached apogee as a parade of unmarked armored vehicles sped past at highway speeds.

Her eyes glued to what she could see of them, Jade let out a breath. "I don't think they spotted us."

Ken pressed the FLIR monocular to his window. "Nope. Not after that Evel Knievel shit you just pulled. Well done, fam."

"Agreed. Way to drive, Jade," Alan praised. "What the hell were those miscreations?"

"Category two Cougar MRAPs," replied Jade.

Alan leaned in and repeated the acronym.

"Stands for 'mine resistant, ambush protected'," Ken filled in. "They're overbuilt infantry mobility vehicles, kind of like this one. Highly resistant to land mines and improvised munitions. Saw them often in the Middle East; my unit had a few."

"Looks like the Pentagon allotted DHS their share," Jade said. "The paint looked black as night, and I didn't see any insignias or markings on them of any kind. They're definitely *not* military."

"No, they're not." Ken set his monocular down. "So this is what martial law looks like, huh? Cool."

Jade sighed. "All those nights of crashing in this thing might pay off for me, after all. Find a spot and get comfortable, boys. With all that enemy armor crawling around, we'll be camping here tonight."

# CHAPTER 22

**Trout Run Valley**
**Wednesday, January 5th. Late evening. Present day**

LAUREN LOOKED TO THE SKY and inhaled deeply, exhaling a sigh. After the roller coaster this trip had become, she was finally home, and it appeared likely her journey would end on a high note.

Then her heart sank when she saw John. He was standing by himself on the opposite side of the gate facing the road, his arms draped over the top rung, an anticipative yet morbid look on his face.

"Shit." Lauren rolled her lips between her teeth and sighed. She sauntered toward him hesitantly, indecision in every step.

John didn't look her way at first. "Did you just get home?"

She nodded, setting her rifle down followed by her pack, feeling the weight depart her shoulders. "A few minutes ago."

"How did you get here? Did you drive?" He sent glances along the road. "Or did someone drive you?"

Lauren considered his question. "We drove *most* of the way…and got stuck, more or less. We had to hump it in after that."

"We?" John's eyes found her.

"A friend was with me, and we brought a couple in with us."

"A friend, huh?"

"Yes, John. A friend."

"Something you're not deprived of," John remarked. "You and your *friends* didn't have to walk far, did you?"

"Actually, we did. Most of yesterday and all day today."

A brow raised, John beheld her with a disapproving stare. "Sorry to hear that, but you made it and that's good…real good." He paused, nearly sniggering. "New clothes, new gun…new friends. It's a new Lauren."

She leaned on the gate. "No, not quite. New clothes, a couple new guns, an *old* friend…but same Lauren."

John nodded, seeming unconvinced. "Who finally decided to come home. Surprising, I never thought I'd see the day."

"John, it's been an incredibly long trip. I just got here, I'm chilled to the bone, and my feet are killing me. I don't want to argue."

"Oh, neither do I. Arguing is the last thing I want to do," John said. "Truthfully, what I really want right now is to grab you, squeeze you, and never let you go…tell you how much I've missed you and kiss those warm lips of yours. I've been thinking about it for over a month now, how badly I've wanted to hold you and feel you do the same, like you used to, back before this new…persona of yours took over."

Lauren inched closer to him.

"But I can't go through with it," John finished.

"What? Why can't you?"

"Because I don't know who you are. I did there for a while, but not anymore. I thought I knew everything there was to know about you. I let myself fall head over heels in love with you a long time ago. But you've changed, and now I just…" He trailed off. "I can't do this anymore."

Lauren's sore legs felt weak enough to buckle under her weight. "John, please…I'm begging you. Don't do this right now, okay? Please? You don't know what I've had to go through since I've been gone—"

"Sure I do. Christian told me," John cut in. "He told everybody everything. I'm sorry, I know it must've been tough."

"It was more than tough."

John nodded. "It hasn't been much easier here."

"I know and I've heard. And I'm sorry, John."

"Me too."

The couple stared at one another for a long minute, neither saying a word.

Lauren sniffled. "Dammit, John. What is this? Why are you so mad at me? God—all I've wanted for days was to be home, to spend time with you, and with Mom and Grace, and be back where I belong. We've loved each other since we were kids, and you've never once acted like this with me. What's this about? Talk to me."

"It's not an act." John stared at the ground. "I know about Richie."

Lauren stammered. She looked mortified, her brows drawing in. "You know *what* about him? Who told you? Did he—"

"It just matters that I know. It doesn't matter who told me."

"Yes, it does. It *does* matter. Richie is a liar, John…you don't know him. He aggrandizes everything."

"Did the two of you go on a date?"

Lauren leaned away. She didn't answer.

"While we were together?"

She again faltered her reply.

John huffed. "Your lack of response says it all." He slammed his palms on the gate. "Jesus—I can't believe this. I can't believe *you*. How could you do that to us? And to me? And with *that* guy, of all people?"

"John, listen. Richie…he meant nothing to me. Nothing at all."

"That's not what *he* said."

"And for the record, I don't *care* what he said," Lauren growled. "Richie only cares about one person—Richie. He lies and embellishes everything. He practically deifies himself."

"Did you sleep with him?"

Lauren forced out a breath. "What?" She stood there in shock. "John, I—"

"Did you?"

Her lips pinched. "You're not being fair."

John folded his arms and gazed at her mercilessly. He wasn't about to back down.

Lauren shifted her hips. "No," she said, countering his gaze with an unblinking one of her own. "I would like to think you know me better than that. But the answer's no. I didn't."

John merely looked away as if Lauren's reply was good for him, though not good enough.

"John, I was sixteen, I'd just met him. You and I were arguing over something stupid. I don't even remember what it was about, but it put me in a weird place. You kept saying all the wrong things to me, and he was saying all the right ones. He came to the house and picked me up, and we drove around for a couple of hours, and *talked.* I started feeling guilty and I told him to take me home, and he did. That was it. He never touched me the whole time." She paused. "I didn't want anything to do with him after, and he chased me like a lost puppy for weeks."

"He talked about you like you were some kind of conquest," John said. "I mean, you, Lauren! My girl! *You* were his conquest! Hearing him say those things about you made me want to kill him."

"And now, so do I." Lauren softened her stance. "I've never been anyone's conquest, John, nor will I, ever. I'm sorry I upset you. I'm sorry I fucked up. Can you please just accept that? Accept my apology so we can go back to being who we were before I left?"

"I accept your apology," John said. "But I can't forgive you right now. You've been gone all this time and I haven't heard a single word from you, not one word. Grace said she talked to you on the radio just a few days ago, and no one even bothered to come get me. It's like I'm the furthest thing from your mind."

"That's not true. I've had a million things on my mind lately, but you've never once been the furthest thing from it."

"But I've never held the coveted number one spot, have I?"

Lauren looked away, gritting her teeth. "You know the answer to that. Only one person has *ever* held that spot."

"It's different for me though, always has been, because you're all I've ever wanted." John paused expansively. "I hated you being away for so long, but it's been good for me, in a way. It gave me time to put things into perspective. For far too long I've been putting too much emphasis on you and us, and not nearly enough on myself."

"John, I didn't intend to hurt anyone, explicitly you," Lauren said. "Ever since this whole thing started, something inside me has taken control, and I've been beating my brains out trying to figure out what the hell it is. That's why I didn't come home…and you can be mad at me as long as you want about it, but I promise I'll never leave again, John. I won't—I won't leave you again." A pause. "Please don't leave me."

"I hear you. I hear the words you're saying, but I don't feel anything. It's like they don't carry any weight." John slipped off his glove and reached into his pocket, then held his hand aloft, uncurling his fingers. In his palm lay a petite sterling silver ring on which a trivial, marquise-cut diamond was mounted. "This belonged to my grandmother. I asked

Dad if I could have it a few months back, and he gave it to me, no questions asked. Because he knew what I wanted to do with it." A pause. "And now you probably do too, don't you?"

A chill crept up Lauren's spine, causing her to shudder. She felt light-headed and weak in that instant, her knees nearly caving beneath her. "John…I don't know what to say. I-I…never—"

"Saw this coming?" he barged in. "Yeah, I figured that much…but, neither did I, really. Not until you left. I was going to surprise you for Christmas, but lo and behold, you weren't here." John faked a chuckle. "I mean seriously, what the hell was I thinking? Asking *you* to marry me—of *all* people. And now, of *all* times." He returned the ring to his pocket. "Anyway, whatever, not like it matters anymore. What's done is done. Too little, too late."

Lauren tensed as she set her jaw in a straight line. This behavior was out of character for John, but he wasn't being cold now, he was being cruel. "Why did you show me that?" she asked, her voice shaking as she spoke. "Because you wanted me to feel shittier than I already do over everything? Because if so…you win. You win, John. Congratulations!" She threw her arms to her sides at the point of boiling over. "You… fucking win! But…goddamn…what an *asshole* move on your part." She was trembling now. "I get it. You had this whole thing planned out, and you hate me for not being here to fulfil your dream for you. And now you throw it right in my face like it's nothing—like I'm nothing… like everything we ever had between us was nothing. To get me back… because fuck me and all my stupid bullshit.

"Does making me feel like shit make you feel better? Are you satisfied? I almost died…I almost never made it home…and spent a day in hell. I watched a man take a bullet to his head, only to be caged up in some nightmare rathole by a gang of lunatics. I spent the darkest night of my life there, scared to death…helpless…clueless as to what some vile piece of shit had planned for me the next day. And you don't know what it was like—you could *never* know what it was like. *All* I wanted in those moments was to be home…with my family, and with *you*." Lauren took a few breaths, attempting to calm herself. "I get it, okay? I understand…you're hurt. I know why you are and I get that you're mad. You have every right to be. But *damn* you, you have *no right* to treat me this way."

John looked away again, appearing somewhat ashamed. He didn't say anything for quite a while. "Maybe you're right," he whispered. "Then again, maybe this makes us even." He then turned away from her and started off.

"I can't change the things I've done…I can't help who I've become. I can't go back."

"I know. Neither can I."

"And that's it? Now we just walk away?"

"I have to, Lauren."

Her arms fell limp. "Even if I ask you not to?"

Her plea caused John to halt, but he failed to turn around. "I can't. I-I'm sorry."

Lauren shivered and watched helplessly as he strode away from her, his figure growing smaller as the distance between them grew, the physical swelling to compete with the emotional. She started to whimper and sob at the sight of it, never having imagined he'd do such a thing. Other than her father, John had been the only solid surface upon which Lauren had erected her trust. Now his back was to her. And it killed her knowing she was at fault.

Lauren sighed, removed her beanie and wiped her face with it, doing so without realizing a layer of freeze had diffused into the fabric, the frigid dampness mixing with her tears. She pushed the gate open as far as it would go over the snow, then tracked the driveway to the cabin.

A gust of cold wind blew past, freezing Lauren's tears to her cheeks, relieving her of the need to obscure them. She didn't want her mom or Grace to ask if something was wrong right off the bat, though she knew there wasn't any way to conceal her mood after this. For certain, it had been a trying set of days. She had been so eager to be home, had fought to get here on multiple levels, and now she *was* home, only to have her heart ripped to shreds upon arrival.

Reaching for the cabin's front door handle, Lauren took in a deep breath, exhaling it slowly. "Here goes."

Grace leapt from the couch at the sight of her sister entering. She screeched and ran to her. "Holy shitballs! I knew it was you! I knew you'd come home!" She wrapped her arms around Lauren, ignoring fully the frozen precipitation clinging to her sister's outerwear. "Jesus Christ on a polar bear, you're cold."

Lauren absorbed her sister's squeezes. "Well, it's moderately cold outside, Grace."

"Duh." Grace looked her over. "You have icicles in your eyelashes. And your cheeks are frozen. Were you crying?"

"No, it's the cold. Makes my eyes water sometimes." Lauren efforted a smile. "I missed you."

Grace tilted her head and put a hand over her heart. "And I missed you more."

Backing away, Lauren slid her fingers lightly across Grace's stomach. "You're starting to show already."

"Damn! You really need to warm those hands before doing that," Grace said with a shiver. "Not bad for my first baby bump, huh? I'm in my twelfth week now. Little boo is about the size of a lime, but the brat feels more like a softball."

"It looks good on you," Lauren said, beaming, her expression going slack. "How've you been feeling?"

"Like soft-boiled crap. But Mrs. Dr. Vincent says being pregnant is the happiest reason to feel crappy."

"That's no fun."

"And in all fairness, it hasn't been, love. I have literally been throwing up everything. My second trimester starts a few days from now, and I'm told *that* bullshit should go away, but confidence is in short supply."

"It will, Grace. Have faith." Michelle strolled in after hearing the commotion.

"Easy for you to say," Grace quipped.

Michelle looked Lauren up and down with stern, distressed eyes. "Well, look who's here. My daughter, the nomad, in the flesh." She moved in, reached for her and pulled her close. "God—it is so good to see you, toots. I'm glad you're home, but just so you know, you're grounded. You exceeded your curfew by a month."

Lauren smiled execrably. "I know, and I'm sorry. I'll try not to let it happen again."

"And I suppose I'll *try* to forgive you, this time. Ugh, you look like you've been outside for days," Michelle lamented. "Come over here and warm up."

Lauren strolled to the hearth with her mother, stripped off her jacket, and held her hands over the Timberline.

Michelle caressed her daughter's temples and cheeks and combed through the tousles of her hair with her fingers. "You look so different."

"I haven't been gone *that* long, Mom."

"Maybe not, but it's been long enough. And I hope you plan on telling us what you've been up to and what took you so long to come back."

"I'll tell you everything…but not now. I don't have the energy for it."

Michelle rubbed Lauren's chin. "You do look like you could use a little rest."

"A little?" Grace said, plopping down on the couch. "From here it looks like she could sleep for a month."

"Thanks a lot, sister."

"What? Just shooting you straight, not saying you look *bad*, just tired." Grace's look turned…expectant. "Seen anyone since whatever boat you flew in on brought you ashore? Other than us, I mean?"

Lauren spoke hesitantly. "No one worth mentioning…besides John."

Michelle pulled her lips together.

"Oooh," said Grace, her eyes widening. "Yeah, shit. I probably should've tried to warn you about that."

"It's okay, it's not your fault. Nothing I can do about it now."

Michelle rubbed Lauren's shoulders. "Why don't you go to your room and take a load off…get changed and cleaned up. Are you hungry? I can make you something."

"No, not really. Just tired. Very, very tired."

Michelle kissed her head. "Tired it is. I hereby order you to bed. We'll talk more tomorrow. I missed you, toots. And I'm super glad you're home."

"Me too," Lauren said, though not exactly feeling it.

Lauren went to her room and closed the door behind her, dropping her things to the floor. She walked to her window and took a seat on her bed, remembering in that moment how many times she had done that very thing. She was home after longing for it for so long, but home had become a phantom of itself.

Lauren stripped off the clothes she'd been wearing for days and got into the most comfortable sleepwear she could locate, happy to find that Michelle had kept up with her laundry in her absence. She pulled the covers from her bed, crawled in and nestled her head in her pillow.

It felt good to be home, felt even better to be horizontal in her own bed for the first time in weeks. But the sensation of being here was far from what she'd been expecting. And now, all she wanted was to find a dark hole where no one could ever find her, crawl into it and disappear from sight.

She fell asleep in minutes, too exhausted to hold open her eyelids.

# CHAPTER 23

**Woodstock, Virginia**
**Thursday, January 6th. Present day**

JADE EXITED THE MARAUDER ARMORED personnel carrier approximately one hour before sunup. Doing her best not to disturb a snoozing Alan and Ken, she bundled up and set off to reconnoiter the neighboring area due south. Recalling what Valerie had told her not long after arriving at Camp Hill and following last evening's close encounter, Jade had developed a hunch, and she needed to either substantiate it or disprove it before moving forward with the day's plans.

She knew that Alan's primary concern, and perchance his only one, was his family's welfare, leaving his own of little consequence to him. His desire to find his loved ones and see this through, now, was pulling on him harder than it ever had. Yesterday's setbacks were certain to make it worse. Their next stop would lead them roughly fifteen miles west of Woodstock, a pastoral town to their immediate south. And it was those coordinates in specific that had Jade on alert.

Stumbling upon unfriendly or hostile forces along the way had been expected and was in character with this voyage. Valerie had conveyed all the omens and then some, and Butch had followed her up by reinforcing them in his own offbeat way, while neglecting to illustrate anything candidly.

What they had seen while travelling here, or rather, what they *hadn't* seen, hadn't merely caught Jade by surprise, it was inconceivable to her. No signs of life—not one—anywhere along the way had been detected. And something about that was odd, to the point of defying probability.

Jade didn't know much in the way of apocalyptic-event aftermaths, hypothetical or otherwise, but from what little she knew of them, she presumed there had to have been *some* survivors out there somewhere. But where the hell were they?

What they'd witnessed weren't the results of a nuclear holocaust, global bioterrorism, or a war versus a hostile artificial intelligence that had wiped out human existence. A pandemic hadn't occurred here, a supervolcano hadn't erupted, and there weren't any signs of environmental degradation bringing about mass famine. This was supposed to be the product, the aftereffects of a life-altering event triggered by an electromagnetic pulse. But to Jade, it felt distinctive… as if those aftermaths had been supplemented or magnified somehow by something far, far worse.

So she investigated, cognizant that her own footprints in the snow would put her at risk of being detected. She made use of the tree lines on either side of US Route 11 for concealment and jogged south, leaving as little evidence of her foot travel as conceivable along the way.

Just beyond the intersection marking the town limits, she discovered that the entire width of the road had been converted into a blockade. It was lined now with bollards and rows of reinforced star barriers surrounding a crash-rated beam checkpoint barricade. A squad of black-garbed agents in body armor, sporting suppressed carbines and submachine guns, stood near a handful of parked SUVs with tinted windows, some seated inside while running the engines to keep warm.

Jade concealed her face with a shemagh and spent a long moment analyzing the area, taking note of everything, every detail in her field of view, while maintaining awareness to keep out of sight. At the point she'd seen enough, she swiveled and made a rapid, stealthy exodus back to the Marauder.

She pulled her door closed, retook her seat and unzipped her jacket, only to find herself on the receiving end of a startling tongue-lashing.

"Where the *hell* have you been?" Alan roared, the objection in his tone rousing Ken.

Jade snapped her head his way, looking aghast while she removed her gloves. "Jesus! Really? Who do you think you are? My daddy? Calm the hell down."

"Don't tell me to calm the hell down! Where were you?"

Jade was stunned. Alan had never once used this tone with her. "I left for a little while…and went for a walk to gather some intel."

"Where did you go? Intel on what?"

"Dude, seriously." Ken yawned. "You don't have to yell at her."

"Shut up, Ken!"

"Oookay."

Jade's eyes went alight. "Alan, that's enough! There's no sense in this! Why are you so upset?"

"Why? Because I—wake up and you…aren't where I saw you last! And after last night? After what we saw? I got worried! Really worried, so excuse me! Excuse the hell out of me for being concerned about you." Alan exhaled a deep sigh and unfolded onto his seatback.

Jade sighed and unraveled her shemagh. "Hey, listen to me, I'm worried too. About *all* of us. That's why I went. I had to know what we're dealing with here."

"Fine. And would you care to enlighten the rest of us?"

"We're in this thing together, are we not? The circumstances affect all of us equally. And yes, I plan to, but only if you calm down…subdue your tone with me. And apologize to Ken for biting his head off."

Alan folded his arms and took a few breaths. "Sorry, Ken."

Ken held up his hands. "Hey, no problem, fam. Just don't stroke out on us."

Jade waited a long moment. "Okay, listen up, both of you. Everything we witnessed yesterday on the way here has been bugging me. Our close call with the Cougars only solidified it. I didn't sleep a wink all night. We drove for hours yesterday and didn't see a single soul, and the more I thought about it, the more it didn't make any sense. All those people didn't just disappear or vaporize into thin air. I realize a considerable number died off, that's par for the course after a disaster like this. But a total absence of survivors after all those miles? No way. Something or someone else is to blame. And I reason they were taken somewhere."

Ken tilted his head. "Taken? You mean—"

"I mean as in rounded up," Jade snapped, "displaced by force and relocated. To where is anyone's guess."

Alan winced, placing a hand to his chest. "This intuition of yours isn't helping to soothe my anxiety, Jade. Not in the least."

"I know it isn't, and I'm sorry. But we needed to know. From what I've seen, everything Valerie told us was spot-on. This area *is* occupied, and the town looks like it's been sequestered."

"Who by?" Ken asked, appearing engaged.

"DHS and elements of FEMA, FPS, ICE, any federal agency or department, plausibly. Homeland could've absorbed any entity of their choosing if granted autonomy under executive order. The highway into town is barricaded at the city limits." She then filled in the particulars.

"Good grief, Jade. You're talking FOB-style security," Ken said.

Jade nodded. "I know. I've seen secured positions before, but nothing quite like what they have. For a civilian operation, it's vastly militarized, mirroring that of foreign consular defenses…in a third world."

"Seems as though *our world* has become just that," Alan said, his tone now mollified. "It's good that we know this, and I appreciate the gamble you made to find out. I'm sorry…for going for your jugular, Jade. It wasn't right."

"It's okay. I know there's a lot eating at you."

"That still doesn't make it right," Alan said, hanging his head. He sighed. "We're really in deep now, aren't we? And what you found out changes a few things. What's our best play from here?"

Jade bit her lip. "I don't think it matters anymore. Any move we make bears serious risks from here on out, the primary one being confrontation. We know they can see us at night just as plain as day, so timing is no longer relevant. It doesn't matter when we go, and I doubt it matters what direction we choose."

Ken chortled. "Sounds to me like you're expecting a run-in with them regardless of what we decide."

Jade nodded her head hesitantly. "Pray for the best, plan for the worst, never take anything too lightly," she said. "That credo has never served me wrong. The odds of finding ourselves in a chance meeting with an opposing force are generous now. We could take any one of twenty routes out of here and any of them could lead to an ambush or be blocked off by an armed barricade like the one I just saw."

"We'll need to think up a way to deal with that," Alan said.

Jade smiled grimly. "I think I already have. Granted, it's unusual as hell and bears a share of risks. And to pull it off, I need you both to trust me, and all three of us must be in agreement."

"Here we go," Ken said, leering at Alan. "Jade's got something up her sleeve at all times."

"Not this time. But it does involve something I have in my bag." Jade crawled into the rear compartment with Alan and acquired her backpack, pulling from it a roll-top dry bag. She dug inside and extracted her old uniform, the one issued to her by the Department of State.

Ken smirked. "Oh, I get it. If we stumble on them, you're just going to stroll up to them wearing that, with a big naïve smile, and holler 'same team, same team', and hope they go for it, right?"

Jade located Ken's pack, unzipped it and dug inside. "No, *we* both are," she said, tossing his uniform bundle to him.

"Oh." He unrolled the items and felt through the wrinkles.

"Travelling at night is no longer viable, and all the same, neither is waiting here. I think being proactive and going dynamic is our best option. In fact, my impulse is heading directly south from here right into town, and right to them."

Ken and Alan both responded with, "*What?*"

Alan looked shocked. "No way you're genuinely considering that an option."

"No shit. What have you been drinking?" Ken prodded. "And why aren't you sharing?"

"Guys, please. I know it's a lot to swallow, but let me quarterback this," Jade pled. "At first contact, we'll anticipate hostility and aggression. Because it *will* happen. We follow their instructions to the letter, exit slowly and smile a lot, go with business as usual. Offer righteous answers to whatever questions they pose and do whatever we can to achieve a common ground, all while presenting these." She held aloft a clear LOKSAK, a waterproof, sealable, plastic storage bag, within which were three folding leather identification wallets, each bearing the Seal of the US Diplomatic Security Service.

"You're shitting me. Are those our credentials?" pondered Ken. "I thought we lost them."

"No, not lost. I stashed them on the towpath about a half a mile shy of Camp Hill. We were in a sticky situation and needed to buy some time. I didn't know who we'd run into or how they'd react to bumping into three federal agents right off the bat."

Ken peered into Jade's pack. "I don't suppose you have our uniform patches hidden in there."

"Unfortunately, no. But valid State Department credentials should carry enough influence to cover that."

Ken took the bag and found his ID, then handed Jade hers. "Alan, if you shaved your head real quick and dyed your facial hair a few shades, you might pass for Walt."

Alan smirked. "Though I *would* still lack the uniform."

"Just tell them it's laundry day."

"I think we can forgo that," said Jade. "Alan will be staying here, leaving you and me to deal with this. Our IDs haven't expired and should serve as proof that we are very much retained by DOS. If we roll up to that checkpoint waving federal creds and hand them a believable story, our unexpected arrival and the exotic armor we're driving should be nonissues. Like Ken said, more or less, we're on the same team, there's no reason not to let us pass. Especially if we refuse to take no for an answer."

Alan deliberated over this. "What if they contact State for verification and learn the contrary? It's been over a year; both of you could be excommunicated by now."

"*If* the cavern is still in operation, which is doubtful, I presume that *would* be the case," Jade said. "Most of our servers failed, and we lost the majority of our comms capabilities at zero hour, most of which hinged on the now fundamentally extinct internet."

Alan shifted in his seat. "What about satellites?"

Jade's brows drew together. "I recall what Butch said, too. And I believe him, most of our birds are up there, still in orbit and operational. But State's utilization of satcom was rare, used intermittently at best, mostly for personal calls, inter-embassy videoconferences and low-bandwidth stuff. Add to that they were complicated as hell; setting them up required bringing in third-party contractor geeks with know-how."

"Like Butch?" Ken joked.

"And you're certain by choosing differently and getting caught in the open, either by a roadblock or patrol, the ramifications would be worse, correct?" Alan asked.

Jade nodded. "Way worse, especially if we're spotted and they moved in to pursue. Even our calmest attempts at reasoning could be misheard or completely ignored with the other side jacked up on adrenaline. And you can bet a lot of automatic rifles will be pointed our way, mostly by inexperienced shooters with hard-ons, shaky trigger fingers, and dilated pupils. Both options are risky, but the direct approach affords us an opportunity to achieve and maintain armistice long enough to disappear from their radar."

"Both options afford a grand opportunity to achieve death, if you ask me," Ken said snidely, scratching his head. "Okay, say we go with running the gamut and drive this hunk of iron right down their craw. We talk sense into them, get them to lower their guns, but they start probing us for info. What story are we going with?"

Jade closed her eyes momentarily. "I've been giving that some thought too. Why would two DSS agents be traveling in the middle of nowhere this late in the game, unannounced, in a foreign-built APC, unaided by security and support elements?" She paused. "On the way back this morning, it hit me. Sugar Grove Station. And the Greenbrier."

Alan's eyes perked up.

Jade went on without further ado. "Sugar Grove is an NSA communication site in West Virginia, not far from where we're headed. It was built to intercept international comms entering the eastern US. The site at one time also contained NAVIOCOM, the Naval Information Operations Command, but the base was shut down and repurposed in 2015, supposedly."

"Repurposed for what?" Ken asked.

"The unclassified narrative portrayed that a privately owned healthcare facility for veterans was taking it over," Jade explained. "The…not-so-unclassified one involved the construction of a one-hundred-twenty-two-acre underground, self-sustaining, hardened bunker complex for CoG, but neither of you heard that from me. Greenbrier Resort made a covert agreement with the government back in the fifties to serve as the same, primarily for senators and congressmen. The program was called Project Greek Island, and it was supposedly mothballed after becoming public knowledge during the Cold War. But the program, the plan, the bunker, provisions, everything…still exists under a new guise."

Ken's face contorted. "Jade, you're talking continuity of government, and no one outside the highest echelons and clearances knows where cabinet members or the joint chiefs actually went. They could've gotten shipped anywhere—to another country or an island, for all we know."

"Exactly, Ken. You took the words right out of my mouth," Jade said. "*For all we know.* My clearance had so many attached designations that my last supervisor used to call it NSC, as in 'no such classification'. I shook his hand dozens of times, briefed him and even got invited to dinner at his estate, but did I know where SecState would go in the event of an officially declared national crisis? Hell no. You're right, he could be anywhere, but the fact remains whoever hears our story is certain to be just as much in the dark as we are. The narrative will be bullshit, and we'll be tasked with conveying the opposite—compellingly."

"And you can do that?" Alan asked.

Jade sent a cautious grin. "Look a man in the eyes and tell a lie to his face?" She nodded. "Yeah, I've done it a time or two before. But, to be clear, never once to either of you." She paused. "So chat me up. I need opinions, so let's hear them."

Alan rubbed his forehead. "Your plan is dicey. There's holes in it, it feels wrong, and I for one don't like it. But I'm far from being the expert here, and miles away from being unbiased. I don't want my frame of mind to pollute what could be a sensible strategic move." He sighed with closed eyes. "Fuck it. I say we go for it."

Jade turned to Ken.

"'We quell the storm, and ride the thunder'," Ken said, quoting his Marine Corps infantry battalion's motto. "Oorah! I'm down for whatever. Let the chips fall where they may."

"And you both understand the risks?"

"I do," Alan said.

"Ken?"

"Are we there yet?" he replied, using a Texan drawl not his own, spawning outlandish looks from his companions. "Sorry. Just...miss my boy that's all." He shrugged, holding Walter's ID wallet between his fingers.

Jade blushed a little. "We miss him, too."

Alan gestured agreeance with a sidelong glance.

"Okay, since it's unanimous, let's get ready to move. And that means two of us need to modify our apparel." Jade redeployed to the opposite side of the rear compartment, removed her boots and started to undress, only to stop mid-stride. "Um, look. I realize this is far from being a co-ed locker room, but seriously, *no* peeking. Either of you."

Alan turned away and shielded his eyes, using his hand as a blinder.

Ken unbuckled his belt. "No promises," he joked, sliding his pants to his ankles. "Damn, this is awkward."

# CHAPTER 24

WITH A QUICKENED PULSE, JADE released the accelerator and allowed the twelve-ton APC to sluggishly idle itself toward the checkpoint. As it crept, a mass of armed guards surged outward on each flank and circled the Marauder, their rifles fitted to their shoulders. They bawled furious orders to stop immediately or they would open fire, for all passengers to disembark with hands raised, and that failing to comply would be met with lethal force.

Jade barely rotated her neck to share a look with Ken, making certain he was in sync with her. She guided the shifter to park and gave Alan a parting notice. "No matter what happens, stay inside and out of sight."

The pair exited in unison, secured their doors on their way out, then hopped down and lifted their arms to the sky, federal credentials folded open and in plain sight.

The guards rallied around them, shoved and manhandled them roughly at first, and with their faces pressed against the APC's hull, they were patted down invasively for weapons. Some of the guards began noticing a familiarity with the subjects' uniforms, and as they whispered amongst themselves, uncertainty filtered through the collective.

Jade strained to speak over the ruckus. "Take it easy, guys! Hear us out, please! We are federal agents! Both of us, federal agents!"

Jade and Ken remained passive, and several unfriendly grimaces gave way to warmer looks, even more so at finding neither had been armed. Two guards ripped the IDs from their hands and escorted them at gunpoint to the far side of the barricade, leaving a dozen or more to picket and inspect the APC.

A man seated in the SUV nearest the gate withdrew, placed a bump helmet bearing a subdued sergeant's chevron on his head, and approached with caution. As he studied the identification handed to him, his expression grew quizzical. "Diplomatic Security Service? Agent Kenneth Winters"—he eyeballed Ken—"and Special Agent Constance Hensley." He studied Jade from her heels to her split ends. "I wasn't aware we were expecting a visit from the State Department." He motioned to his men to lower their weapons. "What brings the two of you here? That's an interesting set of wheels, by the way."

Jade looked for consent before lowering her hands. "Glad you like it; it's a loaner from our motor pool." She shifted to a fleeting smile. "Being honest, we didn't expect to stumble upon you here, or anyone, really. We thought we'd be touring through the town of Woodstock about now, but instead, here we are; and here you are." She indicated their backdrop with her hands. "Pardon my abysmal knowledge gap, but where are we? What is this, exactly?"

"This?" the sergeant responded, clearing his throat. "Well, *this* happens to be the Plantation, ma'am."

"I'm sorry, did you say *the Plantation*?"

He nodded, still focused on the IDs he'd been given.

Jade broadened her smile and strove not to sound condescending. "Sir, you are aware of what 'knowledge gap' means, don't you?"

After a second, the guard peeked up from Jade's credentials. "Forgive me," he said, appearing sheepish. "It's early and I'm just a tad blindsided by this. It's seldom we have this type of encounter, you see." He paused. "At current, you're located at the northern gateway for DHS Shenandoah Outpost, acting HQ for FEMA region three. The Plantation…is just what we call it."

"Oh, I see now," said Jade, giggling. "Like a code name."

"Yes. That's correct."

"Well, as you can probably tell by looking at us, my colleague and I are a little frazzled too. It's been an inordinately long trip for us already. And what we saw along the way…it's almost beyond words to describe."

"How long have you been on the road?"

"The better part of a day and a half, with a few stops in between," Ken said. "We left Washington two days ago."

"Washington?" The guard's brows knitted. "Last thing I heard, the entire district is a lost cause. As in completely done for, nothing there."

"We can attest to that," Jade said flatly. "You heard correctly, the place is a war zone. There's nothing there, above ground anyway."

"I'm sorry?"

She waved a hand at him. "Don't be, I'll explain. Our division is situated in a subterranean complex three blocks from what used to be the White House. We call it 'the cavern'. That's our facility's code name; maybe you've heard of it."

"I might have," the sergeant said. "And what was your division tasked with?"

"Sorry, I can't answer that, Sergeant. It's classified," Jade deadpanned.

"Oh?"

She held back her reply for several long seconds. "Only teasing you. Agent Winters and I are assigned to the Threat Intelligence and Analysis division. We investigate and respond to security threats directly affecting US embassies and SecState."

The sergeant grinned, then nodded. "That's quite a responsibility. By the way, you almost had me there."

"It's freezing out here, figured the humor might warm us up," she went on. "We received our shelter-in-place orders right after everything went haywire. When the federal continuity directive was implemented, every one of us knew we were there for the duration. Most of our internal systems remained operational, thank God. There was plenty to eat and drink, and the air conditioners worked most of the time. And we had a library of books and DVDs to help pass the time." A pause. "We received word a few days ago that SecState had gone off-grid, and were assigned to fish him out and secure him. When we tried to leave, we found the facility's access control systems were down, and that's when the whole nightmare started for us."

"We lost two members of our detachment just getting out of there," Ken said, his tone becoming despondent. "We had to exfil via the city sewer drains. One of our men…he drowned. The other lost his footing and slipped down a chute. We…never saw him again."

The sergeant sent a vacant look. "I'm sorry to hear that. My condolences."

"Thank you," said Ken. "It's been hell getting this far. I know we don't exactly look presentable, but we cleaned up as best we could. Had to dump all our patches and a lot of our gear. It hasn't been easy, but it's really good to finally see some friendly faces."

The sergeant nodded his head and sent a grin along, then folded both ID wallets closed, handing them back to Jade and Ken. "Look, as far as I'm concerned, everything on your end looks legit. I don't mean to hold you up any more than we already have, but I can't let you pass through without calling it in. If you wouldn't mind waiting here for just a few more minutes..."

Jade beamed at him. "By all means. Lord knows, we all answer to someone. We'll wait however long it takes."

He smiled back at her and went to his SUV, then closed the door to a crack and spent the next few minutes talking into a radio handset. When he returned, his expression hadn't deviated, and it appeared as though they'd pulled it off. "I couldn't raise anyone at HQ," he said. "Guess their alarm clocks haven't gone off yet. So, for now, I'm clearing you on my authority. Not sure which way you'll be heading, but you'll need to pass through another checkpoint on your way out." He paused. "I'm curious, what's your destination? I'm not aware of any government facilities or military bases nearby; you're vastly limited for options to refuel."

Jade kept up with the act. "Our orders have us going all the way to the Greenbrier, but we have a planned stop at Sugar Grove for just that purpose, assuming our *No Such Agency* colleagues cooperate...as well as DHS has."

The guard chortled. "Greenbriar? That's a way's off, isn't it? I figured they would've sent POTUS and his cabinet someplace closer. But I bet both of you know differently, don't you?"

Jade cocked her head to the side. "Sergeant...now, you know I *really* can't answer that."

"I assumed so. I apologize for putting you on the spot." He pointed south, then west. "The south checkpoint identical to this one is roughly two miles from here; just go straight and you'll find it. The other one is west just beyond the overpass on forty-two. I'll radio ahead now and let them know you're coming. Shouldn't be any problem. Good luck to you."

"Thank you, Sergeant," Jade said. "Oh, one more thing. Something just dawned on me; I'll be talking it over with Agent Winters once we get going. Neither of us really wants to head back to the sewer, and opportunities these days aren't as abundant as they used to be. After we finish what we set off for, might there be a place for us here?"

"I can look into it. I know a few people," he said. "Swing back by, and ask whoever you run into for Sergeant Adams. That's me. And we'll take it from there." He then motioned for the barricade to be opened.

Jade and Ken thanked him, waved and returned to their seats inside the Marauder, each expelling an exhaustive breath.

"Damn. You were totally in your element, Jade. I think I shit my pants about a dozen times," said Ken.

"I was right there with you, fam. Trust me."

Jade pulled the Marauder through the checkpoint, tossing a friendly hand up as she passed, unaware if anyone could see it. They continued through town, passing multiple defunct stores and abandoned residences, empty streets, overgrown trees and a mile of sidewalks yet to be shoveled.

Passing by a brick-framed billboard that read 'Massanutten Military Academy' on the right, another sign had been sledgehammered into the ground next to it, displaying the DHS Seal and title 'DHS Shenandoah Outpost'. A parking lot of black SUVs, repainted school buses and armored vehicles lay between and behind every building on the campus.

Alan pointed ahead to a set of nonworking traffic lights. "Take a right here. That'll bring us west over the interstate."

Jade proceeded around the turn, and after ascending a small hill and crossing a railroad track, the trio looked upon a ghastly sight to their left. Two steel security fences topped in rows of razor barbed wire, yards apart from each other, rose skyward above the windshield's visible horizon. The fence line ran parallel to the road for a good distance.

"Um, I'm going to assume *that* hasn't always been there," Jade mused.

"You could ask me, but I'd tell you you're asking the wrong person," said Alan. "What in God's name is that?"

"Come on, what else could it be?" Ken quipped. "We just got done talking about it. Jade said she thought all the people we didn't see were relocated. And that's a big damn trellis, like a bad dream come true. Probably marks the boundary of the prison camp they took them to."

Alan bit his lip. "I'm trying to imagine what type of person would dredge up such a thing. I mean, what mentality requires having such a draconian level of domination and control over a populace? Words like *demented* come to mind. *Twisted. Evil.*"

"I don't think a single word in the English language can define what I'm seeing…or feeling right now," Jade said as they passed the corner rampart of the fencing.

The overpass and the exit checkpoint were now coming into view. Jade slowed the Marauder to a snail's pace and crept closer, noticing the guards had indeed been anticipating their arrival. The barricade gate was already in the process of being raised, and she was receiving hand signals to pull on through. The trio passed the gate without incident and trekked westbound on a well-traveled two-lane road for several miles. Their nerves were collectively shot, and they'd only begun to relax, when Alan felt compelled to chance a look behind them.

"Jade, we have contacts on our six."

"Contacts on our six?" Ken mocked. "Since when did you start talking grunt?"

"Alan, tell me exactly what you see."

"I see a column of black vehicles," he said. "A few SUVs in front and some of those MRAP things we saw last night. I can't count how many there are, but it's more than one."

Ken looked to Jade. "What do you think they want?"

She rolled her weary eyes. "Who knows."

"Any particular way you want to handle *this* one?"

Jade's expression turned to stone. She wasn't about to allow her plan to fall apart. "The same way I would any other time my orders were being interfered with. Ferociously."

"Ooh, sounds exciting." Ken grinned like a schoolboy in a winning game of dodgeball. "Let's go legit, then."

"Sidearms only. And don't unholster unless I do."

Ken acquired his Sig and handed Jade her Glock. "Yes, ma'am."

"And don't shoot anyone."

"Okay, now you're taking all the fun out of it."

"Alan, same plan as before," Jade stated. "Nothing changes. You stay in the APC. Watch for my signals." She whipped the wheel left and went off-road through a metal gate leading into a snowy field of folded-over tall grass. She then floored the Marauder for a distance, made a hard right and circled left, skating the rear tires around so they were now facing the oncoming DHS convoy.

At seeing this, the convoy lined up side by side in a skirmish line. Agents soon began pouring out of vehicles, all toting automatic rifles.

Jade studied the lineup. "Alan, listen up. Normally, being told to stay inside one of these things during a battle is horrible advice. They're magnets for antitank weapons, grenades and the like, especially when idle. I don't see anything beyond thirty caliber out there, and this armor can defeat those all day. So, no matter what happens, you stay here and watch for my signals. Hopefully, this will all be over soon."

"And if it's not?" Alan pondered.

With parted lips, Jade hung her head. "Then we improvise."

"Try asymmetric tactics first," Ken offered. "And if none come to mind, go rabid apeshit on them. Drive this twelve-ton beast straight at them and run over any fucker dumb enough to stand in the open. Disable as many of their vehicles as you can without FUBARing this one. Then make a break for it—but pick us up first *before* you leave."

Jade took several rapid breaths to appear more flustered than she already was and made her exit once again in a single jump, doing so with her hands flailing angrily. "Excuse me! But precisely what is this shit? You are all interfering with official State Department business!"

A dozen kitted-up agents exited vehicles and converged on them, their rifles leveled and pulled tightly to their shoulders.

Jade drew her Glock and presented it ahead of a savage glare.

Ken followed suit and drew down on them. "Gentlemen! Several of you are coming really fucking close to becoming really fucking dead for really stupid reasons!"

With all weapons drawn and pointed at each other, both sides slowed and stalemated.

"Shut your mouth and drop your weapon!" an agent shouted.

"Come on, guys…there's no sense in any of this!" Jade exclaimed. "We were given clearance to pass!"

"That's correct," a deep voice thundered amidst the row of agents. "You *were*." A man wearing a button-up shirt, a tie and a wool sweater beneath his body armor emerged from the group. "Now, drop those weapons before I give the order for my men to shoot you both down."

Jade's jaw clenched. "Give the order, because we will do no such thing. You and your men are out of line! This is deliberate interference with official business! Completely outrageous!"

"Ma'am, we're all professionals here, as you can see. This doesn't have to end badly. My men and I are under orders too. We were told to follow you. Some added clarification is needed, that's all. Provide it, and I'm confident we can all go about our day."

"What clarification could you possibly require? We have already provided all there is!"

The lead agent didn't answer. He sighed, appearing frustrated and far too affable to give the order to open fire on a woman. "Tell you what, how about if we—"

"Sir!" an agent half-seated in an SUV called.

"What…"

"HQ is on the line, requesting to speak to you."

"I'm a little busy, at the moment," he snapped. "Who is it?"

"I don't know, sir, she won't identify, but she's using the secured channel, so it can only be from one place."

The lead agent shook his head and gave the signal for his men to lower their weapons. "Excuse me." He went to the passenger side of the SUV nearest him and slid into the seat as the waiting agent handed him the handset.

Ken ogled Jade and spoke through his teeth. "What the hell is going on?"

She shrugged, holding tight to her sidearm. "I have no idea."

The lead agent returned a few minutes later, his flat expression and tone unaltered. "Ma'am? Can I get your last name, please?"

"Like I said, that has already been provided," Jade hissed. "Call Sergeant Adams. Get it from him."

"Ma'am…please? It really isn't an unreasonable request."

Jade knew it wasn't, but the request puzzled her nonetheless. She took a glimpse at every agent present and sent along the answer, realizing that each one had a camera on his lapel.

"Right. Hensley." He presented his hand. "Agent Hensley, might I have a word with you? In private?"

"Absolutely," Jade said, holstering her sidearm. The agent's palm pressed firmly on her lower back and she walked with him. "Provided you explain what this is about."

He escorted her to the SUV where he'd taken the radio call. "Someone has requested to speak with you," he said. "She advises that she's an…old friend of yours."

Jade's skin began to tingle. She racked her brain for clues as to who this could be. She'd made just as many *old friends* as she had enemies in her lifetime, and this person could be just about anyone. She began steeling herself and plotting her next improvised move, whatever it might be, and despite everything inside her screaming to launch an assault, she yielded and forced a smile. For now.

The agent bade her take a seat, and Jade plopped in, feeling the sensation of the SUV's heated upholstery straightaway. He handed her a duplex radio handset that looked like a military-grade flip phone, minus the buttons.

She placed the speaker to her ear. "Hello?"

A sultry, high-pitched woman's voice bearing a delicate Southern accent came back to her. *"How you been, Connie?"*

Jade gritted her teeth. "I've been better…"

*"Well, good gracious me! I declare, it really is you. It's been forever and a day, hasn't it? I didn't know what to think when I first saw you pop up on my screen...I thought some ole gypsy skank filched your credentials and was tryin' to pass herself off as the genuine Constance Hensley. Aah...you do know who this is, don't you?"*

"I do," Jade snarled. "How long have you been whoring yourself out to DHS, Trixie? Bit of a downgrade, even for you, don't you think?"

*"Kind of you to notice. Actually, it was a drag at first. But everything has turned out just peachy for me here, so you know. I would've stayed with the company, but Augie's career led him elsewhere, and I just couldn't bear to be apart from him."* A moment passed in silence. *"So, tell me. Are you as plum dazzled as I am now? I bet hearing my voice surprises you."*

"No, not at all. It aggravates me," Jade said. "As in downright abrading, like sandpaper on silk. So why not spare me the agony of it and tell me what the play is here."

*"The play?"*

"That's right, the play. What's your angle? What do you want?"

Beatrice giggled through her nose. *"You still don't like beatin' around the bush for long, do you? Well, let's see here, I suppose my angle, as you so eloquently put it, is the same as it's always been. I want it all, Connie...lock, stock and goddamn freakin' barrel. And I plan to get it all."*

"So you haven't changed, then. Still the narcissist meth-head ever ready, willing and able to defile herself at the drop of a hat just to stay ahead of the curve. You've always been my role model."

*"Damn! You are such a riot, Connie! Do you recall the last time we ran into each other? I surely do. I imagine it's hard for you to forget, had to be awfully tough losing your job like you did. Shame, shame."*

Jade smiled internally. "Come to think of it, I do remember that. But I also remember getting a bill in the mail for some cosmetic dentistry that I trashed. How many teeth did you end up losing, by the way?"

*"Since you're bein' nosey, three in total, and they're all porcelain veneers now, and they look marvelous. My smile is as beautiful as ever. How's yours doing? Still covered in tobacco and coffee stains? Lookin' all snaggletoothy? I imagine it's a trifle tough keeping those chompers all pearly white as a bona fide member of society's desecrates."*

"Hey, Trix. It's been a real blast. I'm glad we finally caught up, but I'm done with the idle chitchat."

*"Cut me short, then. See if I care. The lead agent on the scene already knows what I want done with you, and your little friend too. Nothing to worry about, Connie. We'll be seein' each other before long. Bye."*

Then the line went dead.

Jade was exploding inside, every ounce of her being wanted nothing more than to kill the man closest to her and move on to the next, not stopping until every last one of them was a corpse. All agents had their guns lowered now, but she knew that would change in a matter of minutes. Beatrice would've ordered it so. If a move was to be made with any success to speak of, it would require creativity, proper timing, and a stroke of luck.

She casually set the handset down and exited the SUV with grace, presenting her best smile, though wholly counterfeit.

"Sounded like you two knew each other," said the lead agent. "Not in a good way, though."

"We haven't exactly been the best of friends."

"Yeah, I gathered. How long have you known her? A lot of the men have been posing questions, especially after seeing how quickly she moved up in the ranks."

Jade grinned and shook her head in disgust. *Same old Beatrice.* "For far too long."

The agent raised a brow. "I see."

Jade studied every face in the crowd. She could feel the lead agent's hand moving toward her holster in an effort to stealthily disarm her. "I can feel that, you know."

"Oh, I know. The lady told me to watch you, said you were real good. And a real good actress." He pointed to Ken and snapped his fingers. "Lock that one up!"

Ken jumped in place as three rifle muzzles leveled at him. "Whoa! Wait a second! What is this?"

"Just relax," the lead agent said, his hand moving to grip tightly onto Jade's wrist.

Her jaw clenched and she immediately tensed every muscle in her arm.

"I wouldn't do that. If you resist, I'll have a half dozen of these fine gentlemen subdue you. And you won't like how they go about it, I assure you. All you have to do now is come quietly."

"This is preposterous," Jade exclaimed. "You have no right to do this. We're federal agents! Not imposters!"

"I never said you were. But my instructions now are to take you both into custody and impound your transport, pending a full investigation."

Rifle barrels in his face, Ken looked to Jade for what to do, but she had reached the end of her rope. Her self-control had vanished.

Other agents en route to restrain her, Jade aggressively went on the offensive. She withdrew and twisted the lead agent's wrist, then dropped him with a rigid elbow to his chin. He hit the ground hard, losing control of her sidearm. She then spun and guided a flying knee into the waiting face of the next black uniform she saw. A third leveled his rifle at her, and she snatched the muzzle, pulled his body into hers and brought a knee to his groin, then smashed his nose with her forehead. After, she swung his rifle about, catching two other agents upside their heads, sending them each down in crumpling heaps.

Jade went unhinged from there, lashing out savagely at any man foolish enough to come within distance. She was fighting for her life now, doing so with everything she had, punching, scratching, tearing, and even biting her way through the fray. She turned the rifle around and snapped off the safety, but couldn't get her finger to the trigger in time. The instant searing pain of two barbed Taser prongs tore into her back, followed by the throbbing, pulsating shock of fifty thousand volts ripping through her body. Jade dropped like dead weight, teeth chattering, tensing and trembling, to the icy snow.

The electrical current coursing its way through her nervous system was excruciating. It ceased only to begin again as angry, incensed voices shouted, "Hit her! Fry her! Hit that bitch again!" from above.

Only minutes later did it stop altogether as several agents hoisted Jade's limp body upright.

The lead agent rose and rubbed his chin, then limped over and clutched Jade by her throat. "That was stupid! All you had to do was not resist! And what did you do?" He drew back and punched her squarely in the mouth, then hit her a second time as she wailed in pain.

"You fuck!" Ken screamed, now being held at bay by four uniformed men. "Battering women get you hard? Is that what gets you off? Come over here! I'll play sissy for you! Come on and get some, you piece of shit!"

"Shut him up," the lead agent ordered, reaching for Jade's chin again as blood oozed from her lips and gums. "Looks like we have ourselves a change of plans. We won't be taking you two into custody after all. This bullshit is going to end right here. Both of you are finished."

"You're going to execute us? On what grounds?" Jade moaned. "We haven't committed a crime."

"Multiple counts of assault on federal agents? That doesn't sound like a crime to you?" he asked. "Sure as hell does to me."

"When a federal agent assaults another, all bets are off," Jade hissed.

"You mean like this?" He drew his sidearm, motioned for two agents to get clear, then shot Ken in the upper leg.

Jade cried out as Ken reached for his leg and tumbled to the snowy ground, writhing in pain. She tried in vain to go to his aid, but the agents tightened their grips on her.

The lead agent laughed and shook his head, then pointed his gun at Jade. "Who else you got in that transport of yours?"

Jade spit blood on the ground and gritted her teeth. "No one."

"Bullshit. You're hiding something, I know it. Tell me now and I'll put a bullet in your friend's head and kill him quick. Otherwise, he bleeds out. That gives him about four and a half minutes."

Her face bloodied and body weakened after repeated blows from the Taser, Jade's struggles only persisted. "If I get one hand free, you're a dead man, I swear to God."

The agent inched closer and set the muzzle of his pistol to Jade's cheek with a sinister grin. "But you won't. Care to decide which of you dies first?"

"Me!" Ken shouted. "Shoot me, pussy!"

"I believe I already did."

"And you did a shit-stain job of it. When's the last time you qualified with your sidearm? Stop picking on the girl…come over here and finish me!"

"Shut him up—for good this time!" he ordered, then pressed his pistol hard on Jade's temple. "I assume you have some last words? You don't strike me as the quiet type. Hurry up…my coffee's waiting and it isn't getting any warmer."

Jade lowered her head and sent a hard stare to the Marauder's windshield, knowing a diligent Alan would be watching for signals behind it. Then, careful to mouth each word so that her lips could be read, she said, "Death blossom."

The agent's brows drew inward. "What's that? Heard something, but couldn't make it out. Try again, please."

Jade unfolded and repeated with more emphasis, "Death blossom."

"Death blossom? The fuck is that? Your favorite flower? The perfume you're wearing?" He leaned in and sniffed her neck. "That's odd, all I smell on you is sweat and fear."

Inside the Marauder, Alan worked at a feverish pace as his chest pounded away, his fingers pressing virtual buttons on the Samson Remote Weapon System's touchscreen. "I hear you, Jade. I hear you… just hold on…hold on one more second." With shaky hands, he punched in the sequence as she'd shown him only days before, and seconds later, the Katlanit's internal programming took over. "I hope to God you and Ken remembered your lifesavers."

*"Good morning, operator,"* an electronic woman's voice uttered.

Alan jumped. "What the?"

*"Thank you for choosing death blossom, the ultimate, highly advanced automatic hunter-killer targeting mode ever brought into being. Please stand by. All hostiles within range will be vaporized momentarily. Have a pleasant day."*

"Heh. Nice touch, Butch."

Alan heard the whirr of gears and the hiss of hydraulics as the motorized above-deck weapon mount went active. Seconds after, he plugged his ears with his fingers as every sound in the immediate world was drowned out by the reverberating, thundering concussions of rapid heavy machine-gun fire.

Empty boiling-hot bullet brass and metal links showered the Marauder's armored chassis as the M2 Browning unleashed a hellfire of oblivion downrange at every enemy target it acquired. Armor-piercing incendiary rounds pummeled the DHS SUVs, transforming them into scrap sheet metal in seconds. Agents caught inside were ripped to shreds by direct hits and spalling near-misses. Cougar MRAPs suffered similar damage, their defenses unable to resist the armor-piercing rounds. Agents caught in the open were mowed down and reduced to nothing.

Jade went berserk and fought her way free from the agents restraining her and dove for cover right in time for the Katlanit to acquire them as targets. The Ma Deuce pummeled them with rounds that liquefied their body armor and carved cavities through them. Before it could acquire and blow away the lead agent, she tackled him, pulled him to the ground with her, and walloped his face with ruthless elbow strikes until the pistol fell from his hand. She took hold of it, placed the barrel under his chin, and turned his brains into batter with one pull of the trigger.

Jade rolled away and crawled to Ken's aid, fighting the agents from him, beating and bloodying them into submission, and as they backed away and rose to their feet, the Katlanit locked on to them and finished the job she'd started, splattering their bodies into lumps of bloody human tissue.

Once death blossom's growth cycle drew to a close, Alan disembarked the Marauder and ran frantically to Jade and Ken through rising dust and smoke, odors of brimstone, burning metal and flesh. With his AR pistol pulled to his shoulder, he scanned the scene, finding the Katlanit had dispensed an apocalyptic hand of destruction to both man and machine. The hostile forces, whoever they were, DHS, FEMA or some federal entity gone rogue, as Valerie had referred to them, had all been reduced to dust and ash. Every sign of the enemy had been superseded by those of death and ruin.

Jade had taken off her jacket and removed her uniform shirt to employ it as an improvised tourniquet on Ken's upper leg. "Good job," she purred, ogling Alan's approach. "*Damn* good job." She looked upon him, her eyes watering, emotions weighing heavily on her.

Alan dropped to his knees. "How bad is he hurt? And how bad are you hurt?

"The round is through and through, but it grazed his artery, so it's not good. Bleeding's barely under control. And don't worry about me."

Ken winced under Jade's strength and the searing pain beneath the tourniquet. "Of course it's not good...but that doesn't mean you two can start...talking *around* me...like I'm not here."

Alan apologized and looked to Jade for what to do next. He was officially out of his element.

"We have to get help, but I'm afraid to move him like this." She gestured to the uniformed men and fragments of same scattered about. "All of them were wearing kits. See if you can find an IFAK, a trauma kit. I need a real tourniquet and a dressing, something to pack the wound with."

Alan rose and scuttled off to search through the tattered bodies of the deceased. The first man he came upon was missing a leg and half his arm, leaving his torso intact, save a large chasm in his abdomen. Alan rolled him over and discovered a blood-covered trauma kit irreparably damaged by a round that had drilled through his body armor. He moved on to the next, only to find comparable damage. Then, twenty feet away, he saw an undamaged black zippered bag with MOLLE webbing and a familiar red cross. Alan retrieved it, then sprinted back to Jade and Ken.

Jade ripped open the kit, dumped its contents on the snow, and went immediately to work. She instructed Alan to hold tightly on the shirtsleeve tourniquet while she used shears to slice through Ken's pant leg. Locating a combat application tourniquet, she slipped it around Ken's leg and slid it all the way to his crotch.

"Hey!" Ken cringed. "Getting a little frisky, aren't you?"

"Keep it up and I'll put it somewhere you *really* don't want." Jade tightened the tourniquet while Alan gradually relieved tension. The C-A-T took over and the bleeding began to subside. She then opened an Israeli bandage and tightly dressed the wound.

After, Jade fell backward onto the cold ground in exhaustion and took a moment to catch her breath. "Alan, get on the radio Butch put in the APC. Try calling for him; maybe he knows what to do or where we can take Ken. The longer we wait, the better the chances are of him losing that leg."

Alan nodded.

"Don't kid yourself," Ken grumbled. "Take your time, Alan. I'm a combat Marine, and tourniquets are a lifesaving measure. The second they're applied, the limb is a lost cause. I'll deal with it."

"I don't want to hear any of that 'pain is weakness leaving the body' shit, Ken." Jade cut her eyes at him. "No matter what, you need medical attention ten minutes ago." She sent a subtle look of urgency Alan's way.

Alan darted back to the Marauder, climbed the ladder and hopped inside. His fingers were wet from the snow and stiff from the bitterness of the air. His whole body was shaking from the effects of adrenaline, but he reached for the microphone anyway, recalling what Butch had told him the day before.

He squeezed the microphone's button. "White Rock, this is mike-zero-one-actual, I repeat, White Rock, this is mike-zero-one-actual." A pause. "Mayday, Mayday, Mayday. We have a medical emergency, I repeat, medical emergency. Mayday, Mayday, Mayday. Over."

Alan made several more calls in the same fashion, but no response came from Butch. He began recalling what Valerie had said to him about line-of-sight transmissions, transmitting, and direction finding. What he was engaging in now, he was certain could be detected by receivers on or near the same frequency. And by continuing to transmit like he was, it created the potential for hostile forces to home in on him, Jade, and Ken. But Alan didn't know what else to do, they had already done so, and a friend's life was on the line.

He made another call followed by another and set the microphone down, then listened to the open squelch emanating from the speaker. Then motion caught his eye. Alan hopped down from the APC again upon seeing that Jade had hoisted Ken and was now carrying him to the Marauder's rear door. "Jade, can I help?"

"I've got him, but you can get the door for me."

Alan jogged to the Marauder's rear door and pried it ajar. He then assisted getting Ken inside.

"Any luck with the radio?" Jade asked.

"None," Alan lamented. "I've tried five or six times, and nothing."

Her tension on display, Jade ran her fingers through her hair then made for the driver's side.

"Are we leaving?"

"Yes."

"Where are we going?"

"We can't stay here—just get in."

They reconvened in the passenger compartment. Jade shifted into drive and floored the accelerator, launching the APC across the field, over remnants of vehicles blown to bits and bodies mutilated beyond mend, the steering wheel aimed toward the interstate.

Alan's hand returned to the radio mic and he made his call again. "White Rock, do you copy? This is mike-zero-one-actual, I say again mike-zero-one-actual. Mayday, Mayday, Mayday. We have a medical emergency, a medical emergency. Over." His fist tightened in frustration. "I don't think anyone in the whole damn world can hear us."

Jade sniffled and fretted with her busted lip. "Just keep trying. Remember what Butch said, it could be our location. We're moving; it might create some magic with the radio."

Alan nodded his head reluctantly.

"Just so you know, I'm putting distance between us and that place. We're going north…back to Camp Hill. I'm sorry, Alan, I really am—I don't know where else to go or what else to do. I'm going on record here that I'm out of answers."

"Don't apologize to me," Alan said. "Ken's life is more important and you know it."

"Hey, guys? Remember what I said about talking *around* me as if I'm not fucking sitting here? I told you I'm fine. Just take me wherever."

"That's admirable, Ken. Very brave. Overruled." Before reaching for the mic again, Alan went for the first aid kit in the Marauder's glove box and took out an instant ice pack. He readied it and offered it to Jade.

She glanced at it, then at him. "How many times do I have to tell you not to worry about me?"

"I'm insisting this time."

Half-heartedly, she took hold of the ice pack and placed it on her lips. "Thank you."

"You're welcome," Alan said, and grabbed the mic again. He made yet another call with far less exuberance than before, his faith in their ability to communicate dwindling.

Then, after a few seconds, a voice came back to them, but it didn't belong to Butch.

*"Mike-zero-one, this is foxtrot-alpha-nineteen returning your call. This station reads you. What is your emergency? Over."*

Jade's eyes widened. "Who the hell was that?"

"I have no idea."

The person calling back to them spoke hurriedly while articulating each word and syllable with precision. The voice was that of a young man, possibly in his mid-twenties. *"Mike-zero-one, mike-zero-one, I say again, this is foxtrot-alpha-nineteen. I have full copy of your Mayday call and your emergency. Please advise status. Over."*

"Well? What the hell?" Ken chided. "Are you going to answer the dude or not?"

Alan gripped the mic. "Foxtrot-alpha-nineteen, this is mike-zero-one. We read you as well, and yes, we *do* have a medical emergency…a gunshot wound to the upper leg. Tourniquet has been applied and the bleeding has stopped, but we need medical assistance. Over." He unkeyed. "If you have it."

The other station came back instantly. *"Mike-zero-one, this is foxtrot-alpha-nineteen. Full copy. We can offer assistance. Please advise your location…direction of travel, also, if germane. Over."*

"Where are we, Jade?" Alan asked.

"Wait, slow down. We don't know who that is," Jade warned. "What if it's those assholes looking to finish us off?"

"On the same frequency?"

"Why not?"

Alan sighed. "Do you ever go with gut feeling over instinct?"

Jade whipped the wheel, pulling onto the highway and fishtailing in the snow. "Not often."

"Well, I'm getting a feeling in my gut about this," Alan said. "And it's not motion sickness. I don't think this person means us harm. I think we should pursue it."

Jade sent him an odd look, then rotated quickly to gauge Ken's expression.

Ken threw his hands in the air. "Like I give a shit, look at me. Walt's already in a goddamn wheelchair and I'm headed for one, not like it can get much worse."

Jade pursed her lips. "I'm against it. But you guys went along with my plan and look where it left us. Make the call."

Alan looked away and gave the returning station their estimated location as best he knew how, using road signs and environmental landmarks.

Jade tapped her fingers on the Katlinit's touchscreen for a time and pointed to it. "Give those to him."

After conveying their latitude, longitude and heading, an extended pause went by before the station came back.

*"Mike-zero-one, I've got you. We'll put together a response team and rendezvous with you. You should change course and bear due west. Road directions to follow. Break."*

Alan stared hard at the map, and his jaw slackened as he took notice of the directions the friendly station had provided.

Jade veered over the median and sent the APC the wrong way up an entrance ramp, took a left and motored to the first intersection. "Right or left?"

"Right," Alan said, his tone denoting total disbelief. "Jade...you're not going to believe this."

"Try me."

"The directions he just gave us..." Alan hesitated. "They take us right where we were planning to go."

# CHAPTER 25

**Trout Run Valley**
**Thursday, January 6th. Present day**

LAUREN AROSE EARLY HER FIRST morning after returning home, her body tender and plagued with aches from the previous days' exertion. She was well-rested but still felt distraught over the manner in which she and John had seemingly ended things. For the first time in years, she was officially single, but the status bore little significance in the world she knew now.

Upon entering the kitchen for a drink, she found Grace was up, and the two took seats at the table and spent the predawn morning hours immersed in a heart-to-heart. Grace filled Lauren in on everything that had happened in the valley since she'd been gone, and Lauren reciprocated, revealing bits and pieces of what had happened during her time away.

An hour or so into it, Grace felt tired and expressed her need for a nap, and disappeared soon after to her room, leaving Lauren alone with the atypical stillness of the cabin, a place that at one time had been the rowdy epicenter of so many lives crammed together.

Michelle strode in and placed a kiss on Lauren's head, expressing once again with loving eyes how much she'd missed her daughter in the time she'd been gone. They made small talk while Michelle assembled the items needed for breakfast, and something about seeing her mother's smile and hearing her voice again after so long began to lift Lauren's spirits. Being back home with her family was calming; it warmed her soul and brought her peace. It had always been a place of sanctity, unconditional love, compassion and affection, even in the toughest of times. And until now, Lauren hadn't realized how much she'd longed for this feeling.

Still, after the week she'd endured, she felt the need to elevate her spirits even higher. Lauren was in need of some therapy: physical, mental and emotional. She knew of one specific pastime with a reputation for sanctioning all of the above, one that would even help alleviate the soreness in her muscles and the stiffness in her joints.

Lauren hustled to her room and changed into a cold-weather running outfit, complete with trail running shoes, gloves, and a custom fleece cap for ear protection that had a unique posterior opening for arranging her ponytail. She donned clothing and accessories adequate to protect her skin from the morning chill, then told her mother she'd try to make it back by the time breakfast was ready.

Michelle looked upon her daughter merrily. "Be careful and watch the traffic. And don't get frostbite."

Lauren hadn't run in a while, and it had been some time since she'd done so atop a slick, wintry surface. It was taking a bit of getting used to. Soon though, she found a comfortable stride, and once warmed up, she sprinted hard southward along Trout Run Road, with no particular destination in mind.

The air was dry, frigid, and callous and surged by in gusty crosswinds, knocking snow and ice from tree limbs and stirring up loose powder beneath her feet. Lauren could feel it chap her lips, sting her nostrils and parch the insides of her mouth on contact with each inhale. She arranged the fabric of her neck gaiter above her nose, pulled her cap to her eyebrows and pressed on, each nuisance only fueling her to run harder.

So much had changed since the last time she had seen this place. She'd left here during a time of panic, worry, pressure, and desperation, when numerous lives were hanging in the balance. Now, all of that had since passed, and most of their difficulties had been rectified. Security had ranked foremost among the list of concerns for those living here, but it didn't seem nearly so critical now. Twenty well-trained, well-outfitted soldiers from Dave Graham's unit were on the job, and their presence provided peace of mind and room to breathe. No one seemed to feel endangered anymore, not even Lauren. In fact, this was the first time in recent memory that she'd consciously left her house without bringing a gun along.

Just before the notorious straightaway where Lauren and her neighbors had put down a band of malicious invaders, she noticed a familiar four-wheel-drive headed her way. It was the Suburban her family had brought here, the one her father had purchased long ago on the off chance something extraordinary were to take place that would levy irreparable damage to modern automobiles.

As the vehicle got closer to her, Lauren slowed her pace and waved when she recognized the driver.

Norman pulled to a stop alongside her and worked to roll down his window. "Good morning, sweetums. Don't you think it's a little cold for a run?"

Lauren blew out a breath of humid air. "Not for me."

"Must be nice having them young bones," he said. "It's real good to see you. I heard you were back around...you've been sorely missed."

Lauren panted. "Who told you I was here?"

"Eh, my youngest spilled the beans...he mentioned a falling-out he had with you last evening. I assumed it must've happened after you got in."

Lauren rolled her eyes. "What else did he mention?"

Norman pursed his lips. "Really not much at all. He mostly sulked, but that's all he's done now for going on a month. He hasn't been thrilled having to wait for you. Can't say I didn't warn you."

Lauren didn't say anything.

"Hey, I'm not in it," Norman continued. "So take what I say at face value, or flush it. It's none of my business. I do want you to know that I'm real sorry about you two. It's a pity."

"A pity, huh." Lauren chortled. "News travels fast."

"Yeah, in a world as small as this one, it does," Norman said. "Speaking of which, not sure if anyone's told you yet, so stop me if you've already heard. I'm...moving out of the cabin. Kristen and I are...well, I'm not exactly sure what we're doing, but being together is making us both real happy. So we're looking to make a go of it."

"Guess that explains why you're driving our truck," Lauren surmised.

"I probably should've said something about that, huh? I bet it looked a little strange seeing it on the road with me behind the wheel." Norman laughed at himself. "I'm leaving on good terms, by the way. No hard feelings between your mom and me; all of us still consider all of you good friends, etcetera. She told me I could borrow the truck and use it as long as I need it. Truth be told, it felt a little weird asking, like I was stepping on toes."

Lauren smiled genuinely at him. "That's ridiculous, Norm. Your family has always been family to us, and this changes nothing. You've been here since Dad's been gone. No one else was around to step up like you did, and we owe you. But you also owe yourself. You deserve a life of your own and to be happy. That's nothing to feel guilty over."

"I'm doing my best with it," Norman said, adjusting his hat. "Just so you're aware, Lee's planning on staying. It's closer to Megan's place and he likes it there. There wouldn't be room for him at Kristen's, anyway. It looks to be a full house. John…asked about going along; I told him he needed to do whatever he felt was best. So he'll be moving out too, it appears."

Lauren's lips stiffened. She nodded and looked away.

"I take it he hasn't told you."

Lauren shook her head.

"Well, sorry I had to be the one to convey the message," Norman said, "but it's better that you know. I, uh, better get going and grab another load. Got to get in and out without waking Grace up," Norman said. "Last time I made that mistake, she came out the front door in her pajamas looking like Medusa. It's…good to see you home, sweetheart. I'll see you around."

Lauren tapped the truck door and smiled grimly. "It's good to be back. And I'll see *you* around." She deliberated the news of John moving out as she watched Norman skid off and away. "Guess that confirms it."

From there, she dropped the hammer and dashed the length of the straightaway, past the Brady homestead, to and past the northern barricade. The uniformed men stationed there threw verbal reprimands and questioning looks her way for having gone outside the wire. Lauren knew better than to go too far beyond it and began a return trip shortly thereafter at a comparable velocity. The endorphins had already began chipping away at her aches and worries.

Immersed now in a euphoric state, Lauren cleared her mind and was reminded of the myriad reasons she enjoyed exercising. The last time she'd been on a run had been with Grace on Thanksgiving, the day they had learned of a rival entity's true objectives. She called those events into mind and remembered how she'd felt then: imperiled, besieged, afraid, and provoked. A hostile force had revealed its new goal. No longer did they wish to deprive Lauren's family, friends and neighbors of their liberty, property and inalienable rights. Their purpose had converted, and they now meant to deprive every last one of them of life itself.

Their actions had been heinous. A percentage of their food supply had been poisoned and was verging on extinction. Their sole water source had been intentionally contaminated with a biological agent. Several of her neighbors had nearly succumbed to illness, including one as young as Liam, Peter and Amy Saunders' five-year-old son.

Lauren could not overlook that. She couldn't allow herself to disremember what had happened here or become complacent, even as ancillary defensive layers swathed the valley, offering an air of repose to those living here. She knew who was responsible: the organization that had gone door-to-door posting orange declarations of martial law in her grandparents' neighborhood. The one that had threatened them with violent repercussions for choosing noncompliance.

Relocating to the valley had added distance between them and had bought crucial time, but the miles were no longer a deterrent, and the time they'd acquired had seemingly run out. Lauren knew it was destined to get worse; upon learning the methods employed hadn't achieved satisfactory results, they would try again and be certain not to make the same mistakes twice.

The organization that meant to exterminate everyone she knew also had Lauren's grandparents incarcerated over fabricated, victimless crimes. They'd been sentenced devoid of a jury and without due process. These actions were inexcusable, and Lauren wished she could do something about it, but what could be done? Woo Tang had been right, she was naturally suited for combat, but she knew nothing of war or how to wage one.

Lauren was home again. She and the others had left the valley to search for ways of mitigating the side effects of a problem, leaving the problem itself unsolved. It would remain an extant threat to her family, neighbors and their way of life. At some point, a solution would need to be found, perhaps in the form of a reckoning or even a war. Until then, she resolved to ready herself for when the time came to right all the wrongs.

Lauren flung herself overtop the gate at her driveway's edge and sprinted fiercely through the yard. She began judging the length for a long jump onto the porch, but a familiar face running nearly as fast as she was stole her attention.

Neo, Dave Graham's RTO, exploded from the shed behind the cabin and looked to be headed in her direction, though he wasn't exactly looking at her. In fact, Lauren wasn't even sure he could see her. It appeared that he'd forgotten his glasses. She detoured and ran to him, waving a hand in the air to snag his attention.

Neo slowed, squinted and lowered his head. "Who goes there? Sorry, I can't see you."

Lauren went to him and put her face inches from his. "How about now? Did you forget something?"

"Oh, hey! Yeah, I forgot my glasses. I was in a hurry—still am—wait—when did you get home?"

"Last night. Where did you leave them? I'll get them for you."

"No! I mean, that's okay. I'm nearsighted, but it's mostly astigmatism." Neo's pupils darted around. "I can't believe you're here—there's something you should know, but you're going to think I'm crazy."

"Why would I think that?" Lauren asked.

"After I tell you, you will, trust me." Neo was incredibly anxious. "I received a Mayday call on the radio—your dad's radios, the ones you asked me to set up—they work great, by the way. The caller reported a medical emergency—a gunshot wound. And I think—I mean, I *know* the person I talked to was *him*."

"Him?"

"Yeah. Your dad."

Time slowed to a crawl as Lauren repeated Neo's words in her mind. She gawked at him. "Wait, slow down—what did you say?"

Neo rolled his eyes franticly. "See? I knew it. You think I'm crazy. I told you."

"Neo—be straight with me." Lauren inched closer. "How do you know it was my dad?"

He leaned away and spoke matter-of-factly. "Because I know him and I know his voice."

"I'm sure you do, but there are probably hundreds of men out there who sound like him."

Neo rattled his head back and forth. "No, no way. You don't get it—I know voices. I *never* forget them. And your dad only sounds like *your* dad."

Lauren looked confounded. "Did you ask him his name?"

"No."

She cringed. "Why not?"

"Because doing so goes against OPSEC, duh."

Lauren sighed at the edge of her breaking point. "Neo, look at me."

"I am looking at you," he said, his eyes wandering.

Lauren maneuvered, attempting to synchronize with him. "This is serious. I really need you to look *at* me, right now. In my eyes."

The young soldier tensed and flustered. "I can't. I can't do that—you know I can't do that."

Lauren reached for his forearms, but he jerked away. "You're right, I'm doing this all wrong. I'm sorry, I just don't know what to think."

"You don't know what to think, other than I'm crazy," Neo muttered.

"I don't think you're crazy, but we're talking about my dad—I have to know how confident you are. I need something definitive." Lauren thought a long moment, then it hit her. "Okay…Neo, rate your level of certainty for me on a linear scale."

Neo's eyes lit up. "Parameters?"

"One to one hundred," Lauren said.

"Whole numbers? Natural numbers? Integers?"

"Whole numbers only, no negatives."

"And do I assign *one* the least or greatest value?"

Lauren sighed. "Neo…work with me, please? Just a little."

"Sorry." He squinted, looked her over and grinned brightly. "One hundred and one."

Lauren gasped, backstepped and nearly tripped over her foot. Her hand moved to conceal her slackened jaw. "Oh my God. Where is he?"

Neo smiled awkwardly. "According to the coordinates he gave? Not far."

"Not far? In which direction?"

The young man pointed to the mountain range due east.

"You said it was a Mayday call, a medical emergency. Is *he* the emergency?"

"I don't think so," Neo said, shaking his head. "Most trauma victims don't call in their own injuries, and he didn't sound in pain, though he *was* panicked."

Lauren's mind raced. He was close indeed, making Wolf Gap the superlative option of getting to him. The gears in her mind spun into motion. "How far have you gone with this? Who else knows?"

Neo sent a blank look at the handheld radio in his grasp. “Not far, I just left the shed; I have them coming this way. I was going to summon the doctor and get Richie for a transport to meet them; then I saw you.”

“Why do you need Richie for that?”

“I don’t. His JLTV is the closest.”

Lauren reached for his shoulders as he reacted clumsily to her advance. Norman had the Suburban and she needed a ride. “Where is the…JLTV?”

His eyes scurried around. “Richie’s? The church. It’s our FOL… Fred authorized it.”

Lauren plotted her next move. “Okay, listen. I’ll handle Richie and corral Dr. Vincent. You get back on the radio, tell them we’re on our way to meet them, and *don’t* lose contact. I’ll bring the doctor to them, just guide them directly to me.”

“Are you sure about this?” Neo asked, his face knotting up.

“Positive.”

He grinned. “Should I advise it’s you who’s coming?”

Paying no heed to his question, Lauren made a daring play for Neo’s sidearm. “Sorry—I need to borrow this.”

Neo glanced down and askance at his now empty holster. “Oh boy. Force multiplier is back for real now, isn’t she? Ready to go ballistic.” As Lauren went to part ways, Neo grabbed her sleeve. “Wait,” he pled. “Let me tell you what they’re driving so you know what to look for.”

# CHAPTER 26

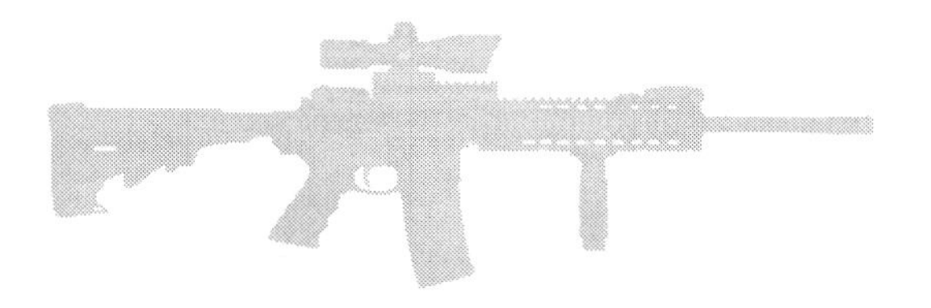

LAUREN DASHED UP THE DRIVEWAY, hurdled the gate again and took off like a shot onto Trout Run Road, with Neo's Sig P320 in hand. Before she knew it, her feet had taken her to the entrance of St. James Church, where a desert tan JLTV sat in the parking lot alongside two other larger, similarly colored transports.

She took a quick look around to gauge the scene and made a break for the driver's door. She opened it and slid into the seat and took a breath before bringing the engine roaring to life.

Lauren reversed the JLTV into the road, and the commotion served to rouse all the soldiers inside the church, including Richie. They marched hurriedly out the main door, waving and shouting, their rifles pulled to their shoulders, having no idea who had pilfered their vehicle or why.

She maneuvered into position and stomped the accelerator, sending the armored truck on a southerly course, passing the cabin's driveway before cutting left at the entrance to the former Ackermann farm, where Dr. Vincent and his wife were staying. She slammed on the brakes, and the JLTV slid diagonally in the driveway, coming to a stop mere feet from the porch.

Dr. Vincent emerged from the house, casting a look of indignance coupled with astonishment. "Young lady! Really! What is the meaning of this? Are you stark raving mad?"

"There's no time to explain," Lauren said, jumping out of the vehicle. She stuffed the Sig in the waistband of her running pants and ran to him. "There's a medical emergency. I need you to come with me now."

Dr. Vincent was taken aback. He folded his arms in defiance. "Oh really? A medical emergency?" he parroted. "Well, I will do no such thing! Not until you, at the very least, tender a suitable rationale for your crude deeds." He scoffed. "I…am truly appalled, miss. You can't just barge in here, demanding from me whatever you want! I happen to be a medical professional, as is my wife, and if you desire our help, you had better damn well entreaty it—doing so respectfully and in the proper fashion!"

Lauren tensed. She could feel mayhem surging inside. There really was no time for this.

Before she realized it, she had drawn the P320 and had it leveled on Dr. Vincent's nose. "Get your medical bag, kit, stethoscope, pocket protector, and whatever else a fucking medical emergency calls for, and get in the goddamn truck!"

Dr. Vincent's jaw went slack, his mouth fell open, though no words escaped. He did as he was told, and with one hand held in surrender, he turned away, retrieved his gear and traipsed with zeal to the JLTV.

Still holding him at gunpoint, Lauren opened the rear passenger-side suicide door and guided him into the backseat. "I'm truly sorry about this. I'll explain everything soon enough, but for now, sit down and shut up." She then slammed the door closed.

Lauren circled the vehicle, jumped in and reached for the door, but before she could pull it closed, a voice called to her. She reacted on instinct before discerning who it was.

With the Sig's barrel pointed in his face now, Christian slowly began raising his hands. "Hey there. Welcome back…and why do I have a gun in my face?"

Lauren hurriedly lowered the weapon. "Sorry about that. No time to talk. I'll explain later."

"Wait…who gave you the truck? Looks kind of like the one that doofus Richie drives."

Lauren sighed exhaustedly. "Christian, I'd love to catch up, but there is *zero* time for this—zero. So either get in or get out of the way, but don't try to stop me. If you do, I'll shoot you, I swear to God."

Christian shrugged. "Twist my arm, then." He rounded the vehicle with excitement and hopped in, and as Lauren maneuvered onto Trout Run Road, found they weren't alone. "Hey, Doc." His pupils shifted sideways. "Um, what's he doing here?"

Lauren didn't say anything, her concentration fully queued up on the matter at hand.

"And the plot thickens," Christian said, looking misplaced. "Did Richie or one of the guys let you borrow the ride?"

Lauren hesitated. "No."

"No?"

"Not exactly."

"Not exactly..." He trailed off. "Okay, you didn't *borrow* it, and I doubt you have one of your own, so I guess...that leaves one explanation. You stole it."

"I didn't steal anything." Lauren vetoed the remark. "I...tactically acquired it."

Christian repeated those last three words to himself. "Well now. I'm getting the feeling this situation, whatever it is, is poised to fall way, way out of control."

Turning the blind left corner, Lauren gasped and pushed hard on the brakes when a figure emerged onto the road before her from literally out of nowhere.

"What the hell?" Christian queried. "Pedestrians? Hey, wait—isn't that your friend from the camp? The one with the sword?"

Lauren nodded. "Oh shit."

Christian's brow furrowed. "Busted already, huh?"

Glowering, Woo Tang marched to Lauren's window with purpose in each step, then pulled her door ajar. "I am aware of many who prefer morning-hour strolls for the purposes of gathering fresh air," he said. "You...apparently prefer morning-hour joyrides in boosted vehicles."

"I didn't boost it," Lauren said. "I need it, Jae—and I don't have time to explain, I really don't."

"Though you *do* plan to tender explanation, regardless."

She nodded. "Of course I do."

The former SEAL evaluated her expression closely. "How serious is this?"

"Dire."

Woo Tang sighed. "Then you may present your motives while Oscar-Mike...to wherever this joyride takes us." He shut her door and opened his, sliding into the back beside Dr. Vincent.

And with a full house now on board, Lauren stomped the accelerator and sped towards the incline, en route to Wolf Gap.

"You know, I've heard these things were way better than Humvees, but I've never ridden inside one until now," Christian mused. "Heh... check it out, it even has a cup holder."

"They are far better in terms of comfort, as well," Woo Tang added, "especially on longer outings. The air-conditioning and extra legroom is noticeable, as is the added padding in the seat cushions."

Christian looked back at their newest arrival. "Hi, we met already…once before, albeit briefly." He stuck his hand out. "I was with Lauren in that death camp you saved us from. Forgive her, she's not the best with introductions. I'm Christian."

"Yes. I remember you being there. You may call me Woo Tang."

Christian grinned mischievously. "Very good to meet you, finally. And let me guess, you…*'ain't nothin' ta fuck with'*. Right?"

Woo Tang's expression went askew. "I beg your pardon?"

"Uh…nothing, forget it." Christian faced forward. "Sorry to bother you."

Several minutes later at the approach of Wolf Gap, Lauren let off the accelerator at the sight of what could only be another tremendous burden. She realized she'd forgotten about the D9T bulldozer that had been parked here to block the road months ago. She slammed on the brakes, punched the steering wheel and shouted curses at herself.

Christian tried consoling her. "Hey, hey! What are you so upset about?"

"I'm not upset! I'm pissed!" Lauren pointed at the snow-covered yellow behemoth. "We can't get to the other side with that thing in the way!"

Christian studied the monstrous earthmover with a casual eye. "Why do we need to get to the other side?"

"A very pertinent question," Woo Tang added.

Lauren rested her head against the wheel, squeezing her eyes closed. "I'm such an idiot."

Christian looked her over, then opened his door.

"Where are you going?" she asked.

"To see if they hid a key somewhere," he said, his tone denoting total lack of concern. "If not, I don't know. Maybe I can hotwire it."

Lauren squinted at him. "You can do that?"

"Please…have I ever failed you before?" He went to close his door but halted. "Never mind. Don't answer that."

Christian tore off, climbed onto the tractor and began wrestling with the controls. Moments passed by, but before long, black smoke spewed from the exhaust stack, indicating success had been achieved.

He motioned with his arm as if pulling an imaginary trucker's horn and drove the monstrous bulldozer ahead at a meager pace to the recreation area's parking lot just beyond the state line.

Stunned at what she was witnessing, Lauren moved in to follow and pulled alongside. A look of victory dawning on him, Christian hopped down and got back inside the JLTV.

Lauren leaned over, placing a kiss on his wind-chilled cheek. "You… are a godsend. Thank you."

"It was either that or watch you suffer a mental breakdown." Christian rubbed his hands together. "Another crisis averted. Think you can explain all this now?"

Lauren began mentally preparing herself to rationalize all this through the anxiety, apprehensions and excitement, but a mile down the road, learned that she didn't have to.

After negotiating the tight turns along the descent and leaving the national forest, a monstrous black armored vehicle turned onto the road and stopped in front of them. Both vehicles stalemated in the middle of the road, barely ten yards from each other's front bumper.

Christian's eyes boggled. "What the hell is that?"

"An armored personnel carrier of some variety," Woo Tang filled in. "Possibly of foreign origin."

Christian nodded. "Look at the size of that machine gun."

The menacing-looking vehicle's passenger door flung open and a second later a middle-aged man jutted his head out and began waving.

Upon seeing his face, Lauren went pale and distant.

"Do you know him?" asked Christian. "He seems to know us."

Lauren didn't answer him; she couldn't answer. Same as it had in her dreams, her voice was failing her.

Woo Tang squeezed between the seats. "Though he does not appear exactly as I remember, there is no question the man waving at us now is Alan Russell."

Christian whipped around. "Are you saying that dude is Lauren's dad?"

"Affirmative."

In utter shock, Lauren shut off the engine and pried open her door. She melted from her seat onto the slick pavement outside, struggling to find footing and support herself on wobbly legs. Barely able to utter a word, her voice trilled, "Dad?"

Jade had halted the Marauder upon seeing the JLTV headed for them after the turn onto Wolf Gap road. Knowing they were here to meet them, Alan didn't hesitate to open his door, stand and offer a friendly wave.

But what he hadn't bargained for was seeing a young woman deliberately exit the driver's side and look upon him as if knowing precisely who he was. Then it all became clear to him in a single spoken word.

"Sweet Jesus. What a day," he said.

"Alan, who is that?" Jade asked, her eyes bloodshot, her tension becoming palpable. "Is that your daughter?"

"Yeah, I think it has to be…"

Jade simpered. After all that had happened today, her emotional self was verging on collapse. "I don't understand…she's here? How is this happening? Here? And right now?"

"Do you recall our talk about fate?" Alan asked. "How did we get here? How did we survive that mess back there?" He descended the ladder. "It's happening because it had to." He then hopped to level ground and secured his door.

Jade reached into her hip pocket and pulled from it a black velveteen bag, the one Valerie had given her right before leaving Camp Hill. The stones that shared her name were still inside. "I'll be damned."

Dr. Vincent let himself out. Medical bag in hand, he made his approach and bellowed to the Marauder, "Hello? I was advised you have a casualty?"

Jade snapped herself out of it. She sprang from her perch and rallied with him. "He's in the back. I'll take you to him."

While Christian and Woo Tang remained in place, Lauren took cautious steps toward a person she hadn't seen since the day the world had gone mad, a man she had written off countless times, only to believe he'd come back to her someday.

But in what was becoming the most surreal moment of her life, she stood frozen in the roadway, a tactical military truck to her aft, another in front of her, facing a man appearing to be Alan Russell, the person she knew to be her father, even though everything about him in that moment felt off beam.

She wanted to go to him, reach for him and hug him and cry with him, while he held her head firmly to his chest, but something wasn't right.

Why was he standing there? Why was his expression so flat and empty? He looked as though he didn't know how to act or even who she was. Why wasn't he running to her to sweep her into his arms? Why wasn't he telling her how much he'd missed her and how much he loved her? And why were no tears erupting from his eyes like they were from hers?

Lauren could feel her lower lip trembling. A flood of emotions was assaulting her, and there were so many things she wanted to say, but she couldn't make sense of the jumble.

Staring back at her, Alan felt something of the same. He looked the young woman over, knowing full well who she was, aware she was his daughter Lauren, but he didn't know what to say to her. What did one say to someone they knew and loved, but failed to recognize and had no memories of? Alan's memory was sluggishly coming back to him, but even now, displaced in a life moment as paramount as his reunification with his daughter, he hadn't a clue how to begin.

He could feel Lauren scanning his every movement and lack thereof. Her eyes were filled with tears and his weren't. She could tell something was off. She knew something was wrong.

Headlights from both vehicles lighting their way in dawn's early light, Lauren started taking steps, inching her way closer to him. When she got to within a few feet, she looked him up and down. "Where… have you been?"

The question, compounded by his burden, the torment etched on her face and the misery and longing in her voice, massacred Alan's heart. "I've…I've been everywhere," he stammered and shook, "everywhere, other than…where I should've been." And with that, his tears began to fall.

She edged closer still, her soggy eyes narrowing into slits. "Something's wrong. You're not yourself," she whimpered. "Did… something happen to you?"

*More than you'll ever know*, he thought. But the words still escaped him.

"Are you sick? Talk to me, Dad. Tell me something."

Alan looked away, attempting to ready himself. He wanted so much to confess all to her, take her into his arms, hold her and tell her how sorry he was for not being there, but an unfamiliar face bearing an urgent expression flanked them, disrupting the moment.

"Excuse me, miss? We must go *now*," Dr. Vincent said. "I believe I can save the gentleman's leg, but we must get him to the infirmary. I need a sterile environment in which to operate, and that isn't here on this road. Are you hearing me?"

Lauren didn't respond. Her whole being was transfixed on her long-lost father having recently returned, only to have done so not as she remembered him. She wasn't about to go anywhere.

The brunette driver of the black APC approached Alan from behind, and Lauren's eyes tracked her, gauging her every move, every expression, taking distinct notice of her eyes and the way the woman looked upon her father.

The doctor became persistent. "Miss? Excuse me, I'm talking to you. I said we must go. And we must go now."

"I got her, Doc," said Christian, moving in with a gentle hand. He tugged Lauren's elbow. "Hey, come on, we can finish this at home." He sent acknowledging nods to both Alan and the brunette. "Follow us. It's not far."

"Alan, let's go," Jade said, and the pair made their reentry.

Dr. Vincent boarded the Marauder as Christian guided Lauren into the JLTV's passenger side, her stare never once leaving her father.

Christian then took the controls. He made a turnabout and guided the duo of armored vehicles toward Wolf Gap and into the valley.

# CHAPTER 27

CHRISTIAN TURNED THE CORNER AT the driveway leading to the Ackerman farm, then pulled into the yard to provide room for the other driver to maneuver. An infirmary had been built within a portion of the farmhouse's lower floor to accommodate the treatment of patients not long after Dr. Vincent and his wife had moved in.

The black APC pulled in immediately behind them and reversed to the porch. Jade jumped out to assist Ken inside, and Alan followed behind her.

Lauren remained stoic, her eyes drilling holes through the passenger window, watching her father follow the doctor and the brunette, who had hoisted the other man into her arms and was now carrying him inside.

Christian absorbed the moment with a raised brow. "I gotta say, all this comes as quite a shocker, even for me. It's crazy, right? Of all things…your dad is home, like totally out of the blue."

"I know."

"Grace is gonna freak." He hesitated, minding Lauren. "But I'm sensing you're not particularly thrilled about it, for some reason."

"I'm ecstatic."

"You don't sound it. Seriously…I would've expected a *way* more cheery reaction from you."

"Sorry to disappoint you."

Christian shut off the engine. "Hey, did I say something wrong?" he asked, hearing more engines approaching from the road, a look left serving to confirm it. "We've got incoming. Looks like the heat on its way to investigate a certain tactically acquired JLTV." He snorted. "I'm driving it *now*, but you started this mess. How should we handle it?"

Lauren hung her head. "I-I don't know. I guess I'll just explain—"

"That will not be necessary," Woo Tang broke in. "No explanation is compulsory on your part. You will see to your father now that he is home. I will make this my problem."

Lauren nodded, biting her lip. "I owe you, again, Jae. Thank you."

He smiled grimly. "You are welcome, again. And you owe me nothing. Christian, it would be kind of you to return the JLTV once you are finished with it."

"Consider it done."

Woo Tang exited from the rear suicide door and approached the pair of oncoming trucks, immediately directing them to halt their advance. Minutes later, he got into one of them, and the pair backed out of the driveway, disappearing onto the road.

Normally, Christian would be the first to offer further comment, even if only serving to fill the silence. But instead, he held back, allowing Lauren to sort through the storm of emotions building inside her.

"I know you and Grace are about to become parents, and who knows what else," Lauren began in a shaky voice. "You're family now, and that gives you every right to be here and be a part of this." She turned to face him, her lips pressing together. "But I would really appreciate some time alone with him."

Christian leaned into his seat. "Incredible. You can be awfully sincere when you want something bad enough."

"Christian…"

"I'm kidding. No worries. I'll leave you to it."

"Thank you, but I also need a favor."

Christian restarted the engine. "Let's hear it."

"I need your help…priming Mom and Grace for this."

"Priming them? You mean like delivering the news? You trust me to handle that?" Christian chuckled. "How much should I tell them? Everything or next to nothing?"

"Neither," Lauren said. "Tell them what I did, for the simple fact that rumors spread so quickly around here, and I don't want them hearing I went crazy, even though I did. And, in the gentlest way you can, which I know won't be easy for you, tell them I'll be home soon…and Dad is coming with me."

"Whoa." Christian's eyes widened. "Damn, are you sure about that?"

Lauren laughed uncomfortably. "Hell no. But you and I both know how unstable Grace is. And Mom is prone to lose consciousness at anything over the top. It might be good to give them a little notice before *he* walks through the door."

"If you think I can fine-tune *that* delivery, you really *did* go crazy."

Lauren pled with him, "Can you just *please* help me out? I'm running on emotional fumes here."

Christian nodded and gave a confident smile. "I'll take care of it. No promises on the results, though." He reached for her. "Cheer up, okay? Your dad's home."

Lauren opened her door and stepped out, and as she went to close it, he called for her to wait.

Christian pulled his jacket off and tossed it to her. "We've...been through this before, I know. But you're a tad underdressed for the occasion."

Lauren looked herself over. She was still in her running outfit. She'd completely forgotten.

She thanked him, and Christian pulled out of the driveway and headed for home, leaving Lauren to wait for her father to show his face again, though the postponement was brief. While slipping Christian's jacket on and zipping it up, Alan appeared on the front porch, the screen door smacking behind him.

The look of uncertainty he'd been casting began to evaporate upon seeing that his daughter was expecting him. He smiled and marched cautiously to her, his hands concealed in his jacket pockets. "I was hoping I'd find you here," he began delicately. "My day hasn't been short on surprises, but you were the last person I ever expected to see get out of that truck." A pause. "For the longest time, it's like I've been wandering aimlessly through a dream. But when I saw you, I knew it was over. Like the dream finally came true."

"I know what you mean. It feels like I'm dreaming right now." Lauren hesitated. "Is your friend going to be okay?"

Alan turned his head, regarding the home to his aft momentarily. "The bullet hit him in a bad spot, but he's tough. I think he'll pull through all right. The doctor is a little strange...has a peculiar bedside manner, so I'm clueless about his leg. Then again, it might be too soon to tell."

Lauren's lower lip began to tremble. She pulled her hands from her pockets and went about cracking her knuckles.

"I bet you have a lot of questions for me," said Alan.

"Thousands. Only, I don't know where to start."

"That makes two of us. I…missed you, Lauren."

"And I missed you," she whimpered. "More than I'm capable of expressing."

Alan beamed at the remark. Maybe this encounter wouldn't be as daunting as he anticipated.

Lauren evaluated him. "Can you start by telling me why you're so off?"

Or maybe he wasn't out of the woods quite yet. "Off?"

"Yeah. I know it's you. I can see that, but everything about you is… wrong, misaligned. You're physically here, but everything I remember about you isn't. It's like a part of you, a big part of you, is somewhere else."

Alan sighed. He presumed questions such as these would manifest, but he hadn't the time to rehearse his answers. All his focus had been shifted to his journey home. Once there, he'd hoped that everything else would harmonize and the pieces would mysteriously fall into place, but they weren't. He wanted so much to tell her the truth, explain everything that had happened to him, but his story wasn't going to offer her any pause, bearing in mind the veritable universe of details that lay missing. "I guess that's…one way of describing it."

Lauren looked disheartened. "Tell me why."

"I wish I could." Alan gritted his teeth. "I wish I could tell you everything, all the way down to the last minute detail. But I can't. I can't because…I don't remember anything. And I hate that I don't."

"Dad, why?" Lauren's eyes flashed. "Why don't you remember?"

"Because something happened to me," he admitted, looking away at first, only to have his daughter pursue and lock on to his eyes. "I got hurt. Rather badly."

"How bad?"

Alan beheld her gravely. "So bad that I almost died."

Lauren covered her mouth with her hand and shook. The possibility of her father departing this life had crossed her mind scores of times. "What…happened to you?"

"It was the worst scenario imaginable," Alan said, his lower lip trembling. "I was…on my way home and there was an accident, an explosion. And I was the victim."

Lauren altered her stance, her distress building. "You?"

"Me." Alan nodded. "If you were to ask how it happened, I couldn't begin to tell you, and I can't recount anything leading up to it…I have no memory of that, either. The only reason I know anything is because I was…told."

Lauren sniffled and turned away slightly. "This whole time…ever since I saw you, you've been looking at me like you don't know who I am. Is it…memory loss?"

Alan's expression went somber. He nodded. "It's post-traumatic amnesia, resultant of a brain injury."

"How bad is it? Is there anything you *do* remember? Anything at all?"

"Some memories have recently begun flashing back…a lot of others have yet to. There's still a lot missing."

"So that's it, then," Lauren said. "You *don't* know me."

"Lauren, don't say that. I'm your father—I know who you are."

She held up a hand. "But you don't remember me *at all*. You don't know anything about me, and you don't remember any of us…not even Mom or Grace."

"I know all of your names, but I don't remember your faces," Alan began. "And, kid…it *kills* me to admit that to you. I didn't even know yours until I saw you again. I've been trying to get back to you for months, and coming here was our last stop. Seeing you…it blew my mind, knowing who you were the instant you called for me. And knowing right then that you were still *alive*. I'm sorry, Lauren. I wish to God things were different, but none of this changes how I feel. I'm overjoyed to be here…home, with you."

Lauren didn't know what to think. She knew this man was Alan Russell, a person she hadn't seen in over fifteen months. He both looked and sounded like the father she knew, but his mannerisms had changed; his demeanor had changed. And the way he looked upon her wasn't nearly the same as it'd once been. She was on cloud nine over having him back, but she couldn't help feeling disappointed. "I don't know what to say to all this…or how to feel about it. I'm sorry."

"Can you at least tell me if your mother and sister are here with you?" Alan pled. "That they're just as alive as you are?"

Lauren pressed her lips together. "Mom and Grace are at home, and they're fine. We're all fine."

"Thank God," he said, exhaling a breath. "Look, maybe I should fill in a few of the blanks for you."

"By all means."

"After the accident, I spent four months in a coma," he began. "I woke up in a strange place, paralyzed, barely able to speak, surrounded by people I didn't know. Every memory of the life I'd lived, of who I used to be was gone. I didn't know what day it was or where I was, how I'd gotten there, or what had happened to me, nothing. I didn't even know who I was. And for almost a month following, I didn't know I had a family, a wife, and daughters."

Lauren scowled. "Then how did you get here? How—"

Alan halted her. "Hey, for this to work, I need you to hear me out. Offer me some benefit of the doubt. It's been forever since we've talked, and there's a mountain of catching up to do. I have a great deal to tell you, but there's a lot I won't be able to."

Jade stepped out onto the porch stoop and sent a thoughtful glance to the reunification taking place in the wintry, rural setting ahead of her.

Lauren's eyes moved away from her father and tracked her instantly. "Who is she?" She gestured to the brunette. "She hasn't stopped surveilling us since we met on the road."

Alan rotated. "That's Jade. She's a friend, Lauren. Someone very special to me. I'll call her over so you two ca—"

"No, wait. Someone special to you?" Lauren interrogated. "What does that mean? You've been gone all this time, and when you finally decide to come home, you bring a woman with you who looks at you like *that*?"

"Lauren, what on earth are you talking about?" Alan grimaced. "In what way is she looking at me?"

"The way a woman looks at a man when she's in love with him, Dad. I saw it the second I laid eyes on her, and I see it right now. Who the hell is she?"

Alan was taken aback. He'd never anticipated this line of questioning. "Okay, hold on. First off, Jade is a dear friend to me. She and I have been through a lot together, but I've never considered her as anything other than a friend. Nothing, not one thing exists between us beyond that affinity, trust me on that. And I didn't just *decide* to come home. It's been the *only* thing on my mind since I was told I had a family.

"Jade was one of a mere twofold who knew me and knew about me prior to my accident. She was integral in helping me relearn the person I was. And ever since knowing, being home with you, Grace, and your mother became a mission for me, and I've been doing everything in my power—everything, short of killing myself—to find you."

Alan felt a sharp pain rise into his head. "I'm sorry—I'm trying hard to help you make sense of this, and I realize it's not working. All I want is for you to believe me and not take the things I say out of context."

Lauren's first impulse was to hold him in contempt and everything he said as an excuse. She desired to take his account at more than simple face value, but there was no cohesion to any of it. This twist of fate today had taken her completely by surprise and wasn't becoming any less convoluted. She felt mystified in the moment.

While casting a hard stare at the resolute brunette, Lauren began to recall her encounter with a man in a black uniform in the middle of the national forest several months ago. She'd had no intention whatsoever of believing a word he'd said either. She hadn't wanted to trust him or know him, and the following day, he'd saved her life. Lauren had injured herself and was helpless, and Christian had taken a stand for her. Something deep within had told her to have faith in him, and she was rewarded for it. He'd protected her selflessly. He had shown up at the right place and time when Lauren had needed someone. Was it unfair for her to believe her father's situation had been any different? And against that backdrop, was this Jade person any different?

Whether the woman possessed an ulterior motive remained to be seen and, like everything else in life, would manifest in due course. Lauren had confided in someone, shorn of knowing his intentions, and if Jade had been there for her dad when he'd needed someone, the woman deserved the same consideration. Her dad deserved her faith because he was her dad. And maybe Jade did, too.

"I'm not trying to make this difficult for you," Lauren said. "*This* is just a lot…harder than I ever imagined it would be."

"I know what you mean. It shouldn't be that way, but you're right. It is," Alan said. "I met Jade where I was working in Washington, and if it wasn't for her, I never would've made it out of there. Four of us walked out of DC using plans I made up, and we made it about halfway home before my…accident. It happened right around the corner from a compound called Camp Hill, where Harpers Ferry used to be; my friend Valerie runs the place now. Between her and Jade and a few others, they stood by me and nursed me back to health from my deathbed. And that's no exaggeration. That makes these people very special to me, Jade in particular. She was there for me the whole time when I was helpless, and if it wasn't for her…" He trailed off in sobs.

"She…saved my life, Lauren. Along with a chosen few whom you've yet to meet. My friend Ken"—Alan pointed to the farmhouse behind him—"who might end up losing his leg over all this, was one of them. These people are special to me because they helped give me back my life. I was a goner, I'd lost everything—my life, my family, everything I ever was or knew. Without these people, without their willingness to stick by me, I wouldn't be here. I'd be dead."

Lauren nodded her head solemnly, taking everything in. "I believe you, and I'm sorry. But…I've been *dreaming* of this day. I've written you off dozens of times, only to hate myself for doing it…only to write you off again and have you appear in my dreams. You protected me there and said things that made me feel strong again, just like you used to. In the last dream I had, you told me you never left. And now you're here and I don't know what to make of it."

She sniffled and her eyes welled up. "You're right, it is like a dream come true—but you don't even know me. You don't remember the hikes we used to take, any of my birthdays, or any of the talks we had. And you don't remember how *close* we were. You're calling me by my first name now, and you *never* used to do that. I…miss the emotion and passion in your eyes; I used to see it every time we spoke. And right now, I don't see anything."

A cascade of tears slipped down Alan's cheeks. "I'm trying, okay? And I won't stop trying. I'm still me, Lauren. I'm still your dad. There's a good chance my memories will come back, and if they do, the old me might return with them. But I'm here now, and until that happens, I'm going to need your help. Guide me back…to who I was with you."

The two fell silent a moment and wept together while the cold void of air remained unnaturally between them.

Lauren soon began again in monotone. "After all this time and everything that's happened, it's a miracle you came back to us. And it's good to see your face…it looks a little different, though." She forced a smile. "There's some new scratches and dents, and you really need to work on your beard."

Alan smiled grimly. "Thanks. It's good to see you, too. Now I can finally put a face to a name."

Lauren snickered and sniffled and her father inched closer.

"Look, I realize this rendezvous is turning out to be far from perfect," he said. "I wish there was something I could do to take back all the time we missed, and I'm really sorry about how things went down. By God, if I knew of a way to fix this, I'd be on it…and if I could go back and prevent it from happening, I would in a heartbeat. I never should have left you that day. I know my memory is screwed and it's going to take time for me to warm up to things, but that doesn't mean I'm not your dad."

"I know that."

"Then you know how long it's been since I've gotten a hug from you," Alan said. "I've come a really long way to be here…if you're up for it, I think it might be good…for both of us."

Lauren gazed up at her father as several heavy tears escaped her lower eyelids. "I *know* it would." She reached out and fell limply into him, feeling his arms pull her in. Her heartbeat slowed and a feeling of calm began to overtake her. In a world that had turned on her and had taken him from her, he'd somehow found a way back.

Lauren never wanted the feeling to go away. But in that moment, a premonition washed over her. As good as it felt to be reunited with him, the difficulties that had plagued her life since his disappearance hadn't gone anywhere and wouldn't. And at some point, her father needed to know.

"I love you, Dad. And I'm sorry for being a bitch to you."

Alan smiled and squeezed her. "I love you, too. I missed you more than you'll ever know. Even more than *I'll* ever know." He kissed her head, rubbed her hair with his nose, and inhaled through his nostrils.

Feeling that, Lauren pulled away suddenly and wiped her tears. "Where did that come from?"

"What? What did I do?"

"You said you've forgotten a lot of yourself, but do you realize what you just did?"

Alan shook his head, his lower lip protruding. "No. What?"

"You…sniffed me. You smelled my hair." Lauren grinned. "You used to do it all the time, almost like a reflex. I used to think it was creepy, and even went through a spell when I thought you had some strange obsession with shampoo. But later on, I learned what it really was."

Alan sent along a look, urging her to explain.

"Affection," Lauren said. "It's one of your ways of showing affection for the ones you love. You're the only person I know who's ever done it."

"Me? I'm the only one, huh?" Alan's expression softened. "Amazing. An hour reunited and you're already helping me become the old me again."

Lauren giggled.

Alan exhaled some relief. "Look, I know it's going to take time to rebuild everything we've lost…but I also know it's not going to happen in one day. I could stand with you, right here, for an eternity. But I'd love just as much to see your mother…and your sister, if they're around."

Lauren turned and reached for his hand. "Come on, I'll take you home." She motioned to Jade. "Let your friend know she's welcome to come along."

# CHAPTER 28

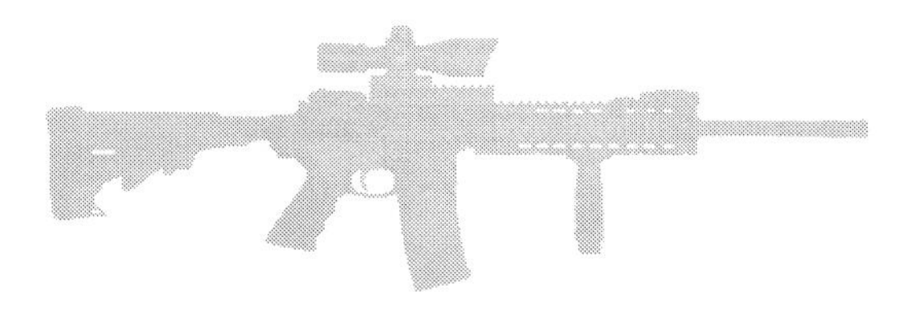

LAUREN GUIDED ALAN AND JADE along Trout Run Road the short distance to the cabin. Upon arrival, the inviting scents of breakfast being prepared and coffee brewing tugged on Alan's nose.

As Lauren went for the door handle, Alan halted her upon noticing how far Jade was lingering behind. "Whatever's cooking in there smells incredible," he said. "I should introduce the two of you before we go any further." He beckoned Jade to come closer. "I want you to meet my daughter Lauren. Lauren, this is Jade, one of the special someones who've been there for me…every step of the way."

Jade smirked. "Literally," she said, tendering her hand. "It's good to meet you, finally."

"I take it you've heard a lot about me," Lauren said, noticing now the woman's busted lips and bloodied gums.

"I have." Jade nodded, concealing her smile. "But not one bit of it did you justice. You're a…striking young woman."

The reply came bashfully. "That's…kind of you to say. Thank you." She looked to her father. "Ready for this?"

Alan exhaled a stressful breath. "No. But it feels like I've been waiting forever for it."

Lauren pushed the door open and guided Alan and Jade into the cabin, to find Grace and Christian in the kitchen, working to get breakfast going.

When Grace saw her father make his entrance, she expelled a loud "Eeek!" and let loose the stack of plates in her hands. They fell to the floor and shattered calamitously on impact, sending shards and shavings in abstract patterns about her bare feet. Torn now between standing fast and injuring herself to go to him, she reached for Christian with fingers flailing. "Well, shit. Honey! Honeeey! I need help."

Christian turned on his heels and hove her into his arms, then carried her over the danger zone, crushing pieces of broken dishes under his boots.

The second her toes touched the floor, she sprang to Alan with outstretched arms. "Hey, Daddy-o! Oh my gosh…it's so exhilarating to see you! I'm glad you're back!" She jerked away, sniffing, looking him over sideways. "You smell funny. And you're cold as balls. Brrr! So how was your trip?"

Alan looked upon her strangely, not knowing how to react. "My trip? It was…okay, I suppose."

"Okay? That's it? Hmm…noticeably anticlimactic. After all this time away, I was *expecting* a veritable kiloturd more from you." Grace put a finger to her chin and studied him. "You look pretty good, all doomsdays considered. And it's very pleasing to know my future hubster wasn't being a disingenuous twat when he told us you were here a bit ago." She grabbed her beau's right arm and dragged him forward. "Speaking of whom, have you met my Christian yet?"

"Uh, no. I mean, not formally," Alan said, taking the younger man's hand. "Alan Russell."

Christian humbly introduced himself. "It's a pleasure, sir."

"Likewise. And you don't have to call me sir."

"Oh, yes he does," Grace countered. "Trust me, Daddy-o, there's a splendid rationale for the added formality. Though, it appears…no one has informed you, hitherto." She flicked Christian's funny bone and cut her eyes at her sister.

"Nuh-uh." Lauren pointed away. "Direct that hormonal hate of yours elsewhere."

Christian rubbed his elbow, looking befuddled. "Sorry, Grace. I just assumed you'd rather wait…you know, for the right moment."

"Right moment?" Grace shot back in misplaced disdain. "Right moment?! *What* right moment? Just spit it out, one of you, or somebody! Why am I always the one to do it?"

The younger man despairingly tossed his hands in the air. "Grace, come on. *Jesus*."

"No! No Jesus! Don't do that, Christian!" Grace exclaimed. "Don't you dare demean me! I'll sign the divorce papers *before* you propose!"

"Grace..."

"Don't say another word! You'll only further embarrass yourself! I swear to—"

"Hey!" Alan balled in a thundering tenor, muzzling the room, its occupants, and the house. "Can all of you *please* calm down? I just got here!"

Grace lowered her head and bit into her lips. "Sorry, Daddy."

"I apologize too, sir," said Christian.

"Apologies accepted, and please stop calling me sir." Alan scanned the faces in the room. "Okay, seriously. What on earth is so important that I've yet to be informed about?"

A few seconds passed in the silence before a forlorn, downhearted voice emitted from the hall. "That you're going to be a grandfather." With one hand to her chest and the other pressed to the wall for support, Michelle glided in with short steps. Her skin was blotchy and pale, and her lower eyelids looked ready to burst. "Congratulations."

Alan's eyes locked onto her figure and he shuddered. He'd prayed and begged God to get him this far. Despite his uncertainty, he was staring now into the damp, swollen eyes that could only belong to his wife. It was a moment for which he never could have prepared, one he'd known would come had he made it home. Alan didn't recognize her and he didn't know her face, but he could feel her presence pulling on him with a force stronger than gravity. Even the sound of her voice felt like it was drawing him in. "I'm...speechless. I don't know what to say."

"Neither do I." Michelle wiped her nose with a tissue as more tears fell. Then she crashed into him, almost knocking him to the ground. "Welcome home." She held on for dear life and exploded into sobs. "Christian said you were here...I didn't believe him...I thought it was a cruel joke. I've been in bed with my face in a pillow, crying like a baby about it. Until I heard your voice. I thought I was hallucinating. But I'm not, right? This...really is you, isn't it?"

"It's me."

"Well, I don't believe it." Michelle backed away a few inches to survey the man appearing to be her husband. "Jesus, Alan. This doesn't seem real to me. It feels like you and looks like you, but you look like hell."

"I feel how I look, then."

Michelle's lips quivered. "And you didn't give up on us."

"Not for a second." While struggling to absorb the moment, Alan deliberated all the faces in the room, save Jade's. "I'm sorry, I don't mean to put a hold on this, but I don't want to miss anything either." He paused. "Now, which one of my daughters is pregnant?"

Lauren shook her head feverishly. "Definitely not me."

Grace proudly raised her hand and pointed to her belly, her mood having achieved an about-face. "This baby bump certifies you a soon-to-be granddaddy-o."

Alan nodded and grinned proudly. "I…suppose it does," he said, then faced Christian. "And you're the father, I imagine?"

The young man nodded avowal. "Yes, sir—I mean, yes. Minus the sir."

Alan drew back, smiled broadly and took a breath, his hands having never left his wife. "Congratulations to both of you."

Grace curtsied. "Why, thank you. It was nothing, really."

The room went quiet after the exchange. All present moved to allow the out-of-touch husband and wife some extra space. Christian carried Grace back into the kitchen and set her down close to the stove, safely away from the shards of peril. He then went to cleaning up the shattered mess of dish remnants at her direction.

Alan rotated and was preparing to introduce Jade, who'd yet to leave the foyer, to the family. But at seeing Lauren's glare, he decided to postpone.

Lauren then went to her. "Can you and I talk outside for a minute?"

"Of course," Jade said with a nod, and followed the younger woman outside to the porch.

The women took positions opposite each other, and a breeze fluttered by, tossing Lauren's hair around. She moved to square off with Jade, doing so in innocuous fashion. "What happened to your face?"

Jade hesitated, looking sheepish. "I…got in a little fight."

Lauren tilted her head curiously. "A little one?"

"Mm-hmm. I won, though. In case you're wondering."

"And your opponent looks worse than you, I take it?"

"Oh, by far," Jade said, grinning with zeal. "He sort of…lost his head over it."

The witticism coupled with the look on Jade's face served to break the ice. Lauren grinned back at her, then said, "My reasoning for pulling you out here wasn't to prevent you from meeting everyone. You will, soon. But a lot of suppressed emotions are flying around right now, and

I didn't want my mother to see…what I've been seeing. Because she would have."

Jade folded her arms. "Okay…"

"For the record, a large part of me is fighting this. I don't know you. But evidently you've been with my dad the whole time he's been gone, the whole time I haven't been. I don't know if it's protectiveness or some form of envy on my part, but this whole situation feels wrong to me, and I can't switch that off just yet." Lauren exhaled a humid breath that condensed into a fog. "Dad said that you saved his life. Is that true?"

Jade looked away, her grin waning. "That's not an easy question to answer."

"From where I'm standing, it is. Either you did or you didn't. It's black or white, doesn't leave a lot of room for gray."

"I only did what anyone else would have done."

"Not just anyone," Lauren corrected. "And if you did, it's admirable. There's no reason to play it down."

"I'm not," Jade stated. "But I do refuse the full credit. If I explain, you'd understand better. But I'm not about to waste my time if you don't plan to hear me out."

"I'm listening." Lauren bade her continue.

Jade took a deep breath. "I was there when he got hurt, came to his aid not long after it happened. And it wasn't good; I didn't think for a second he'd pull through. But he did, he surprised everyone, especially me, and I took care of him throughout his recovery." A pause. "But I should've taken better care of him before. Saving a person's life *can* be cut and dry, but it wasn't in this case. Not for me. If I would've been doing a better job that day, your dad would've never fallen prey to anything."

"I don't understand. What job?"

"Protection. Preventing those under my watch from falling prey to bad shit," Jade said flatly. "I was a professional; I lived and breathed the life for years, even became top tier, one of the best at it. But, in your dad's case, when the moment came, I wasn't there. I failed him."

"So, in recompense, you felt obligated to care for him after he got hurt?"

"Yes, but there's a lot more to it than that."

"I'm sure there is." Lauren squinted. "What were you? A bodyguard? Someone's private security?"

"In some respects, but not exactly."

The direction this chat was heading was making Lauren all the more curious about Jade, but the mystery woman's story could wait. She needed to know her father's full backstory. "So what happened to him?"

"Are you sure you want to know?" Jade asked frankly. "The details aren't pretty."

"I don't doubt it. Whatever happened kept him away from us a long time."

Jade rolled her lips. She spent the next few minutes outlining the details of her relationship with Lauren's father, beginning with how things had initially gone down on the day of the EMP that had served as reason for their interaction to begin with. Jade told her about Walter and Ken and the foursome's escape from Washington, to include the dreadful scenes they'd witnessed, as forever etched in her memory. "Fortunately for us, your dad already had a plan plotted out. We used the C&O towpath and walked our way out of there."

Lauren felt a chill unrelated to the weather, recalling her conversation with Bernie scarcely days before.

"If it hadn't been for your dad, we wouldn't have had anywhere to go. And all the same, none of us would have left." Jade hesitated, casting her stare out and beyond. "We slept in shifts, rotated watch, and spent a week on the trail without incident. Fifty miles in, we got ambushed. There was a firefight. We were…pinned down at first. They were shooting at us from overhead, from positions on a bridge overpass. And that's a shitty environment to fight a gun battle.

"But we had automatic weapons, training and every advantage you could dream of, minus the high ground." She regarded Lauren. "Your dad was in a good spot. He chose an old sycamore tree for cover. Its roots were exposed from floodwater erosion, and they hemmed him in. He chose well; from that spot he could shoot all day long and never get hit. But there was a culvert not far behind him that had been fortified with a binary explosive."

"Like Tannerite," said Lauren.

"That's right. The opposition had taken a lot of casualties and we were nearing the deciding point. They were getting desperate; they weren't even aiming their shots anymore. We assumed they would either give up, run off and hide, or do something stupid, but they didn't. They pushed their big red last-resort button." Jade paused. "I won't bore you with the science on how blended ammonium nitrate and powdered aluminum reacts when struck by a bullet, but I watched your father soar about twenty feet after detonation, and it scared the life out of me." She paused. "Of our group, he was the only one who'd never been in combat, and he had no place being there. And if I would've been doing my job, he wouldn't have been a casualty."

Lauren folded her arms and put her weight on a heel, finding herself riveted.

Jade continued. "We finished those fuckers off after that, every goddamn one of them. We chased them down and snuffed them out like cockroaches. Then we hoofed it six klicks, taking turns lugging your dad and his stuff to the nearest resupply waypoint on your dad's map. His friend Valerie lives there. It was a town once, but they'd locked it down not long after the blackout and converted it into a compound. That's where we found help for him. A doctor treated him, and Valerie and I took care of him during his coma."

"And you were there when he woke up?" Lauren asked.

Jade nodded. "Admittedly, I haven't left his side. I couldn't."

"Not once?"

"Okay, obviously, there were intermissions," Jade said coyly.

"I'm sure there were." Lauren stared hard at Jade. She searched her eyes and studied her expression and mannerisms, utilizing levels of inherited scrutiny. "You should know, I can see it, Jade. The way you look at him."

Jade stammered. Her lips parted, but she didn't answer.

"There's no point in denying it," Lauren said. "All things considered, it's good my sister was in one of her off-the-wall moods. I don't think my mom caught on, between her state of shock and the...distractions."

Jade furrowed her brow and turned away. She dug for and pulled out a partial pack of out-of-date cigarettes and placed one between her lips, remembering then where she'd found them. "Dammit...you wouldn't happen to have a light, would you?" She fidgeted, searching through every pocket in her clothing for an apparatus capable of igniting a flame. "As if this day couldn't get any worse."

"Worse? I didn't say any of that to call you out."

"Yet that's precisely what you did," Jade snapped. "Look, it's okay. I'm used to it. I'll just split. I'll run along and go back to doing my own thing. It was stupid of me to ever believe any of this."

Lauren took a few steps closer and held up a mini Bic while Jade looked warily at her.

“I always keep one on me,” Lauren said, flicking it to life. “It was one of the things Dad used to preach, among others.”

Jade leaned in and pulled the flame into the desiccated tobacco, and it crackled to life. “Thanks.”

“Where would you go if you left here?”

“I don’t know,” Jade said, shivering now. “It wasn’t part of the plan, but I’ll figure it out.”

Lauren looked curiously at her. “But staying here was?”

Jade hesitated. “Yes.”

“By my father’s invitation?”

Jade eyeballed her, then nodded and took a long drag, smiling uncomfortably. “You know, normally, I would be appalled at this. But this whole day has been a far cry from normal, and I’m making an exception because of who you are. You’re just like your father—big on the truth, no matter how sacrosanct, and that’s fine. I’ll tell you whatever you want to know, because that’s fine too—my reputation here doesn’t mean shit, so why not?”

Lauren’s eyes crinkled into slits. “You can tell me whatever you want, but keep your voice down.”

“Sorry.” Jade exhaled, recalling where she was now. “I’ve met thousands of people in my life, but not a single person like your dad. He’s a diamond in the rough. And your mom is lucky as hell to have him. To lose him like that, for as long as she did, I don’t know how she lived through it. Seeing them reunited a few minutes ago was magic. I’ve never felt more satisfied in my life. It was like I finally accomplished something good for a change.

“Your father was the first person to ever show me he cared and never once turn his back on me. And he had no reason to do that. He owed me nothing; he just did it anyway. He gave me a chance that no one else ever bothered to. And no one has ever made me feel more like a person than he has. I didn’t come here to cause problems, Lauren. I swear I’m not here to toss a wrench in your parents’ marriage. I came because I have nowhere else to go. And yes, your dad invited me to come and be a part of this.”

“A part of what?”

Jade hesitated, now on the verge of tears once more. “Family. It’s a long story, lots of unpleasant details, but I’ve…never known one myself.”

Lauren regarded her counterpart thoughtfully. No person was truly invulnerable, not herself, or even Jade. Eventually, there comes a time when humans feel the need for companionship, for fellowship, and that which exists exclusively within the realms of family. The universe was built that way by design. If we chose, one of us could wander the world and fight our way through life's tangles on our own, but it just wasn't meant to be that way.

"Well, it appears you do now," she said. "Dad always speaks his mind, but everything he says comes from his heart. And when he says something, he means it."

"Boy, do I know it." Jade smiled at Lauren, receiving one in return, and the two women shared a stare, both realizing their eyes were the same color.

"I won't grill you anymore about this," Lauren said. "But I needed to know. Dad told me there's nothing between you, and I believe him. But that's only his side of things." A pause. "In the future, you might do an enhanced job of masking how *you* feel."

Jade smirked. "Sounds like good advice."

"Also, if you wouldn't mind keeping a line of communication open between us, I'd appreciate it. It might help me better understand my dad's ailments."

"You can call on me anytime," said Jade. "For now though, I think I'm going to make myself scarce. I need to check on Ken's progress and get back to the Marauder and get our things situated."

"Sure you won't join us for breakfast?"

"Maybe some other day. I'm not much on family reunions, and it's probably best to give your parents some space." Jade looked away a moment. "Would you mind passing a message to your dad from me?"

"Not at all."

"Tell him I said promise fulfilled. And thank you." Jade smiled. "He wants to credit me for saving his life, then he deserves the same for saving my butt this morning. I don't think Ken would disagree."

Lauren's brow furrowed as she switched gears. "Wait—what happened this morning?"

Hearing her tonal change put Jade on alert yet again. "We had a… mishap. How much do you know about what's materializing on the other side of that mountain?"

Lauren went stone-faced. "Plenty. Why?"

"Then you know about the DHS and FEMA presence?"

Lauren's jaw clenched. She nodded. "We've had our own mishaps with them. Is that how Ken got shot and you got hurt?"

Jade nodded, then recounted and disclosed the most recent turn of events along their trip here.

At the culmination, Lauren's eyes grew wide with patent urgency. The southern barricade had been left wide open upon their hasty return, and it mustn't remain that way. Jade's report needed to be passed along and distributed. Woo Tang, Fred, Neo, Christian, even the likes of Richie needed to be briefed on this, and in due course, every soul in the valley had to be brought up to speed.

She turned away and started off. "I'm sorry, I have to go. Excuse me."

"Lauren, wait. Was it something I said?"

"Absolutely."

Jade hopped from the porch into the yard and gave chase. "Hey! Hold up. Let me give you a ride."

# CHAPTER 29

**The cabin**
**Trout Run Valley**
**Friday, January 7th. Present day**

THE DAY HAD BEEN SPENT getting Alan acquainted with the acreage spanning the valley, his neighbors, their livelihoods and the routines occurring within, which also involved reacquainting him with old friends and their families. In doing so, a primer on the ins and outs of daily life had been afforded, and Alan gathered that living here was nothing short of an ongoing struggle. Hard work was an obligation, and survival and subsistence was the name of the game, both requisite rules of nature in their world. But the efforts put forth bolstered commitment, created trust and solidarity, and were therefore rewarding.

During his tour, Alan had grown to think of his new home much in the way he had Camp Hill. The communities were proving to have a lot in common, though the valley did have more room and more familiar faces, while holding no hellishly steep roads on which to stumble and relearn his walking stride, and no Valerie with whom to raise dispute.

The Russell family, no longer divided, elected to put together an evening celebration, something that hadn't been done since being here. Michelle made her rounds and invited every two-legged beating heart in the valley to the cabin for an impromptu coming-home party for Alan. Kim Mason and Kristen Perry helped to arrange a feast for the attendees; and as the confines of his home crammed with guests, Alan was put on a pedestal to answer questions, overhear stories of the past, and converse with those he hadn't spoken to in over a year's time, though he failed to recall ever having chatted with any of them.

Michelle went against protocol and had broken out the remaining airplane bottles of liquor her husband had amassed long ago in their preparations, for use as currency and for barter. The invaders who had appropriated the valley over a month prior had partaken from the cream of the crop for their amusement, but that didn't hinder any guest from enjoying a cocktail or two, or more.

Friends gathered together after dark in the Russell cabin to enjoy each other's company amidst glowing lanterns and candlelight. They talked and told jokes, laughed, carried tunes and even danced. They spoke of old memories, trying times and hopeful futures.

Alan did his best to be hospitable and find enjoyment as the party's guest of honor, but the commotion soon became a little too much for him, and he excused himself.

Escaping from the crowd, Alan went outside to the front porch, failing to put on a jacket first. He swirled around the drink he'd brought with him and stared into his yard, into the cold, shadowy woodlands beyond, wondering for a time if everything that had happened recently, and was happening now, was even real.

It felt as though he'd spent a lifetime away from these people, the friends he was getting to know again, and even his own family—his devoted wife of many years and his two exquisite daughters. It was a lot to swallow in one sitting; the former existence of Alan Russell was no more and a new one had begun. He was home now, but everything and everyone felt foreign to him, though the feeling of unfamiliarity itself was far from being so. Alan attributed all this to his infirmity, this damned amnesia, and while sipping the sweet, stinging emulsion from his glass, he stirred internally and wondered if a day would ever come that might return to him all that he had lost.

Alan knew that outside his grievances, he was indeed a lucky man. This chapter in his life had found a satisfying conclusion; he'd made it home to his estranged family after swindling death. He had tried second-guessing the future, attempted to plan for every worst-case scenario imaginable, and then some. But in the end, all that planning and preparing hadn't counteracted the inevitable. Alan's wife and children had been torn from his grasp, and him from theirs; and what had ultimately served to reunite them was his love for them and theirs for him. Undeniably, he knew of no other force more powerful or more capable of doing so in the known universe.

Alan wasn't aware of what the future held from this day forward, but he was surely never to forget that; just as certain as he was never to leave this place or those he loved ever again. Not without having their souls forcibly pried from his cold, dead hands.

Michelle had seen Alan move away from the crowd and make his way outside. She had seen everything he'd done throughout the day, having never taken her eyes from him. She figured it possible he'd gone to look for some fresh air, or like every other man she knew, to use the outdoor facilities. But after being gone for a time longer than she'd expected, she grew uncomfortable and went looking for him.

Michelle put on a jacket, took another for her husband and went outside to the porch, relieved to find him there. She glowed both inside and out at seeing him, and at the sensation of his presence. She'd never thought this day would come, that this man who'd pestered her with his silly orations on conspiracy theories, hidden political agendas and potential end-of-times scenarios would return to her.

Michelle called to mind the times she'd hated him for it, when all she'd wanted was to find some way of shutting him off. And she recalled the times she'd given up and left him to his devices while pretending to enjoy some book or pointless show on television so she wouldn't have to listen to his ramblings.

Looking at him and considering all they had been through, it astounded her how differently she felt now. Though it hadn't gone off as he'd planned, the preparations in which Alan had invested and procured, in unison with the plans he'd crafted, had bestowed his family with a buffer. And that buffer had enabled them to continue life beyond that of the majority, in the wake of the collapse of civilization.

This man had also done something else Michelle couldn't put into plain words, something that still, even to this day, threw her for a loop. Alan had involved Lauren in this and had made her an integral part of his plan, to include a list of undertakings he'd concealed from his own wife. Much of the specifics remained a mystery, but his doing so had been one of the key reasons his family had remained unharmed to this day. Their youngest possessed extraordinary talents that kept her and those around her alive, accentuated her courage and made her strong—stronger than anyone Michelle had ever known. And this man, this husband of hers a short time ago returned, had perpetuated all of this.

She wanted to despise him for it. She wanted to hate him for all that he'd done, hadn't done, and hold against him everything he'd screwed up, but Michelle couldn't bring herself to feel that way. Alan was here now, and that in itself was a miracle. He'd somehow come home to her, and the thought of that alone brought peace to Michelle's soul and soothed her aching heart, bringing an end to a searing pain that had begun on the day he'd failed to return.

Michelle was beginning to recognize that his purpose for going to those lengths were far more intrinsic than for which she'd originally given him credit. He hadn't done all this for his ego, it wasn't avarice, and it hadn't been just so his family could reign superior or simply outlive, outgun, and outlast the underprepared and less fortunate. Rather, he'd done so merely because he loved them and wanted the best for them. Alan Russell had wanted his family to live their lives safely and happily, come what may, should the worst of times ever befall them. And who was she to condemn him for wanting that?

Michelle moved in behind her husband and encircled him with her arms, slipping the jacket she brought for him over his shoulders. "Hey… you've been out here a while. Aren't you cold?"

Alan shivered and a brow shot up. "Now that you mention it."

"Are you doing okay? Looked like you were having fun in there."

"I was, and I'm good," Alan said. "It's just a little overwhelming. I've grown accustomed to interacting with people who know me, when I know nothing about them. But tonight, there's been a lot more of *them* than I'm used to."

"You were never good with crowds, or large groups of people, if it's any consolation."

"That sounds about right. Every time I opened my mouth, I got nervous and my throat dried up like a desert." Alan slipped his arms into the jacket sleeves. "In addition to these tasty adult beverages, I know I've put down at least a gallon of water tonight; more than I've drank in months."

Michelle gestured to his glass, noting the emptiness. "Want me to warm that up for you? Or make you a nightcap? I don't mind."

"No, I'm okay for now," Alan said. "I've been meaning to thank you for everything you've done today. You've gone out of your way to get me settled in and help me feel at home, and it's working."

"Alan, I'll do whatever it takes. I know this is a lot for you to deal with. Everything and everyone is...foreign to you. And the last thing I want is you wandering around and getting lost." She squeezed him. "And you're welcome."

Alan grinned. "You might consider hunting me down a map, just to be safe," he said. "The area around here is beautiful. And the cabin and our property is markedly cozy. I think I'm going to like living here."

"That's good, I'm glad you think so. I don't think we'll be moving anytime soon."

"And believe it or not, I'm perfectly okay with those plans." Alan finished his drink off. "It was thoughtful of you to allow Jade and Ken to stay here. That really means the world to me. We've been through a lot together."

Michelle's brows raised. "So I've gathered. Conveniently enough for them, we had two vacancies open up recently," she mused. "Ken's a little unusual, but after learning to cope with Christian's quirks, it's nothing I can't handle. And it wouldn't be right of me to let your girl sleep in the yard."

"My *girl*?"

Michelle nudged him and grinned sheepishly. "I'm kidding, sort of. You promised her a place here...and I suppose, as your wife, I have an obligation to abide by that." A pause. "But it's not easy for me. I don't know much about her, and I'm not particularly fond of another woman living under my roof who's...*seen* as much of *you* as I have."

Alan snickered. "You have nothing to worry about."

"I know. You've said that."

"It's the God's honest truth, Michelle. I was either comatose or catatonic the whole time. What's more, a urinary catheter was involved," Alan clowned, "making foul play highly unlikely, if not downright impossible."

"Foul play?" She punched his arm. "For fuck's sake, Alan! We need to work on this—there are certain things a man should *never* say to his wife, even teasing."

The couple shared a laugh. Alan reached for her and Michelle snuggled into him. They swayed together and vocalized their devotion for each other for the umpteenth time since reunifying.

Alan placed his lips against her temple, sensing her quickened pulse. “I saw Christian take Grace downstairs a while ago, but I don’t remember Lauren leaving. Feels like I haven’t seen her in hours.”

“It probably feels that way because you haven’t. She’s a lot like her father when it comes to crowds. You must’ve rubbed off on her at some point.”

“She’s already gone to bed, then?” Alan asked.

“I doubt it.”

“Where is she?”

Michelle’s features softened as a grim smile set in. “Knowing her, she’s as overcome by all this as you, but in her own way.” She glanced right to the porch’s edge, to a set of fresh boot prints in the snow. They intermixed with a jumble of others deposited by their party guests hours ago and split off, moving away in single file toward the bridge over Trout Run. Michelle reached for Alan’s arm. “Come with me.”

She led him behind the cabin to the bridge, where the prints went missing in the areas shoveled out and reappeared on the opposite side. They tracked them together past the shed until they disappeared in the darkness marking the tree line.

“If I know my daughter, those belong to her,” Michelle said.

Alan squinted. “What’s back there?”

Michelle shrugged her shoulders a tinge. “I’m not sure. Solitude? Tranquility? Enlightenment, maybe? I’ve asked, but Lauren’s never given me a straight answer. I doubt she ever will either. She’s always felt at home amongst nature…we practically raised her in it, but most of what she knows about it is owed to you.” A pause. “But I think this place is different for her.”

Alan homed in on Michelle’s tonal change. “What makes it different?”

She ushered him inbound. “You should ask her,” she said, then patted him on the butt. “Go. Find your daughter and talk to her. Then come home…and bring her with you.”

“I think I’ll do that,” Alan said, somewhat shocked at the smack she’d given him. He literally could not remember the last time he’d been on the receiving end of such an unprovoked attack from a loved one.

Alan followed the set of boot prints, taking his time to allow his eyes to adjust to the dimness. He wasn’t sure how far he’d be able to go at first, as it was almost proving too dark for his maturing eyesight. After a hundred yards or so, he caught sight of a gleaming light in the distance.

Arms outstretched and hands held before him, Alan used the light to guide himself between trees, and after a few minutes, the terrain leveled and opened into a grove. The light he'd been following had been the smoldering mantels of a dated Coleman lantern, one that was now suspended from a branch, serving light to areas around and below. A few feet away, swathed by the lantern's flickering radiance, her face concealed inside her hood, was Lauren.

Not wishing to startle her, Alan got ready to announce his presence, but she beat him to the punch, having heard his approach a ways off.

"Are you lost?" she asked, turning her neck to face him.

Alan took a quick look around and shrugged. "No, just felt like taking a little walk. It was getting stuffy in there; thought the fresh air would do me some good." He slid his hands in his pockets and studied her. "You look immersed in thought. Am I interrupting something?"

"No, not at all."

"Everything okay with you?"

Lauren sighed and grinned shyly. "Not really. But I'm fine, so don't worry. It's become the new norm for me."

"Oddly enough, I think I can relate." Alan took a few hesitant steps closer. "Are you sure I'm not intruding?"

Lauren shook her head, her expression affable. She turned away soon after and sent her stare into nothingness.

Alan went quiet too. He spent a moment hunting for a segue, failing to locate one. "Well, I didn't come here to bother you, I was just wondering where you'd run off to. I'll leave you alone."

"No, Dad, you're fine. Please stay."

Alan's forehead wrinkled, indicating a yearning for validation. Lauren conveyed a fleeting smile and he accepted the invite. "I loved what your mother did tonight; it was a little over the top for me…lots of new faces and names to remember. It got hectic with all the handshakes, catching up and awkward hugging…I didn't even see you leave."

"I doubt anyone did," Lauren said. "I sort of slipped out when no one was watching. I've never been a big fan of crowds.

Alan smirked. "Your mother informed me of that just a few minutes ago. She said I was no different, but damned if I ever knew until tonight. Guess it's something we have in common."

"You and I have countless things in common."

"Yeah, I'm coming to that realization." Alan harrumphed. "Damn. Listen to me…what kind of father says shit like that to his kid?"

Lauren giggled. "I only know of one."

"Yeah, so do I. I'm hoping that'll change someday, preferably soon, like before old age sets in. Otherwise, how will any of you distinguish normal, oblivious Dad from the one who's going senile or developing progressive dementia?"

Lauren cackled again. "Stop it."

"Stop what? Making fun of myself?"

"No, making me laugh," she cooed.

"Oh, that." Alan faked disappointment. "But I never knew I was so good at it."

Lauren snickered and wiped her nose, sending him an endearing look. "You haven't lost your sense of humor. You're still a goofball."

Alan almost looked proud. "Thanks for noticing, and thanks even more for telling me." He sighed. "I guess that's *something*, isn't it?"

"It's a start."

Alan veered away from his daughter and evaluated their surroundings. He soon took notice of a crude crucifix made of sticks angling up from the snow-covered earth some feet away, the name Angel carved onto the crossbeam. A morbid curiosity dawned on him. "Lauren, where are we? What is this place?"

She took her time responding. "It doesn't look like much, but this is hallowed ground we're standing on. After what happened, I hated the thought of this place; I didn't want to set foot anywhere near it. But I suppose time heals, and I got over feeling that way. It's become…very special to me."

Alan hesitated. "Who's buried here?"

Lauren wavered and spoke with a quiver. "A little girl."

Shocked at her reply, Alan's stare left the grave marker and instantly fixed on his daughter.

"I never knew how old she was, but she couldn't've been more than six or seven. She…died a few months ago. I met her and her mother on a trail a few days before; they were foraging for food. I didn't know anything about her, none of us did; we didn't even know her name." A pause. "An armed faction that had raided the valley last summer attacked us again without warning. They shot up vehicles and houses, set fire to one, then came here to do the same. We fought off a dozen or more of them. Some had tried to break into the shed out back, and after the fight was over, I went to check on it. The little girl was inside with her mother, and the woman had a gun in her hand."

Lauren paused briefly. "I tried reasoning with her, but she wouldn't bend. She was callous and irrational and had no compassion to speak of. She was one of the types of people you used to warn me about. She pointed her gun at me like there was no other option…and that left me with one. I shot her…right in front of her own daughter. I'll never forget the sound of her screams. But I'll never forget what happened after that…it torments me to this day. And probably will forevermore."

Alan's concern and worry for his daughter were fully engaged. "Tell me," he said, closing in on her.

Lauren's lips trembled and her eyes welled. "The woman…she shot her—killed her own daughter, put a bullet in her head like she was *nothing*, right there in front of me. It was the most brutal, hateful thing I've ever seen; nothing could've ever prepared me for it." A pause. "I'd only shot and killed one person in my life before then, and I did it to protect Mom. But I took the lives of at least a dozen men that day. I even shot that little girl's mother…but for some bizarre reason, I didn't kill her, even though I wanted to, especially after what she did. Sometimes, I think it's my fault that Angel's life ended when it did and how it did… I'm the reason she's interred here."

Alan put a hand on Lauren's shoulder. "No, Lauren. You're not. What happened is her mother's fault; the woman murdered her child. There's no way you or anyone else could've predicted that outcome, so don't you dare waste another second of your time beating yourself up over what might've been. Not one of us knows the future, and you only did what you knew was necessary in that moment. The decisions you made then affected what was most important. They kept you alive and safe."

"That sounds like the old you talking."

"That might be," Alan said, "but old or new me, I mean every word." A pause. "This can't be easy to talk about, but I'm grateful and glad you're choosing to open up to me. I felt *beyond* detached from you the other day."

"You were my best friend growing up. Not because I wanted you to be, but because you *chose* to be. You demanded the truth and never once judged me over it, no matter how bad it was. I knew I could always talk to you about anything…I'm just a little off my game."

"I think we both are," Alan said, his shoulders slumping. "This is good practice for us."

Lauren hung her head. "I know you don't remember this. You took me shooting for my first time when I was eleven. I was hitting paper with your .22, and while reloading, I asked you if it could kill someone. You never sugarcoated anything and didn't hesitate to tell me yes and that all guns were capable of killing." She paused, looking away a moment. "I remember how it felt to hear that; it was reassuring, empowering, and downright terrifying, all at the same time.

"It worried me that a gun could kill someone all of a sudden, but you clarified by explaining that guns were inanimate and brainless and merely a tool. Killing is the act of causing death, and it must be carried out by decision or even indecision. I told you then that I never wanted to kill anyone…I remember those words as if spoken yesterday. Ever since you've been back, I can't get them out of my mind…along with a million other conversations we've had."

"Why do you think that is?"

"I don't know." Lauren's brows elevated. "Maybe because I've spent so long subduing my memories of you. But I think it's mostly because of what I've done and…who I've become since you've been gone. I was a different person the last time I saw you. I'd never killed anyone, but I've taken more lives than anyone my age should *ever* have to since then. I know the whys and wherefores, and I know what I've done was justified. But you're back now…and it's all crashing in on me."

"Lauren, I—"

"Let me talk this out, please," Lauren pled, now nearing tears. "I want so much to blame you for this. You got me involved and started me on a path. You educated me and taught me how to think. You showed me how to look at everything and everyone differently, taught me skills and had others teach me. You readied me to make war with hell, Dad…and then…you never came home. This person I've become…*you* created her; everything suppressed and lying dormant was awakened by what you did. And now, I can never get those days back. I'll never get my childhood or late teens back. I'll never be normal again. And I want to blame you for all of it. And I'm sorry."

A tear slipped down Alan's cheek and crashed to the snow at his feet. He looked away into the laurel grove and beyond. "No, I'm the one who's sorry. Obviously, I don't know all the details. And I won't know unless you tell me, and I'm hoping you will, eventually. It certainly doesn't have to be now." A pause. "But if I'm to blame, so be it. I'll shoulder every responsibility…just ask yourself this; if I hadn't prepared you for this world and you hadn't become this person and acted as you had. If you hadn't taken those lives…would you still have yours? Would you still be alive to tell me how you felt about all of this? Would you and I even be having this conversation?"

Lauren sniffled and shrugged. "I don't know. You taught me to expect the least expected, that life is ridiculously unpredictable. And you're right, there's no telling where any of us would be if I hadn't done what was needed or what I knew I had to. But it never used to bother me; it's almost as if I took responsibility for everything, myself and the family, in your absence. In the short time you've been back, something's changed. I've been hurting. I feel what I've done, Dad. If you only knew…God—there's so much I want to get off my chest, but I don't want you to think badly of me or hate me. I only want what I've always wanted, for you to be proud of me."

"Hey, listen. It's your turn to hear me out," Alan said firmly. "I *am* proud of you. And I could never hate you, Lauren. If anything, I should hate myself for not being here. You're feeling this way for the simple reason that I wasn't, and dammit, I should've been—the entire time. I should've been here to defend you, protect you, supply and provide, but I wasn't, due to my own shortsightedness. It's always been my job to handle all the dirty work so you wouldn't have to, and anything you've had to do—good, bad or indifferent—has kept you alive, making it necessary.

"Look, Dad is home, okay? I'm here now. Granted, not all of me is, but the memories I've lost are a small part of who I am. I am still Alan Russell and you are still my daughter. I never resigned my place as your father or the head of this household, and I'm hereby back to resume my post. You don't have to be afraid, and you don't have to hurt or be ashamed of anything you've done. As your father, I won't allow it. Whatever we've done apart from each other from this point forward no longer matters. This family is together again, and nothing is going to change that. I promise you."

Lauren closed her eyes and nodded, accepting his words in their entirety with approval. "I believe you, and I believe *in* you. And I pray you're right, but you've been wrong before, like the time you told me you thought we were indivisible. You were *way* wrong about that." She nearly snickered. "Being fair, you also said that if anything ever served to keep us apart, you would stop at nothing to find your way back to me, so I guess you were both wrong and right." She locked eyes with him. "I never expected to see you again, Dad. And I've been so torn over what to think, one day waking up and writing you off and the next day believing you'd find a way home, and all the *not* knowing.

"I know I can't go back, and blaming you for something you had no control over is stupid, especially now, after everything we've both been through. All those nights crying, begging God to find you, thinking you were dead, everything we went through, all the moves, all the dangers we've encountered and thinking the worst. You're here and you're in one piece and the only thing missing, the only thing you didn't bring back are your memories of us. And I suppose, all things considered, that isn't so bad."

"Easy for you to say," Alan jeered. "You still have yours."

"Stop."

"Sorry."

Lauren hesitated. "I watched you gun two men down to protect Mom and me once. I never thought I would have to do that, until the day came when I had no other choice. You weren't there to protect us, so I had to. It's been like that ever since, until I saw you again. My dad came home. My protector was back. And for a moment, I got this feeling that maybe I wouldn't have to kill again, maybe I wouldn't need a gun anymore. Then I talked to Jade. She told me what happened to you guys on the way here, and I realized what I was feeling was too good to be true."

"It was rough. We almost didn't make it out of there." Alan's brow furrowed. "What else did you two talk about?"

"You, mostly," Lauren said. "But our conversation got me back on track." She gestured to the Glock handgun attached to her thigh. "I'm glad we're reunited and I want this feeling to last forever. But the same people you encountered have made their intentions known here. They don't just want to harm us, they want us dead. No one knows why, and I don't care why. I won't lie down and let them run us over. I'm not naïve;

I know what has to be done. I know I have to fight, and I'll do so as long as I have to, as long as it takes. But I pray for a day when I won't have to. I want that day to come when I can put my guns down and won't kill again."

"Sounds to me like your heart is in the right place, and I also think that would be a very beautiful thing," Alan said. "Hearing you say this tells me a lot about how your mother and I must've raised you. But I guess it's good that I'm home, so I can fight alongside you. For what it's worth though, I'm sorry I wasn't around to keep the blood off your hands." He paused. "God put me on this earth for a reason, to support, love, cherish, and protect my family, and that is exactly what I intend to do. So dry your tears, okay? Turn them into something else, because Daddy's home."

Lauren nodded her head and nearly beamed after hearing her father utter those words. She knew he'd done so inadvertently, unaware of how often he'd used a similar phrase with her in the past.

"That sounds like the Dad I know. It's good to have you back."

"It's good to hear you say that...especially since you're not exactly getting a total package."

"I'll take what I can get." Lauren rotated and wrapped her arms around her father's waist. Alan reciprocated and pulled her into an embrace. "I love you with all my heart, Dad. But you have to promise me something."

"Anything. You name it."

"Don't ever leave us," Lauren said, her tone succinct. "More to the point, don't ever leave *me*. Please. Ever again."

"Lauren Jane Russell, not a chance. I will do no such thing. Not on your life. Or mine."

# ACKNOWLEDGMENTS

2019 has been a bear.

That said, the reception for the What's Left of My World Series, Lauren and Alan Russell and their story, has been nothing short of breathtaking. My creativity has been goaded since the moment book one was published, and that is owed primarily to readers and fans. I simply cannot thank you all enough for making this dream a reality for me. With your praise, kind words, epic reviews, Facebook tags, and constructive criticism, you push me to write through the toughest of days without even knowing it. You have my eternal appreciation.

To the fam: Thank you for once again tolerating my eccentricities during one of the busiest years I've ever encountered. I love you and your loyalty to me means more than you'll ever know.

Special thanks to Sabrina, Pauline and Felicia. All I do is talk to myself, type words and garbled nonsense. You guys align and make sense of them somehow while revealing to me what little I know about punctuation. Thanks also to #VOXAPOC Kevin Pierce for being my spokesman, for the laughs and encouragement.

A big thanks goes to Deranged Doctor Design for killing it once again with another round of captivating cover designs - and of course, to Darja, for making an appearance on her fourth consecutive cover, with a fifth on the horizon.

Finally, shout-outs to fellow authors Franklin Horton, Steve Bird, Tom Abrahams, Jeff Motes, R.E. McDermott, Doug Hogan, W.J. Lundy, Chris Weatherman, Boyd Craven and Lisa Akers. Thanks for your advice and guidance, for the inspiration, and for the teamwork.

# ABOUT THE AUTHOR

C.A.Rudolph is a self-published novelist who lives and writes within the pastoral boundaries of Virginia's northern Shenandoah Valley. He spends most of his limited spare time pursuing outdoor adventures with his family. He is an avid backpacker, proud gun owner, and an amateur radio operator.

His first book, What's Left of My World, published in December 2016, became an Amazon post-apocalyptic and dystopian best seller..

To be briefed on Mr. Rudolph and his books, his life, and future exploits, find him loitering outside the wire on Facebook, Twitter, Instagram, and via his website at http://www.carudolph.com

Made in the USA
Middletown, DE
30 September 2019